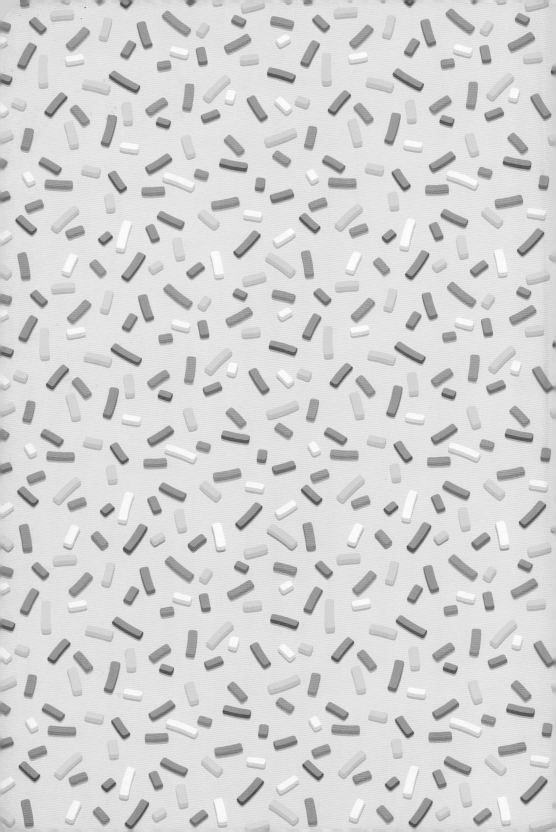

Alexis
and the
Perfect
Recipe

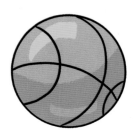

This book is a work of fiction. Any references to historical events, real people, or real places are used fictitiously. Other names, characters, places, and events are products of the author's imagination, and any resemblance to actual events or places or persons, living or dead, is entirely coincidental.

SIMON SPOTLIGHT
An imprint of Simon & Schuster Children's Publishing Division
1230 Avenue of the Americas, New York, New York 10020
This Simon Spotlight edition June 2023

For information about special discounts for bulk purchases, please contact Simon & Schuster Special Sales at 1-866-506-1949 or business@simonandschuster.com.
Text by Tracey West
Cover and Character Design by Manuel Preitano
Art by Giulia Campobello at Glass House Graphics
Assistant on inks by Marzia Migliori
Colors by Francesca Ingrassia
Lettering by Giuseppe Naselli/Grafimated Cartoon
Supervision by Salvatore Di Marco/Grafimated Cartoon
Designed by Laura Roode
The text of this book was set in Comic Crazy.
Manufactured in China 0323 SCP
10 9 8 7 6 5 4 3 2
ISBN 978-1-6659-3322-3 (hc)
ISBN 978-1-6659-3321-6 (pbk)
ISBN 978-1-6659-3323-0 (ebook)
Library of Congress Catalog Control Number 2022943225

CUPCAKE DIARIES

Alexis and the Perfect Recipe

By
Coco Simon

Illustrated by
Giulia Campobello
at Glass House Graphics

Simon Spotlight
New York   London   Toronto   Sydney   New Delhi

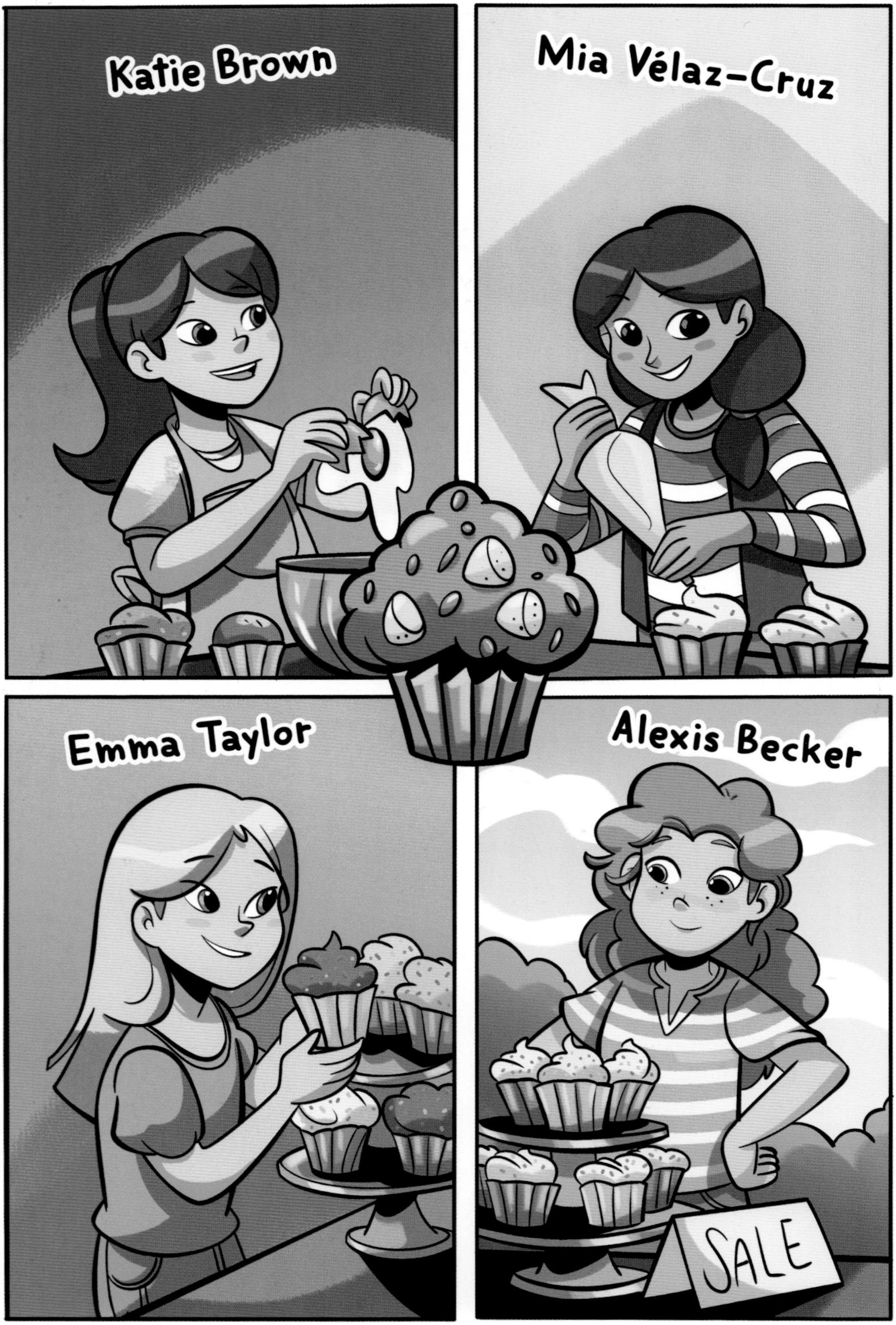
Katie Brown
Mia Vélaz-Cruz
Emma Taylor
Alexis Becker
SALE

Chapter 1

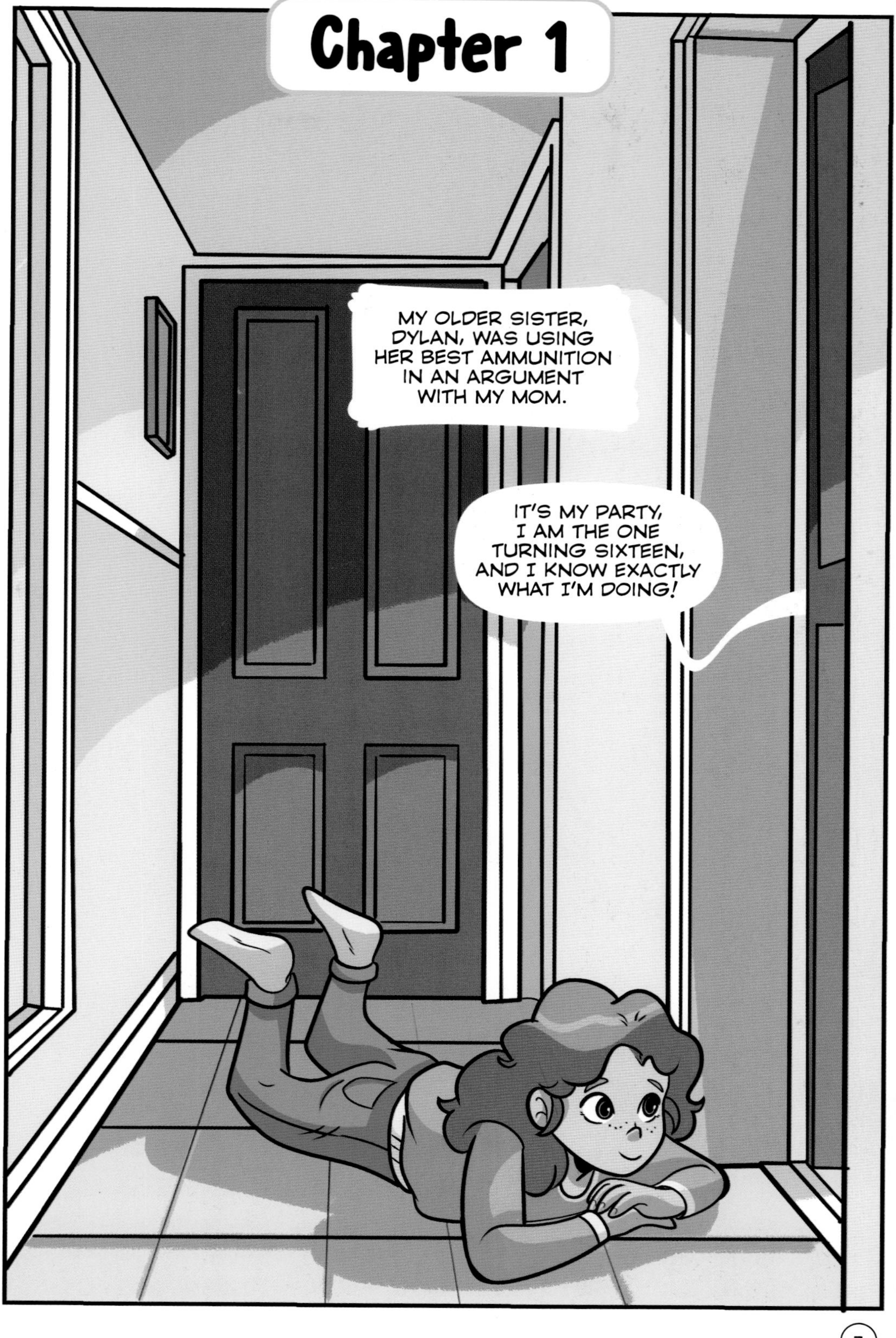
MY OLDER SISTER, DYLAN, WAS USING HER BEST AMMUNITION IN AN ARGUMENT WITH MY MOM.
IT'S MY PARTY, I AM THE ONE TURNING SIXTEEN, AND I KNOW EXACTLY WHAT I'M DOING!

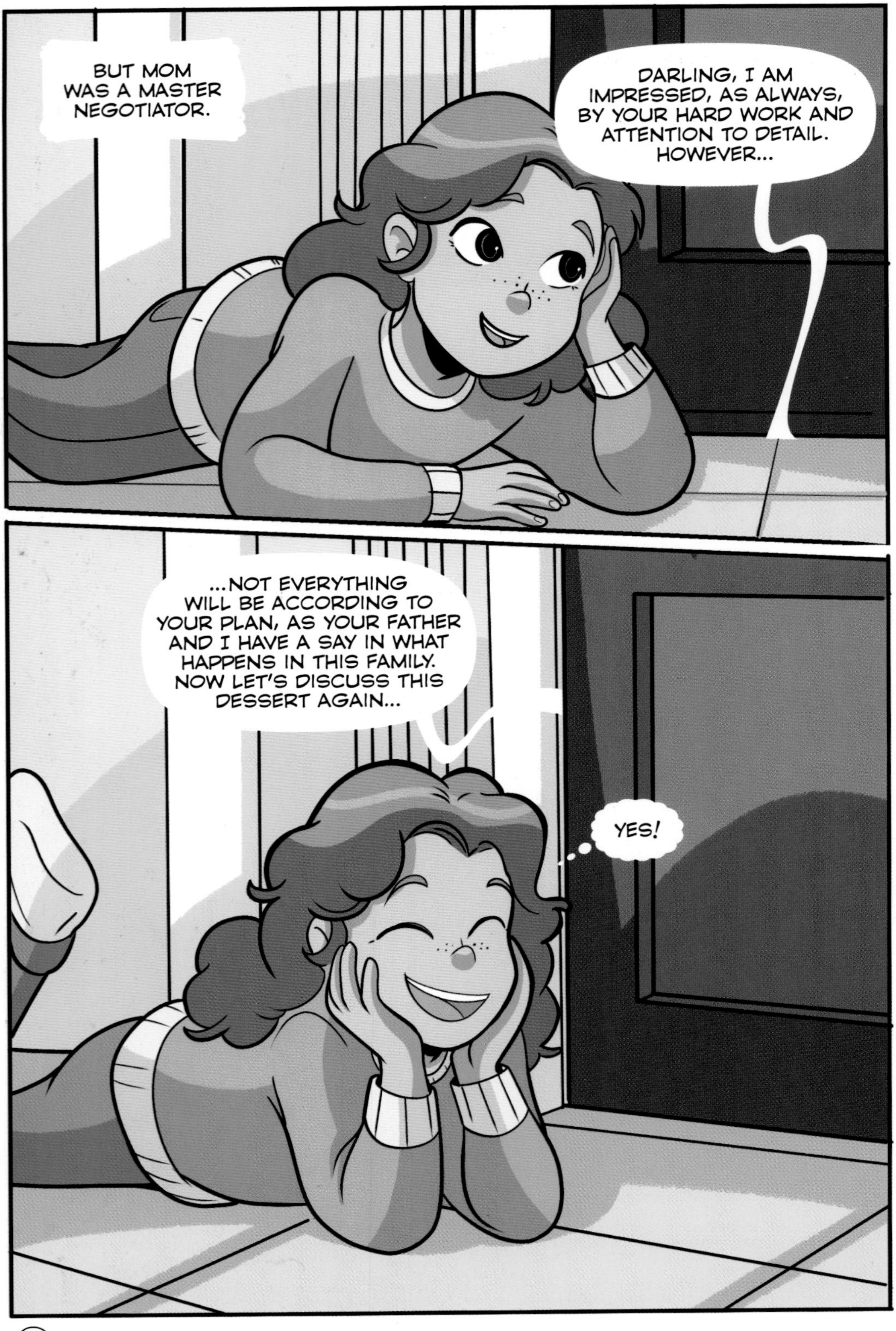
BUT MOM WAS A MASTER NEGOTIATOR.
DARLING, I AM IMPRESSED, AS ALWAYS, BY YOUR HARD WORK AND ATTENTION TO DETAIL. HOWEVER...
...NOT EVERYTHING WILL BE ACCORDING TO YOUR PLAN, AS YOUR FATHER AND I HAVE A SAY IN WHAT HAPPENS IN THIS FAMILY. NOW LET'S DISCUSS THIS DESSERT AGAIN...
YES!

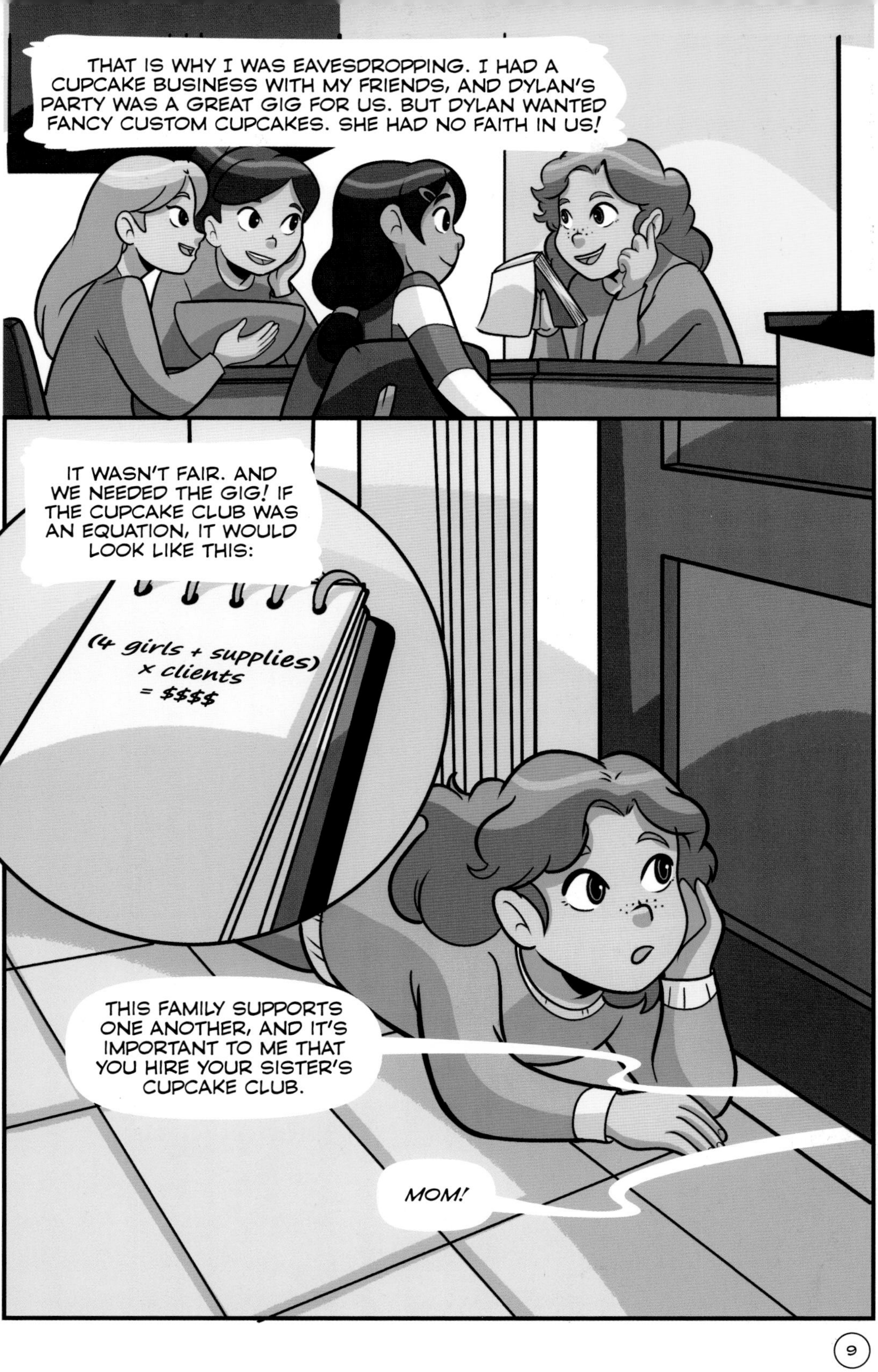
THAT IS WHY I WAS EAVESDROPPING. I HAD A CUPCAKE BUSINESS WITH MY FRIENDS, AND DYLAN'S PARTY WAS A GREAT GIG FOR US. BUT DYLAN WANTED FANCY CUSTOM CUPCAKES. SHE HAD NO FAITH IN US!
IT WASN'T FAIR. AND WE NEEDED THE GIG! IF THE CUPCAKE CLUB WAS AN EQUATION, IT WOULD LOOK LIKE THIS:
(4 girls + supplies) x clients = $$$$
THIS FAMILY SUPPORTS ONE ANOTHER, AND IT'S IMPORTANT TO ME THAT YOU HIRE YOUR SISTER'S CUPCAKE CLUB.
MOM!

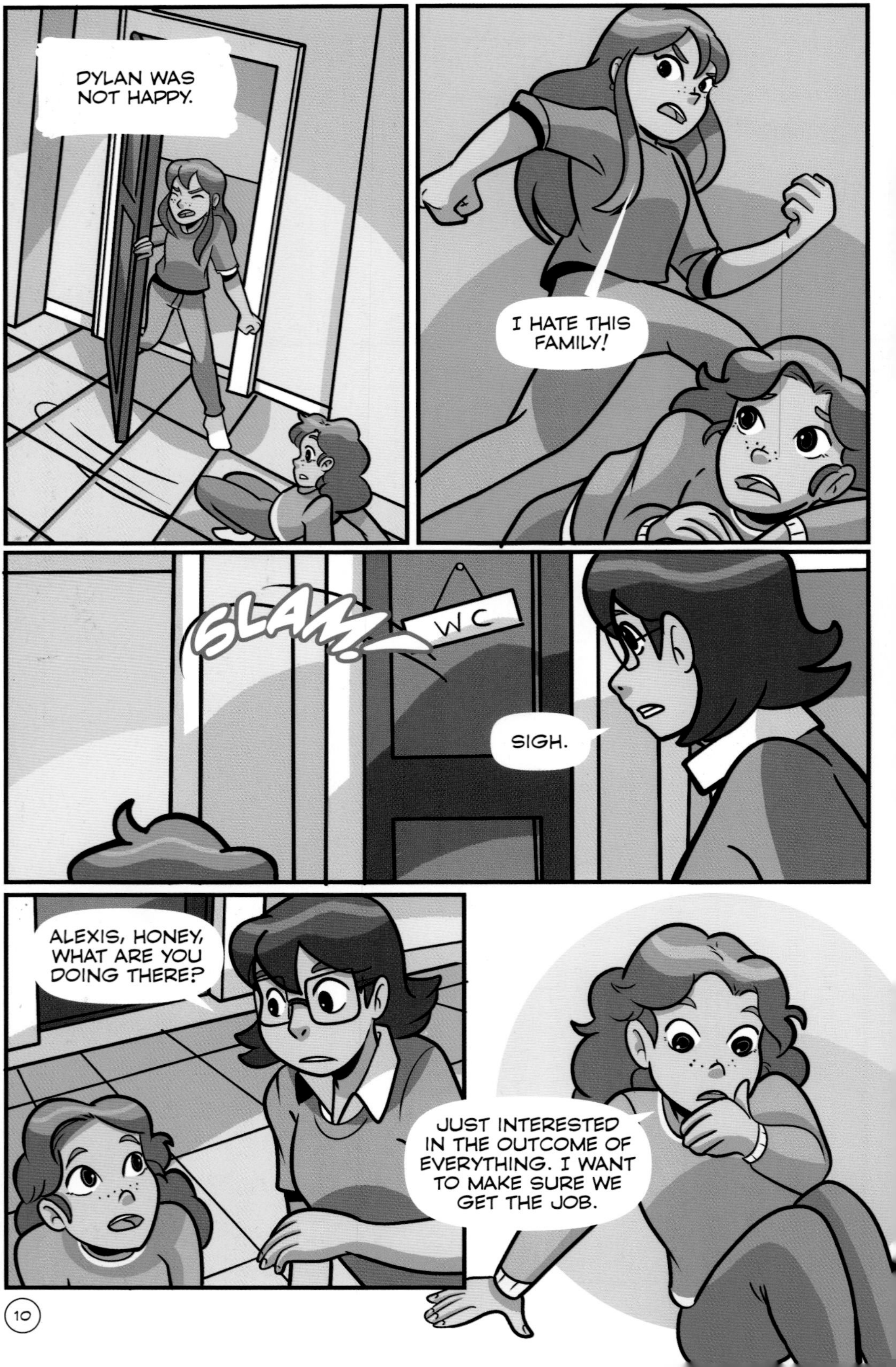
DYLAN WAS NOT HAPPY.
I HATE THIS FAMILY!
SLAM!
WC
SIGH.
ALEXIS, HONEY, WHAT ARE YOU DOING THERE?
JUST INTERESTED IN THE OUTCOME OF EVERYTHING. I WANT TO MAKE SURE WE GET THE JOB.

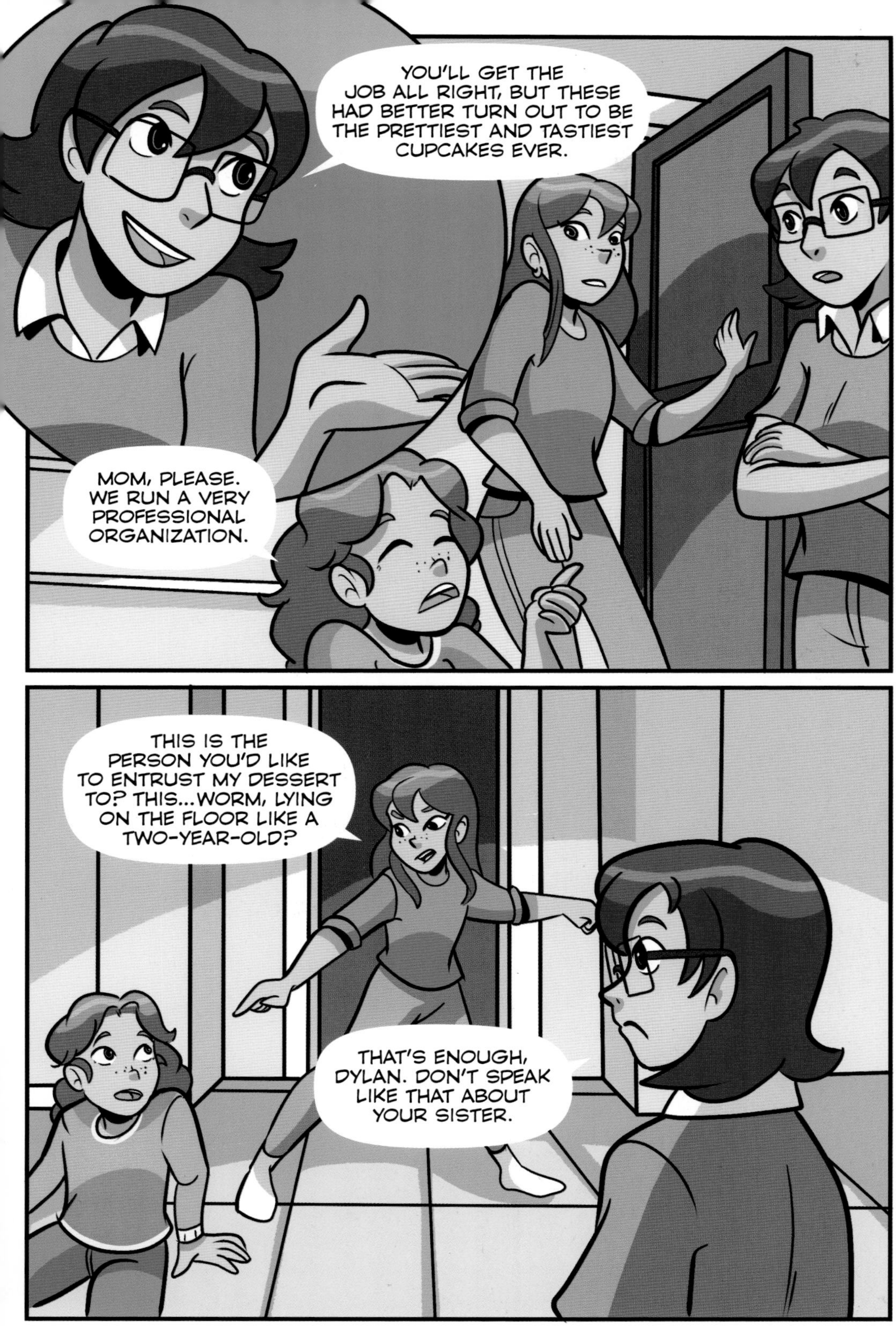
YOU'LL GET THE JOB ALL RIGHT, BUT THESE HAD BETTER TURN OUT TO BE THE PRETTIEST AND TASTIEST CUPCAKES EVER.
MOM, PLEASE. WE RUN A VERY PROFESSIONAL ORGANIZATION.
THIS IS THE PERSON YOU'D LIKE TO ENTRUST MY DESSERT TO? THIS...WORM, LYING ON THE FLOOR LIKE A TWO-YEAR-OLD?
THAT'S ENOUGH, DYLAN. DON'T SPEAK LIKE THAT ABOUT YOUR SISTER.

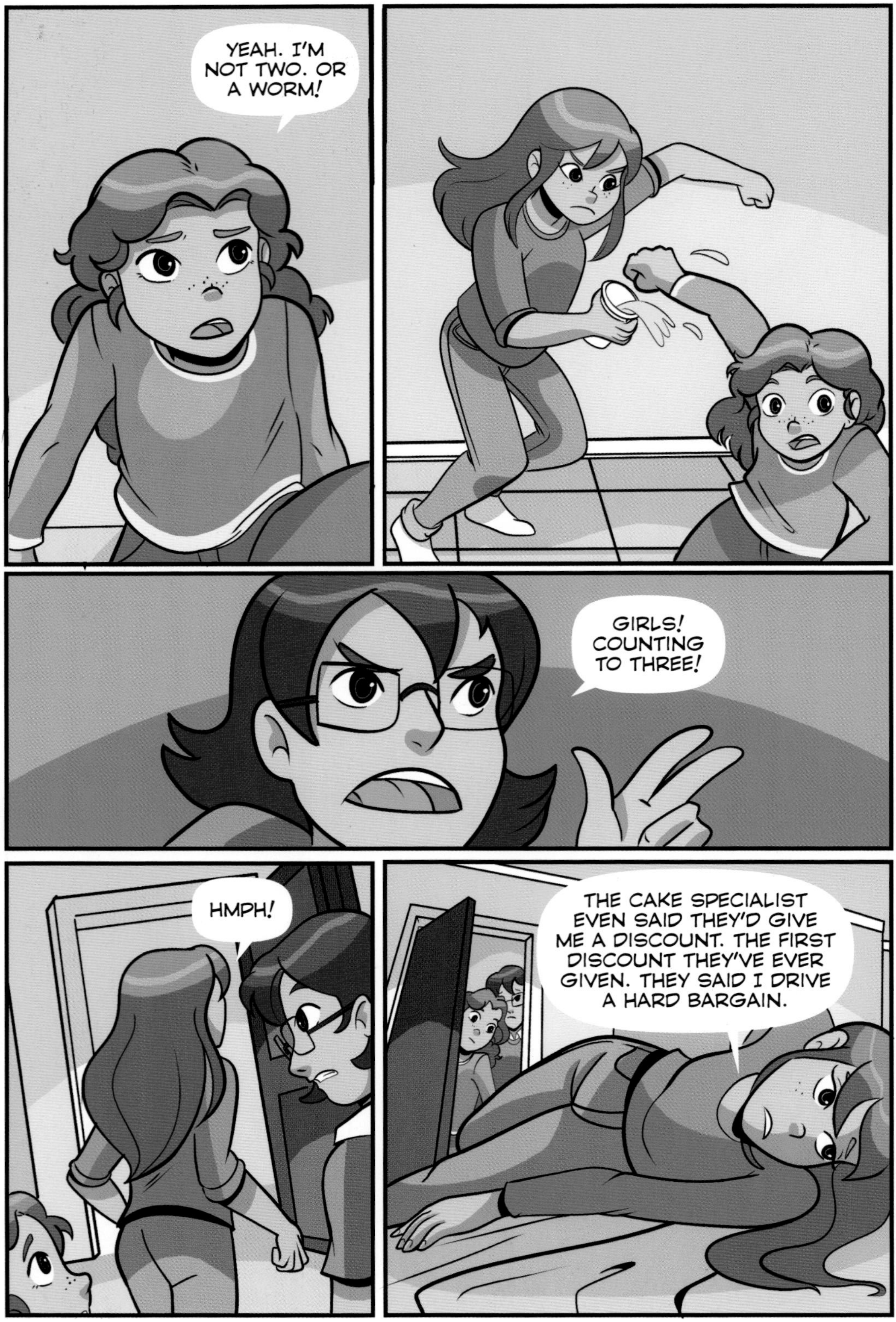
YEAH. I'M NOT TWO. OR A WORM!
GIRLS! COUNTING TO THREE!
HMPH!
THE CAKE SPECIALIST EVEN SAID THEY'D GIVE ME A DISCOUNT. THE FIRST DISCOUNT THEY'VE EVER GIVEN. THEY SAID I DRIVE A HARD BARGAIN.

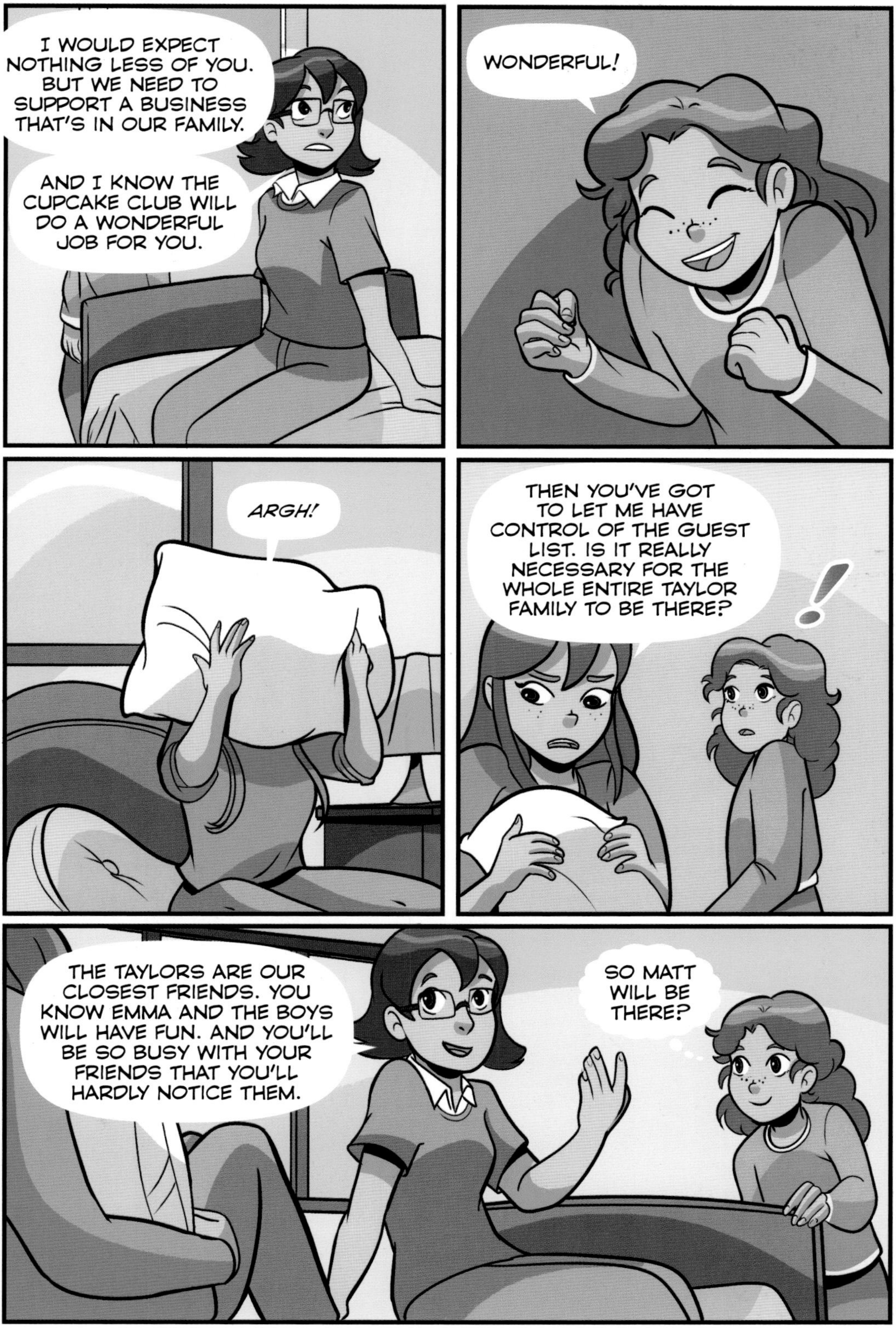
I WOULD EXPECT NOTHING LESS OF YOU. BUT WE NEED TO SUPPORT A BUSINESS THAT'S IN OUR FAMILY.
AND I KNOW THE CUPCAKE CLUB WILL DO A WONDERFUL JOB FOR YOU.
WONDERFUL!
ARGH!
THEN YOU'VE GOT TO LET ME HAVE CONTROL OF THE GUEST LIST. IS IT REALLY NECESSARY FOR THE WHOLE ENTIRE TAYLOR FAMILY TO BE THERE?
!
THE TAYLORS ARE OUR CLOSEST FRIENDS. YOU KNOW EMMA AND THE BOYS WILL HAVE FUN. AND YOU'LL BE SO BUSY WITH YOUR FRIENDS THAT YOU'LL HARDLY NOTICE THEM.
SO MATT WILL BE THERE?

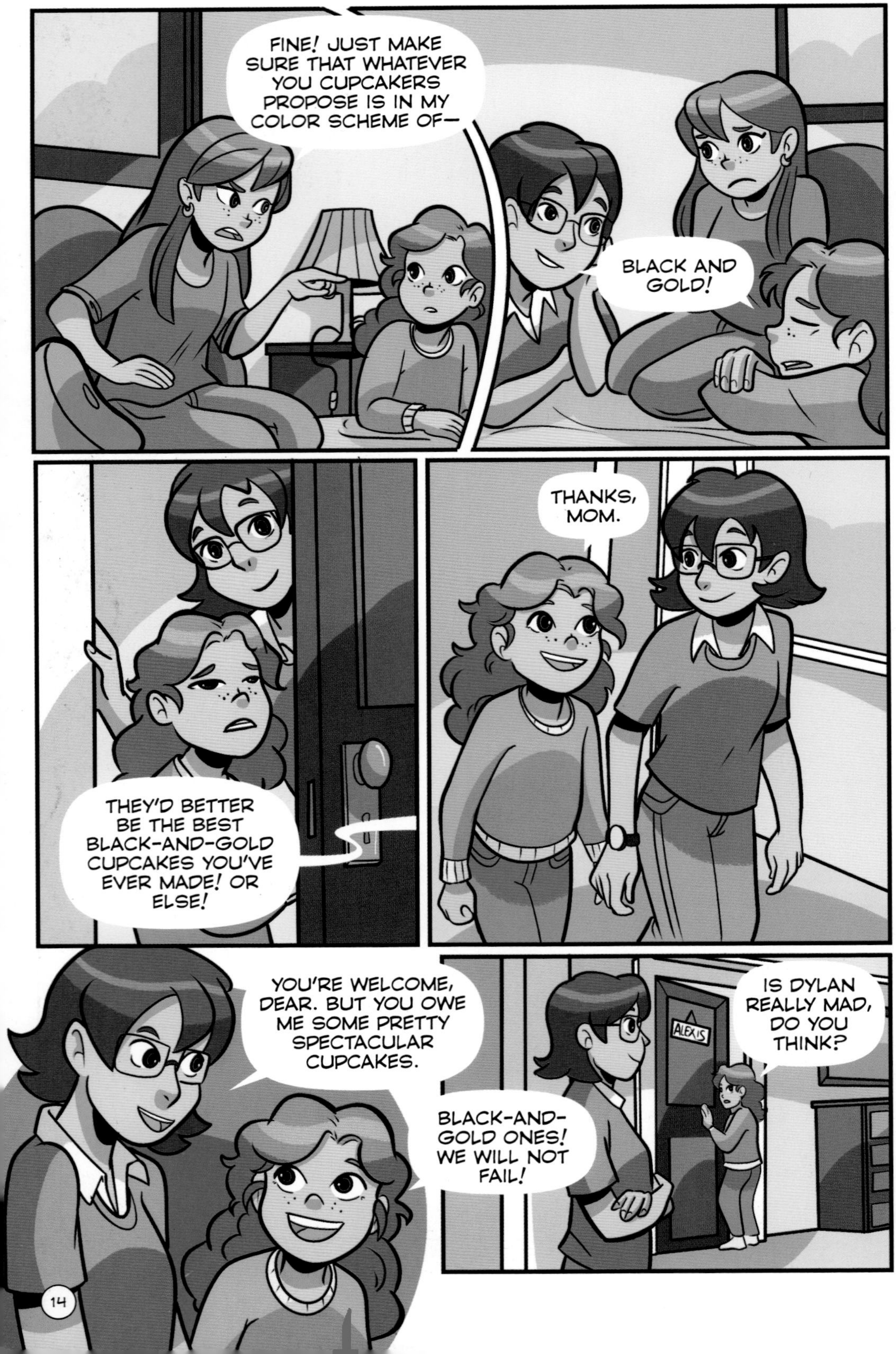
FINE! JUST MAKE SURE THAT WHATEVER YOU CUPCAKERS PROPOSE IS IN MY COLOR SCHEME OF—
BLACK AND GOLD!
THEY'D BETTER BE THE BEST BLACK-AND-GOLD CUPCAKES YOU'VE EVER MADE! OR ELSE!
THANKS, MOM.
YOU'RE WELCOME, DEAR. BUT YOU OWE ME SOME PRETTY SPECTACULAR CUPCAKES.
BLACK-AND-GOLD ONES! WE WILL NOT FAIL!
ALEXIS
IS DYLAN REALLY MAD, DO YOU THINK?

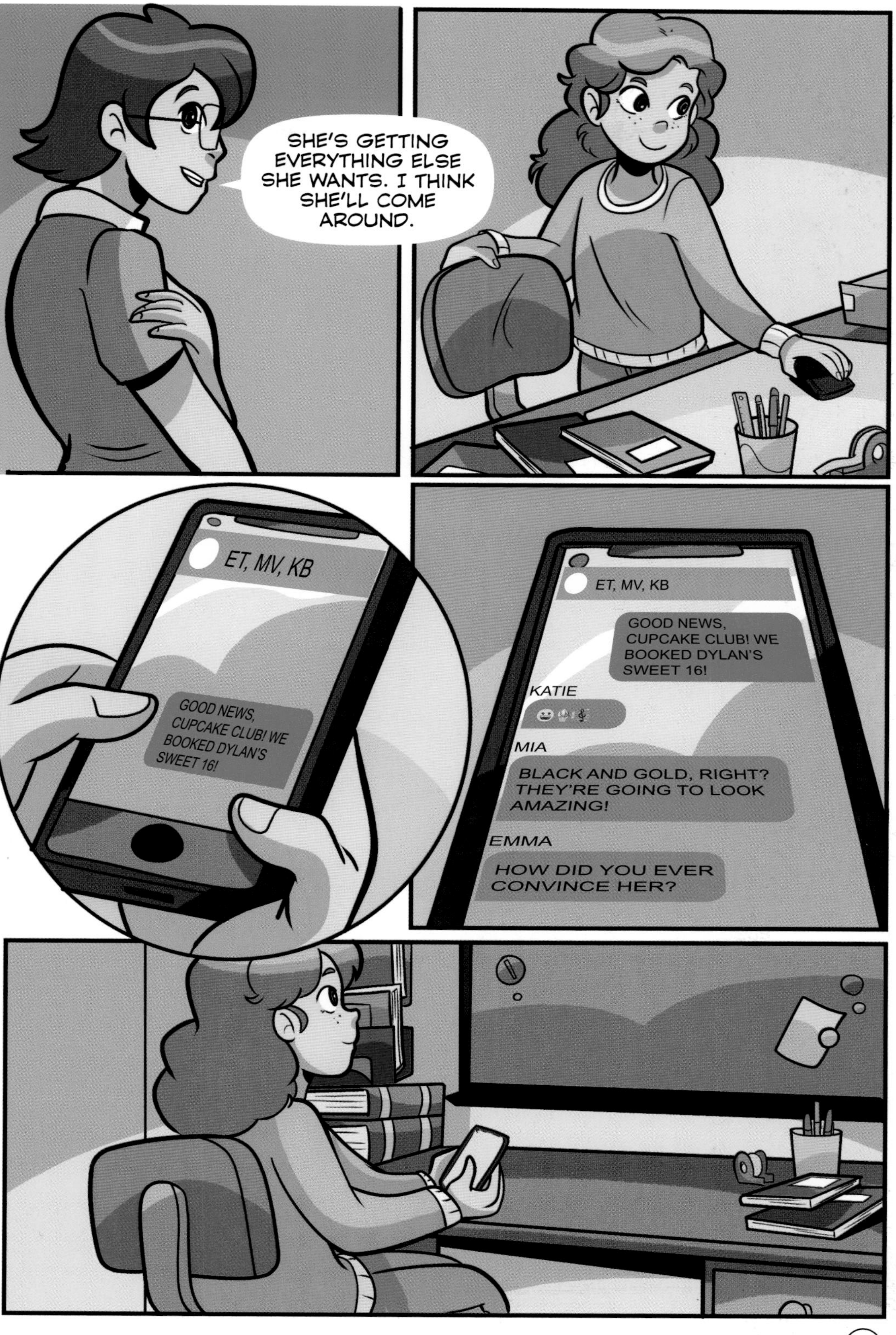
SHE'S GETTING EVERYTHING ELSE SHE WANTS. I THINK SHE'LL COME AROUND.
ET, MV, KB
GOOD NEWS, CUPCAKE CLUB! WE BOOKED DYLAN'S SWEET 16!
ET, MV, KB
GOOD NEWS, CUPCAKE CLUB! WE BOOKED DYLAN'S SWEET 16!
KATIE
MIA
BLACK AND GOLD, RIGHT? THEY'RE GOING TO LOOK AMAZING!
EMMA
HOW DID YOU EVER CONVINCE HER?

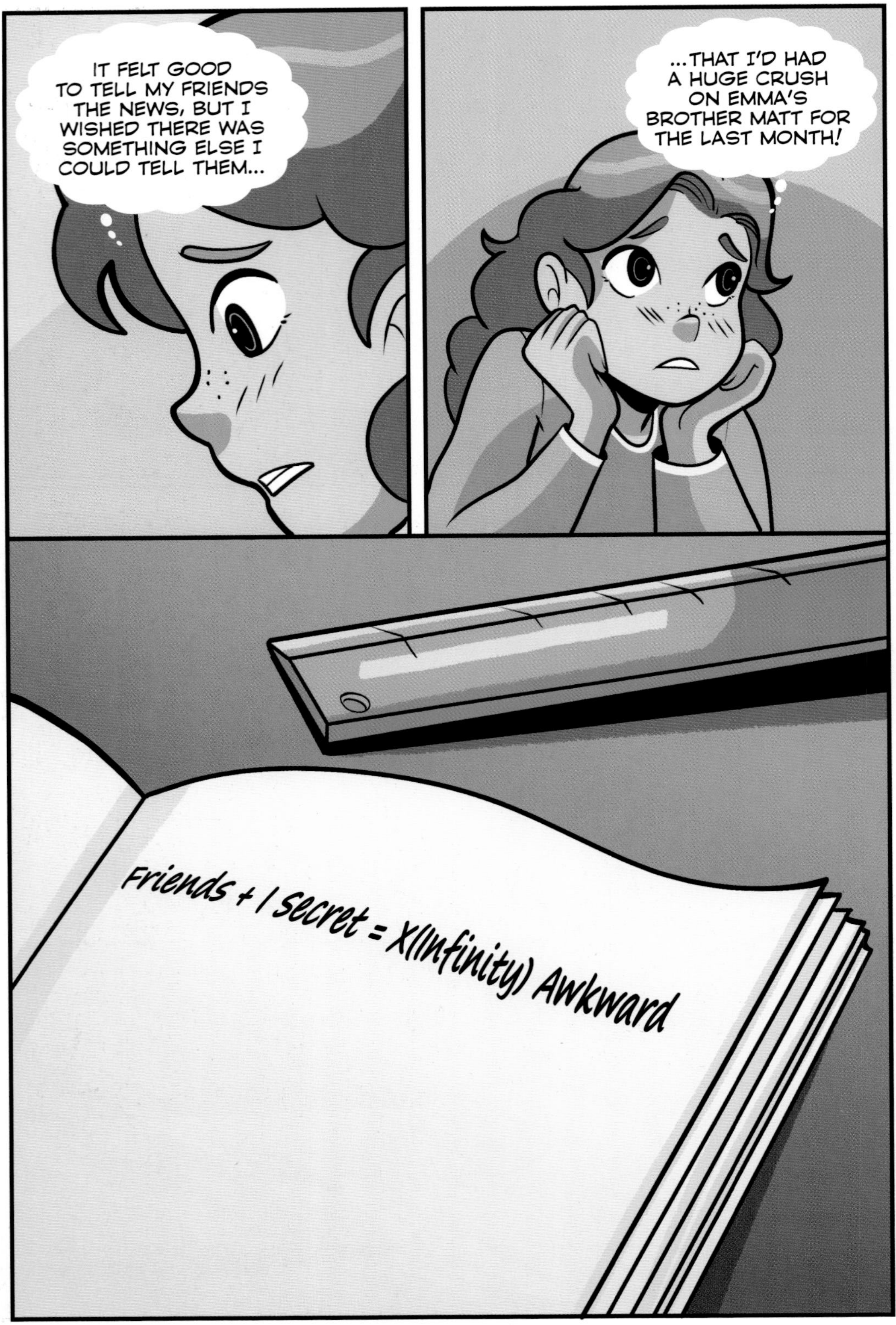
IT FELT GOOD TO TELL MY FRIENDS THE NEWS, BUT I WISHED THERE WAS SOMETHING ELSE I COULD TELL THEM...
...THAT I'D HAD A HUGE CRUSH ON EMMA'S BROTHER MATT FOR THE LAST MONTH!
Friends + 1 Secret = X(Infinity) Awkward

Chapter 2

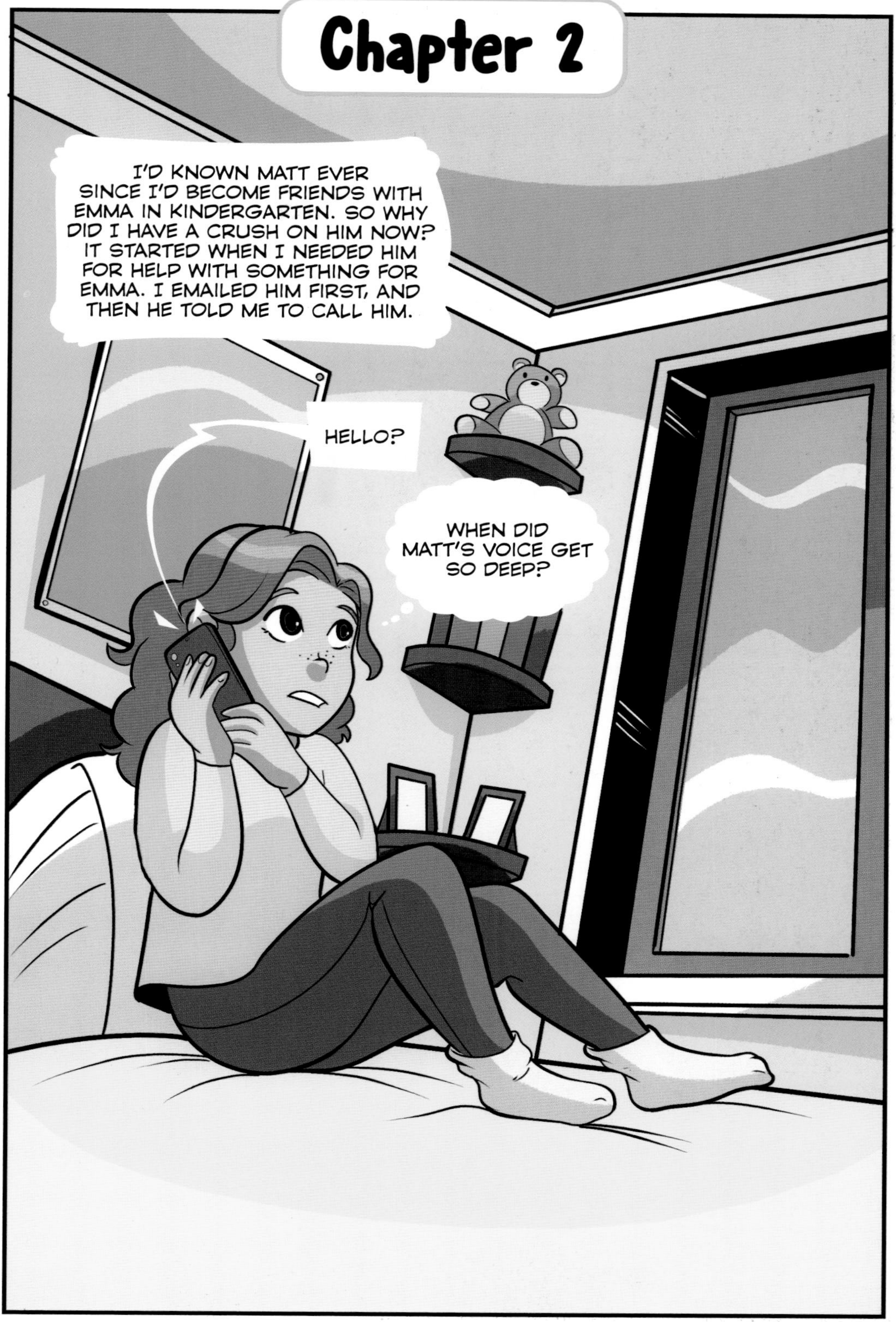
I'D KNOWN MATT EVER SINCE I'D BECOME FRIENDS WITH EMMA IN KINDERGARTEN. SO WHY DID I HAVE A CRUSH ON HIM NOW? IT STARTED WHEN I NEEDED HIM FOR HELP WITH SOMETHING FOR EMMA. I EMAILED HIM FIRST, AND THEN HE TOLD ME TO CALL HIM.
HELLO?
WHEN DID MATT'S VOICE GET SO DEEP?

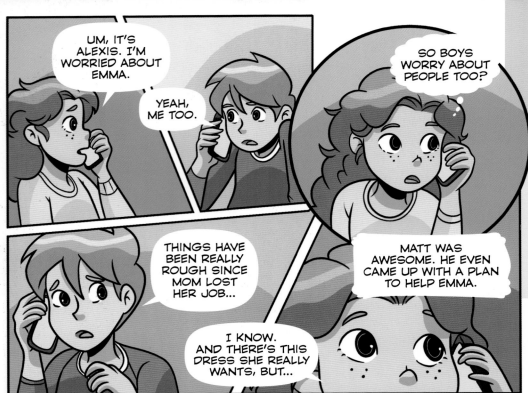

UM, IT'S ALEXIS. I'M WORRIED ABOUT EMMA.

YEAH, ME TOO.

SO BOYS WORRY ABOUT PEOPLE TOO?

THINGS HAVE BEEN REALLY ROUGH SINCE MOM LOST HER JOB...

MATT WAS AWESOME. HE EVEN CAME UP WITH A PLAN TO HELP EMMA.

I KNOW. AND THERE'S THIS DRESS SHE REALLY WANTS, BUT...

THAT'S THE MOMENT WHEN I STOPPED THINKING OF MATT JUST AS EMMA'S BROTHER...

MATT MATT MATT

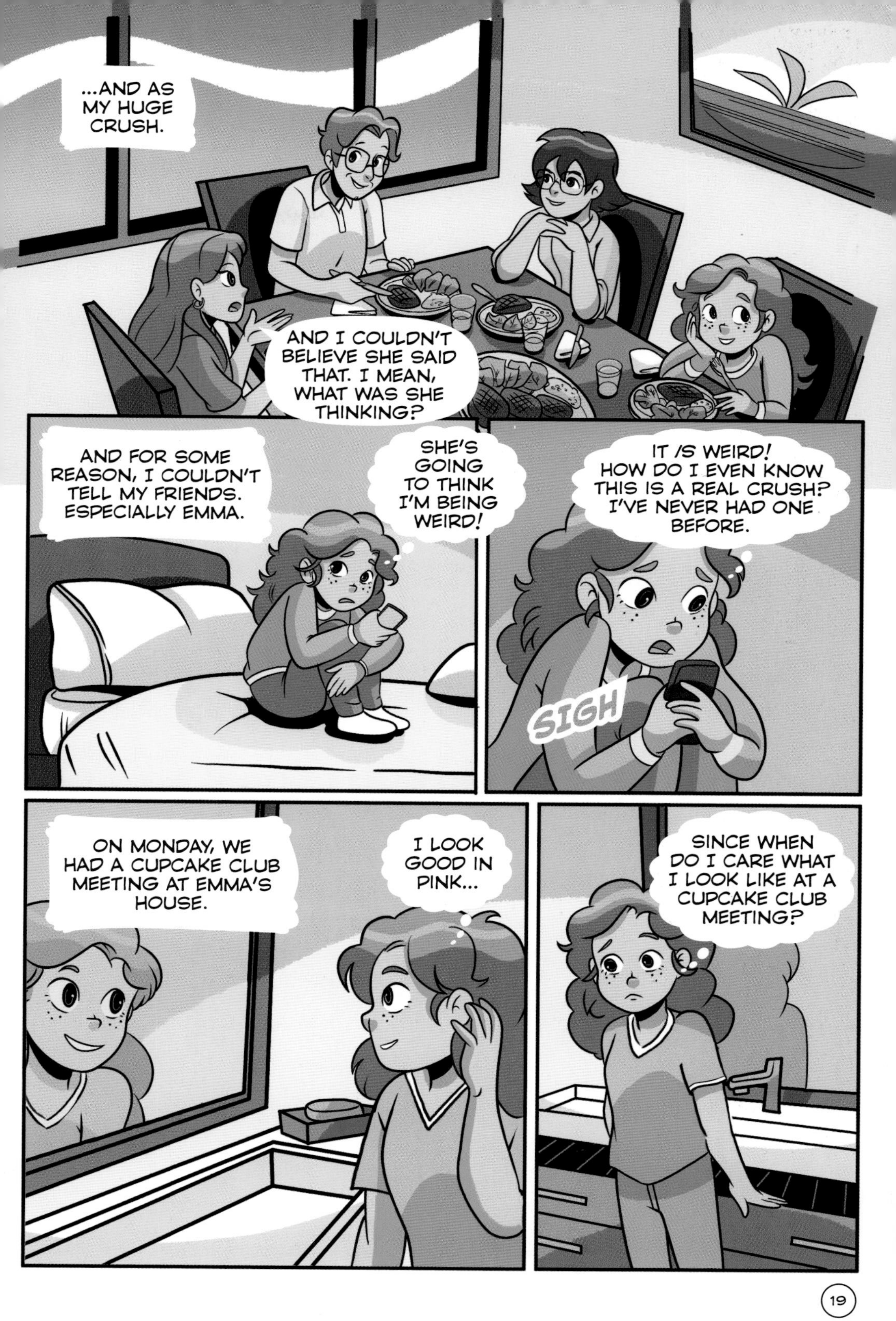

...AND AS MY HUGE CRUSH.
AND I COULDN'T BELIEVE SHE SAID THAT. I MEAN, WHAT WAS SHE THINKING?
AND FOR SOME REASON, I COULDN'T TELL MY FRIENDS. ESPECIALLY EMMA.
SHE'S GOING TO THINK I'M BEING WEIRD!
IT *IS* WEIRD! HOW DO I EVEN KNOW THIS IS A REAL CRUSH? I'VE NEVER HAD ONE BEFORE.
SIGH
ON MONDAY, WE HAD A CUPCAKE CLUB MEETING AT EMMA'S HOUSE.
I LOOK GOOD IN PINK...
SINCE WHEN DO I CARE WHAT I LOOK LIKE AT A CUPCAKE CLUB MEETING?

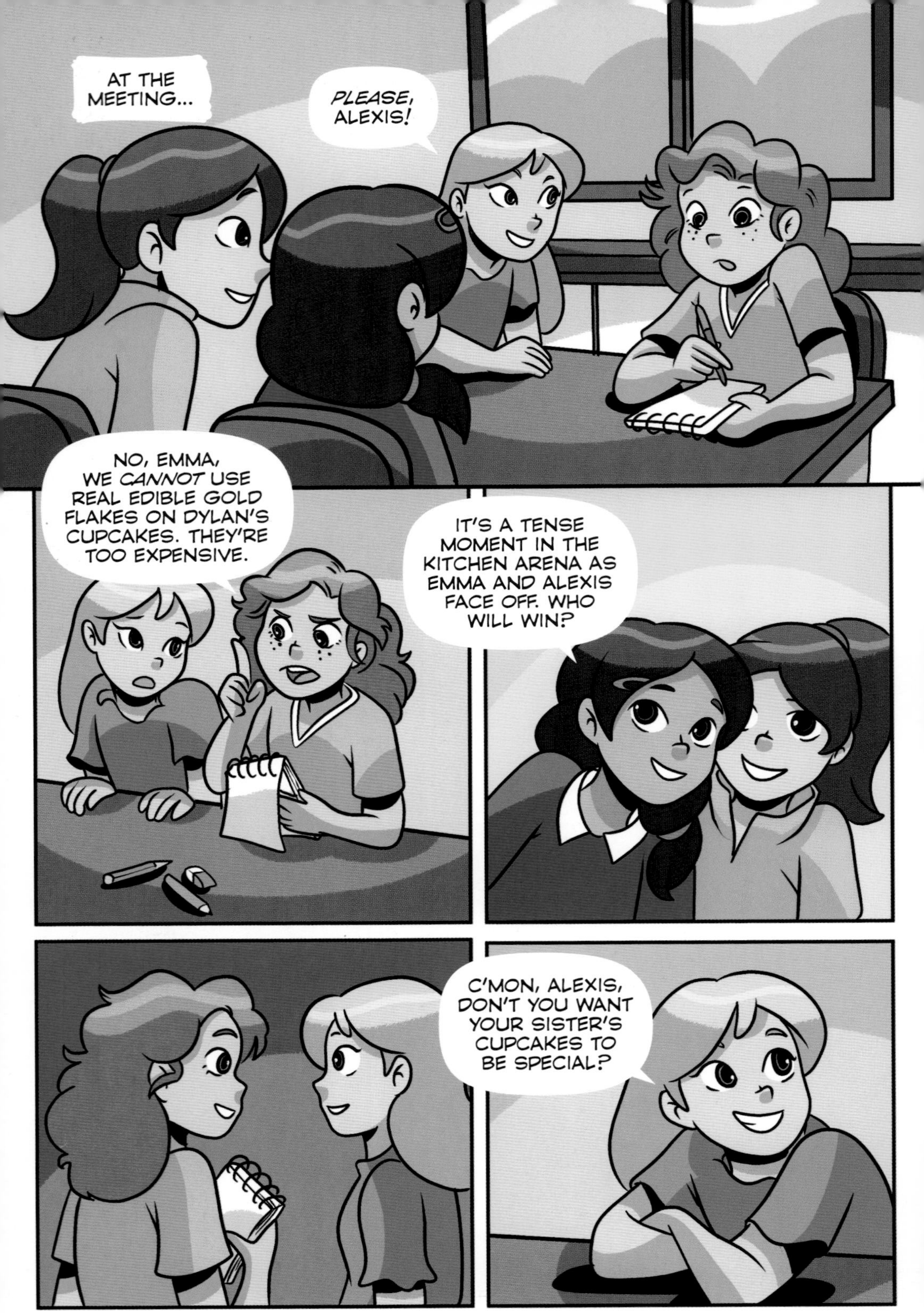
AT THE MEETING...
PLEASE, ALEXIS!
NO, EMMA, WE CANNOT USE REAL EDIBLE GOLD FLAKES ON DYLAN'S CUPCAKES. THEY'RE TOO EXPENSIVE.
IT'S A TENSE MOMENT IN THE KITCHEN ARENA AS EMMA AND ALEXIS FACE OFF. WHO WILL WIN?
C'MON, ALEXIS, DON'T YOU WANT YOUR SISTER'S CUPCAKES TO BE SPECIAL?

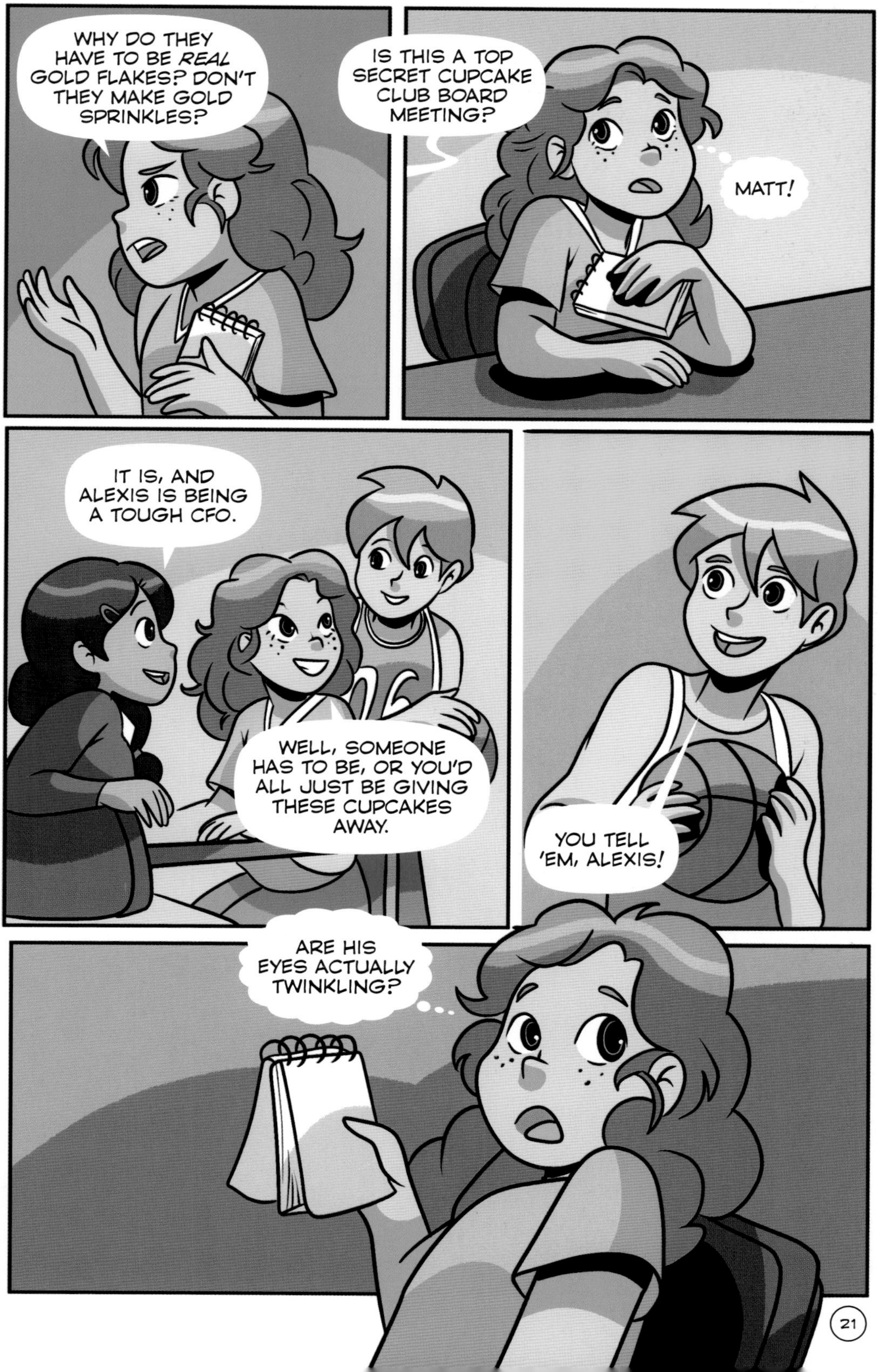
WHY DO THEY HAVE TO BE *REAL* GOLD FLAKES? DON'T THEY MAKE GOLD SPRINKLES?
IS THIS A TOP SECRET CUPCAKE CLUB BOARD MEETING?
MATT!
IT IS, AND ALEXIS IS BEING A TOUGH CFO.
WELL, SOMEONE HAS TO BE, OR YOU'D ALL JUST BE GIVING THESE CUPCAKES AWAY.
YOU TELL 'EM, ALEXIS!
ARE HIS EYES ACTUALLY TWINKLING?

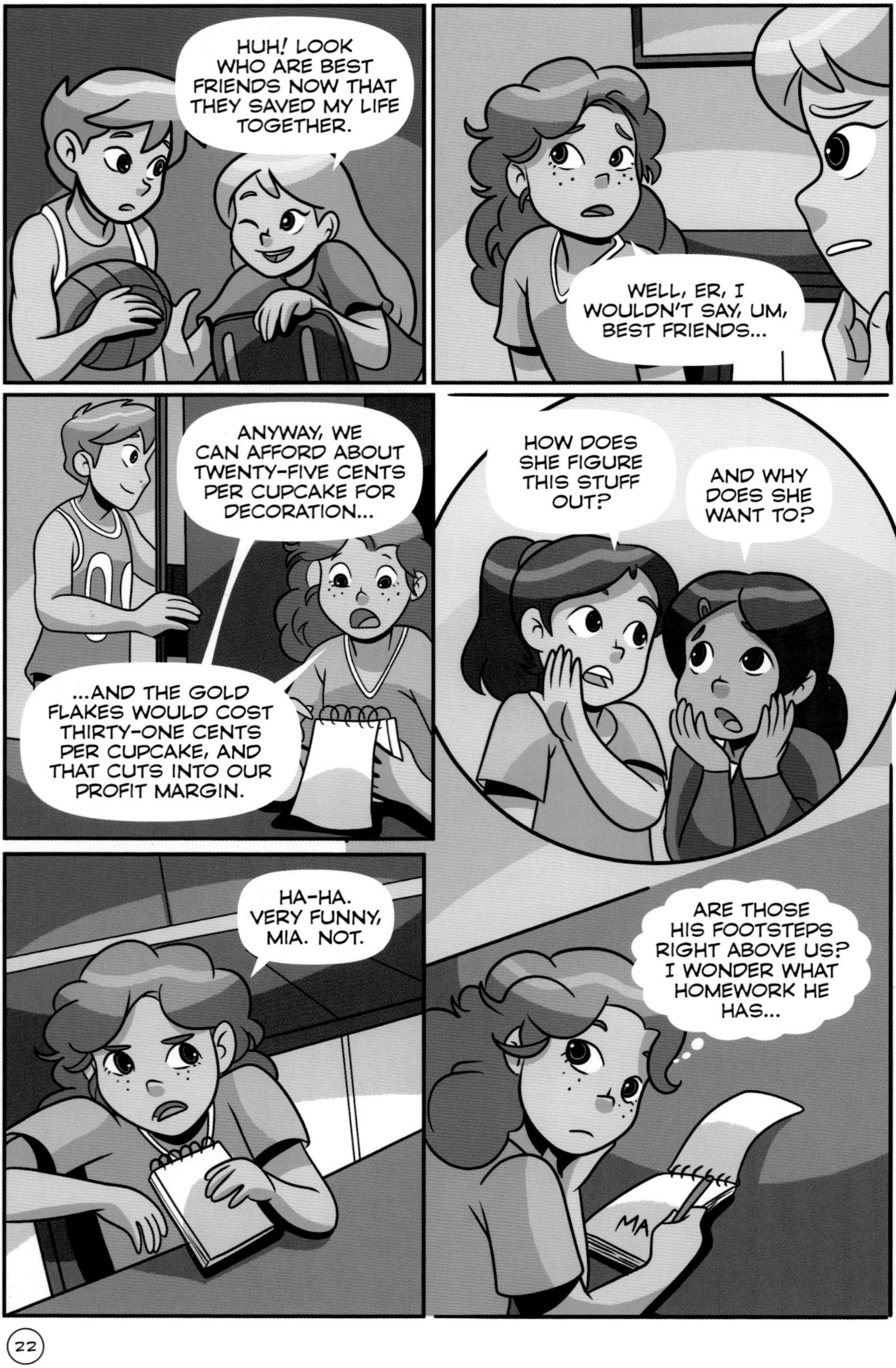
HUH! LOOK WHO ARE BEST FRIENDS NOW THAT THEY SAVED MY LIFE TOGETHER.
WELL, ER, I WOULDN'T SAY, UM, BEST FRIENDS...
ANYWAY, WE CAN AFFORD ABOUT TWENTY-FIVE CENTS PER CUPCAKE FOR DECORATION...
...AND THE GOLD FLAKES WOULD COST THIRTY-ONE CENTS PER CUPCAKE, AND THAT CUTS INTO OUR PROFIT MARGIN.
HOW DOES SHE FIGURE THIS STUFF OUT?
AND WHY DOES SHE WANT TO?
HA-HA. VERY FUNNY, MIA. NOT.
ARE THOSE HIS FOOTSTEPS RIGHT ABOVE US? I WONDER WHAT HOMEWORK HE HAS...
MA

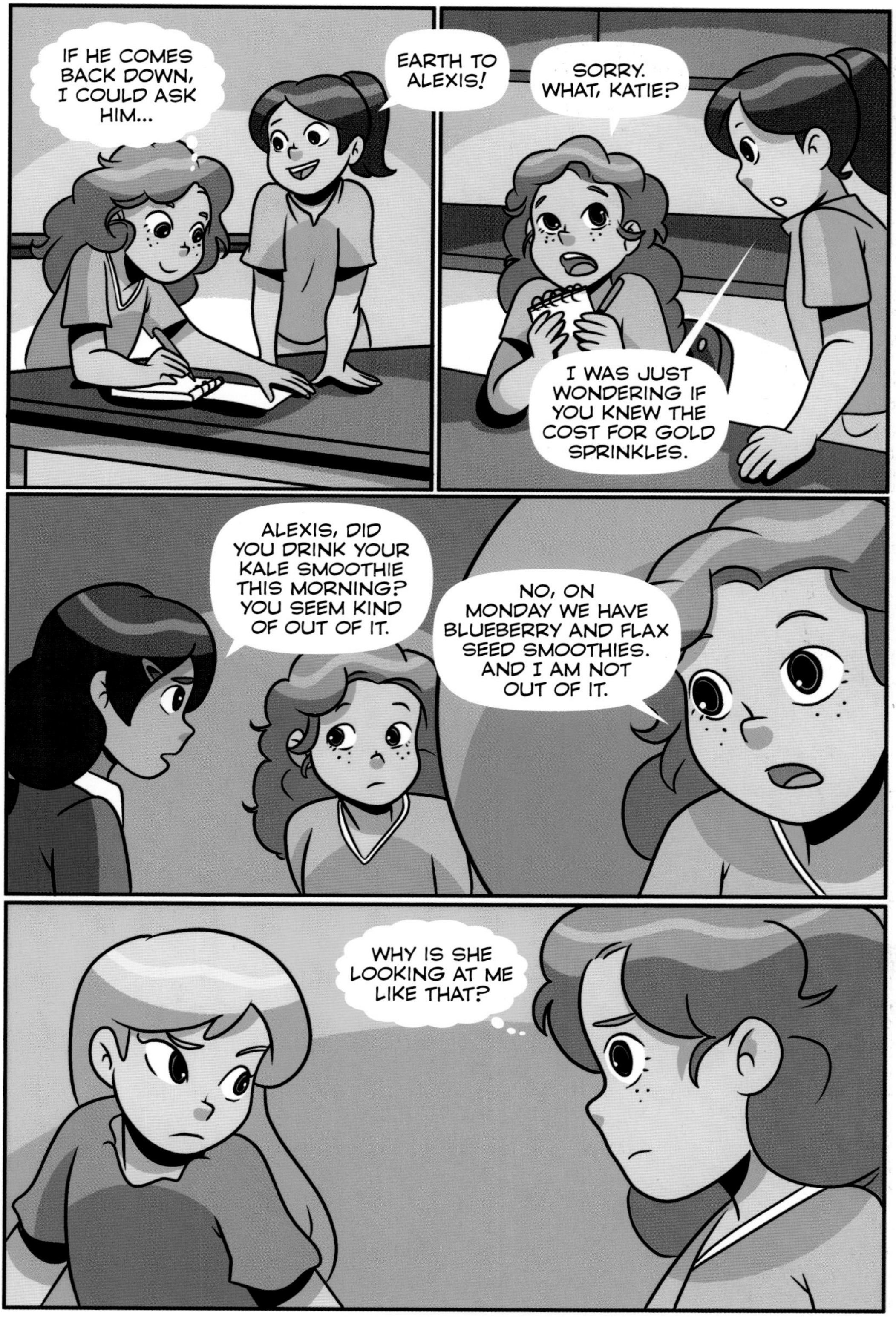
IF HE COMES BACK DOWN, I COULD ASK HIM...
EARTH TO ALEXIS!
SORRY. WHAT, KATIE?
I WAS JUST WONDERING IF YOU KNEW THE COST FOR GOLD SPRINKLES.
ALEXIS, DID YOU DRINK YOUR KALE SMOOTHIE THIS MORNING? YOU SEEM KIND OF OUT OF IT.
NO, ON MONDAY WE HAVE BLUEBERRY AND FLAX SEED SMOOTHIES. AND I AM NOT OUT OF IT.
WHY IS SHE LOOKING AT ME LIKE THAT?

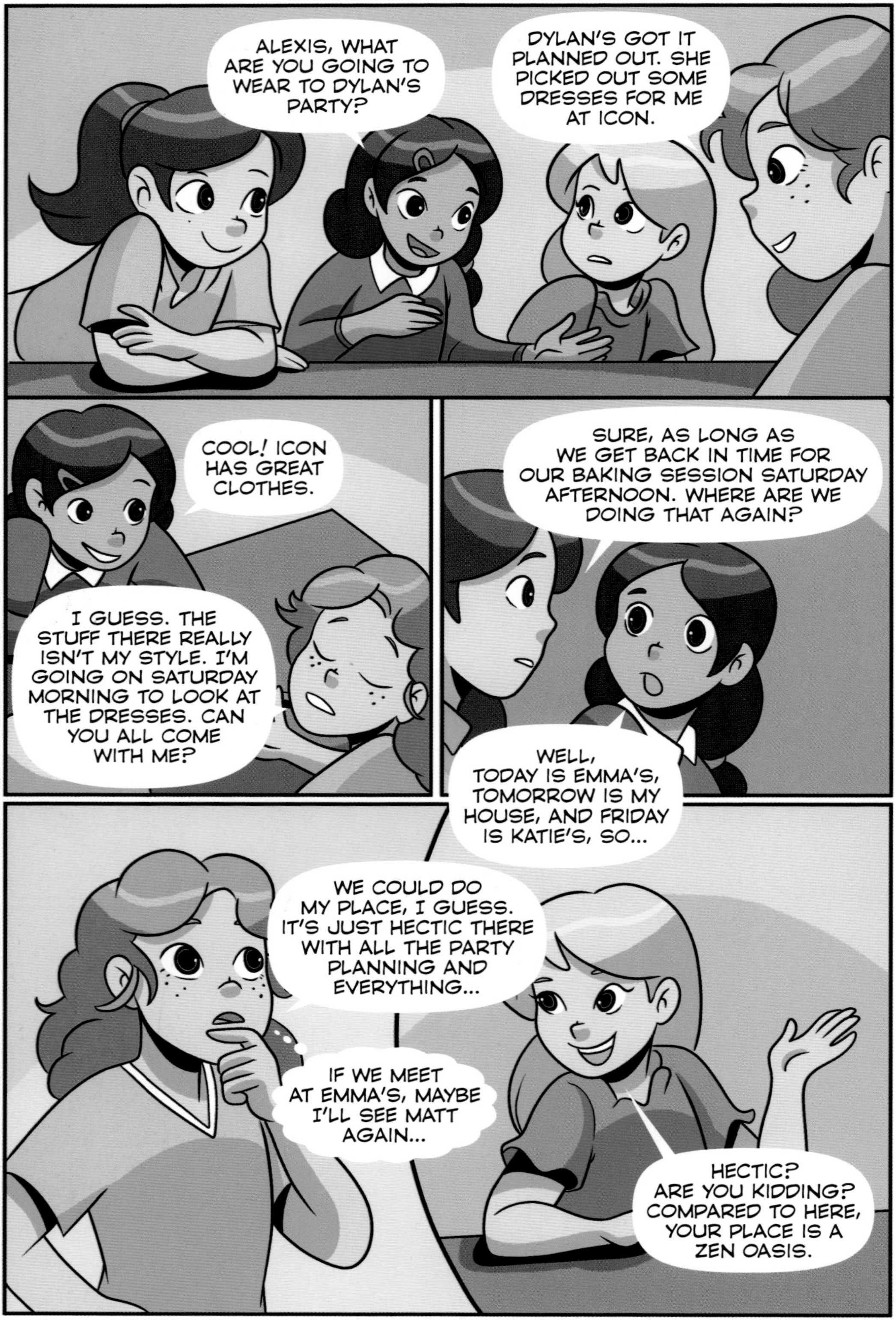
ALEXIS, WHAT ARE YOU GOING TO WEAR TO DYLAN'S PARTY?
DYLAN'S GOT IT PLANNED OUT. SHE PICKED OUT SOME DRESSES FOR ME AT ICON.
COOL! ICON HAS GREAT CLOTHES.
I GUESS. THE STUFF THERE REALLY ISN'T MY STYLE. I'M GOING ON SATURDAY MORNING TO LOOK AT THE DRESSES. CAN YOU ALL COME WITH ME?
SURE, AS LONG AS WE GET BACK IN TIME FOR OUR BAKING SESSION SATURDAY AFTERNOON. WHERE ARE WE DOING THAT AGAIN?
WELL, TODAY IS EMMA'S, TOMORROW IS MY HOUSE, AND FRIDAY IS KATIE'S, SO...
WE COULD DO MY PLACE, I GUESS. IT'S JUST HECTIC THERE WITH ALL THE PARTY PLANNING AND EVERYTHING...
IF WE MEET AT EMMA'S, MAYBE I'LL SEE MATT AGAIN...
HECTIC? ARE YOU KIDDING? COMPARED TO HERE, YOUR PLACE IS A ZEN OASIS.

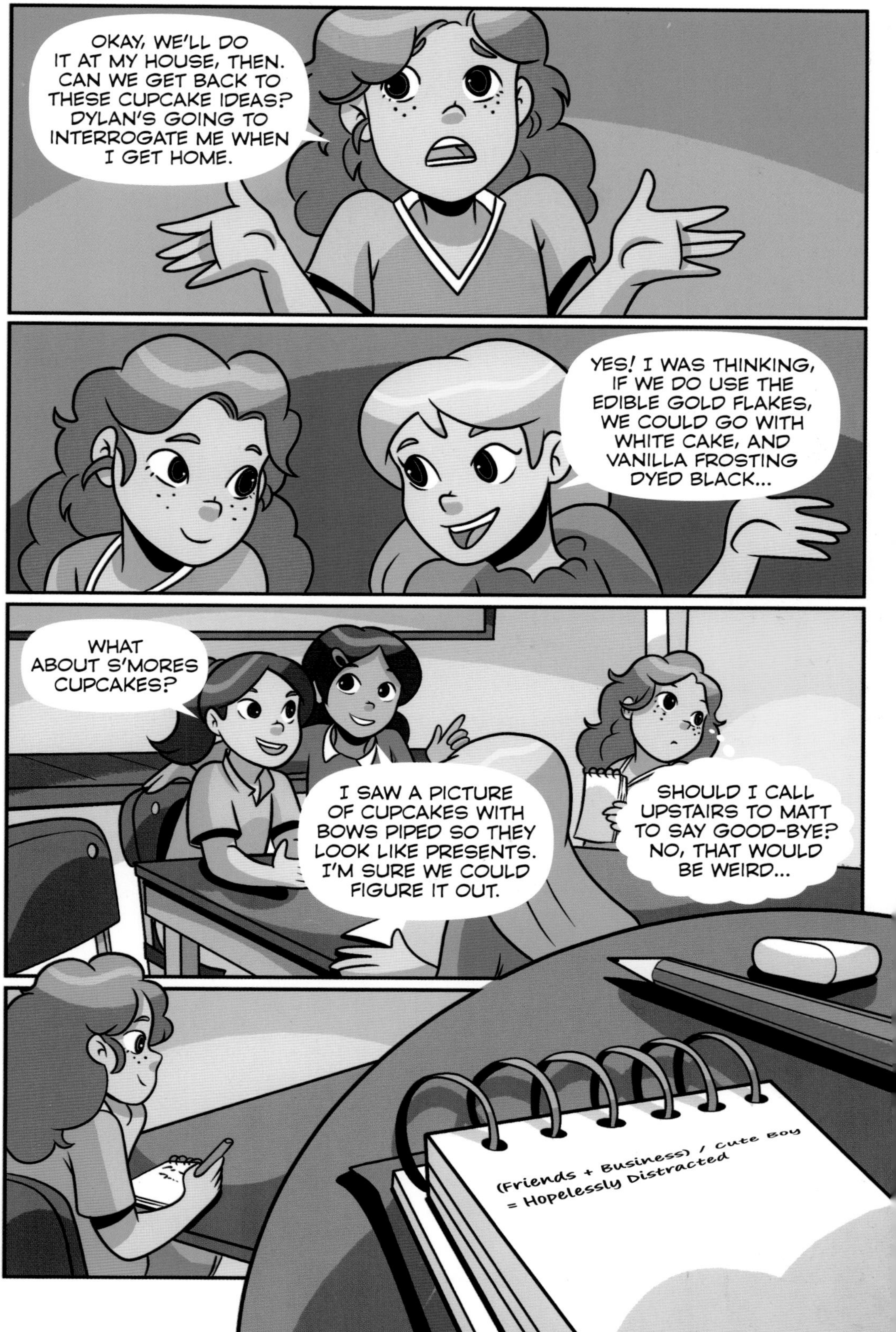
OKAY, WE'LL DO IT AT MY HOUSE, THEN. CAN WE GET BACK TO THESE CUPCAKE IDEAS? DYLAN'S GOING TO INTERROGATE ME WHEN I GET HOME.
YES! I WAS THINKING, IF WE DO USE THE EDIBLE GOLD FLAKES, WE COULD GO WITH WHITE CAKE, AND VANILLA FROSTING DYED BLACK...
WHAT ABOUT S'MORES CUPCAKES?
I SAW A PICTURE OF CUPCAKES WITH BOWS PIPED SO THEY LOOK LIKE PRESENTS. I'M SURE WE COULD FIGURE IT OUT.
SHOULD I CALL UPSTAIRS TO MATT TO SAY GOOD-BYE? NO, THAT WOULD BE WEIRD...
(Friends + Business) / Cute Boy = Hopelessly Distracted

Chapter 3

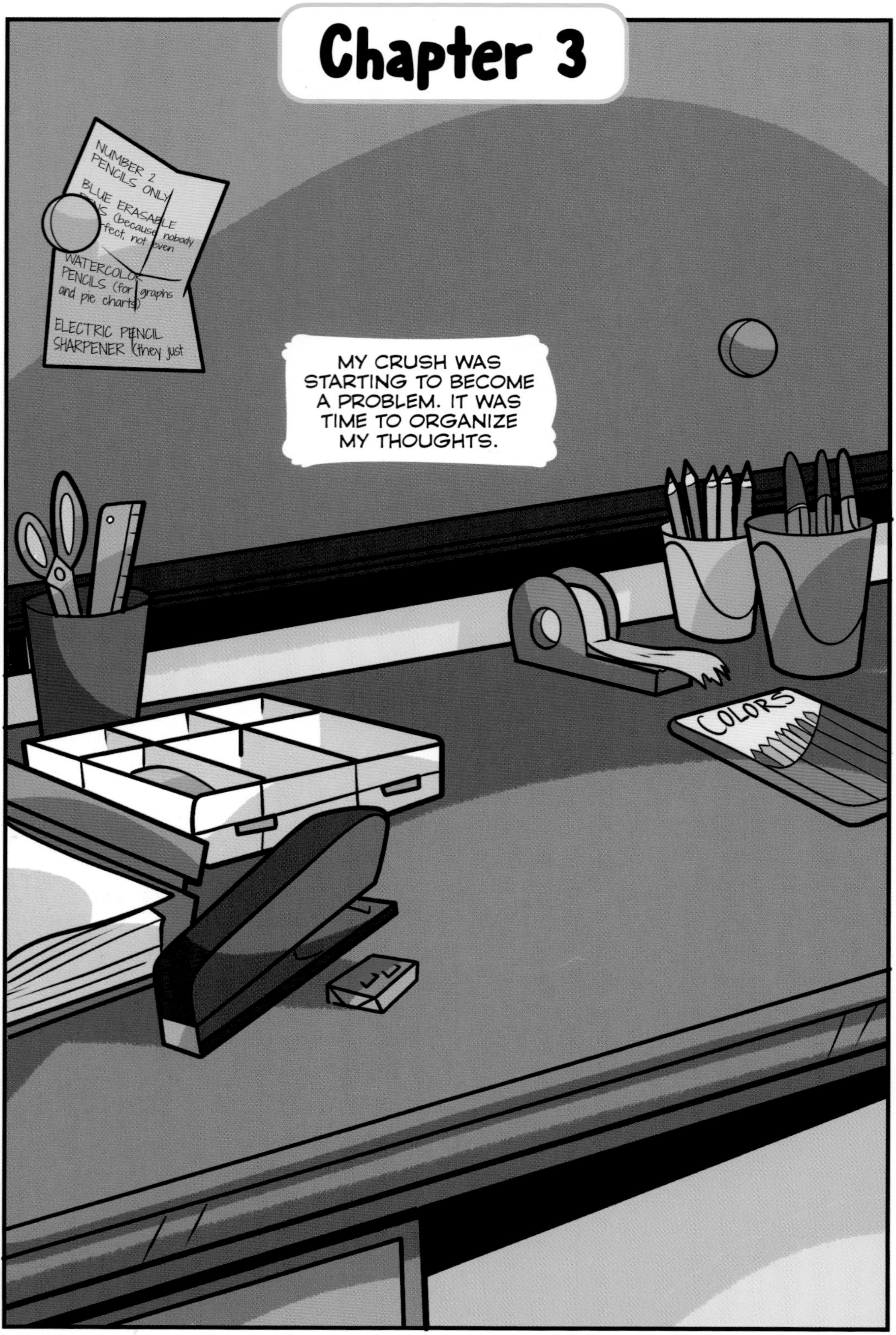
NUMBER 2
PENCILS ONLY
BLUE ERASABLE
WATERCOLOR
PENCILS (for graphs
and pie charts)
ELECTRIC PENCIL
SHARPENER (they just
MY CRUSH WAS STARTING TO BECOME A PROBLEM. IT WAS TIME TO ORGANIZE MY THOUGHTS.
COLORS

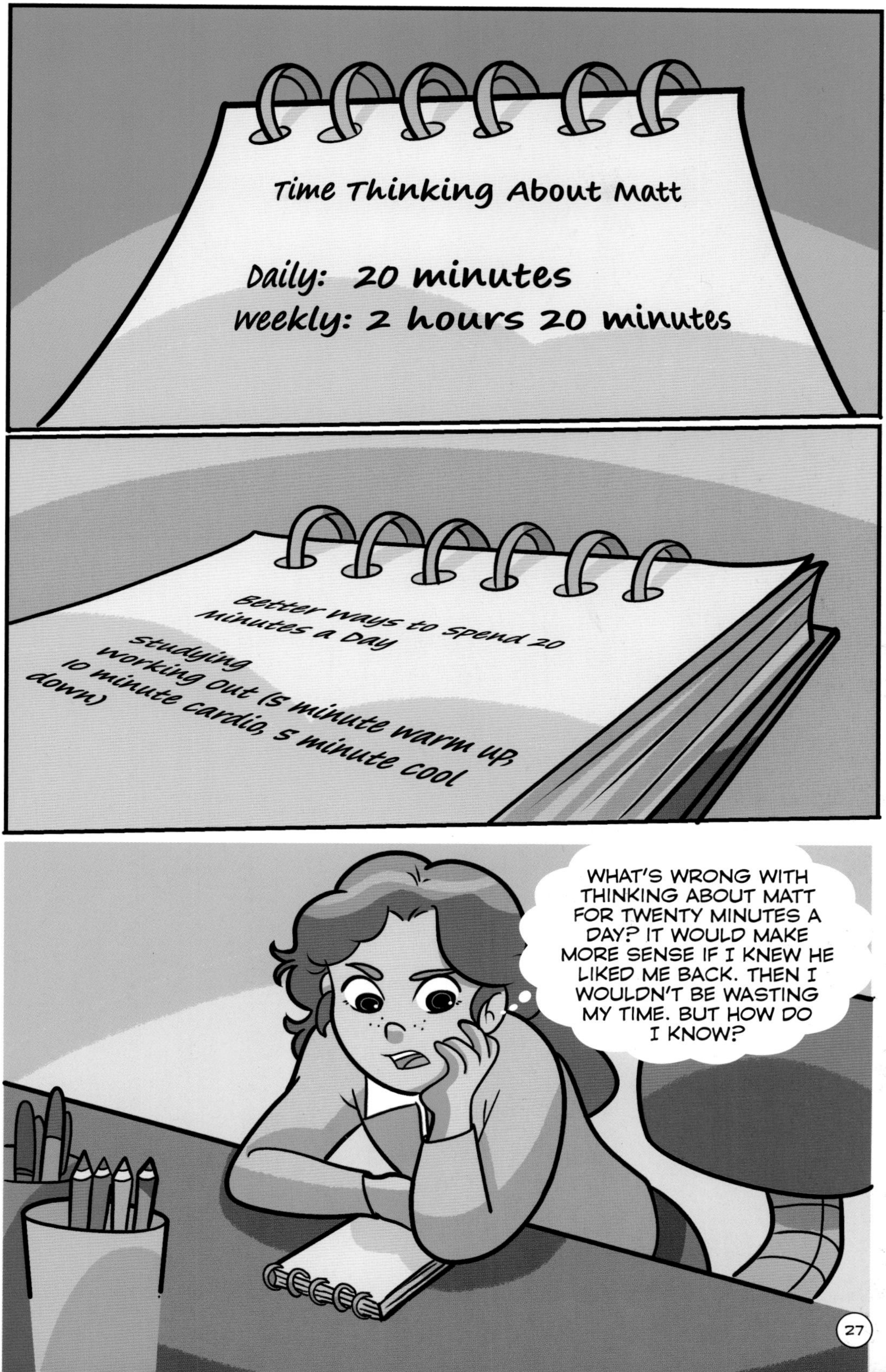
Time Thinking About Matt
Daily: 20 minutes
Weekly: 2 hours 20 minutes
Better ways to spend 20 minutes a Day
Studying
working out (5 minute warm up, 10 minute cardio, 5 minute cool down)
WHAT'S WRONG WITH THINKING ABOUT MATT FOR TWENTY MINUTES A DAY? IT WOULD MAKE MORE SENSE IF I KNEW HE LIKED ME BACK. THEN I WOULDN'T BE WASTING MY TIME. BUT HOW DO I KNOW?

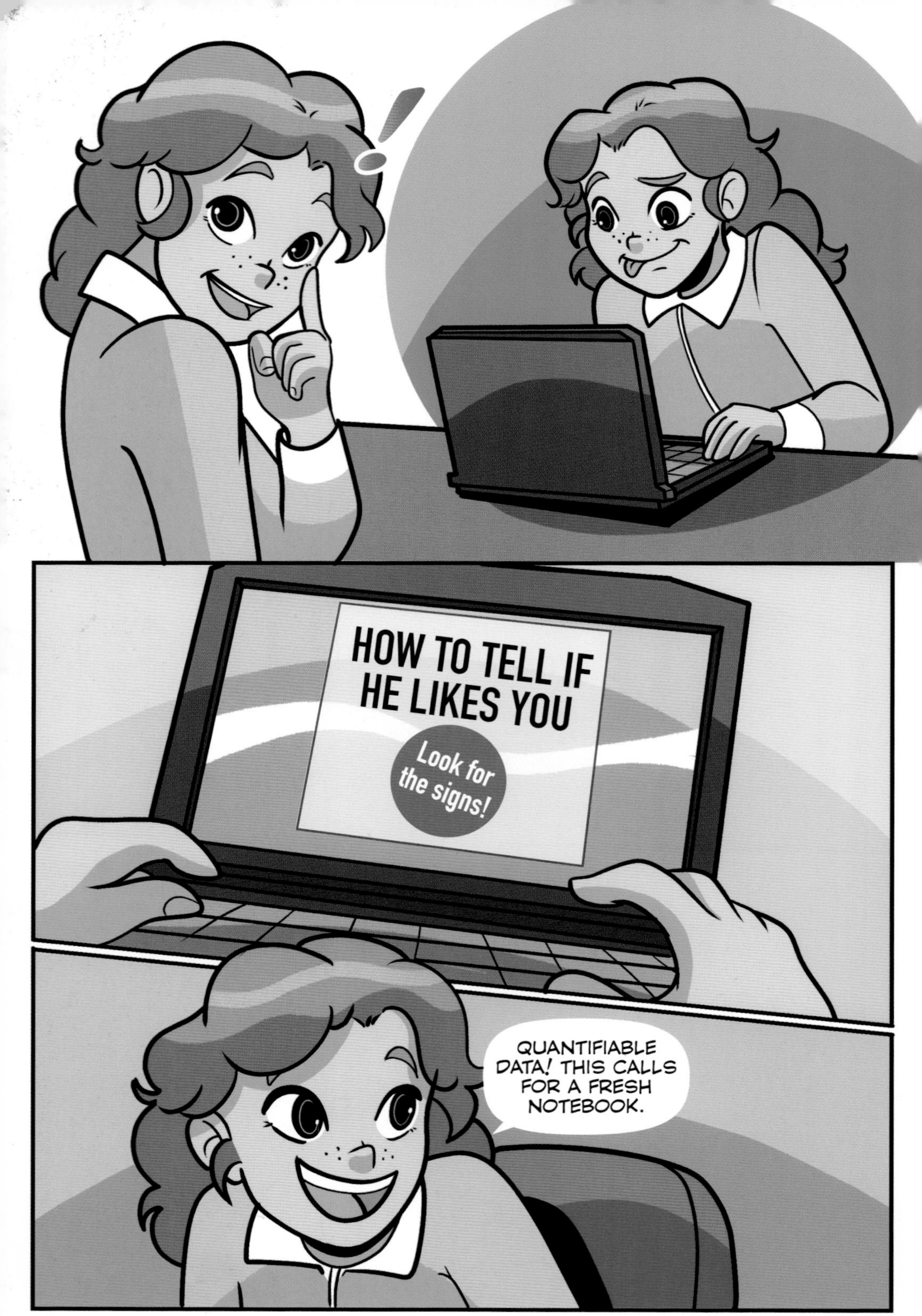
HOW TO TELL IF HE LIKES YOU
Look for the signs!
QUANTIFIABLE DATA! THIS CALLS FOR A FRESH NOTEBOOK.

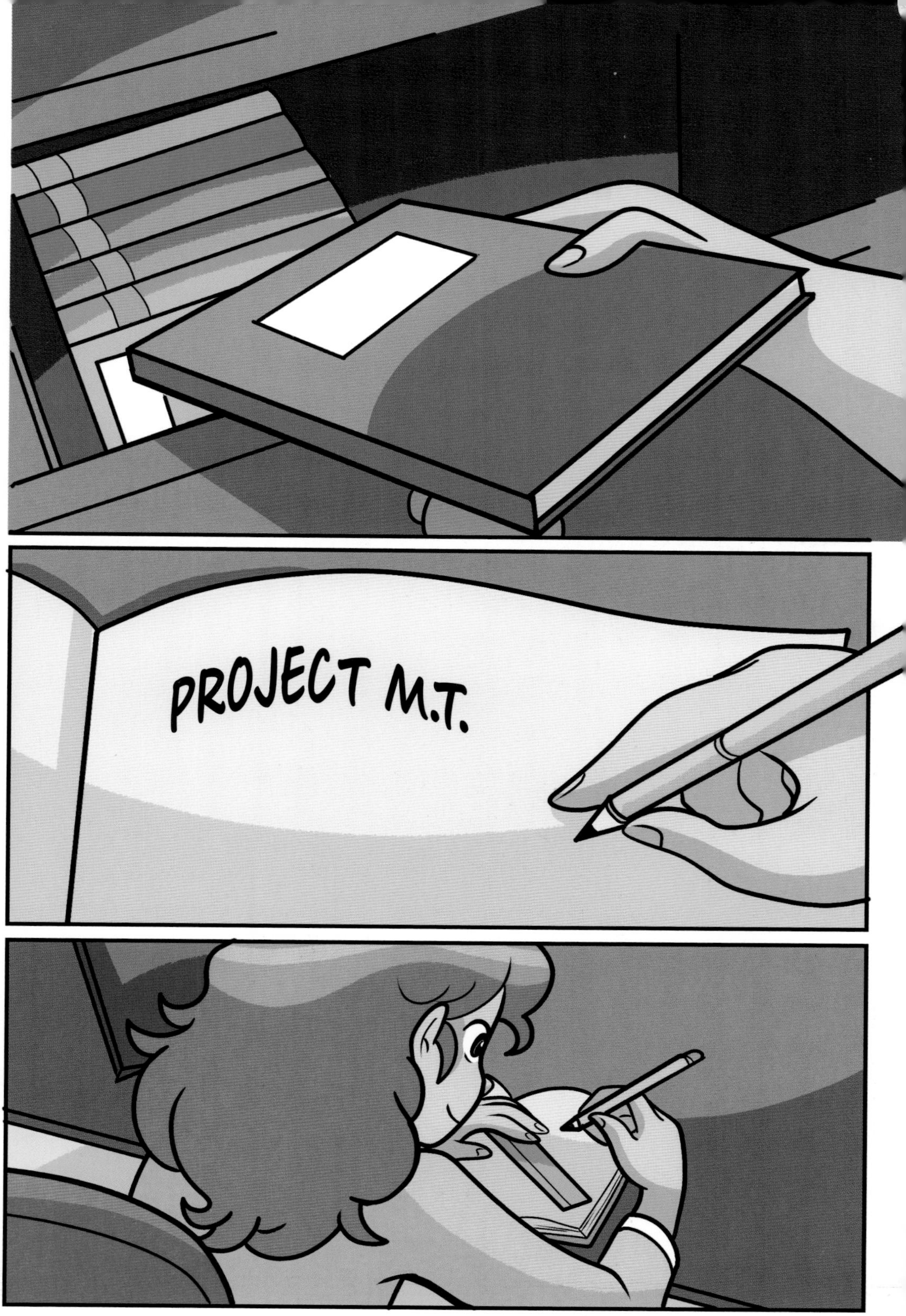
PROJECT M.T.

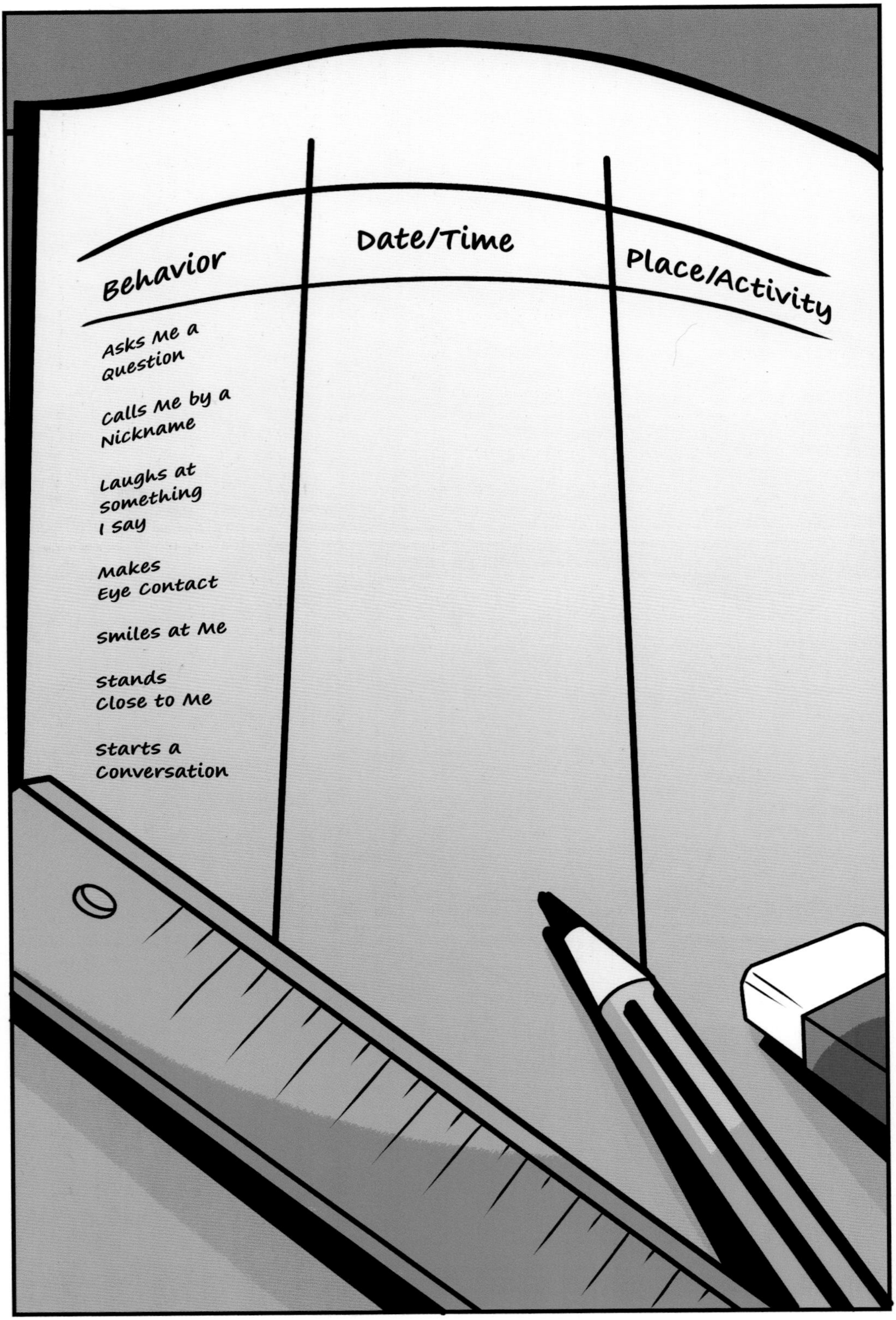
Behavior
Date/Time
Place/Activity
Asks Me a Question
Calls Me by a Nickname
Laughs at Something I Say
Makes Eye Contact
Smiles at Me
Stands Close to Me
Starts a Conversation

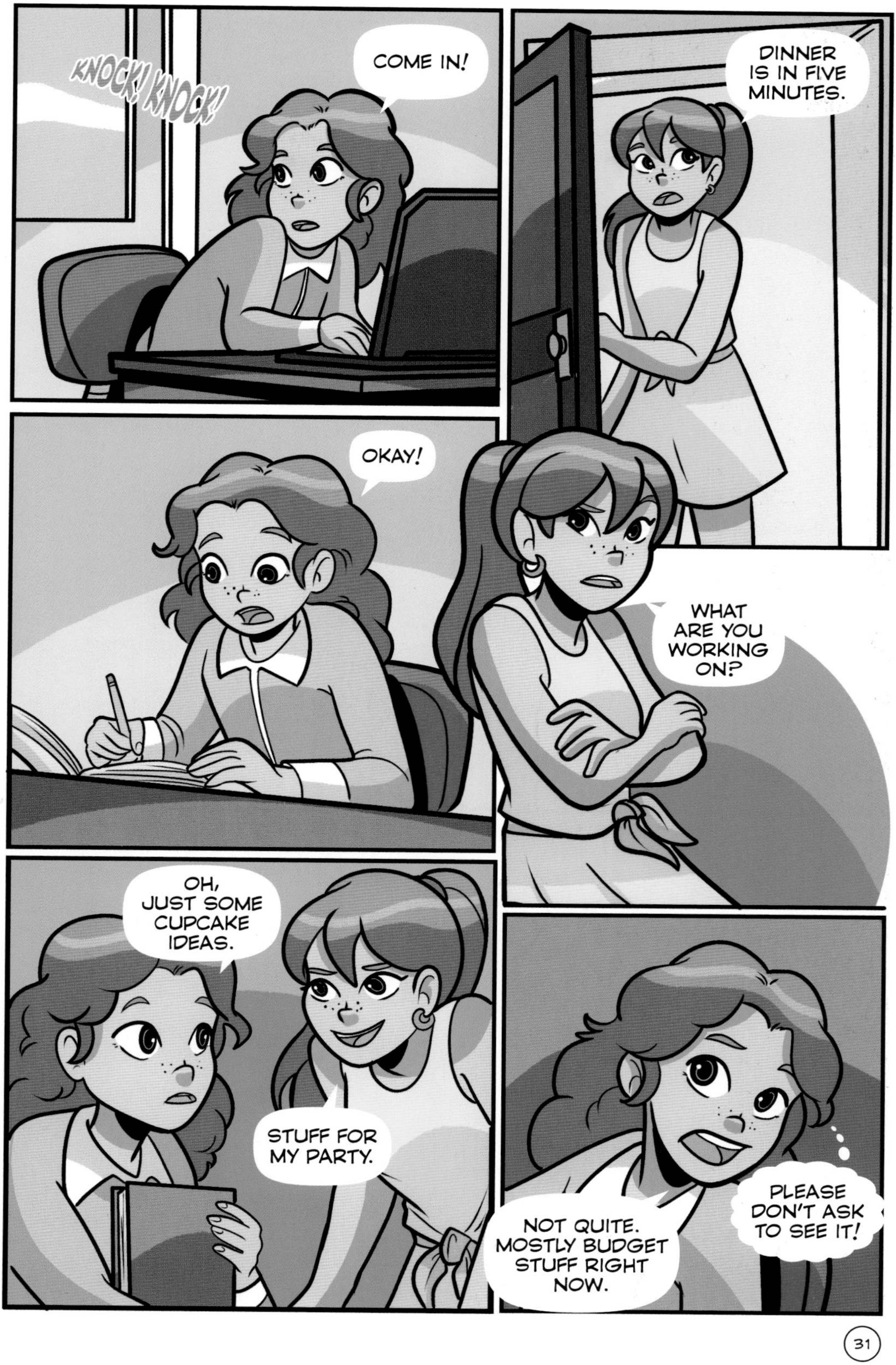
KNOCK! KNOCK!
COME IN!
DINNER IS IN FIVE MINUTES.
OKAY!
WHAT ARE YOU WORKING ON?
OH, JUST SOME CUPCAKE IDEAS.
STUFF FOR MY PARTY.
NOT QUITE. MOSTLY BUDGET STUFF RIGHT NOW.
PLEASE DON'T ASK TO SEE IT!

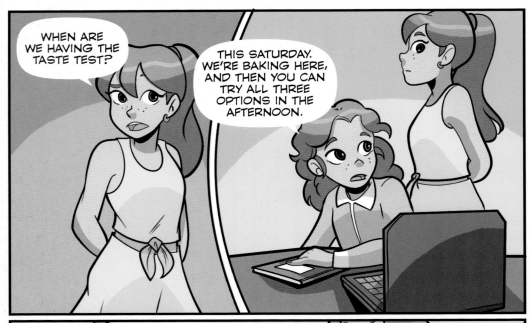

WHEN ARE WE HAVING THE TASTE TEST?

THIS SATURDAY. WE'RE BAKING HERE, AND THEN YOU CAN TRY ALL THREE OPTIONS IN THE AFTERNOON.

BUT I HAVE CHEERLEADING PRACTICE ON SATURDAY!

WELL, WHAT TIME?

IS SHE REALLY THE OLDER SISTER? SHE SOUNDS LIKE A WHINY TODDLER.

FOUR O'CLOCK!

NO PROBLEM. WE'LL BE DONE MAKING THE SAMPLES BY THREE FOR SURE.

YEAH, BUT I CAN'T EAT ALL THAT SUGAR AND THEN GO OUT AND EXERCISE! THIS WILL NOT WORK! I'M GOING TO TALK TO MOM.

WHATEVER, DYL PILL.

I HEARD THAT!

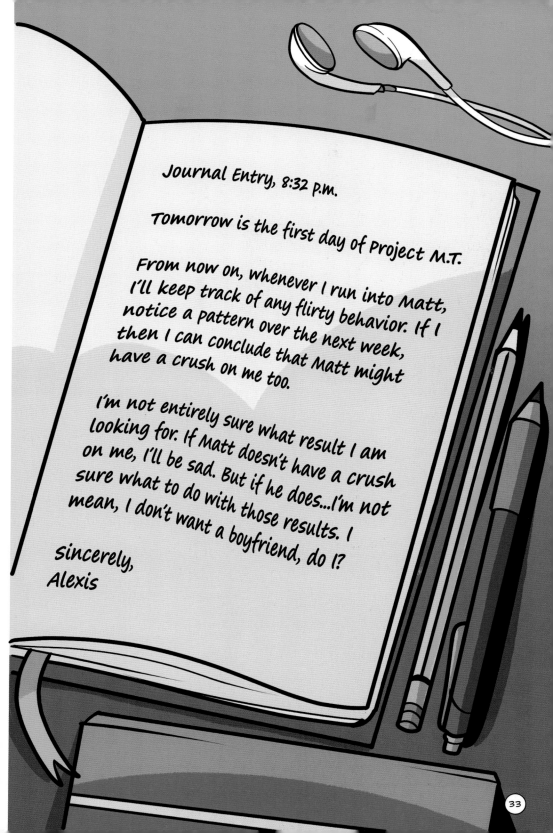

Journal Entry, 8:32 p.m.

Tomorrow is the first day of Project M.T.

From now on, whenever I run into Matt, I'll keep track of any flirty behavior. If I notice a pattern over the next week, then I can conclude that Matt might have a crush on me too.

I'm not entirely sure what result I am looking for. If Matt doesn't have a crush on me, I'll be sad. But if he does...I'm not sure what to do with those results. I mean, I don't want a boyfriend, do I?

Sincerely,
Alexis

Chapter 4

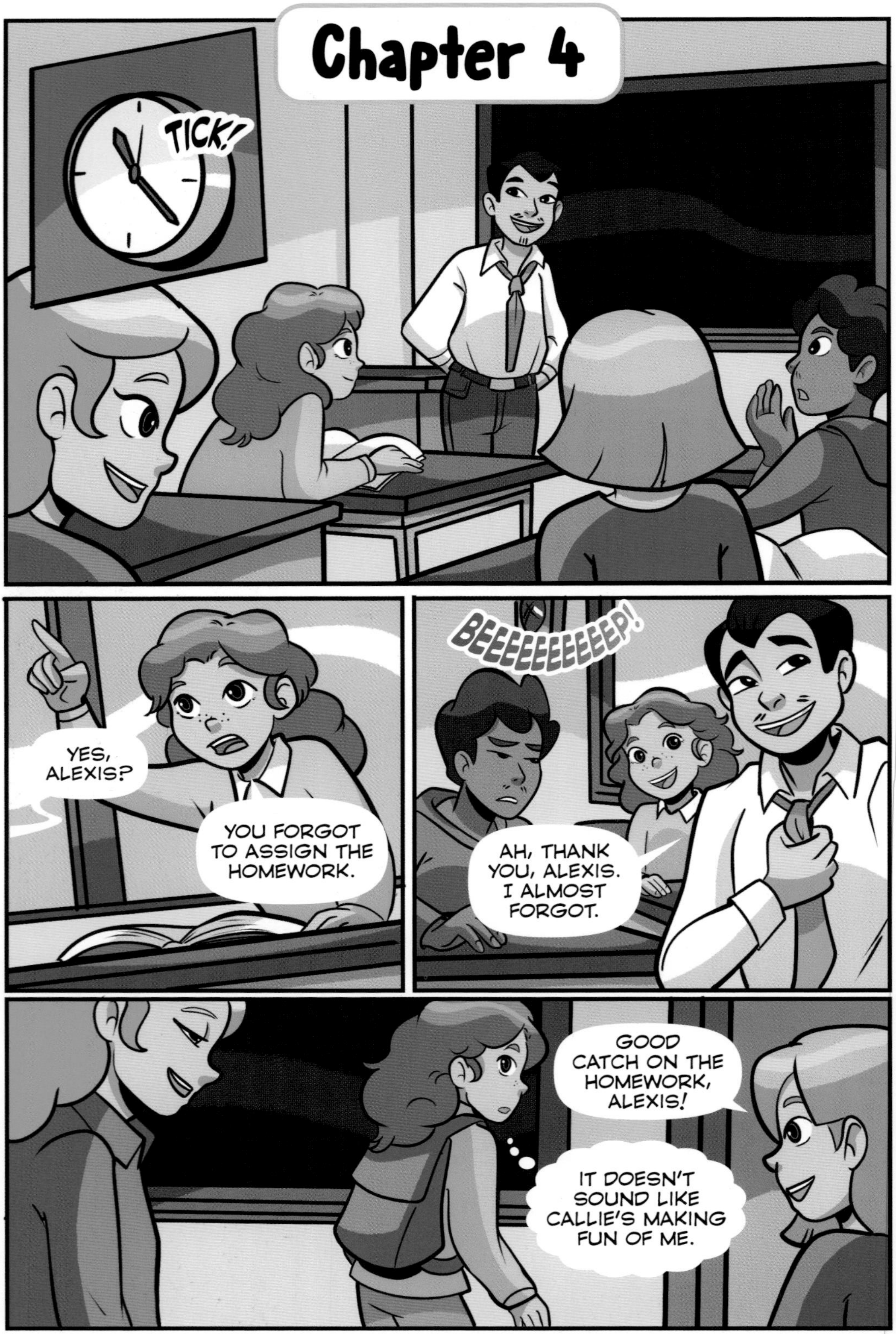
TICK!
YES, ALEXIS?
YOU FORGOT TO ASSIGN THE HOMEWORK.
BEEEEEEEEEEEP!
AH, THANK YOU, ALEXIS. I ALMOST FORGOT.
GOOD CATCH ON THE HOMEWORK, ALEXIS!
IT DOESN'T SOUND LIKE CALLIE'S MAKING FUN OF ME.

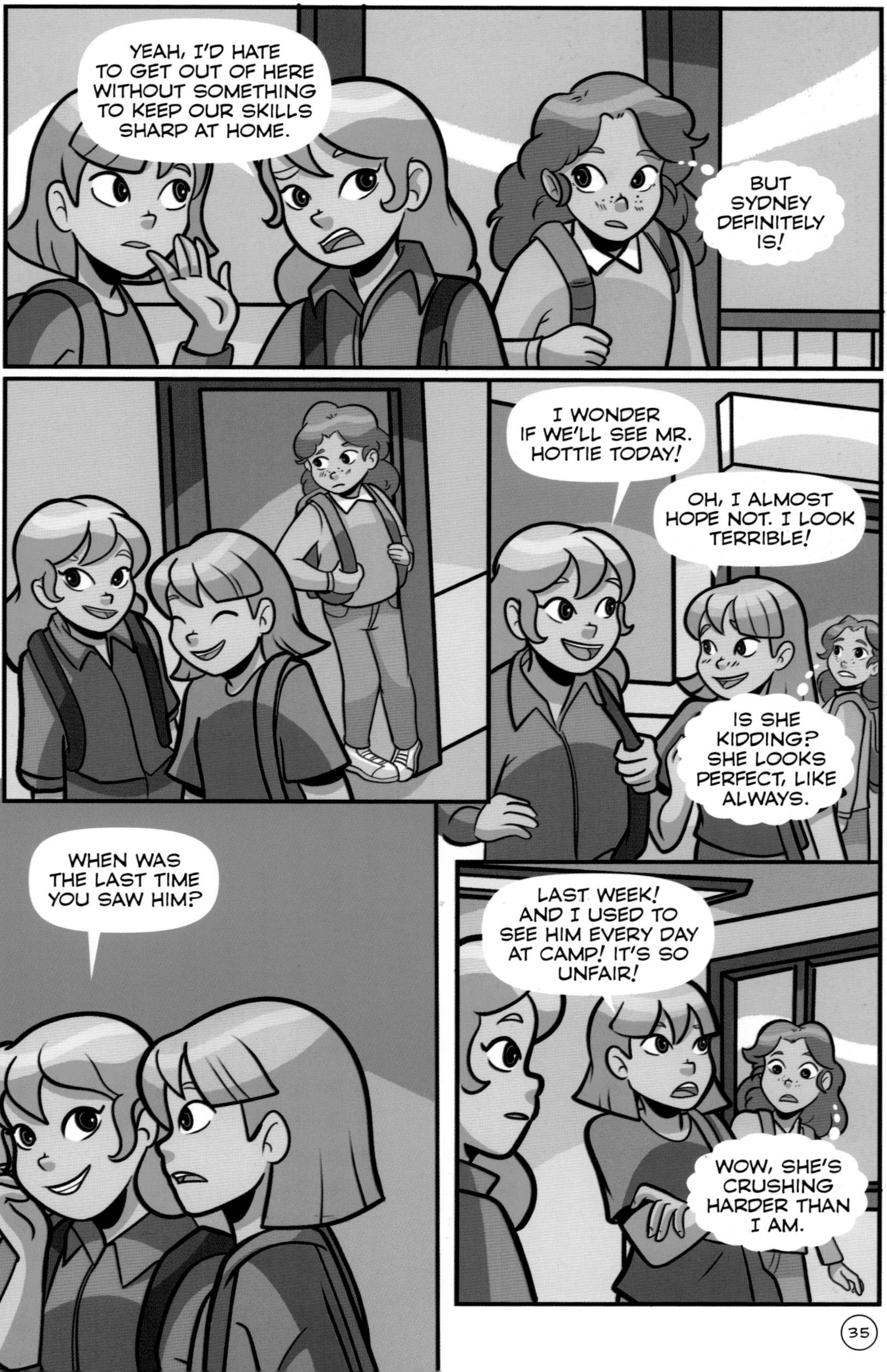
YEAH, I'D HATE TO GET OUT OF HERE WITHOUT SOMETHING TO KEEP OUR SKILLS SHARP AT HOME.
BUT SYDNEY DEFINITELY IS!
I WONDER IF WE'LL SEE MR. HOTTIE TODAY!
OH, I ALMOST HOPE NOT. I LOOK TERRIBLE!
IS SHE KIDDING? SHE LOOKS PERFECT, LIKE ALWAYS.
WHEN WAS THE LAST TIME YOU SAW HIM?
LAST WEEK! AND I USED TO SEE HIM EVERY DAY AT CAMP! IT'S SO UNFAIR!
WOW, SHE'S CRUSHING HARDER THAN I AM.

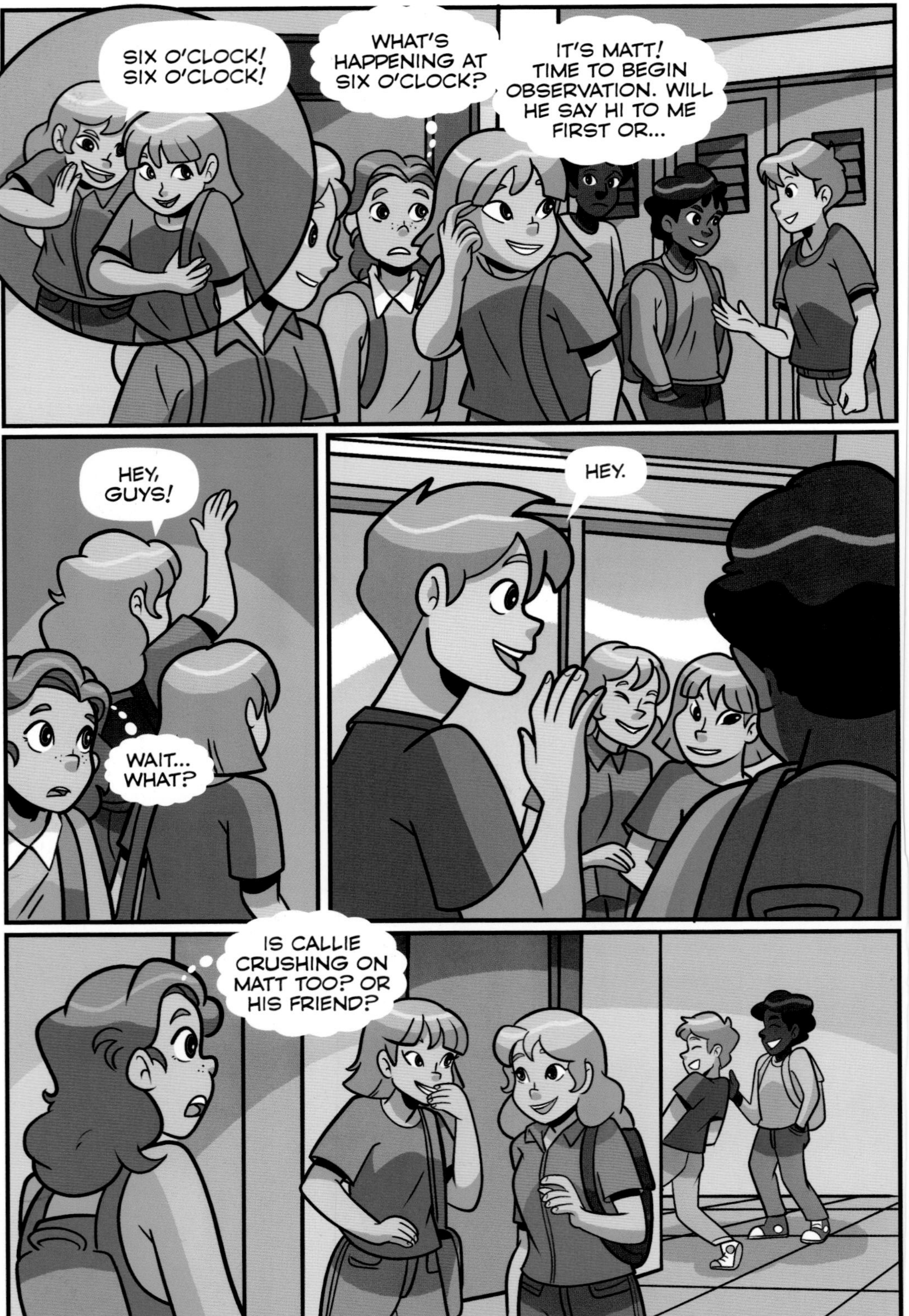
SIX O'CLOCK! SIX O'CLOCK!
WHAT'S HAPPENING AT SIX O'CLOCK?
IT'S MATT! TIME TO BEGIN OBSERVATION. WILL HE SAY HI TO ME FIRST OR...
HEY, GUYS!
WAIT... WHAT?
HEY.
IS CALLIE CRUSHING ON MATT TOO? OR HIS FRIEND?

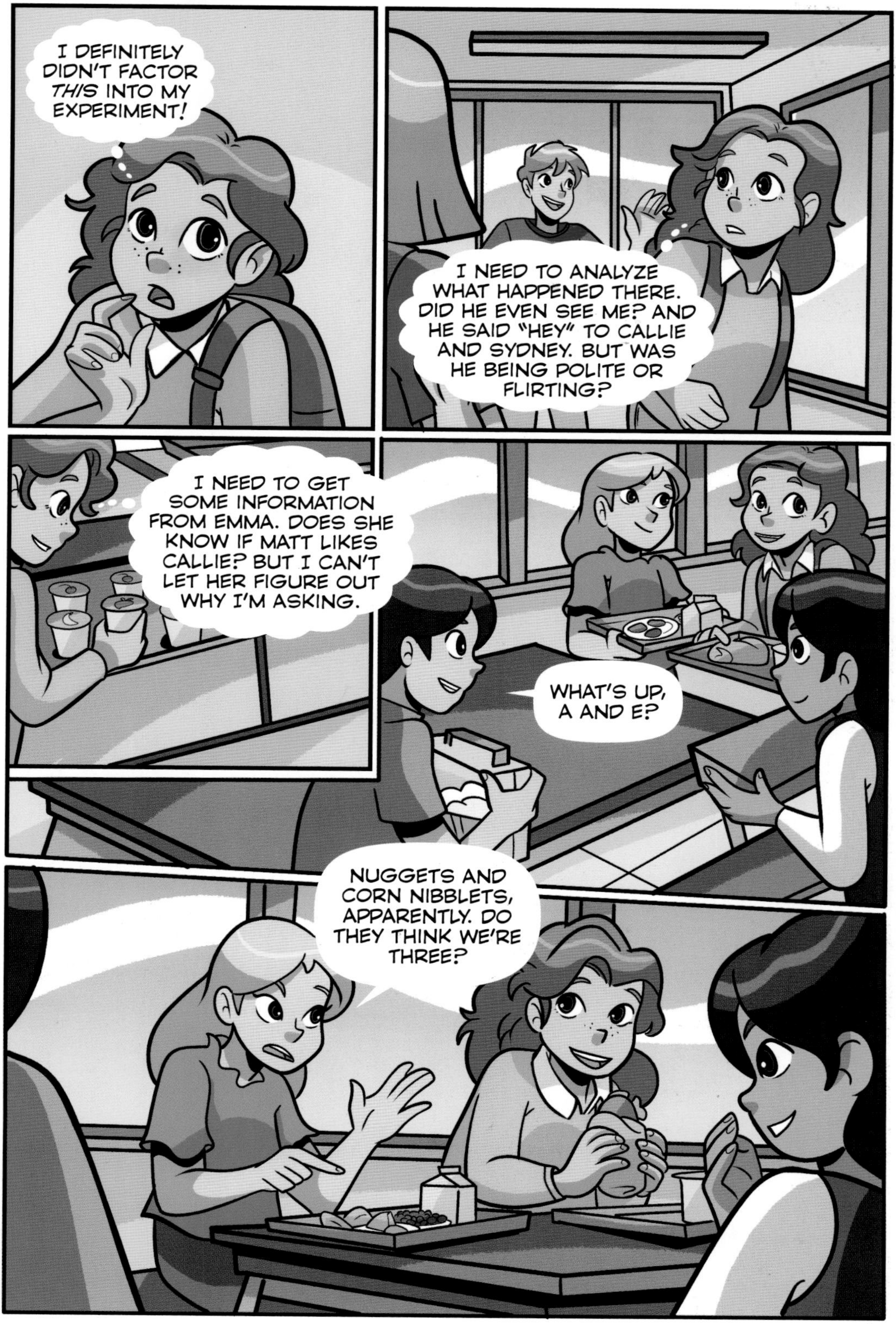
I DEFINITELY DIDN'T FACTOR *THIS* INTO MY EXPERIMENT!
I NEED TO ANALYZE WHAT HAPPENED THERE. DID HE EVEN SEE ME? AND HE SAID "HEY" TO CALLIE AND SYDNEY. BUT WAS HE BEING POLITE OR FLIRTING?
I NEED TO GET SOME INFORMATION FROM EMMA. DOES SHE KNOW IF MATT LIKES CALLIE? BUT I CAN'T LET HER FIGURE OUT WHY I'M ASKING.
WHAT'S UP, A AND E?
NUGGETS AND CORN NIBBLETS, APPARENTLY. DO THEY THINK WE'RE THREE?

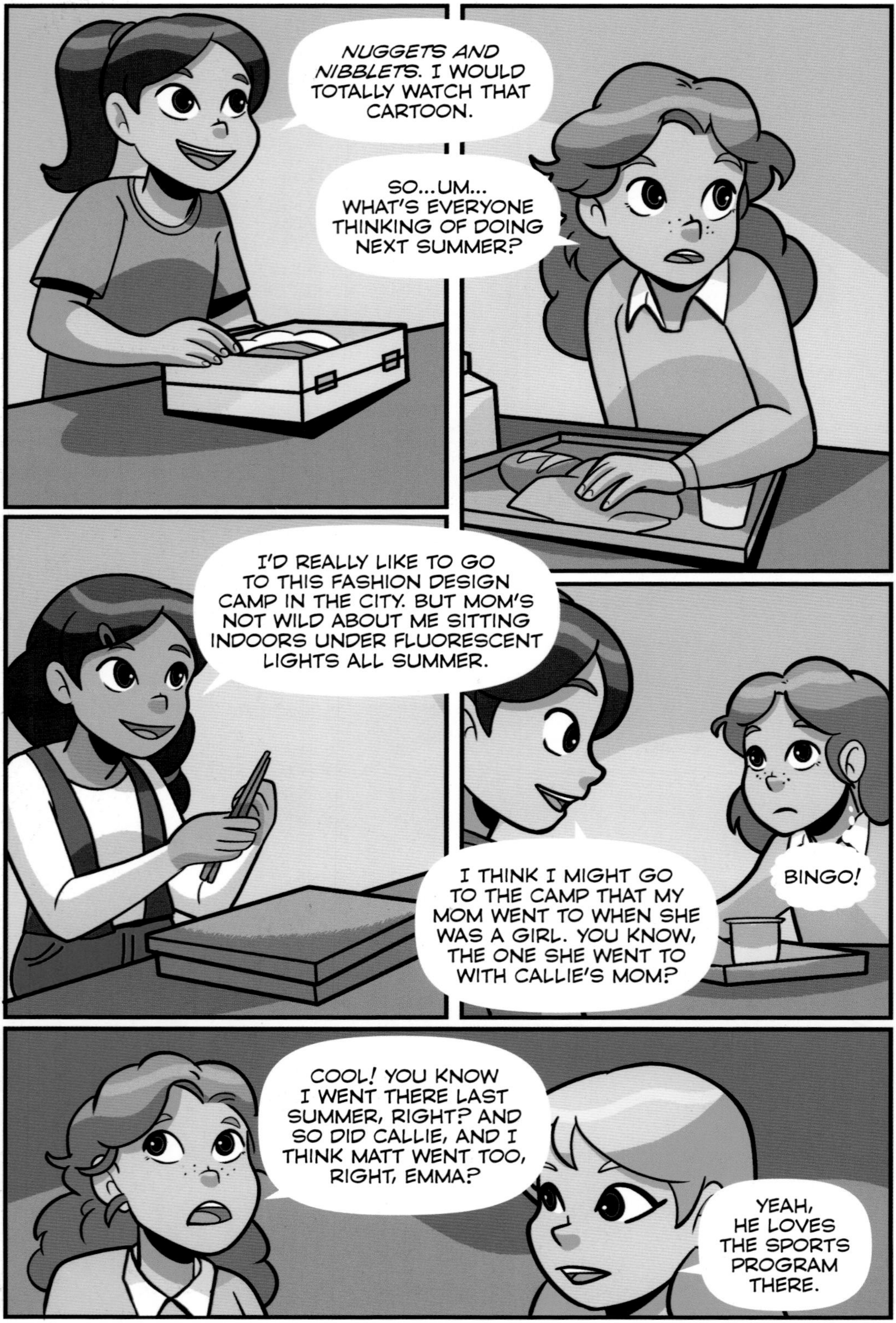
NUGGETS AND NIBBLETS. I WOULD TOTALLY WATCH THAT CARTOON.
SO...UM... WHAT'S EVERYONE THINKING OF DOING NEXT SUMMER?
I'D REALLY LIKE TO GO TO THIS FASHION DESIGN CAMP IN THE CITY. BUT MOM'S NOT WILD ABOUT ME SITTING INDOORS UNDER FLUORESCENT LIGHTS ALL SUMMER.
I THINK I MIGHT GO TO THE CAMP THAT MY MOM WENT TO WHEN SHE WAS A GIRL. YOU KNOW, THE ONE SHE WENT TO WITH CALLIE'S MOM?
BINGO!
COOL! YOU KNOW I WENT THERE LAST SUMMER, RIGHT? AND SO DID CALLIE, AND I THINK MATT WENT TOO, RIGHT, EMMA?
YEAH, HE LOVES THE SPORTS PROGRAM THERE.

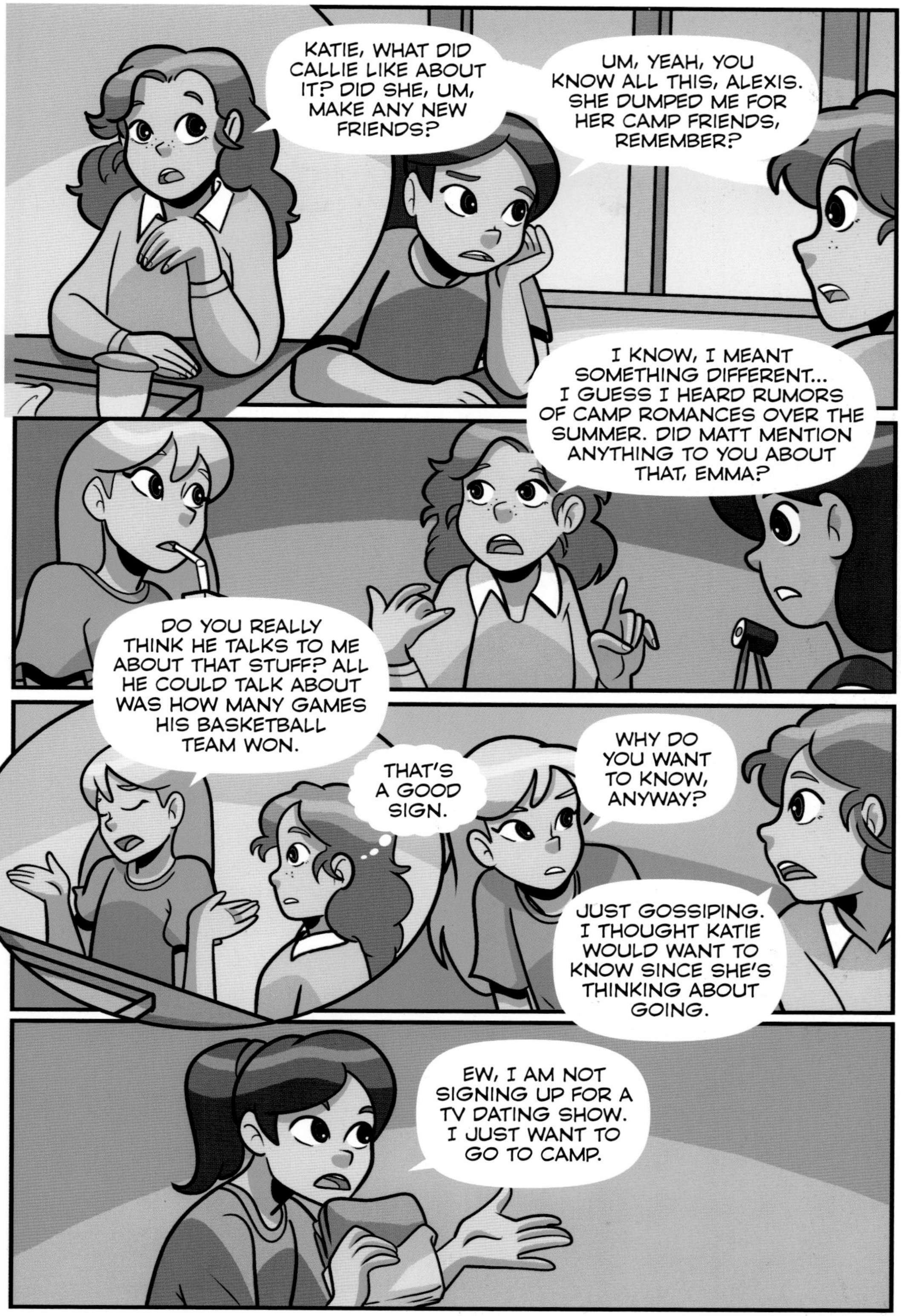
KATIE, WHAT DID CALLIE LIKE ABOUT IT? DID SHE, UM, MAKE ANY NEW FRIENDS?
UM, YEAH, YOU KNOW ALL THIS, ALEXIS. SHE DUMPED ME FOR HER CAMP FRIENDS, REMEMBER?
I KNOW, I MEANT SOMETHING DIFFERENT... I GUESS I HEARD RUMORS OF CAMP ROMANCES OVER THE SUMMER. DID MATT MENTION ANYTHING TO YOU ABOUT THAT, EMMA?
DO YOU REALLY THINK HE TALKS TO ME ABOUT THAT STUFF? ALL HE COULD TALK ABOUT WAS HOW MANY GAMES HIS BASKETBALL TEAM WON.
THAT'S A GOOD SIGN.
WHY DO YOU WANT TO KNOW, ANYWAY?
JUST GOSSIPING. I THOUGHT KATIE WOULD WANT TO KNOW SINCE SHE'S THINKING ABOUT GOING.
EW, I AM NOT SIGNING UP FOR A TV DATING SHOW. I JUST WANT TO GO TO CAMP.

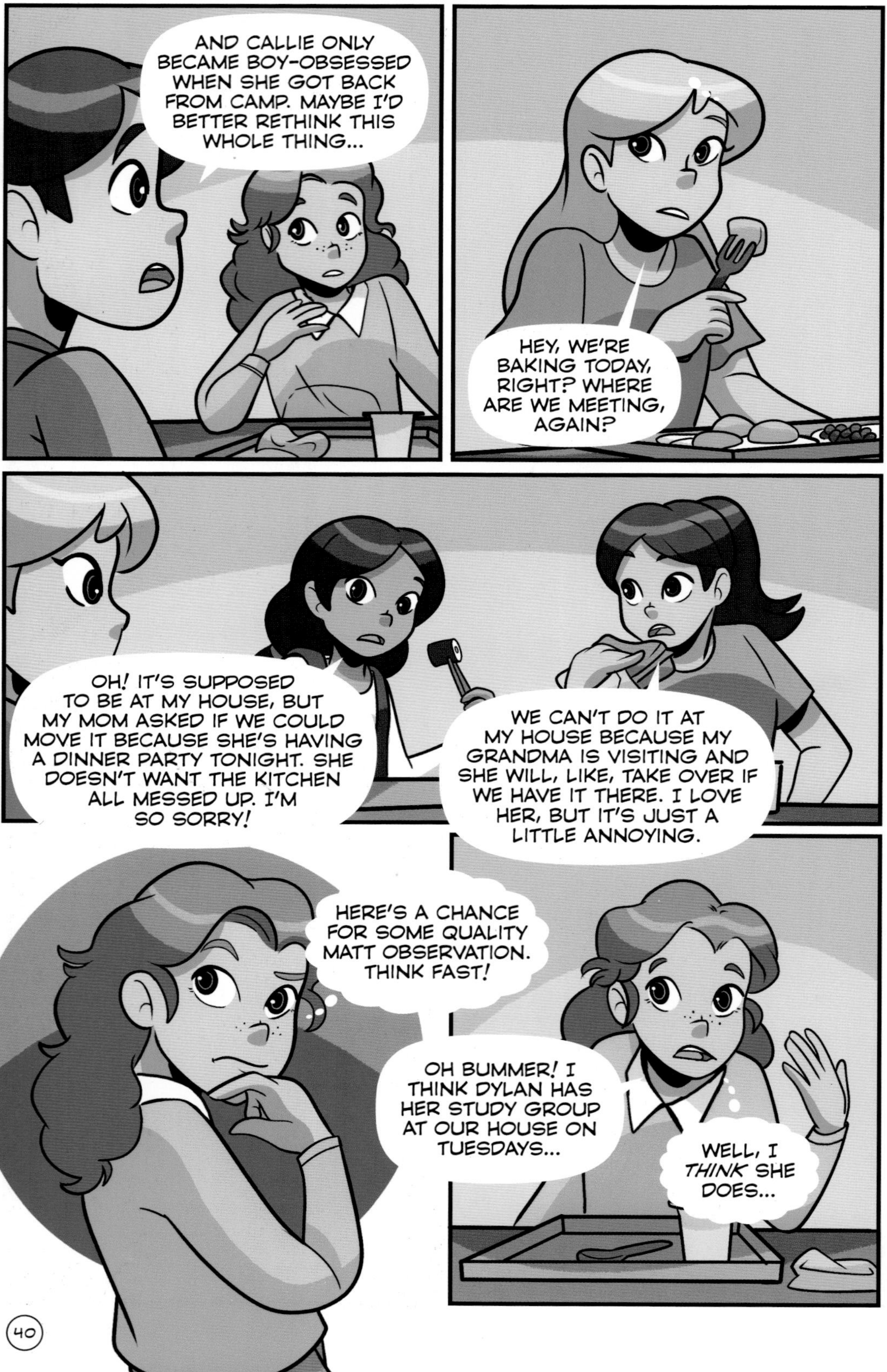
AND CALLIE ONLY BECAME BOY-OBSESSED WHEN SHE GOT BACK FROM CAMP. MAYBE I'D BETTER RETHINK THIS WHOLE THING...
HEY, WE'RE BAKING TODAY, RIGHT? WHERE ARE WE MEETING, AGAIN?
OH! IT'S SUPPOSED TO BE AT MY HOUSE, BUT MY MOM ASKED IF WE COULD MOVE IT BECAUSE SHE'S HAVING A DINNER PARTY TONIGHT. SHE DOESN'T WANT THE KITCHEN ALL MESSED UP. I'M SO SORRY!
WE CAN'T DO IT AT MY HOUSE BECAUSE MY GRANDMA IS VISITING AND SHE WILL, LIKE, TAKE OVER IF WE HAVE IT THERE. I LOVE HER, BUT IT'S JUST A LITTLE ANNOYING.
HERE'S A CHANCE FOR SOME QUALITY MATT OBSERVATION. THINK FAST!
OH BUMMER! I THINK DYLAN HAS HER STUDY GROUP AT OUR HOUSE ON TUESDAYS...
WELL, I *THINK* SHE DOES...

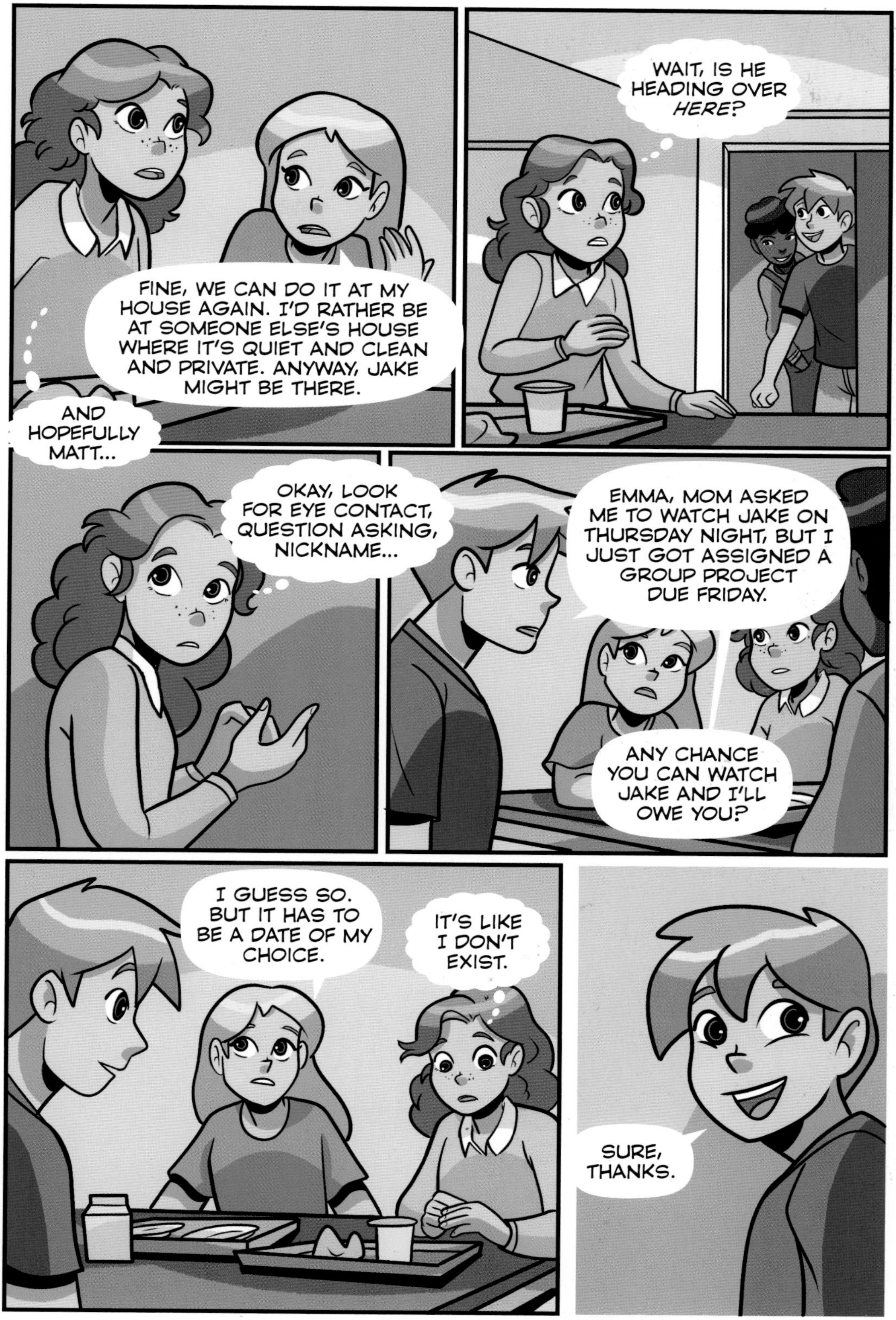
FINE, WE CAN DO IT AT MY HOUSE AGAIN. I'D RATHER BE AT SOMEONE ELSE'S HOUSE WHERE IT'S QUIET AND CLEAN AND PRIVATE. ANYWAY, JAKE MIGHT BE THERE.
AND HOPEFULLY MATT...
WAIT, IS HE HEADING OVER *HERE*?
OKAY, LOOK FOR EYE CONTACT, QUESTION ASKING, NICKNAME...
EMMA, MOM ASKED ME TO WATCH JAKE ON THURSDAY NIGHT, BUT I JUST GOT ASSIGNED A GROUP PROJECT DUE FRIDAY.
ANY CHANCE YOU CAN WATCH JAKE AND I'LL OWE YOU?
I GUESS SO. BUT IT HAS TO BE A DATE OF MY CHOICE.
IT'S LIKE I DON'T EXIST.
SURE, THANKS.

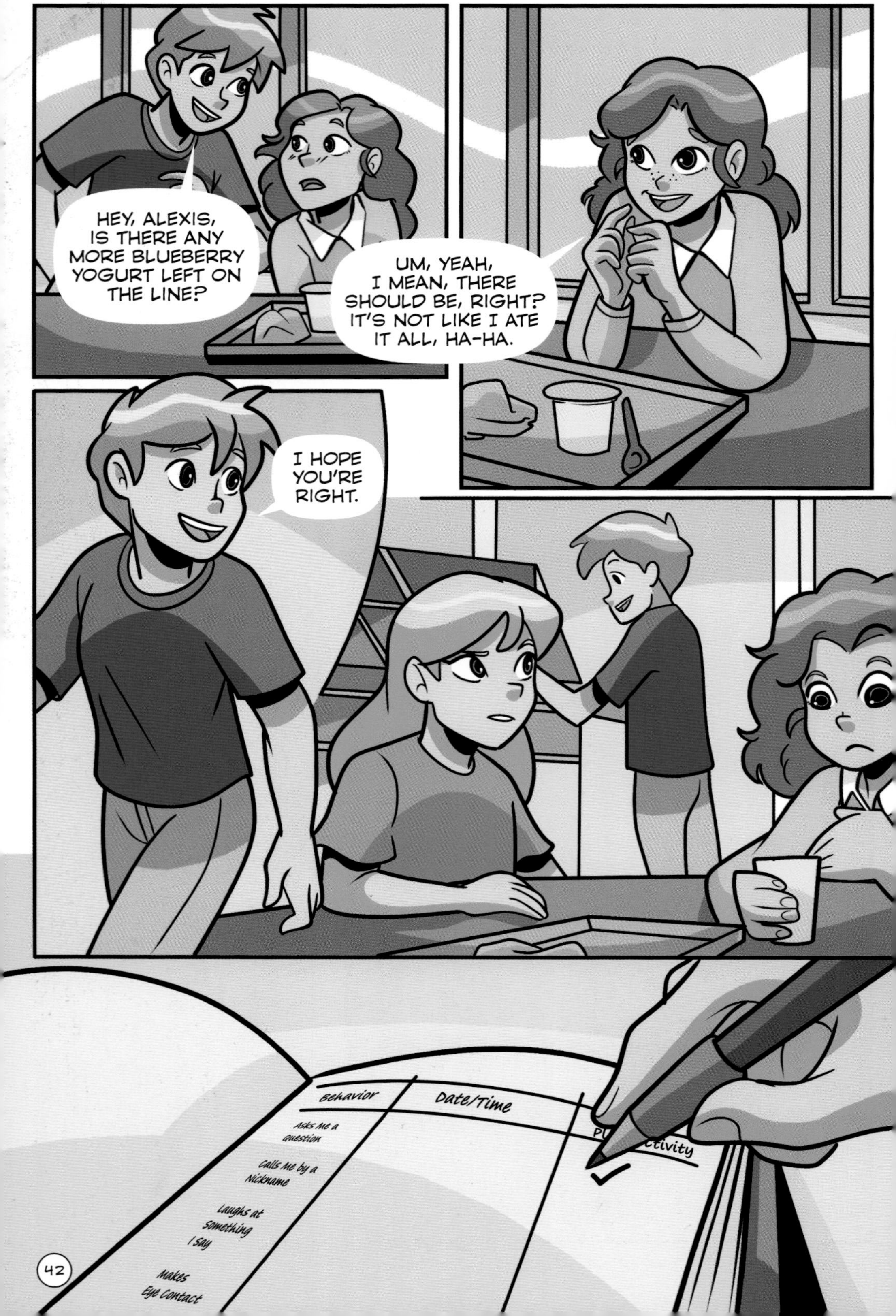
HEY, ALEXIS, IS THERE ANY MORE BLUEBERRY YOGURT LEFT ON THE LINE?
UM, YEAH, I MEAN, THERE SHOULD BE, RIGHT? IT'S NOT LIKE I ATE IT ALL, HA-HA.
I HOPE YOU'RE RIGHT.
Behavior
Date/Time
Asks Me a Question
Calls Me by a Nickname
Laughs at Something I Say
Makes Eye Contact

Chapter 5

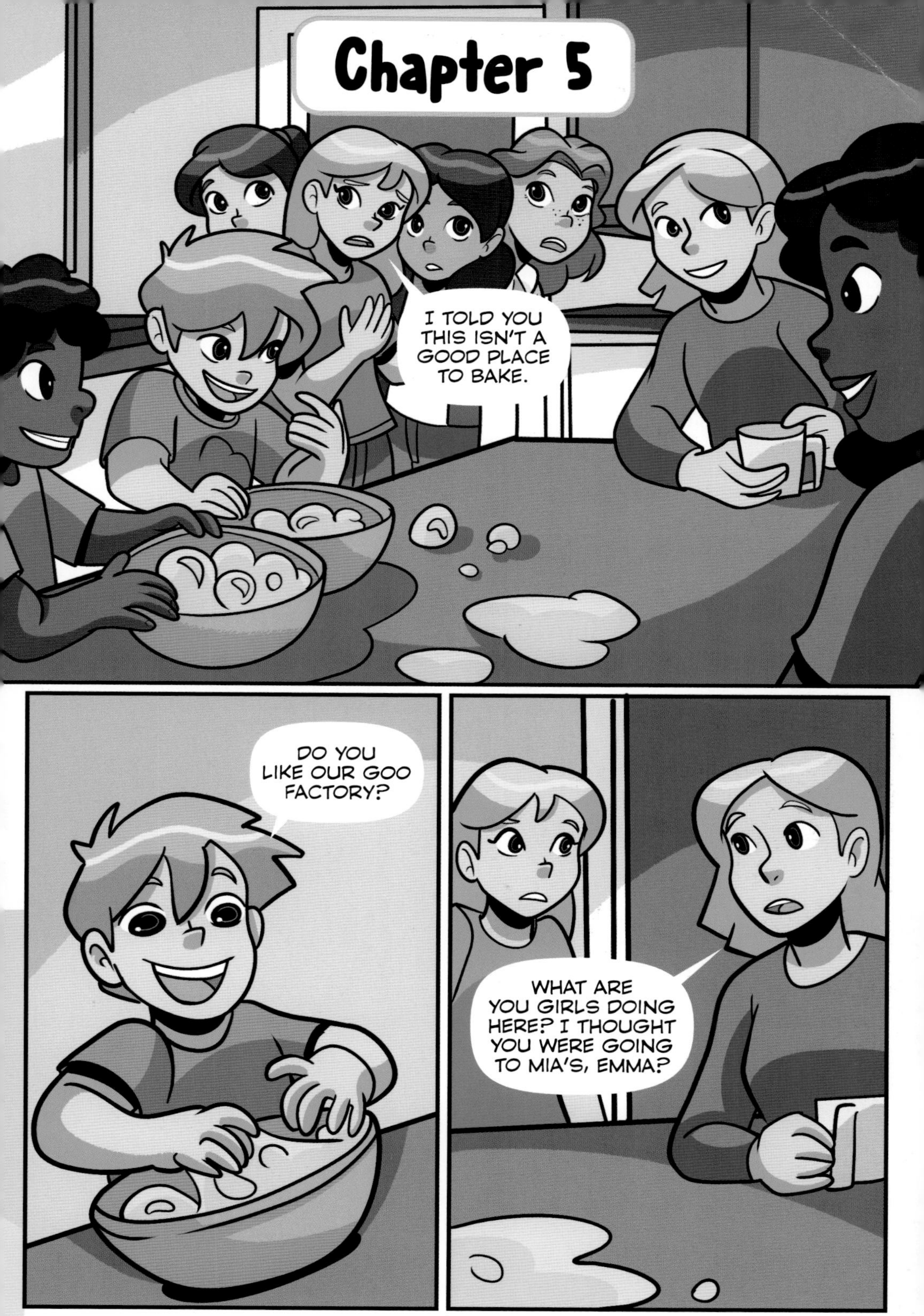

I TOLD YOU THIS ISN'T A GOOD PLACE TO BAKE.
DO YOU LIKE OUR GOO FACTORY?
WHAT ARE YOU GIRLS DOING HERE? I THOUGHT YOU WERE GOING TO MIA'S, EMMA?

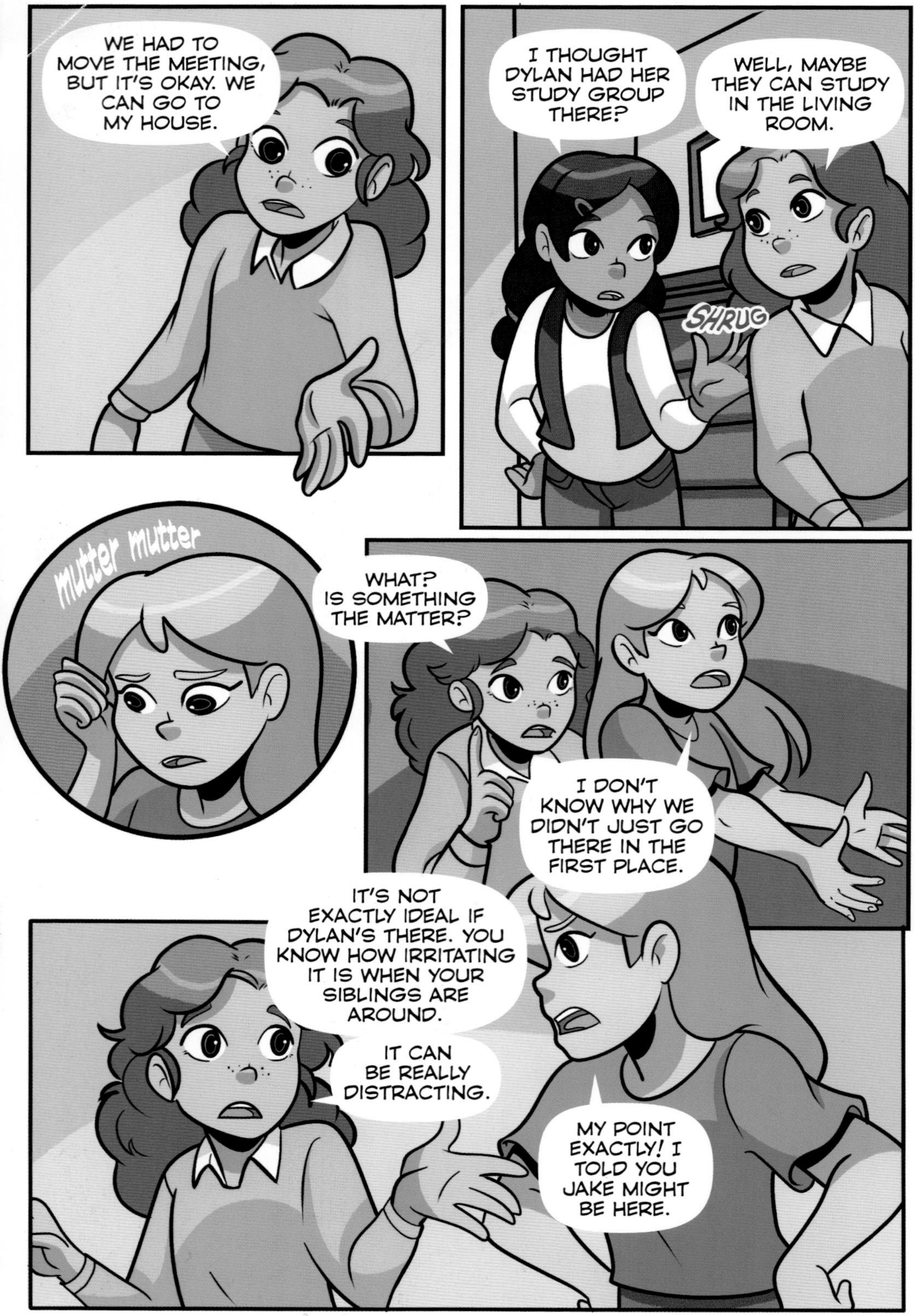
WE HAD TO MOVE THE MEETING, BUT IT'S OKAY. WE CAN GO TO MY HOUSE.
I THOUGHT DYLAN HAD HER STUDY GROUP THERE?
WELL, MAYBE THEY CAN STUDY IN THE LIVING ROOM.
SHRUG
mutter mutter
WHAT? IS SOMETHING THE MATTER?
I DON'T KNOW WHY WE DIDN'T JUST GO THERE IN THE FIRST PLACE.
IT'S NOT EXACTLY IDEAL IF DYLAN'S THERE. YOU KNOW HOW IRRITATING IT IS WHEN YOUR SIBLINGS ARE AROUND.
IT CAN BE REALLY DISTRACTING.
MY POINT EXACTLY! I TOLD YOU JAKE MIGHT BE HERE.

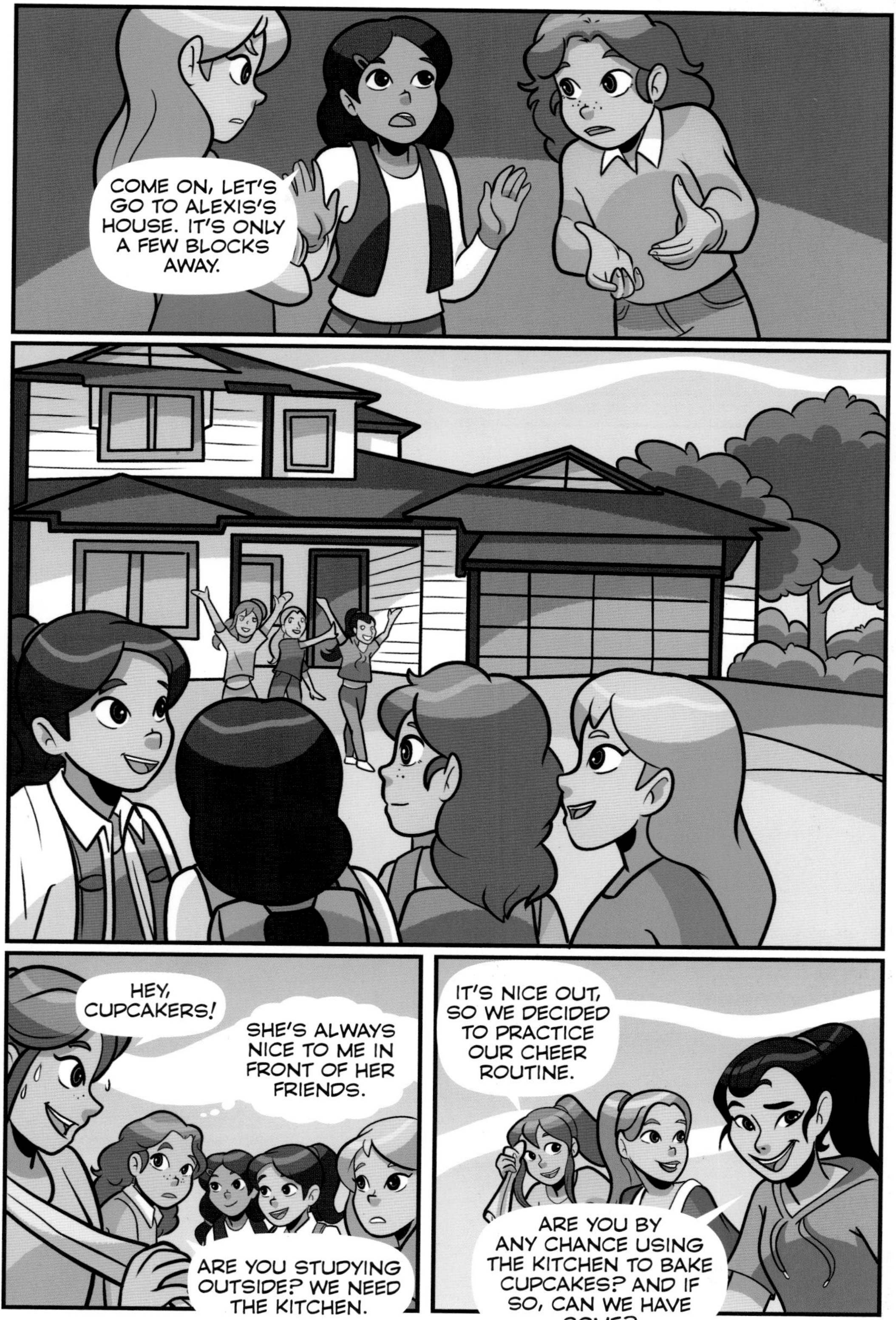

COME ON, LET'S GO TO ALEXIS'S HOUSE. IT'S ONLY A FEW BLOCKS AWAY.
HEY, CUPCAKERS!
SHE'S ALWAYS NICE TO ME IN FRONT OF HER FRIENDS.
ARE YOU STUDYING OUTSIDE? WE NEED THE KITCHEN.
IT'S NICE OUT, SO WE DECIDED TO PRACTICE OUR CHEER ROUTINE.
ARE YOU BY ANY CHANCE USING THE KITCHEN TO BAKE CUPCAKES? AND IF SO, CAN WE HAVE SOME?

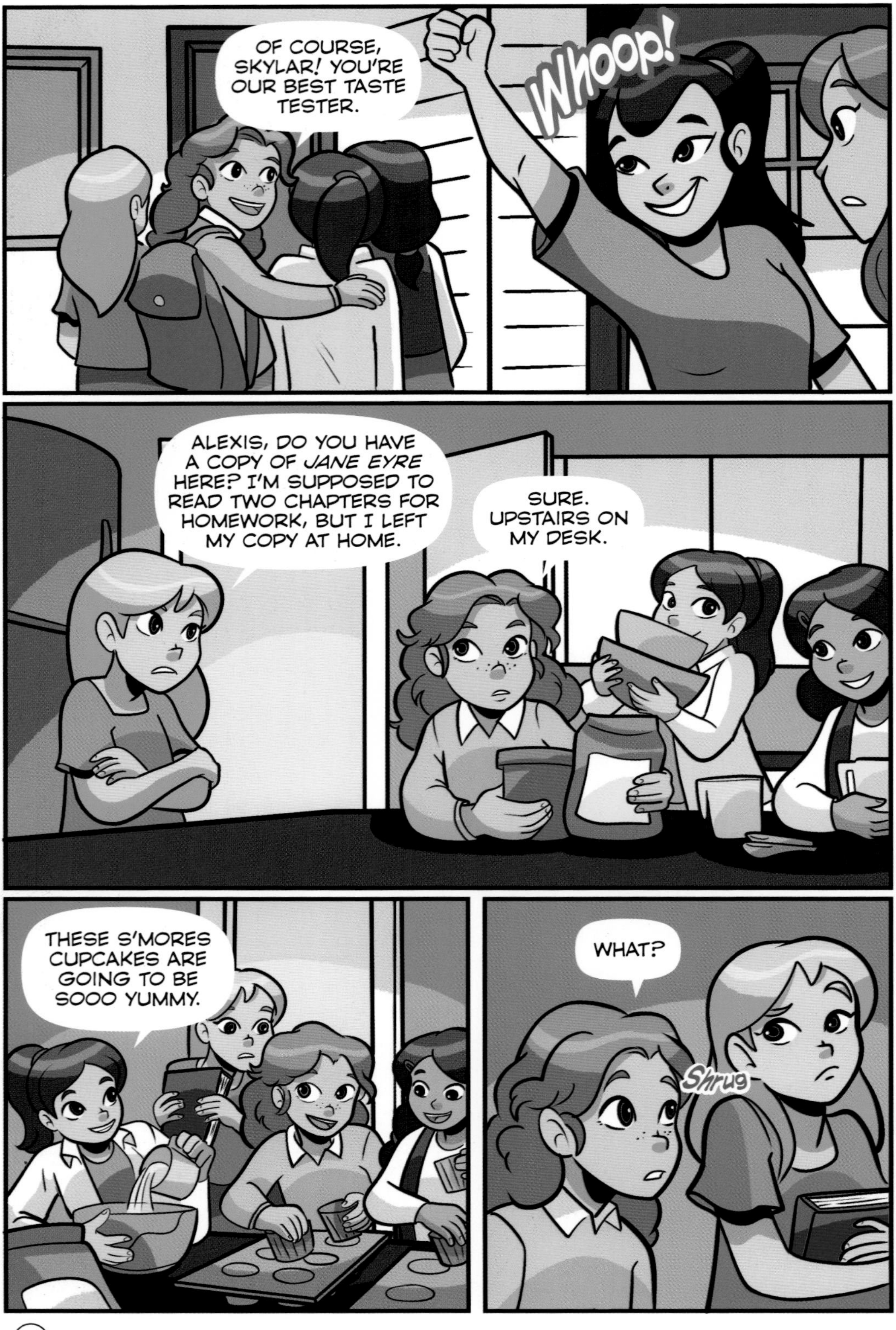
OF COURSE, SKYLAR! YOU'RE OUR BEST TASTE TESTER.
Whoop!
ALEXIS, DO YOU HAVE A COPY OF *JANE EYRE* HERE? I'M SUPPOSED TO READ TWO CHAPTERS FOR HOMEWORK, BUT I LEFT MY COPY AT HOME.
SURE. UPSTAIRS ON MY DESK.
THESE S'MORES CUPCAKES ARE GOING TO BE SOOO YUMMY.
WHAT?
Shrug

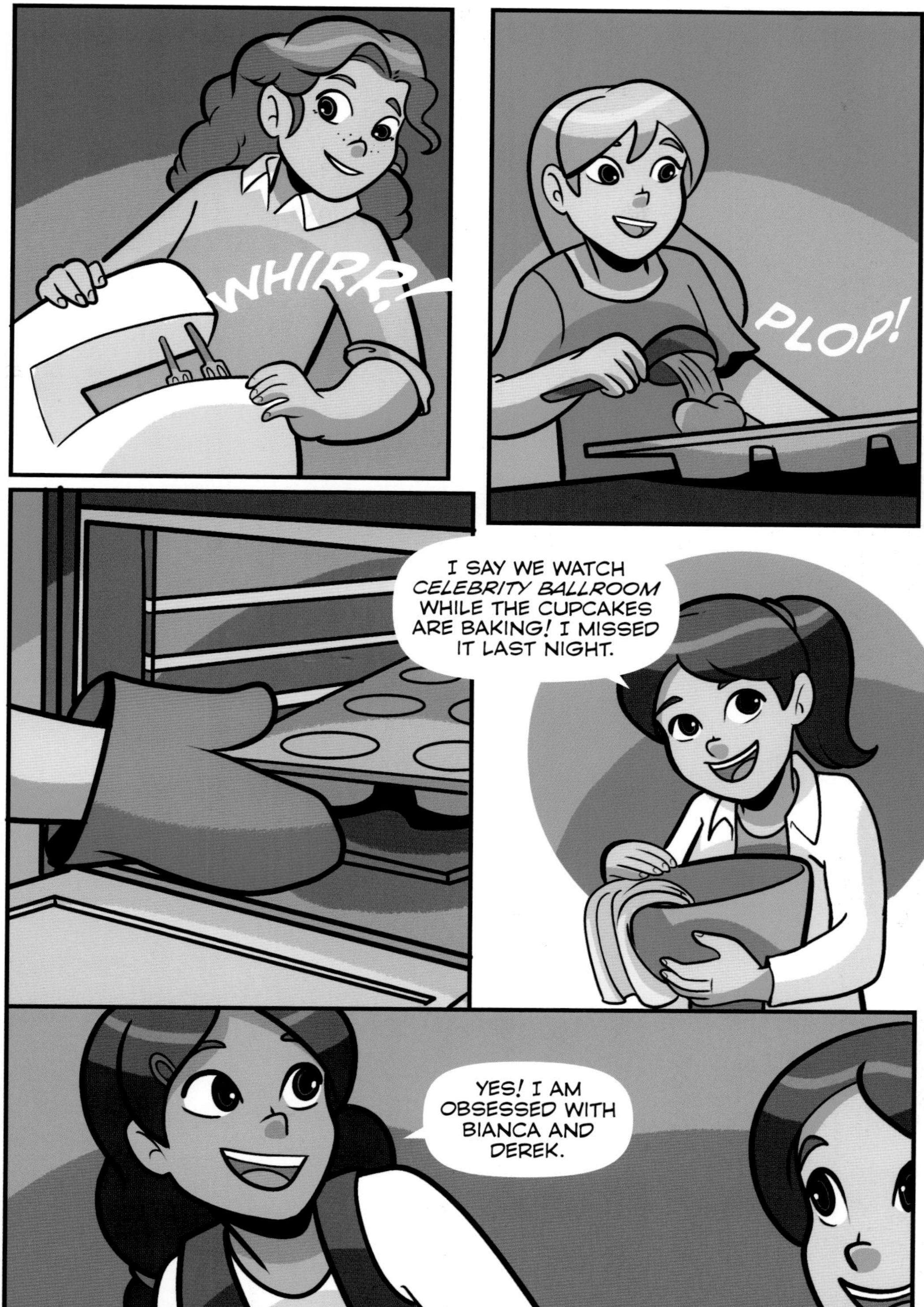
WHIRR!
PLOP!
I SAY WE WATCH *CELEBRITY BALLROOM* WHILE THE CUPCAKES ARE BAKING! I MISSED IT LAST NIGHT.
YES! I AM OBSESSED WITH BIANCA AND DEREK.

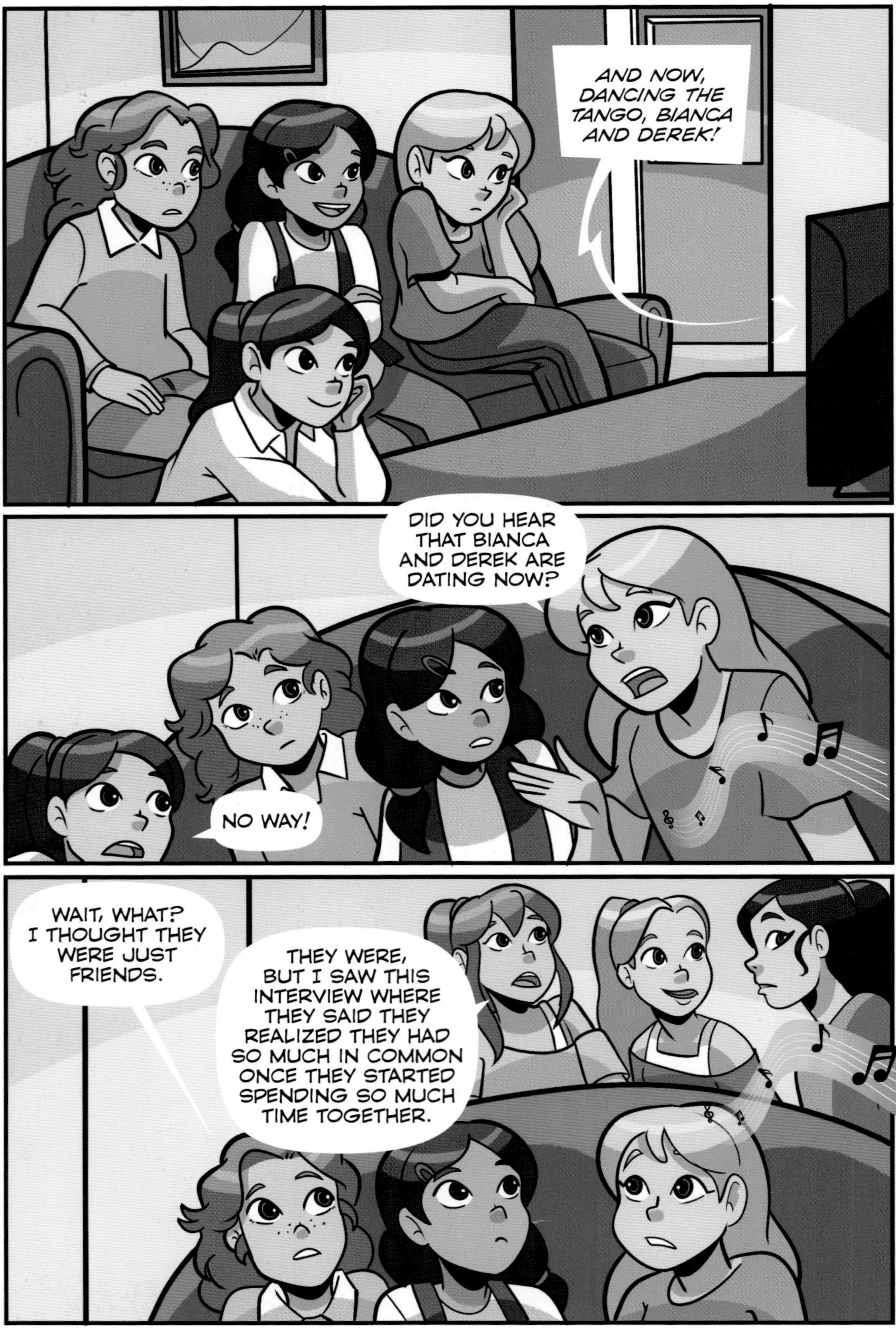
AND NOW, DANCING THE TANGO, BIANCA AND DEREK!
DID YOU HEAR THAT BIANCA AND DEREK ARE DATING NOW?
NO WAY!
WAIT, WHAT? I THOUGHT THEY WERE JUST FRIENDS.
THEY WERE, BUT I SAW THIS INTERVIEW WHERE THEY SAID THEY REALIZED THEY HAD SO MUCH IN COMMON ONCE THEY STARTED SPENDING SO MUCH TIME TOGETHER.

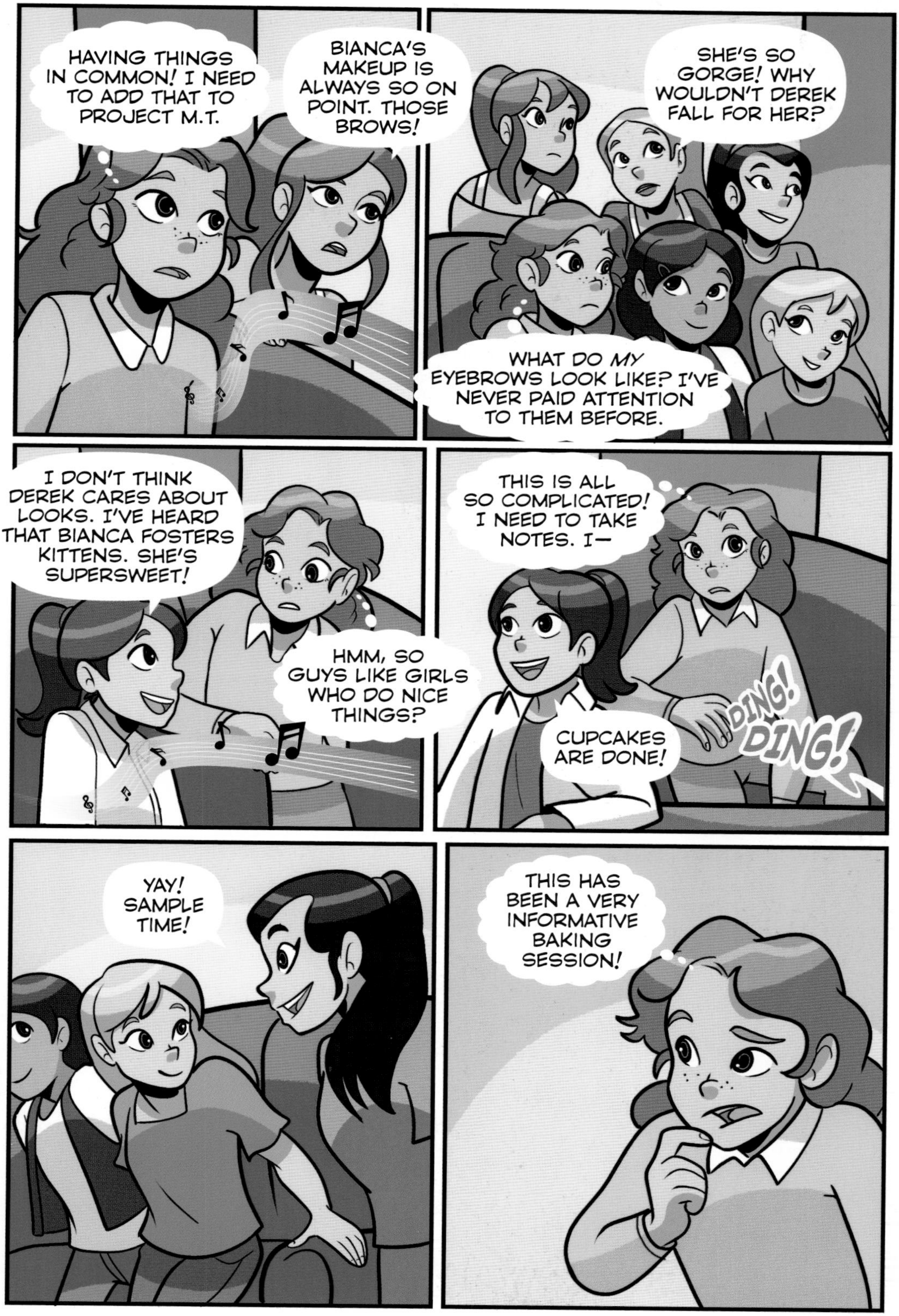
HAVING THINGS IN COMMON! I NEED TO ADD THAT TO PROJECT M.T.
BIANCA'S MAKEUP IS ALWAYS SO ON POINT. THOSE BROWS!
SHE'S SO GORGE! WHY WOULDN'T DEREK FALL FOR HER?
WHAT DO MY EYEBROWS LOOK LIKE? I'VE NEVER PAID ATTENTION TO THEM BEFORE.
I DON'T THINK DEREK CARES ABOUT LOOKS. I'VE HEARD THAT BIANCA FOSTERS KITTENS. SHE'S SUPERSWEET!
HMM, SO GUYS LIKE GIRLS WHO DO NICE THINGS?
THIS IS ALL SO COMPLICATED! I NEED TO TAKE NOTES. I—
CUPCAKES ARE DONE!
DING! DING!
YAY! SAMPLE TIME!
THIS HAS BEEN A VERY INFORMATIVE BAKING SESSION!

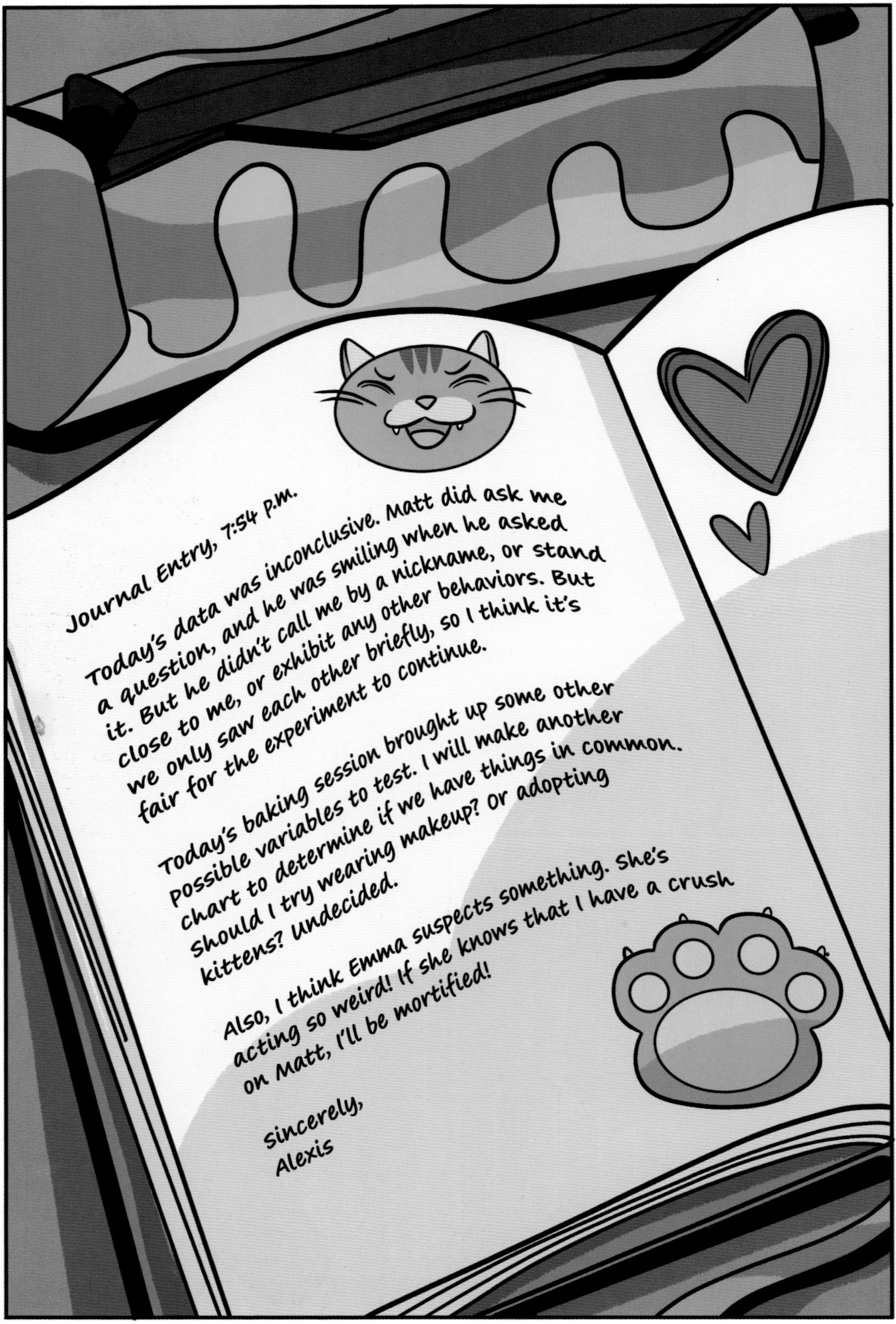
Journal Entry, 7:54 p.m.
Today's data was inconclusive. Matt did ask me a question, and he was smiling when he asked it. But he didn't call me by a nickname, or stand close to me, or exhibit any other behaviors. But we only saw each other briefly, so I think it's fair for the experiment to continue.
Today's baking session brought up some other possible variables to test. I will make another chart to determine if we have things in common. Should I try wearing makeup? Or adopting kittens? Undecided.
Also, I think Emma suspects something. She's acting so weird! If she knows that I have a crush on Matt, I'll be mortified!
Sincerely,
Alexis

Chapter 6

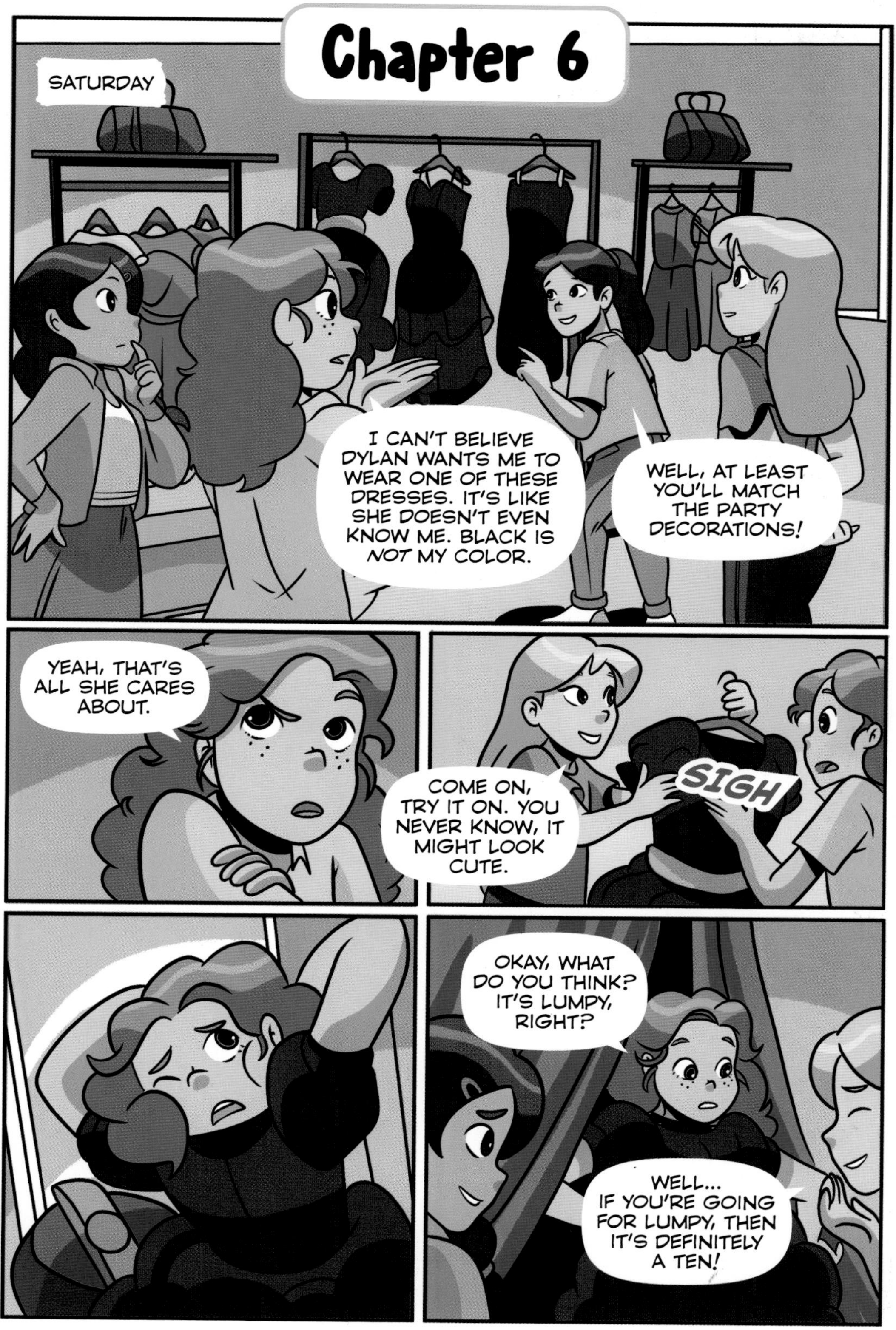

SATURDAY
I CAN'T BELIEVE DYLAN WANTS ME TO WEAR ONE OF THESE DRESSES. IT'S LIKE SHE DOESN'T EVEN KNOW ME. BLACK IS *NOT* MY COLOR.
WELL, AT LEAST YOU'LL MATCH THE PARTY DECORATIONS!
YEAH, THAT'S ALL SHE CARES ABOUT.
COME ON, TRY IT ON. YOU NEVER KNOW, IT MIGHT LOOK CUTE.
SIGH
OKAY, WHAT DO YOU THINK? IT'S LUMPY, RIGHT?
WELL... IF YOU'RE GOING FOR LUMPY, THEN IT'S DEFINITELY A TEN!

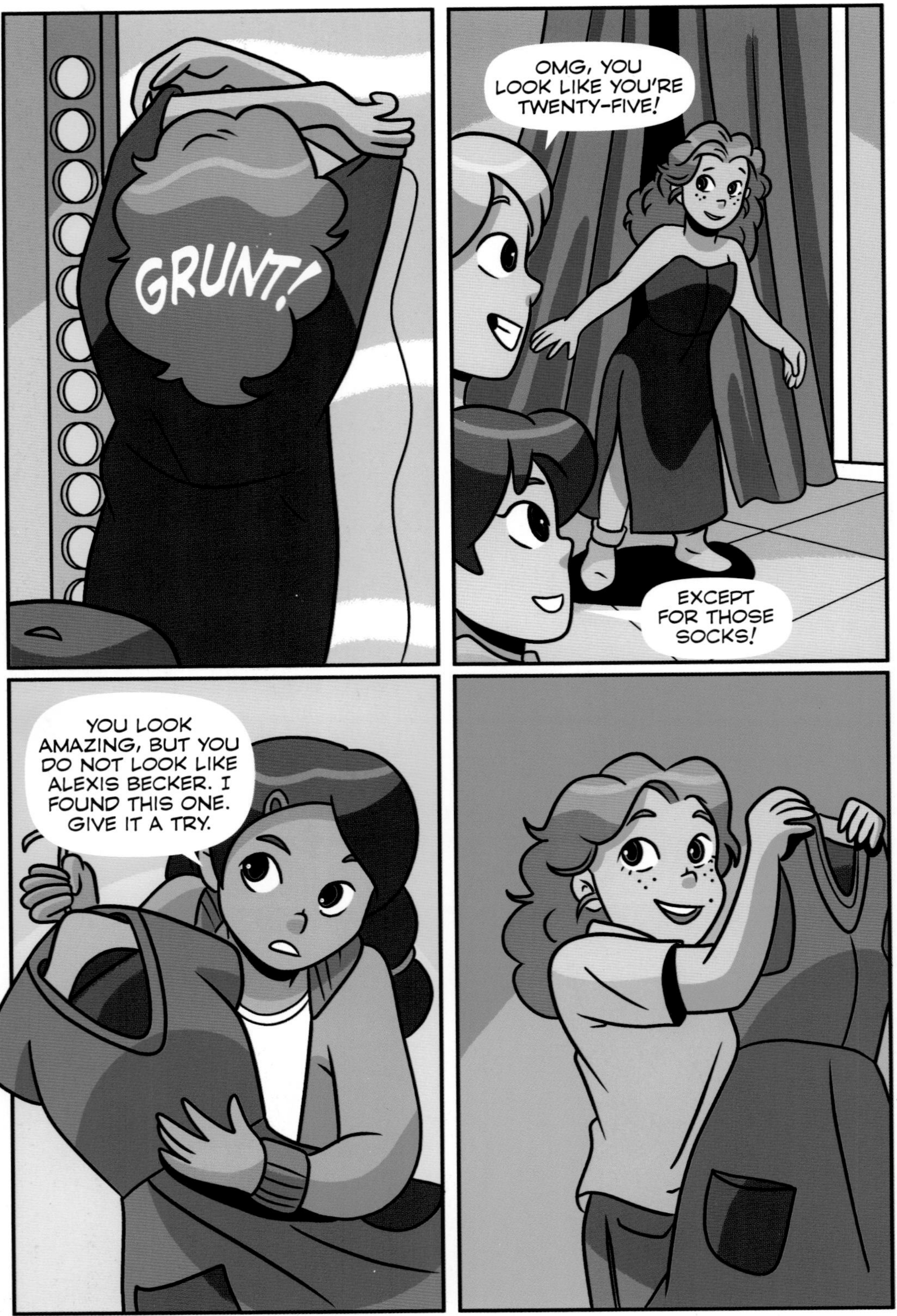
GRUNT!
OMG, YOU LOOK LIKE YOU'RE TWENTY-FIVE!
EXCEPT FOR THOSE SOCKS!
YOU LOOK AMAZING, BUT YOU DO NOT LOOK LIKE ALEXIS BECKER. I FOUND THIS ONE. GIVE IT A TRY.

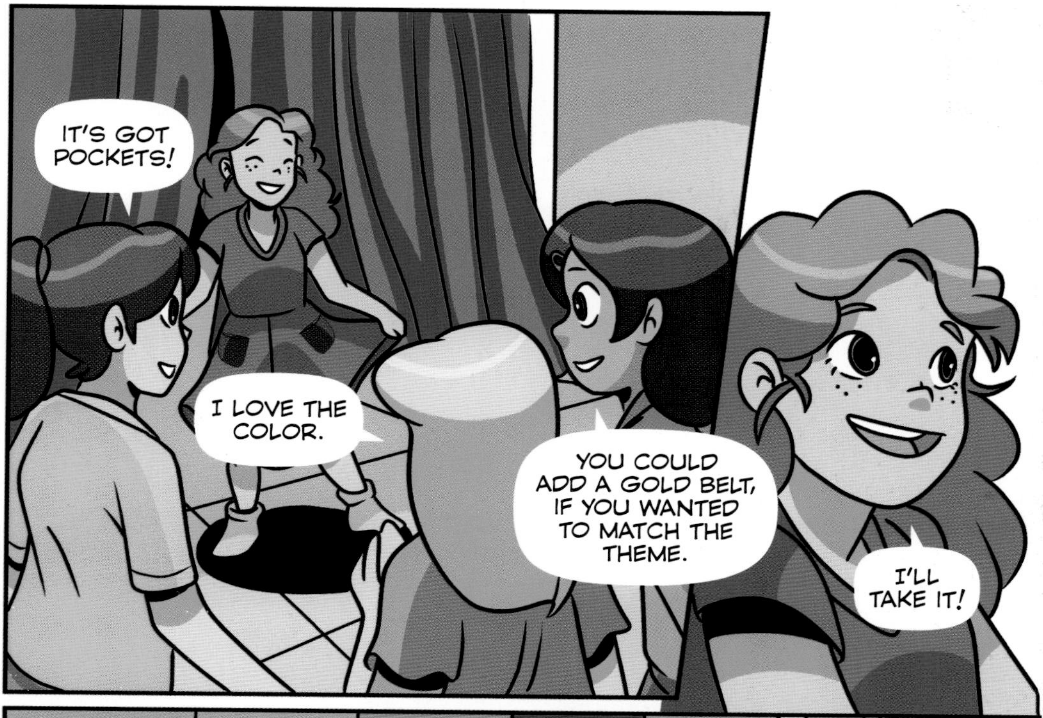
IT'S GOT POCKETS!
I LOVE THE COLOR.
YOU COULD ADD A GOLD BELT, IF YOU WANTED TO MATCH THE THEME.
I'LL TAKE IT!

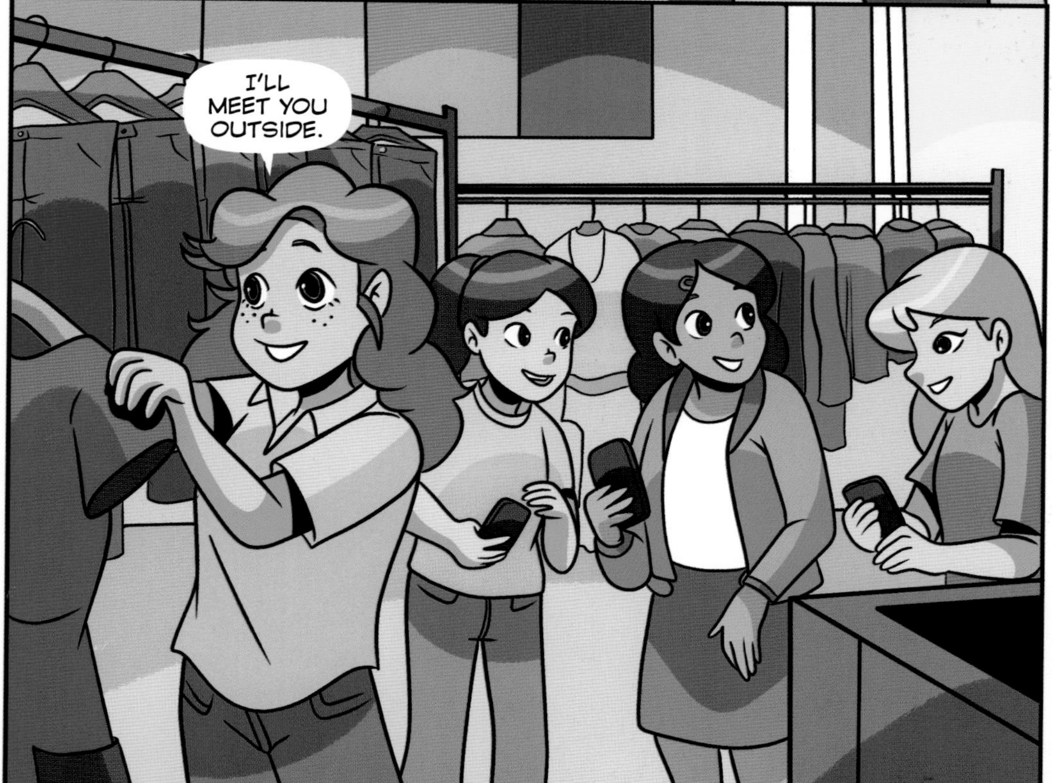
I'LL MEET YOU OUTSIDE.

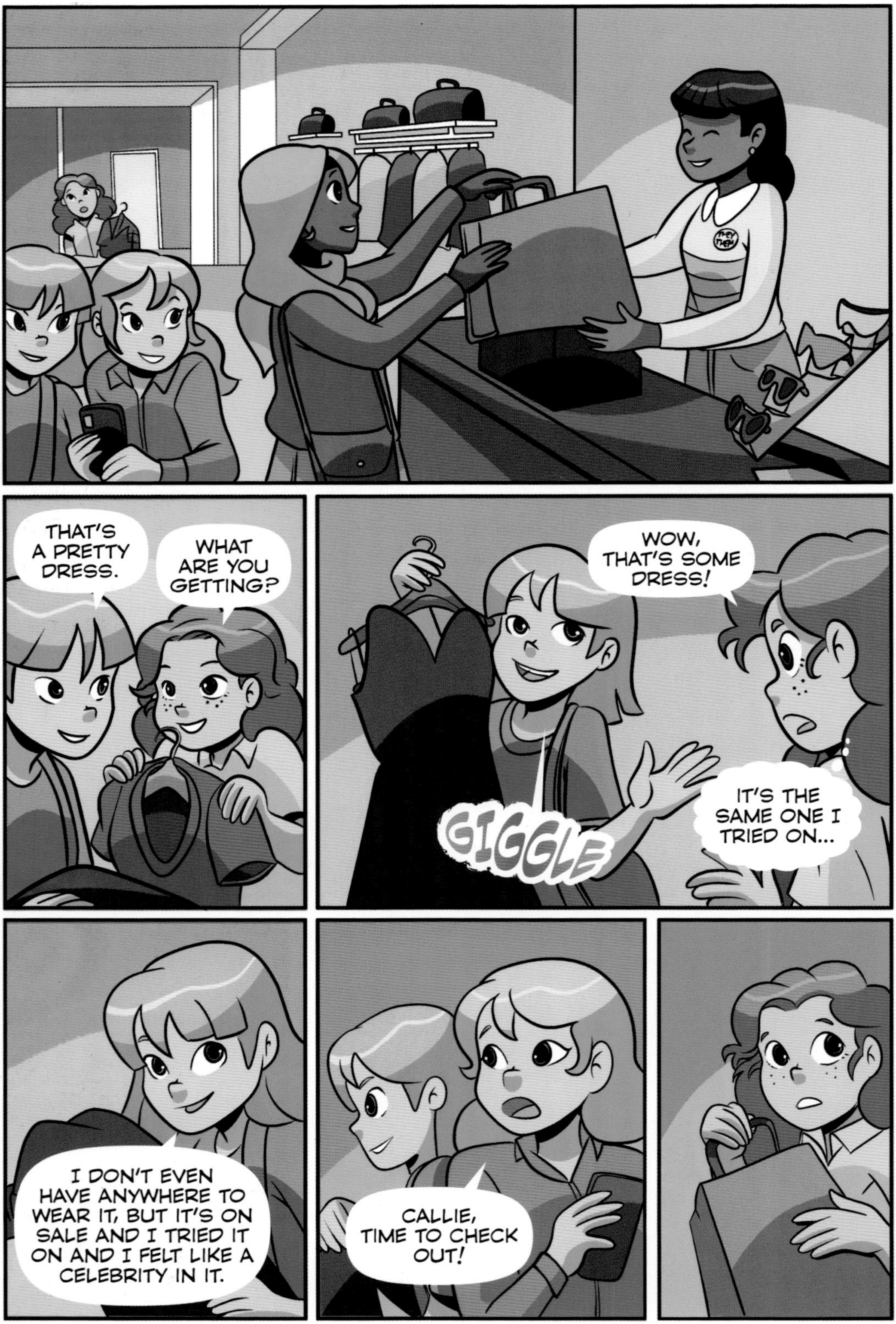
THAT'S A PRETTY DRESS.
WHAT ARE YOU GETTING?
WOW, THAT'S SOME DRESS!
GIGGLE
IT'S THE SAME ONE I TRIED ON...
I DON'T EVEN HAVE ANYWHERE TO WEAR IT, BUT IT'S ON SALE AND I TRIED IT ON AND I FELT LIKE A CELEBRITY IN IT.
CALLIE, TIME TO CHECK OUT!

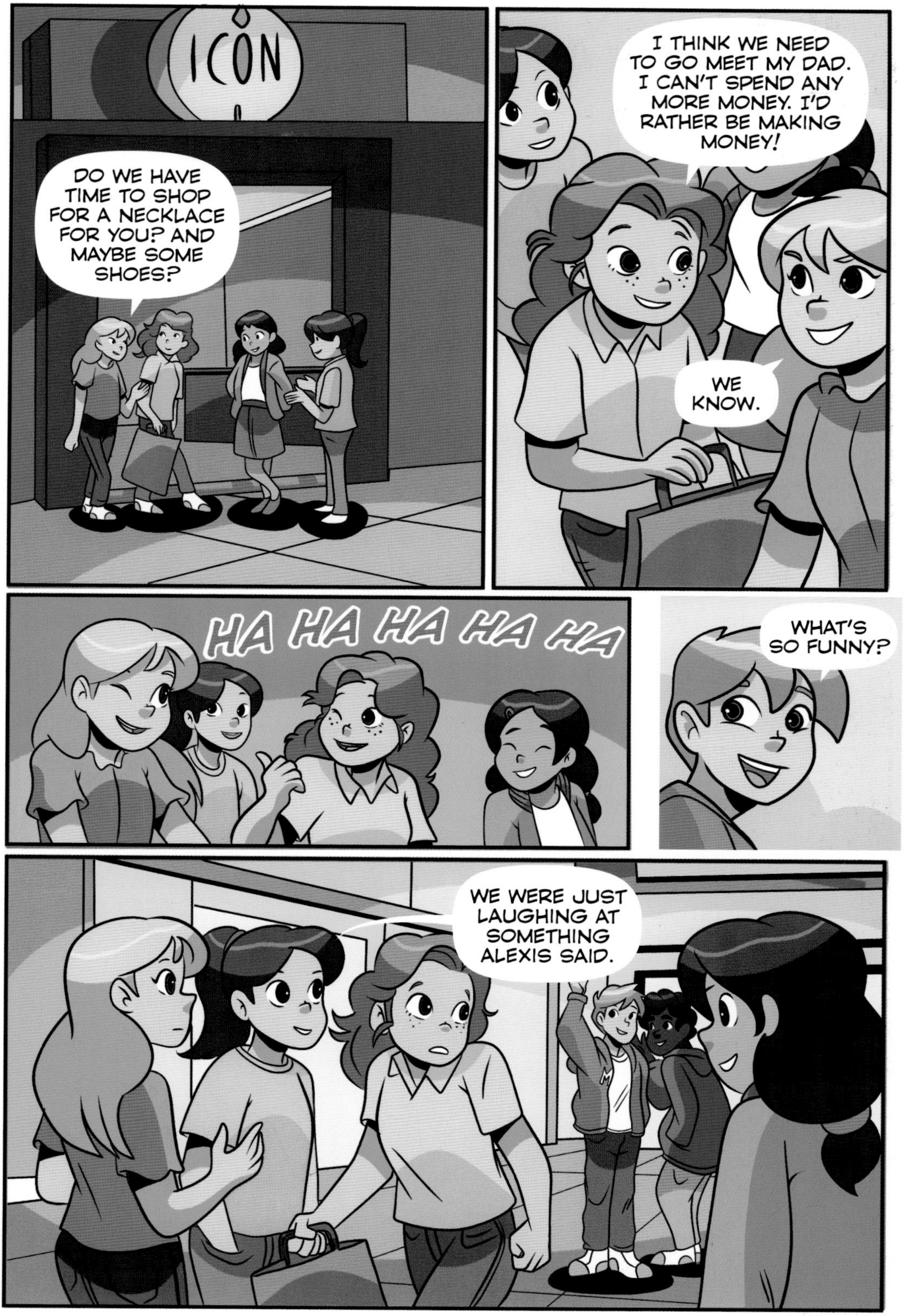
ICON
DO WE HAVE TIME TO SHOP FOR A NECKLACE FOR YOU? AND MAYBE SOME SHOES?
I THINK WE NEED TO GO MEET MY DAD. I CAN'T SPEND ANY MORE MONEY. I'D RATHER BE MAKING MONEY!
WE KNOW.
HA HA HA HA HA
WHAT'S SO FUNNY?
WE WERE JUST LAUGHING AT SOMETHING ALEXIS SAID.

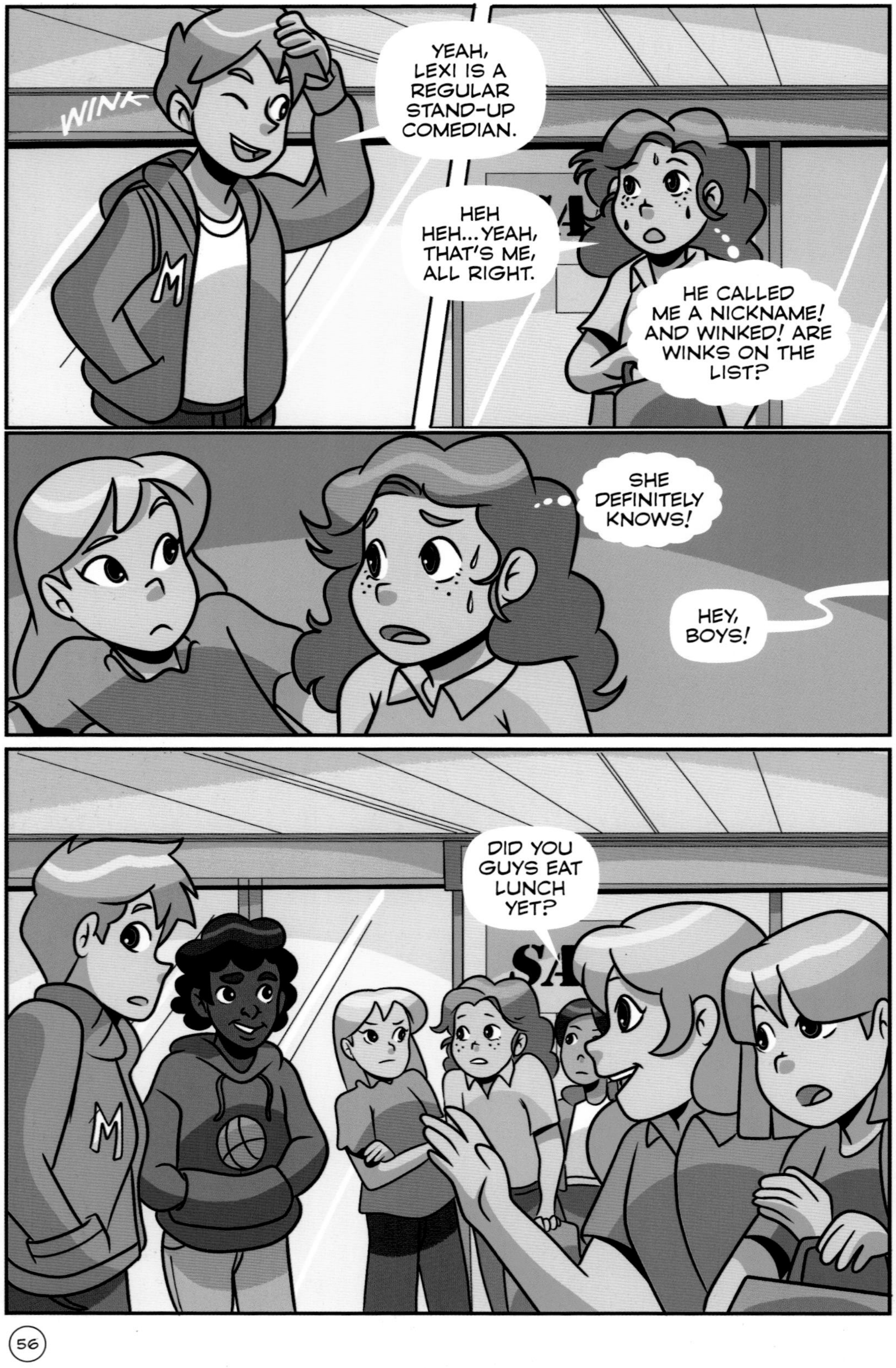
WINK
YEAH, LEXI IS A REGULAR STAND-UP COMEDIAN.
HEH HEH...YEAH, THAT'S ME, ALL RIGHT.
HE CALLED ME A NICKNAME! AND WINKED! ARE WINKS ON THE LIST?
SHE DEFINITELY KNOWS!
HEY, BOYS!
DID YOU GUYS EAT LUNCH YET?

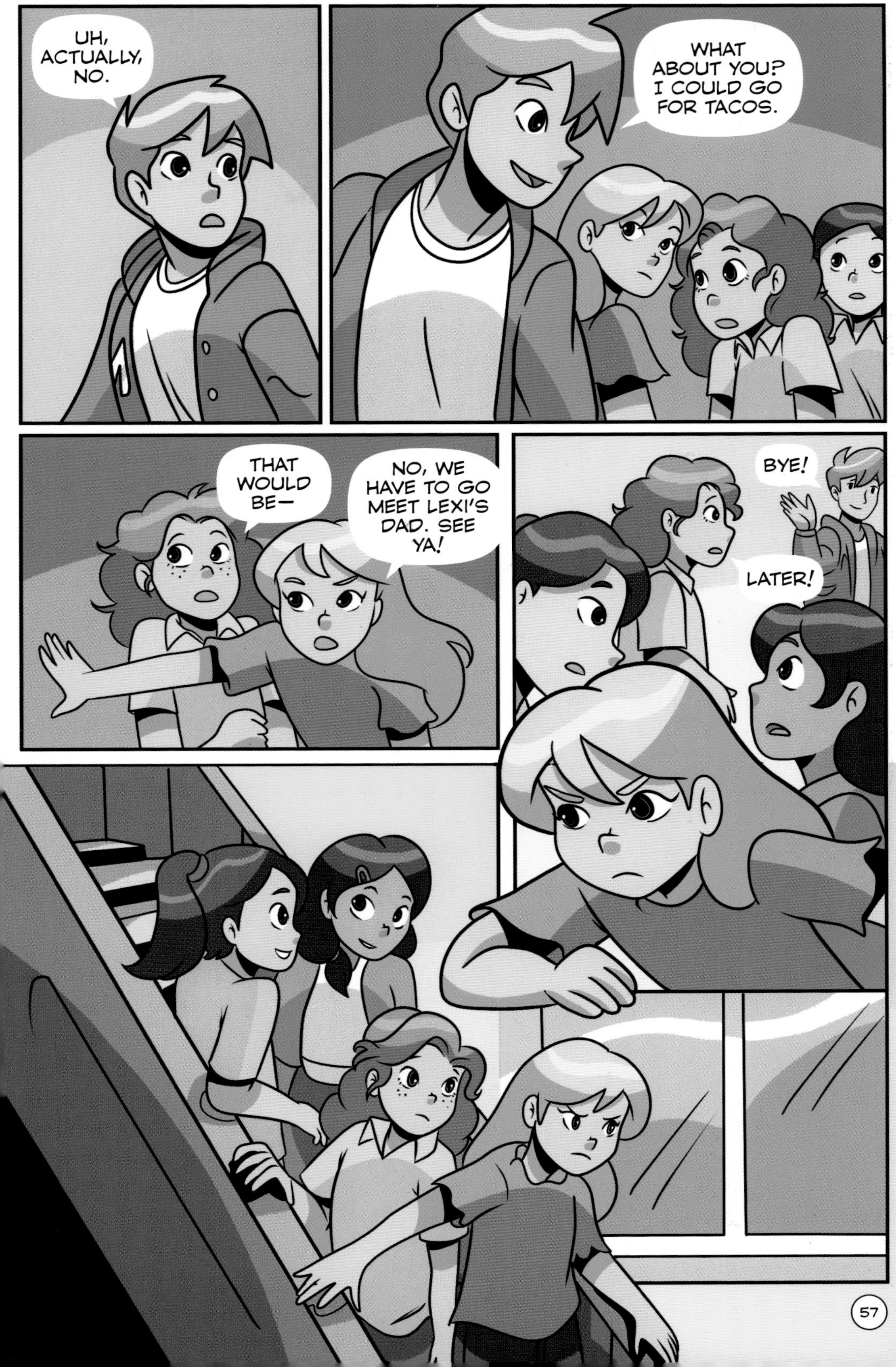
UH, ACTUALLY, NO.
WHAT ABOUT YOU? I COULD GO FOR TACOS.
THAT WOULD BE—
NO, WE HAVE TO GO MEET LEXI'S DAD. SEE YA!
BYE!
LATER!

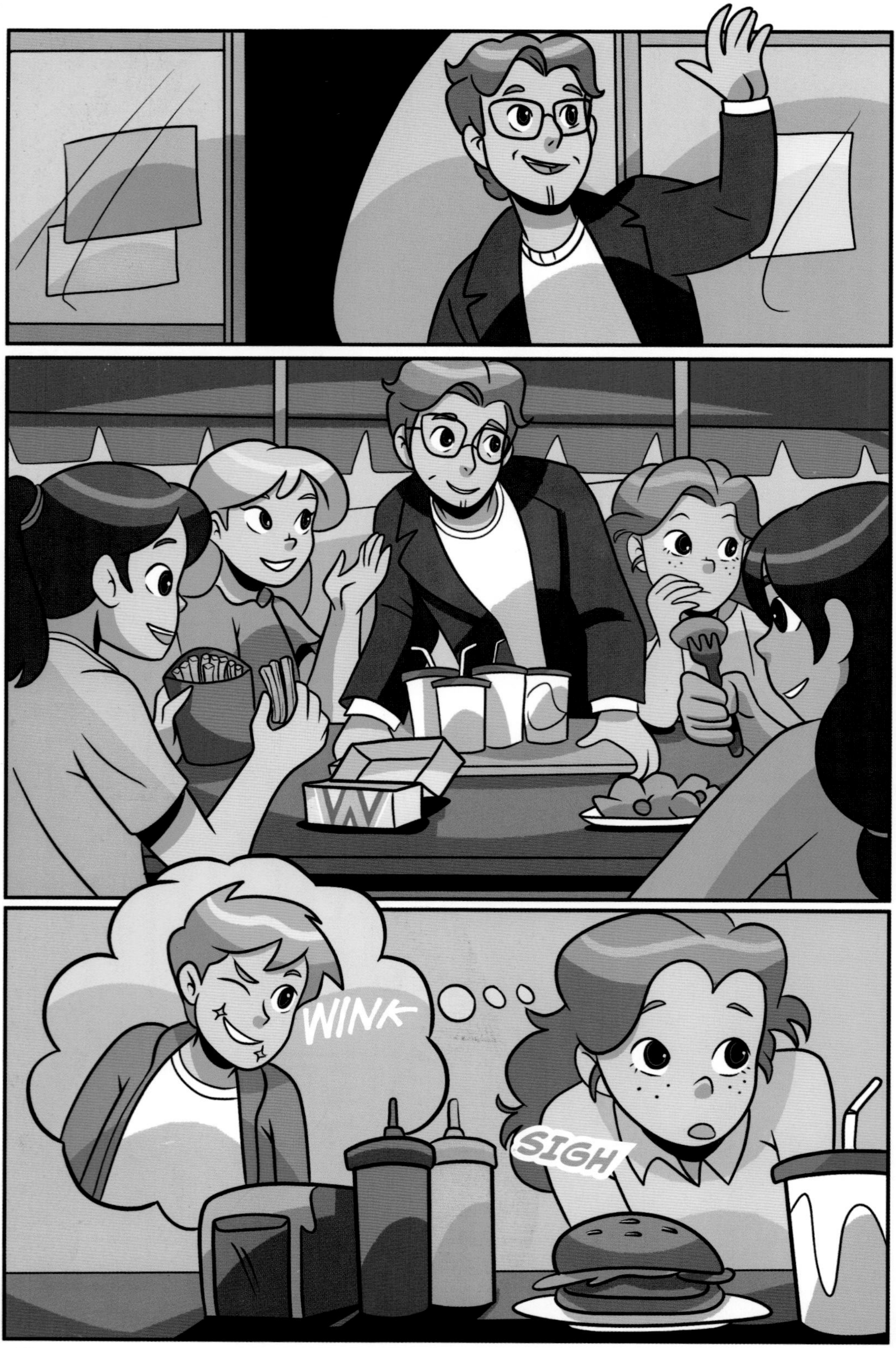
WINK
SIGH

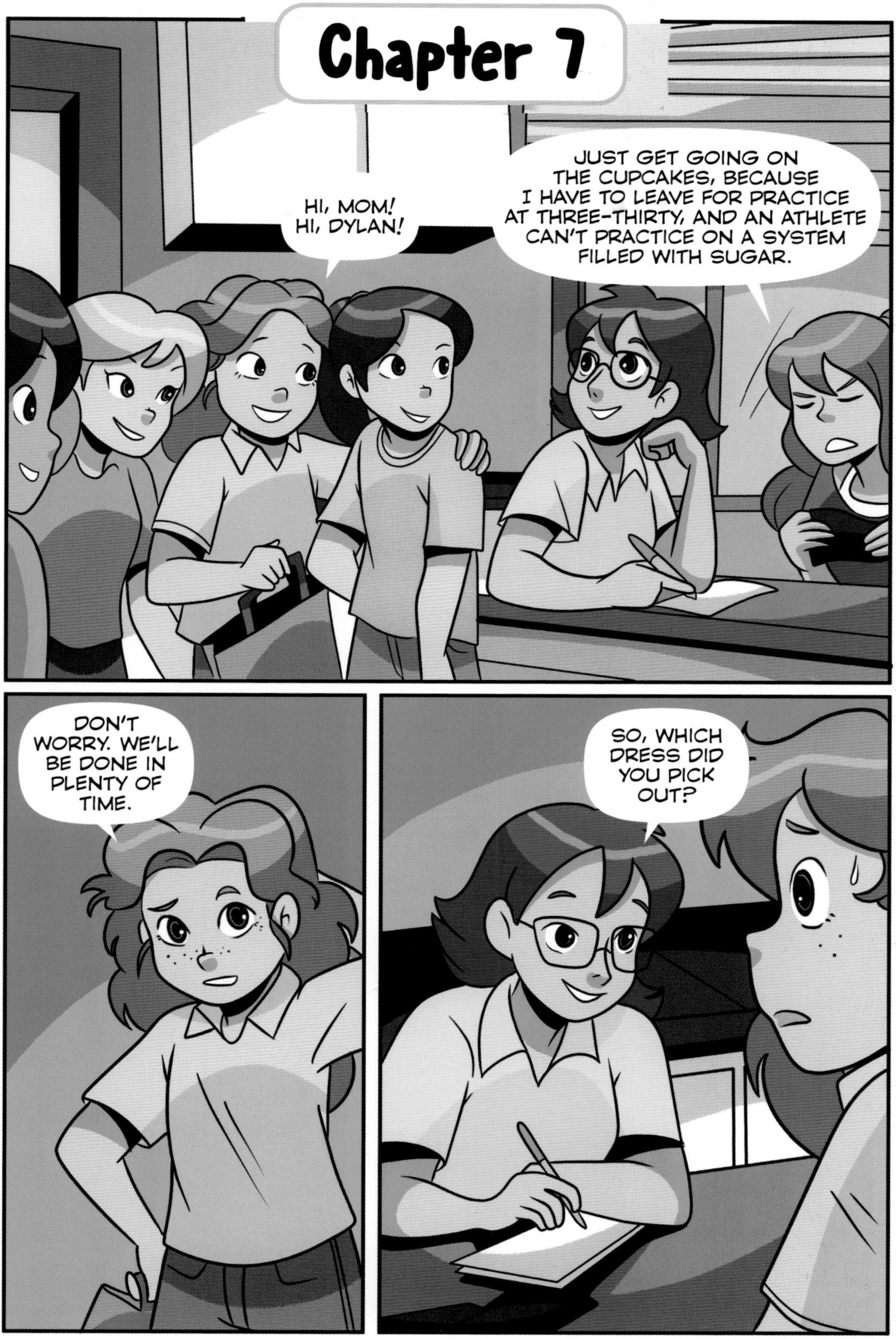
Chapter 7
HI, MOM! HI, DYLAN!
JUST GET GOING ON THE CUPCAKES, BECAUSE I HAVE TO LEAVE FOR PRACTICE AT THREE-THIRTY, AND AN ATHLETE CAN'T PRACTICE ON A SYSTEM FILLED WITH SUGAR.
DON'T WORRY. WE'LL BE DONE IN PLENTY OF TIME.
SO, WHICH DRESS DID YOU PICK OUT?

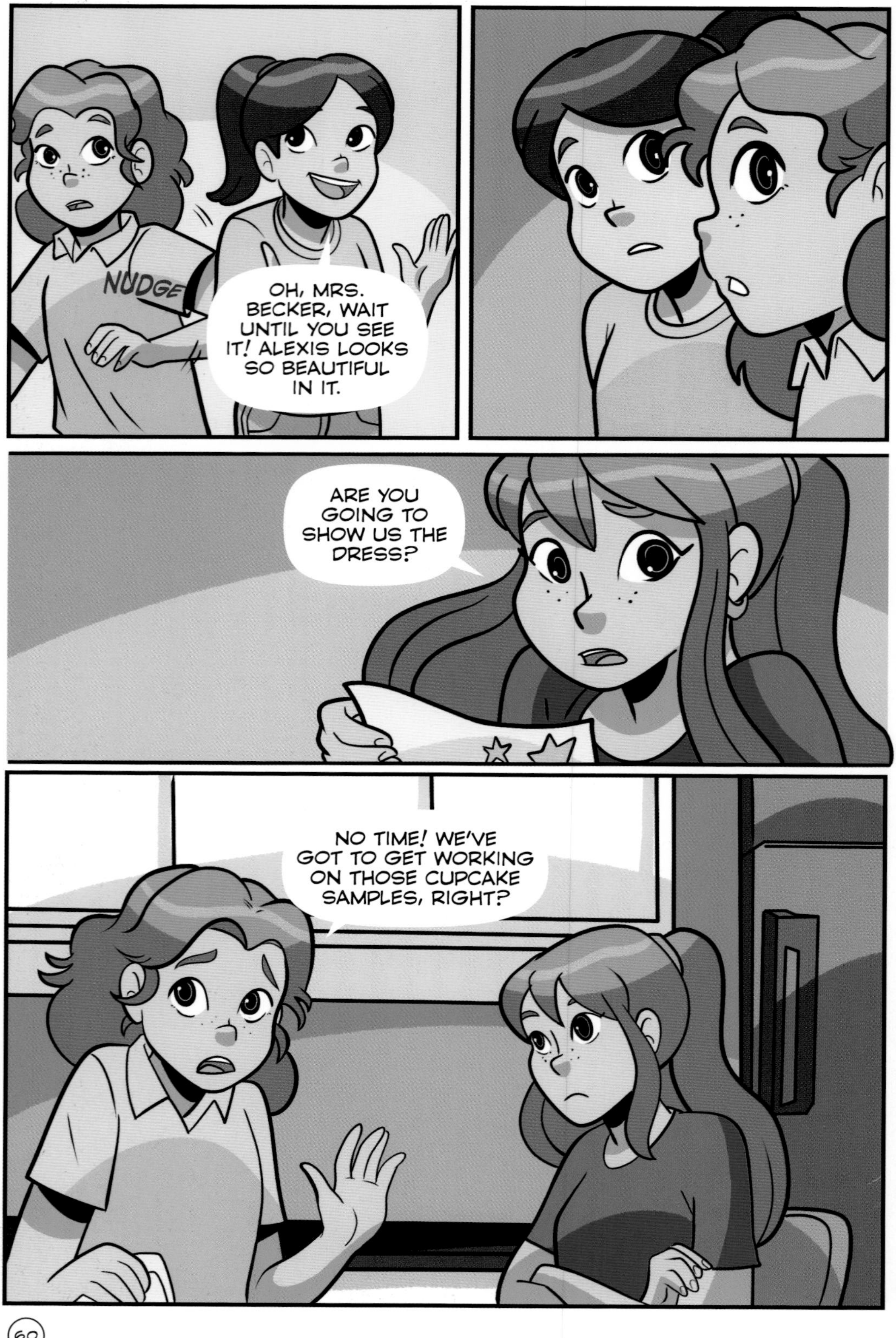
NUDGE
OH, MRS. BECKER, WAIT UNTIL YOU SEE IT! ALEXIS LOOKS SO BEAUTIFUL IN IT.
ARE YOU GOING TO SHOW US THE DRESS?
NO TIME! WE'VE GOT TO GET WORKING ON THOSE CUPCAKE SAMPLES, RIGHT?

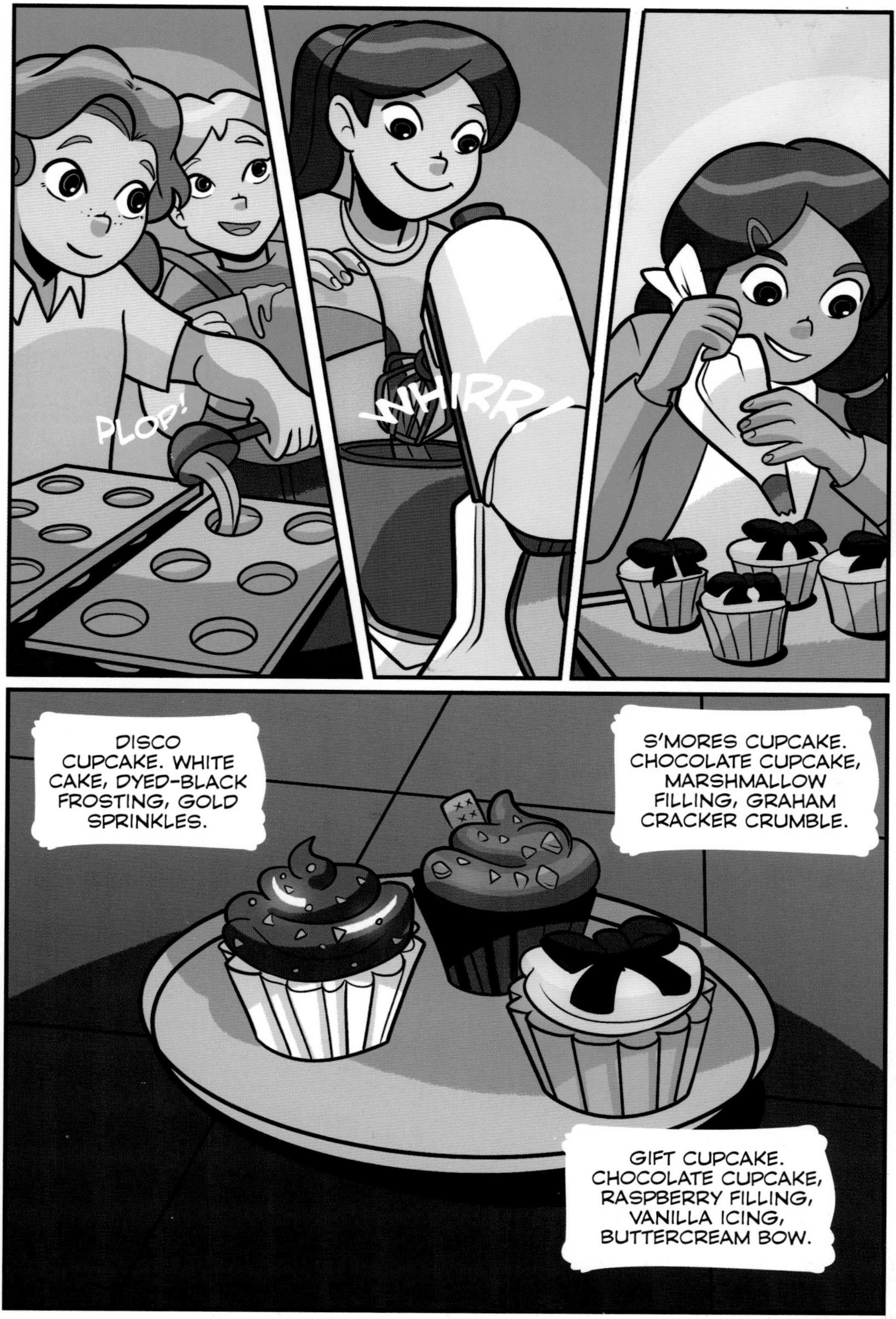
PLOP!
WHIRR!
DISCO CUPCAKE. WHITE CAKE, DYED-BLACK FROSTING, GOLD SPRINKLES.
S'MORES CUPCAKE. CHOCOLATE CUPCAKE, MARSHMALLOW FILLING, GRAHAM CRACKER CRUMBLE.
GIFT CUPCAKE. CHOCOLATE CUPCAKE, RASPBERRY FILLING, VANILLA ICING, BUTTERCREAM BOW.

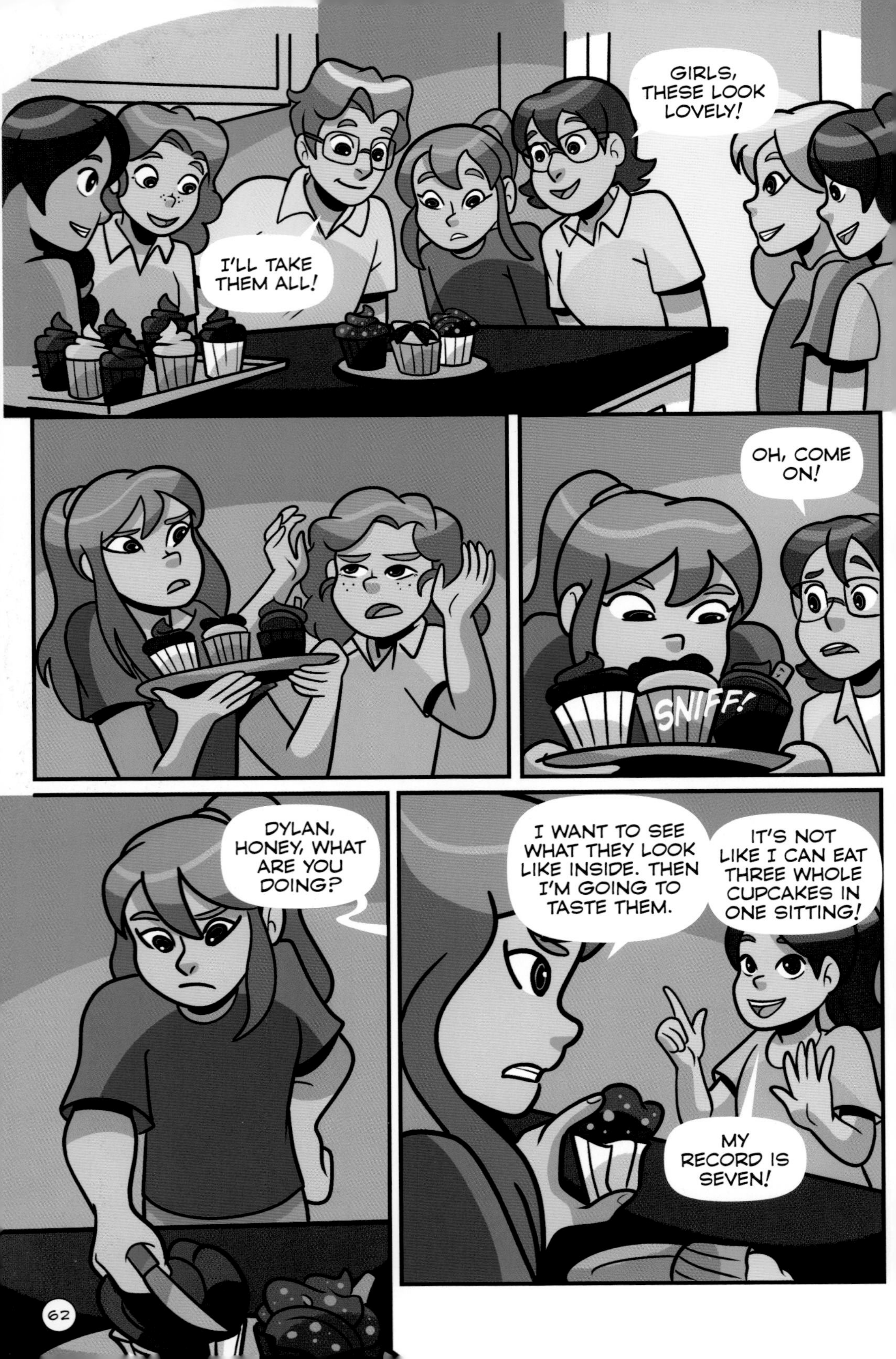
GIRLS, THESE LOOK LOVELY!
I'LL TAKE THEM ALL!
OH, COME ON!
SNIFF!
DYLAN, HONEY, WHAT ARE YOU DOING?
I WANT TO SEE WHAT THEY LOOK LIKE INSIDE. THEN I'M GOING TO TASTE THEM.
IT'S NOT LIKE I CAN EAT THREE WHOLE CUPCAKES IN ONE SITTING!
MY RECORD IS SEVEN!

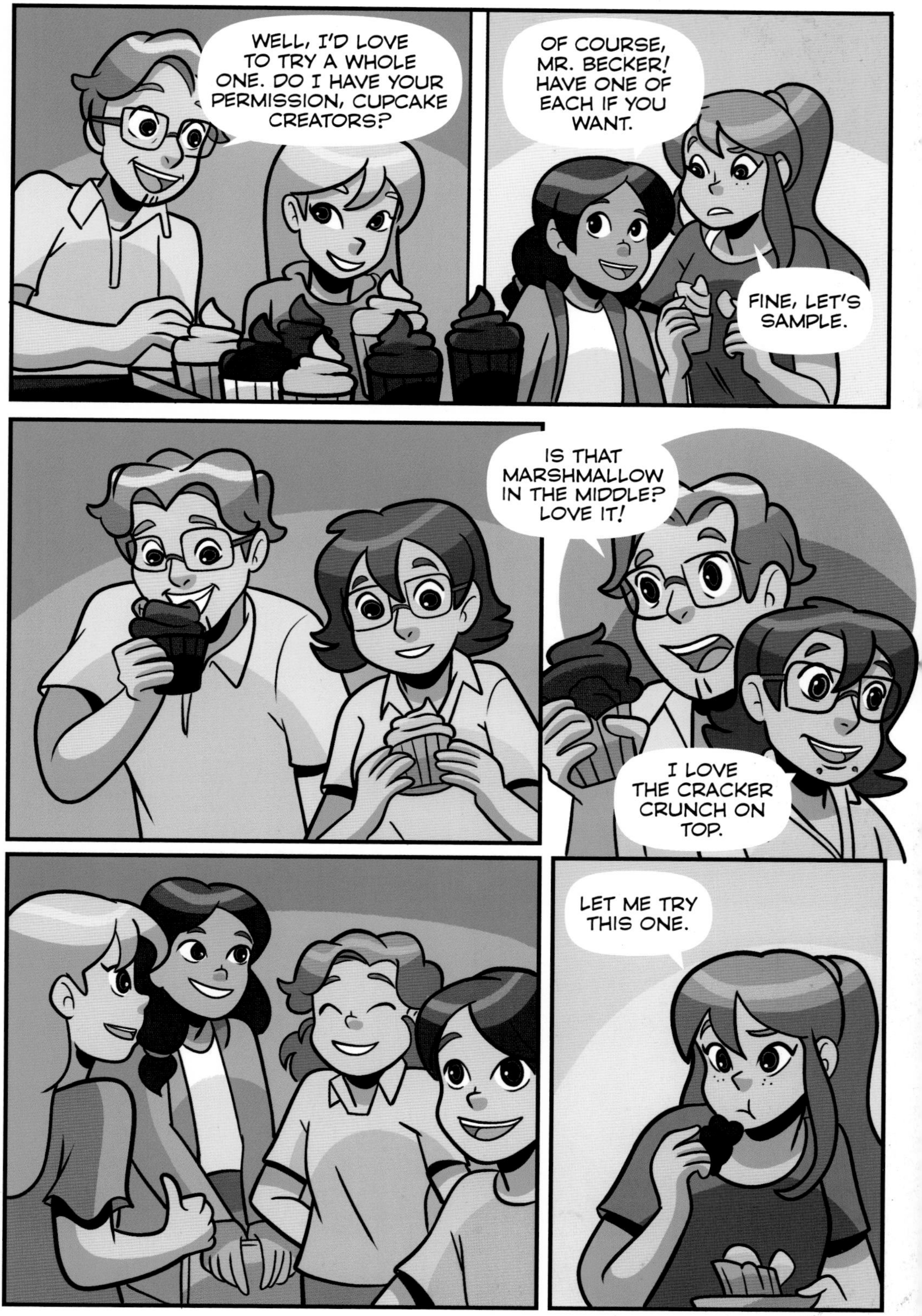
WELL, I'D LOVE TO TRY A WHOLE ONE. DO I HAVE YOUR PERMISSION, CUPCAKE CREATORS?
OF COURSE, MR. BECKER! HAVE ONE OF EACH IF YOU WANT.
FINE, LET'S SAMPLE.
IS THAT MARSHMALLOW IN THE MIDDLE? LOVE IT!
I LOVE THE CRACKER CRUNCH ON TOP.
LET ME TRY THIS ONE.

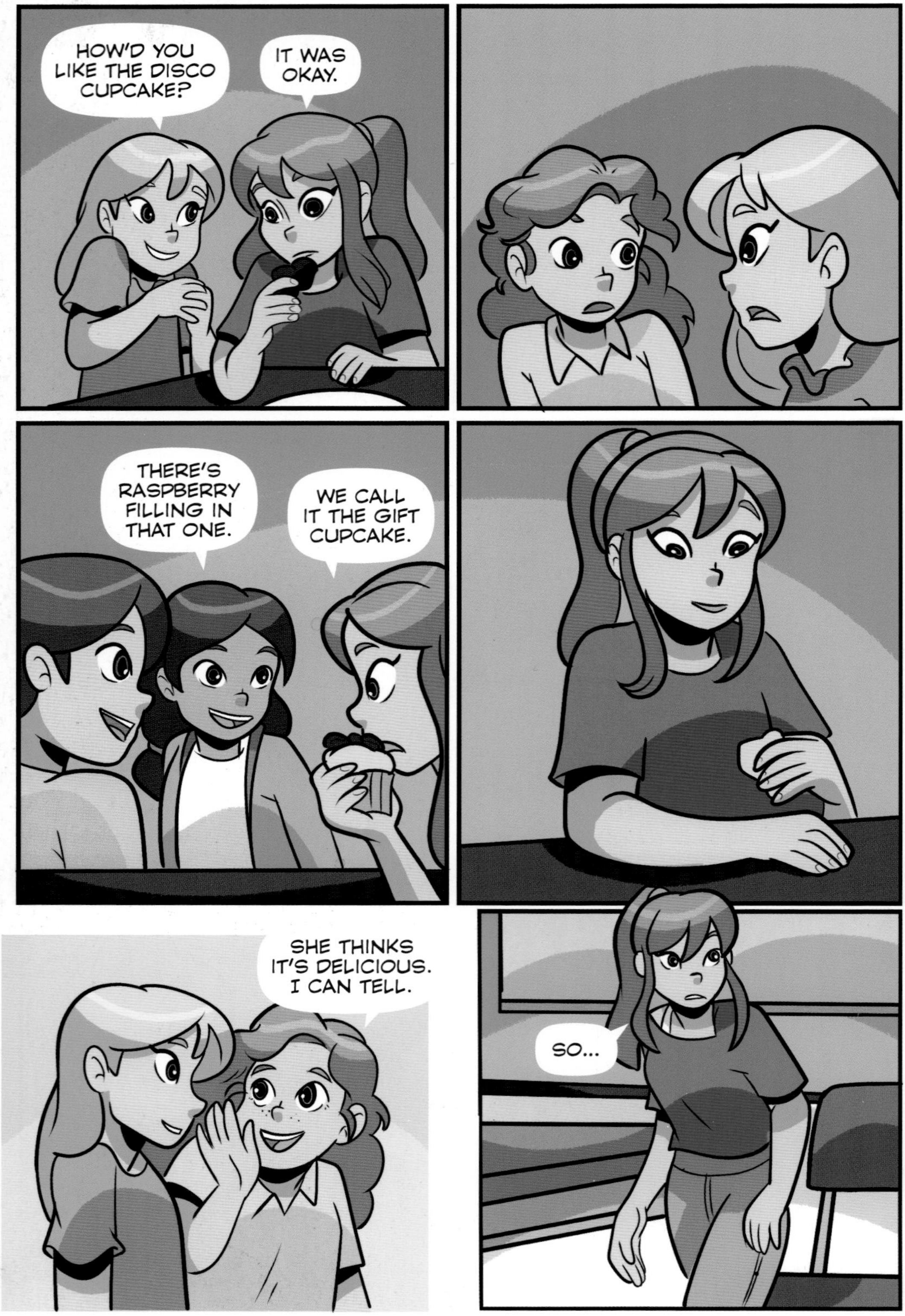
HOW'D YOU LIKE THE DISCO CUPCAKE?
IT WAS OKAY.
THERE'S RASPBERRY FILLING IN THAT ONE.
WE CALL IT THE GIFT CUPCAKE.
SHE THINKS IT'S DELICIOUS. I CAN TELL.
SO...

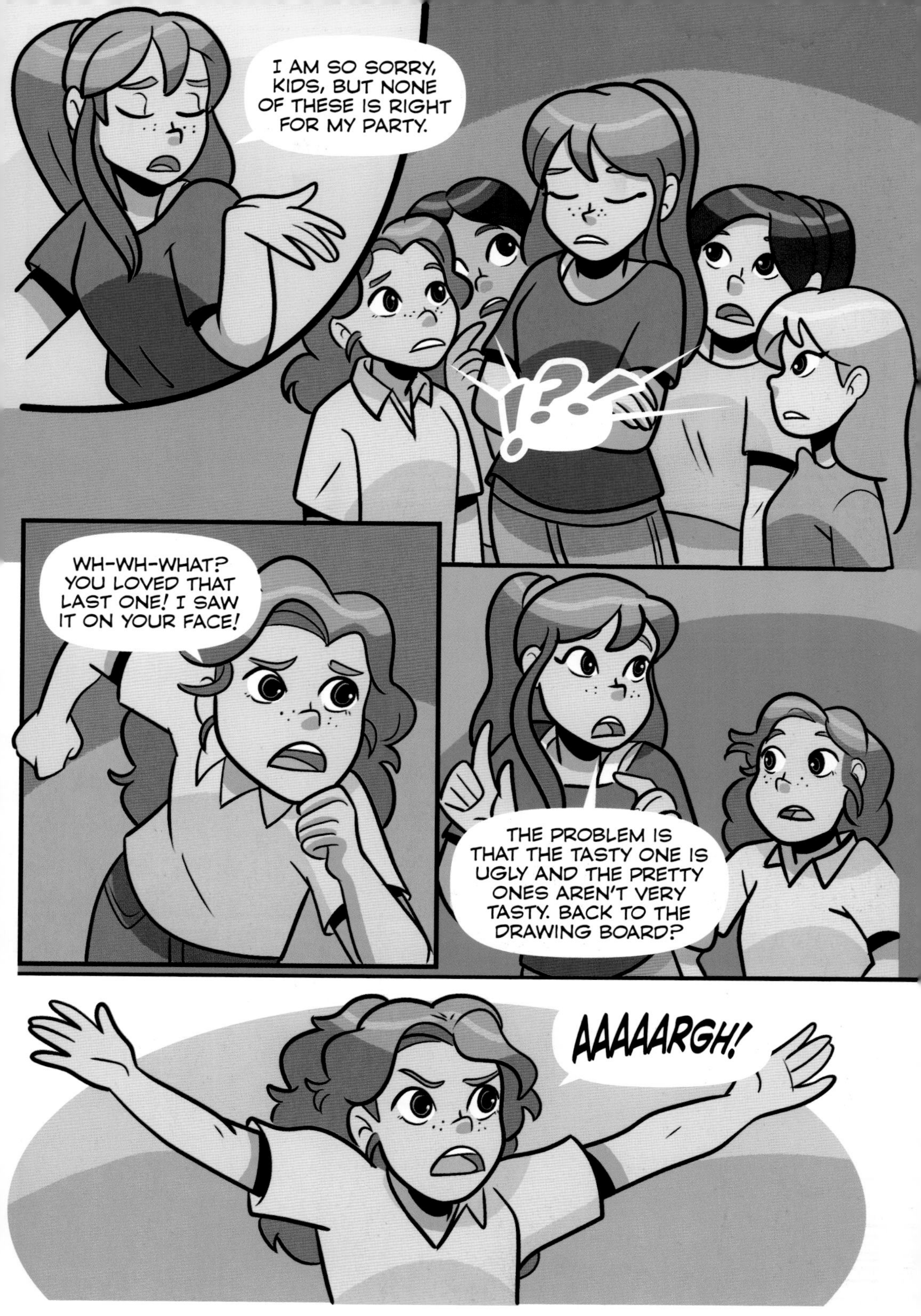
I AM SO SORRY, KIDS, BUT NONE OF THESE IS RIGHT FOR MY PARTY.
!?
WH-WH-WHAT? YOU LOVED THAT LAST ONE! I SAW IT ON YOUR FACE!
THE PROBLEM IS THAT THE TASTY ONE IS UGLY AND THE PRETTY ONES AREN'T VERY TASTY. BACK TO THE DRAWING BOARD?
AAAAARGH!

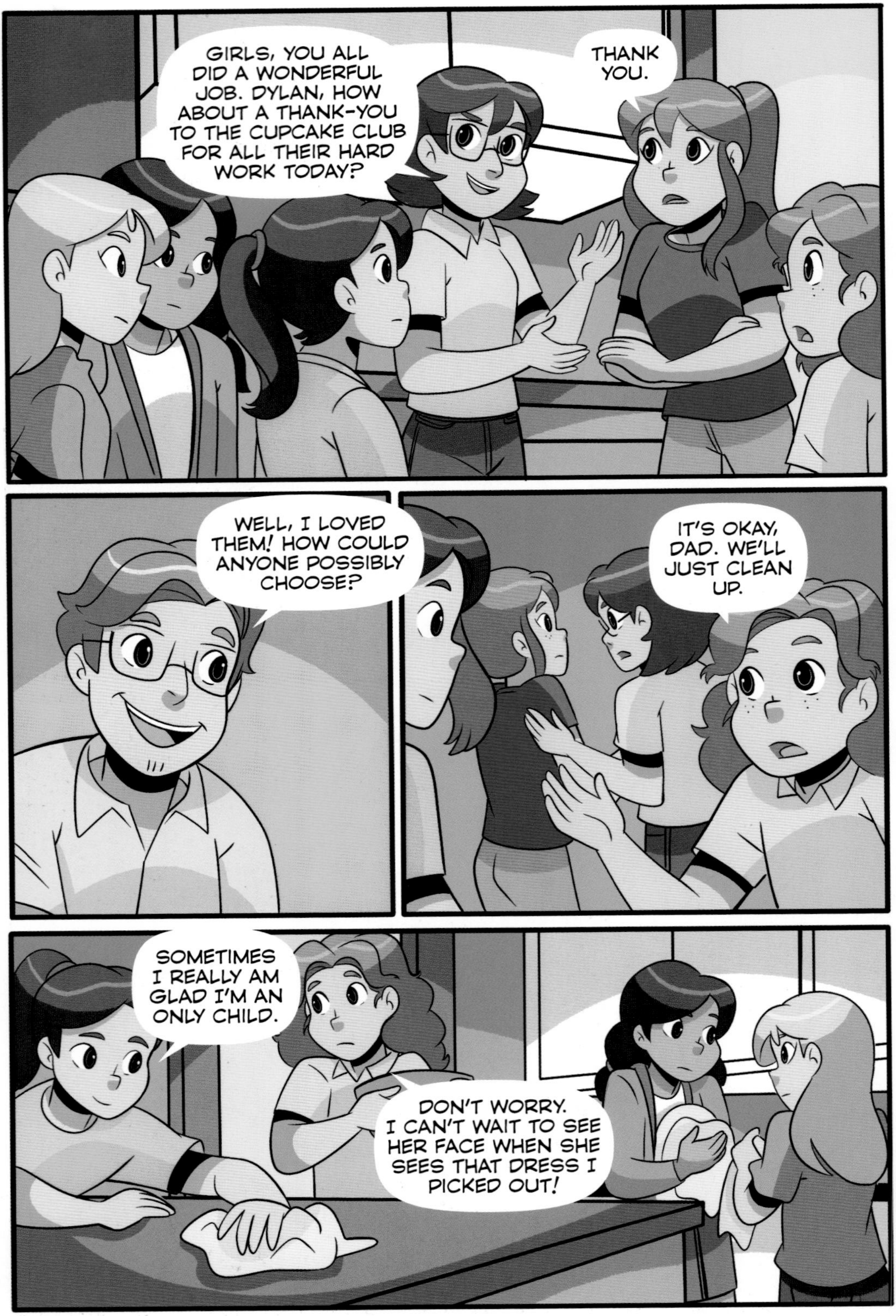
GIRLS, YOU ALL DID A WONDERFUL JOB. DYLAN, HOW ABOUT A THANK-YOU TO THE CUPCAKE CLUB FOR ALL THEIR HARD WORK TODAY?
THANK YOU.
WELL, I LOVED THEM! HOW COULD ANYONE POSSIBLY CHOOSE?
IT'S OKAY, DAD. WE'LL JUST CLEAN UP.
SOMETIMES I REALLY AM GLAD I'M AN ONLY CHILD.
DON'T WORRY. I CAN'T WAIT TO SEE HER FACE WHEN SHE SEES THAT DRESS I PICKED OUT!

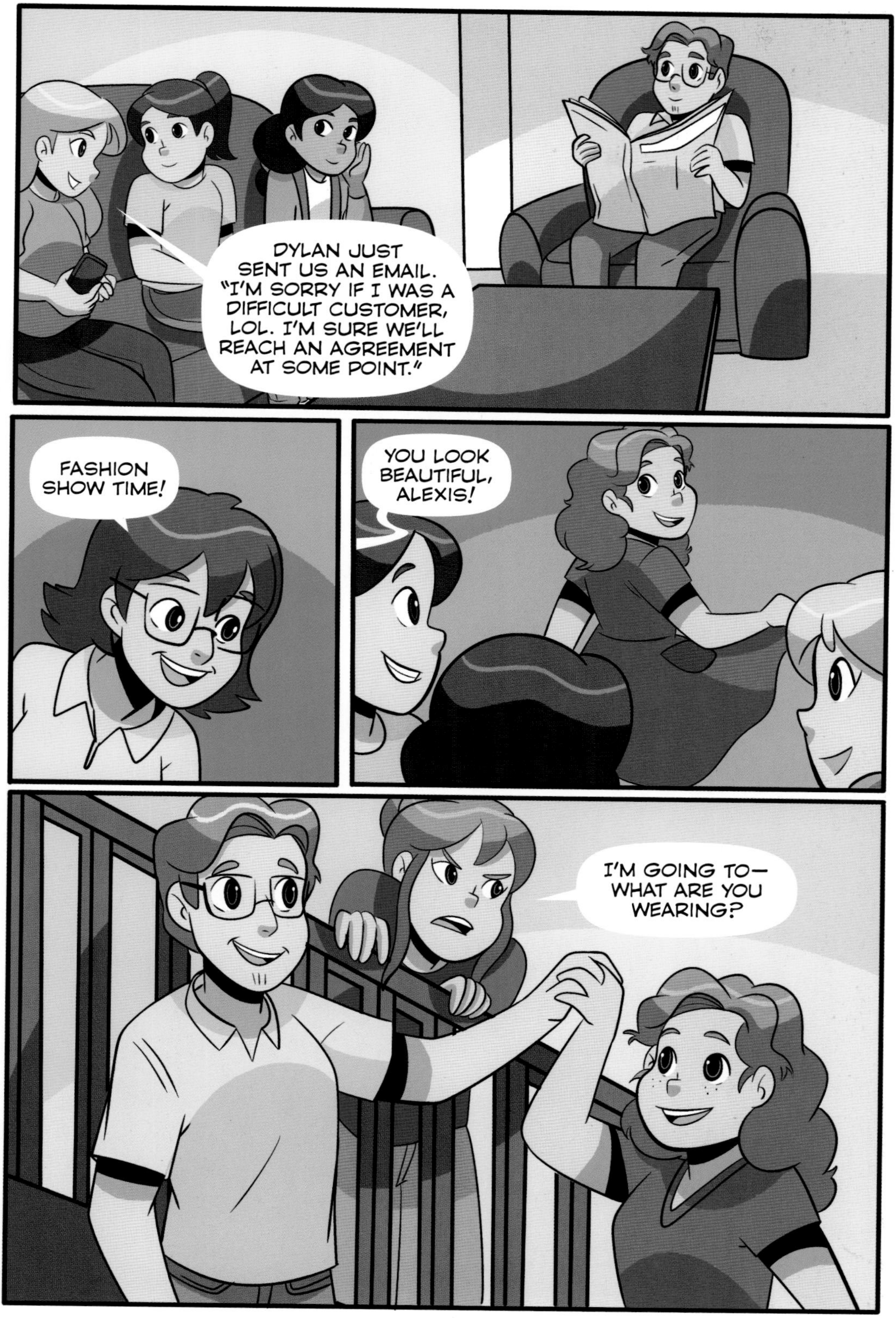
DYLAN JUST SENT US AN EMAIL. "I'M SORRY IF I WAS A DIFFICULT CUSTOMER, LOL. I'M SURE WE'LL REACH AN AGREEMENT AT SOME POINT."
FASHION SHOW TIME!
YOU LOOK BEAUTIFUL, ALEXIS!
I'M GOING TO— WHAT ARE YOU WEARING?

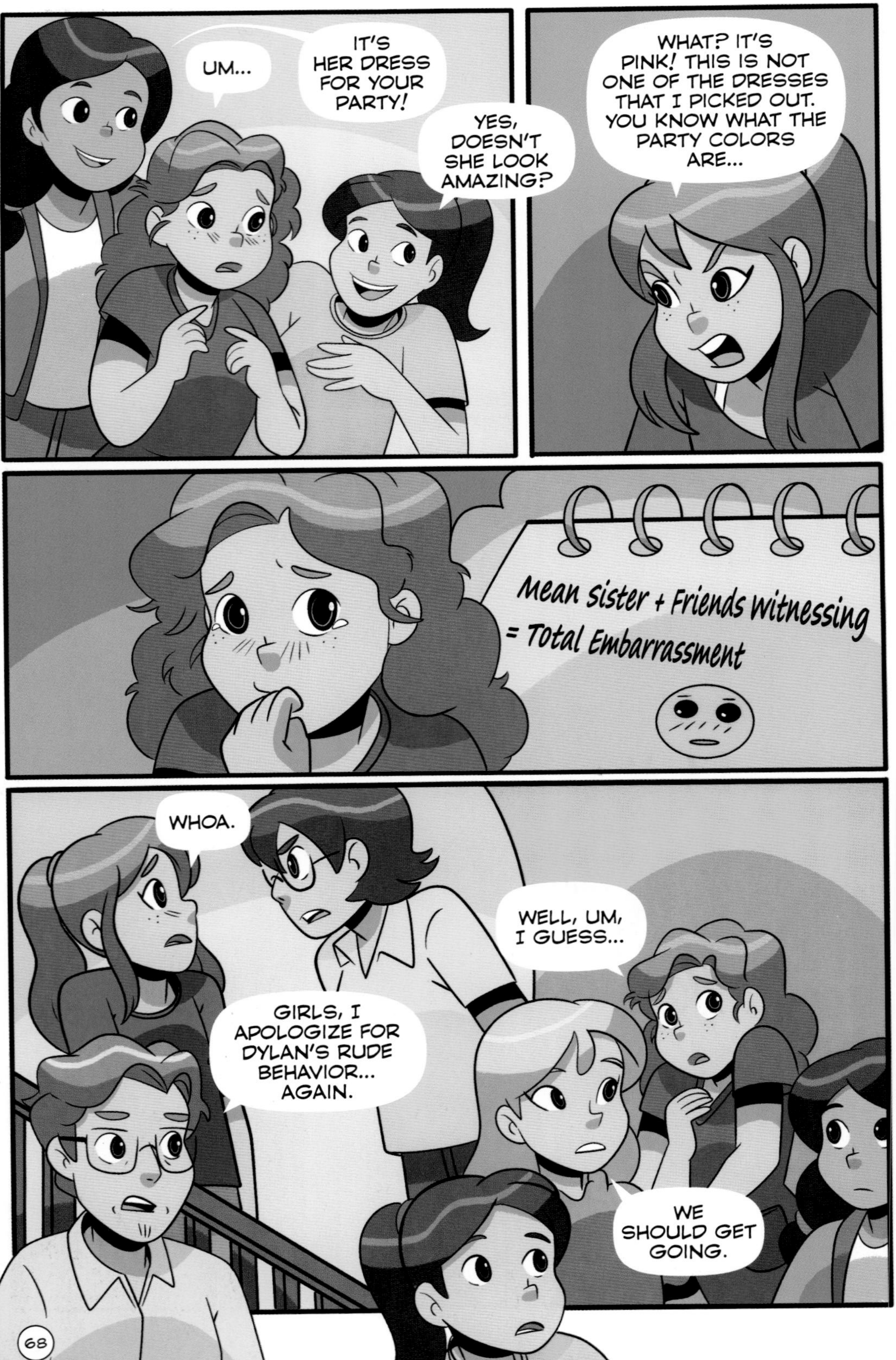
UM...
IT'S HER DRESS FOR YOUR PARTY!
YES, DOESN'T SHE LOOK AMAZING?
WHAT? IT'S PINK! THIS IS NOT ONE OF THE DRESSES THAT I PICKED OUT. YOU KNOW WHAT THE PARTY COLORS ARE...
Mean Sister + Friends Witnessing
= Total Embarrassment
WHOA.
WELL, UM, I GUESS...
GIRLS, I APOLOGIZE FOR DYLAN'S RUDE BEHAVIOR... AGAIN.
WE SHOULD GET GOING.

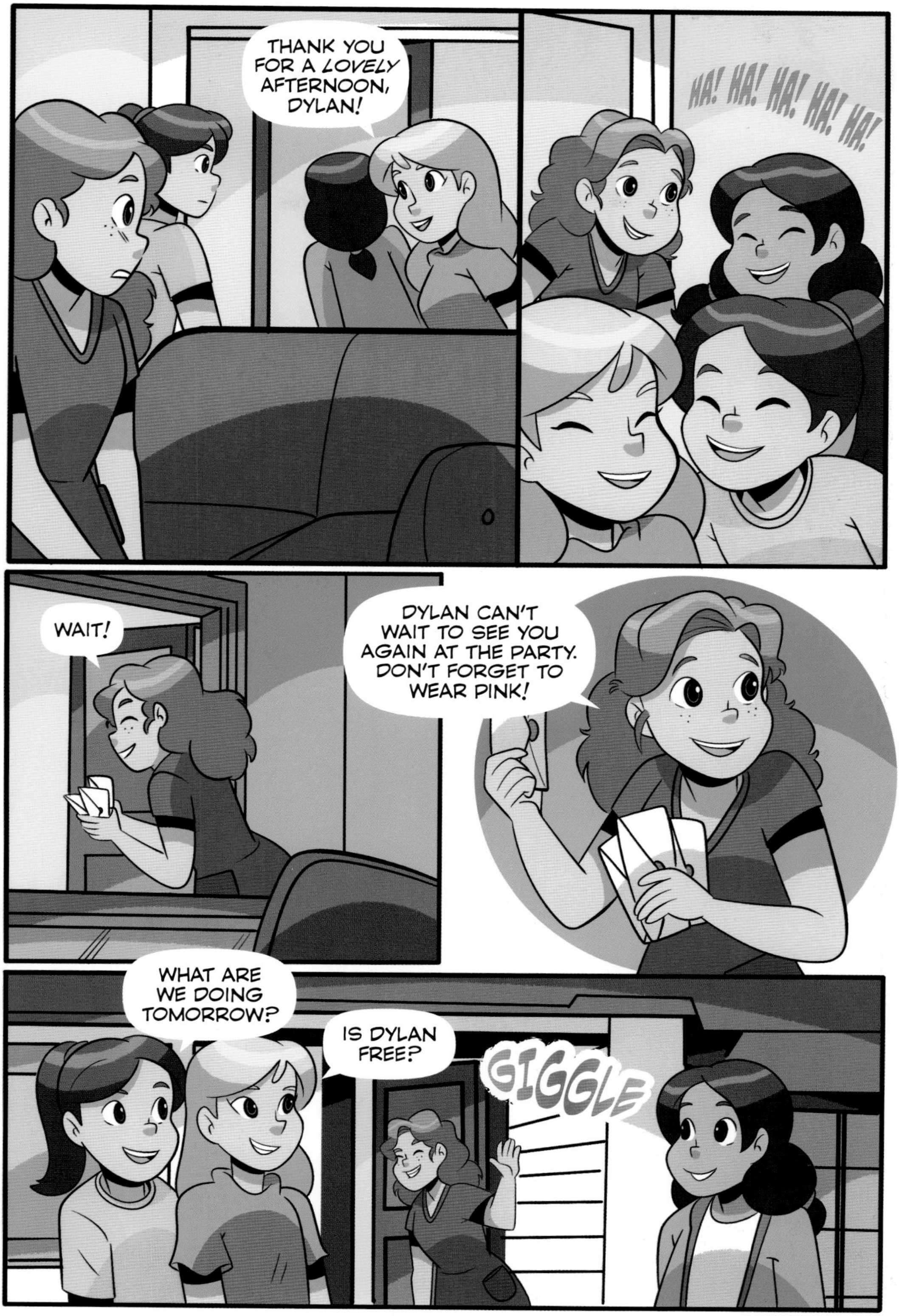
THANK YOU FOR A *LOVELY* AFTERNOON, DYLAN!
HA! HA! HA! HA! HA!
WAIT!
DYLAN CAN'T WAIT TO SEE YOU AGAIN AT THE PARTY. DON'T FORGET TO WEAR PINK!
WHAT ARE WE DOING TOMORROW?
IS DYLAN FREE?
GIGGLE

Chapter 8

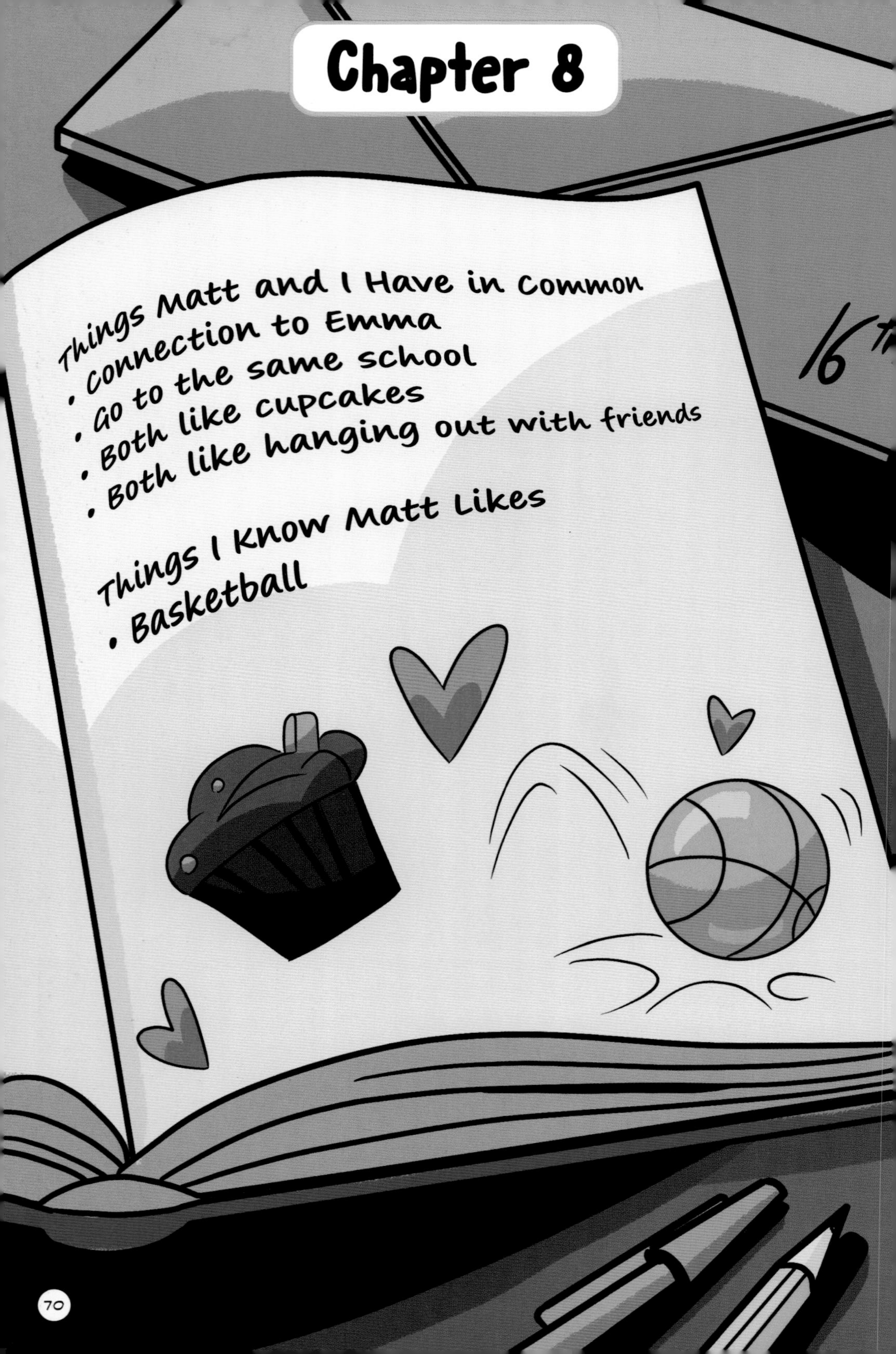
Things Matt and I Have in Common
• Connection to Emma
• Go to the same school
• Both like cupcakes
• Both like hanging out with friends
Things I Know Matt Likes
• Basketball

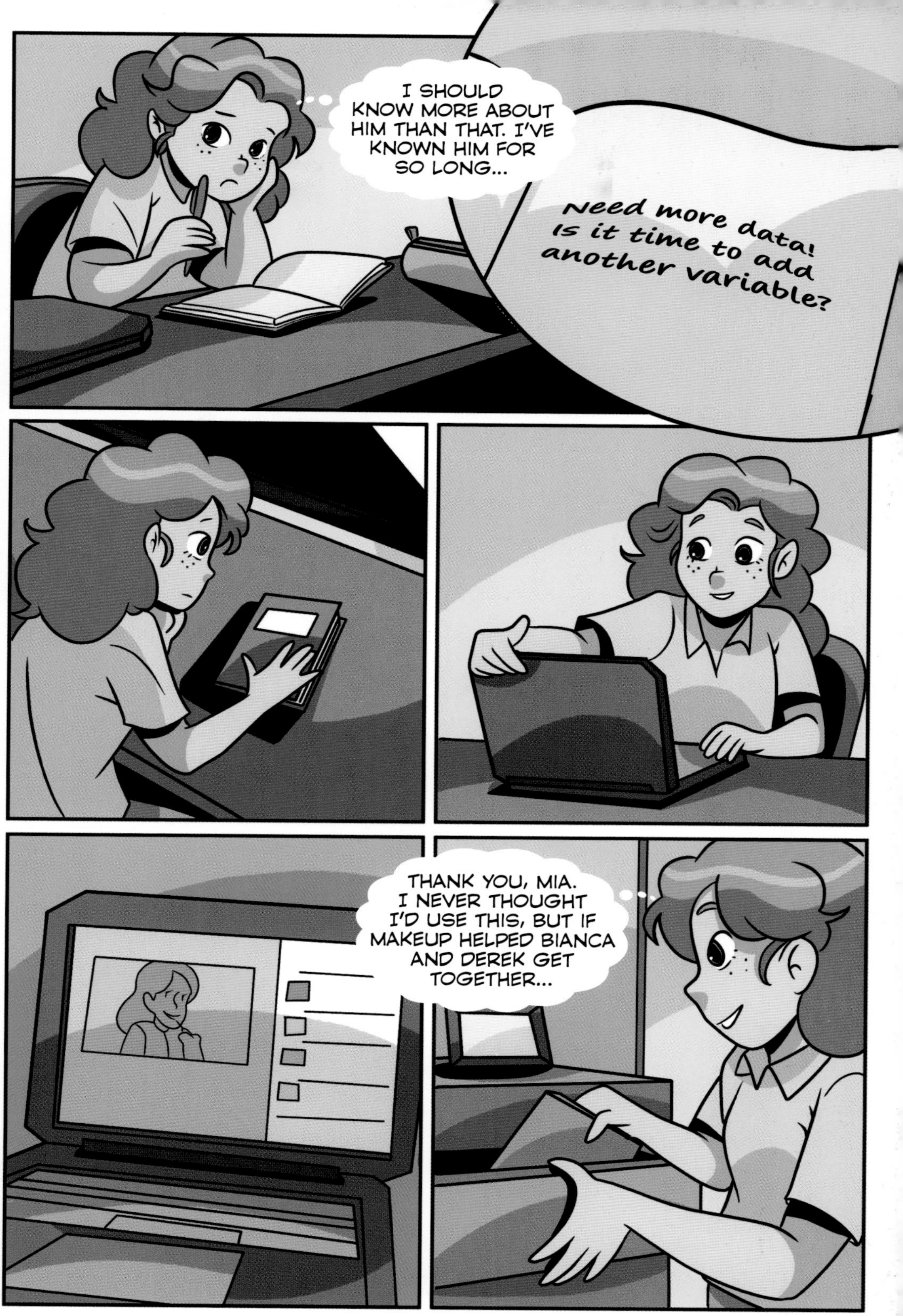
I SHOULD KNOW MORE ABOUT HIM THAN THAT. I'VE KNOWN HIM FOR SO LONG...
Need more data! Is it time to add another variable?
THANK YOU, MIA. I NEVER THOUGHT I'D USE THIS, BUT IF MAKEUP HELPED BIANCA AND DEREK GET TOGETHER...

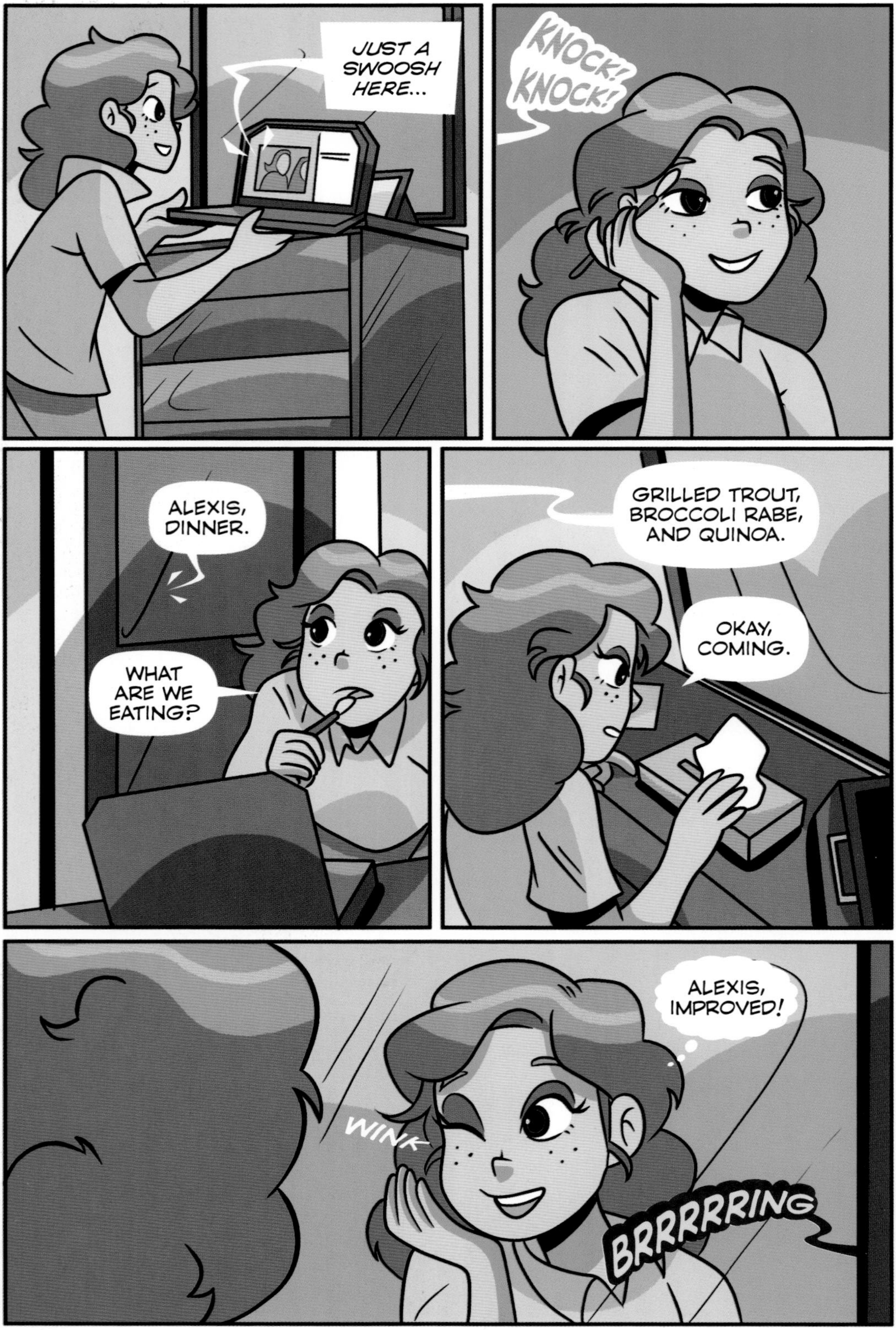
JUST A SWOOSH HERE...
KNOCK! KNOCK!
ALEXIS, DINNER.
WHAT ARE WE EATING?
GRILLED TROUT, BROCCOLI RABE, AND QUINOA.
OKAY, COMING.
ALEXIS, IMPROVED!
WINK
BRRRRRING

ALEXIS, CAN YOU GET THAT ON YOUR WAY DOWN?

RING

HELLO?

HI, ALEXIS?

I'M JUST CALLING TO RSVP TO THE LOVELY INVITATION TO DYLAN'S PARTY!

ALL—ALL OF YOU?

THAT'S RIGHT. ME, MR. TAYLOR, EMMA, AND THE BOYS. PLEASE TELL YOUR MOM FOR ME.

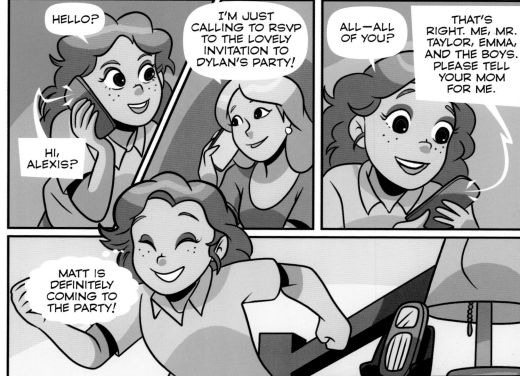

MATT IS DEFINITELY COMING TO THE PARTY!

Chapter 9

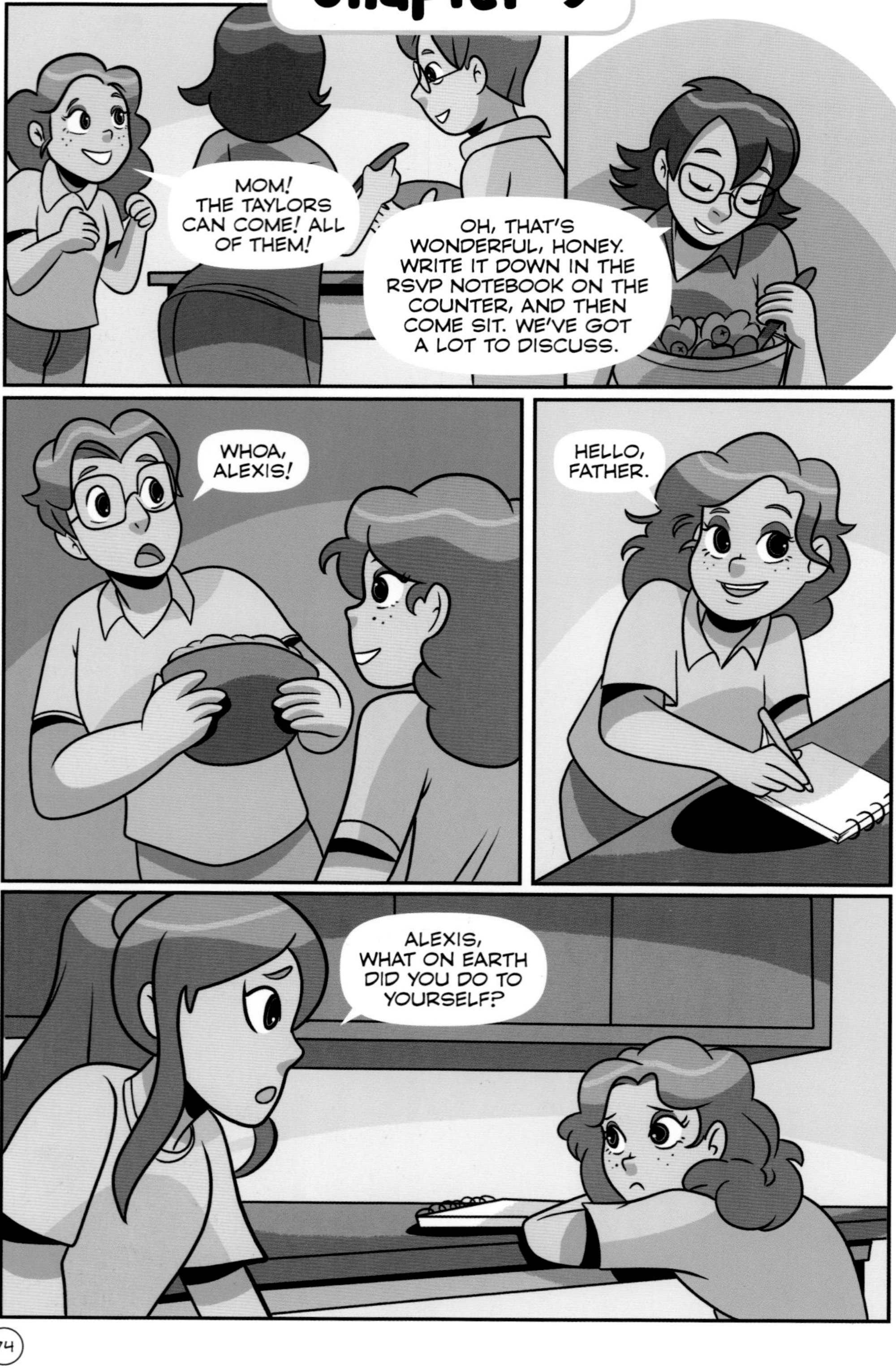

MOM! THE TAYLORS CAN COME! ALL OF THEM!
OH, THAT'S WONDERFUL, HONEY. WRITE IT DOWN IN THE RSVP NOTEBOOK ON THE COUNTER, AND THEN COME SIT. WE'VE GOT A LOT TO DISCUSS.
WHOA, ALEXIS!
HELLO, FATHER.
ALEXIS, WHAT ON EARTH DID YOU DO TO YOURSELF?

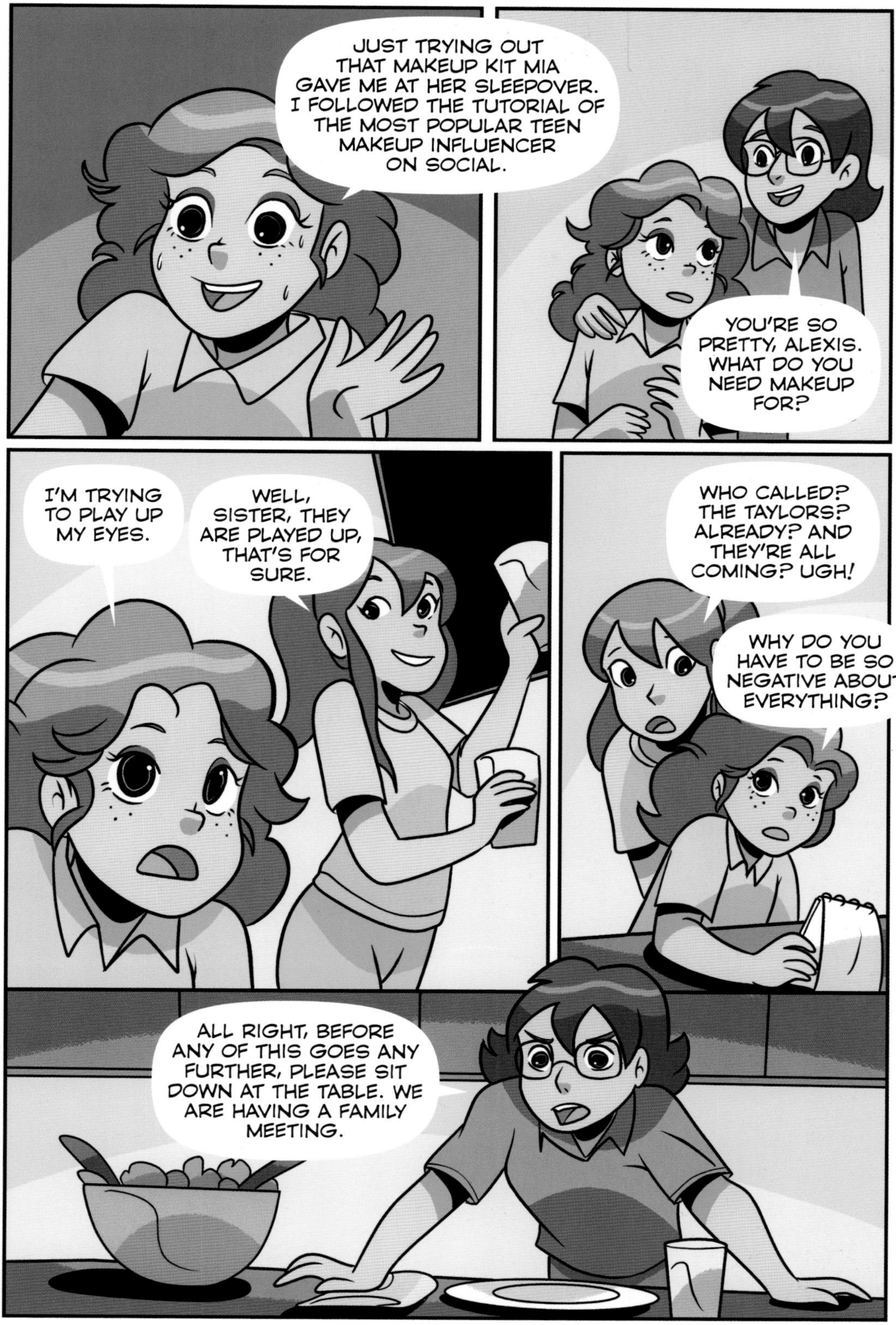
JUST TRYING OUT THAT MAKEUP KIT MIA GAVE ME AT HER SLEEPOVER. I FOLLOWED THE TUTORIAL OF THE MOST POPULAR TEEN MAKEUP INFLUENCER ON SOCIAL.
YOU'RE SO PRETTY, ALEXIS. WHAT DO YOU NEED MAKEUP FOR?
I'M TRYING TO PLAY UP MY EYES.
WELL, SISTER, THEY ARE PLAYED UP, THAT'S FOR SURE.
WHO CALLED? THE TAYLORS? ALREADY? AND THEY'RE ALL COMING? UGH!
WHY DO YOU HAVE TO BE SO NEGATIVE ABOUT EVERYTHING?
ALL RIGHT, BEFORE ANY OF THIS GOES ANY FURTHER, PLEASE SIT DOWN AT THE TABLE. WE ARE HAVING A FAMILY MEETING.

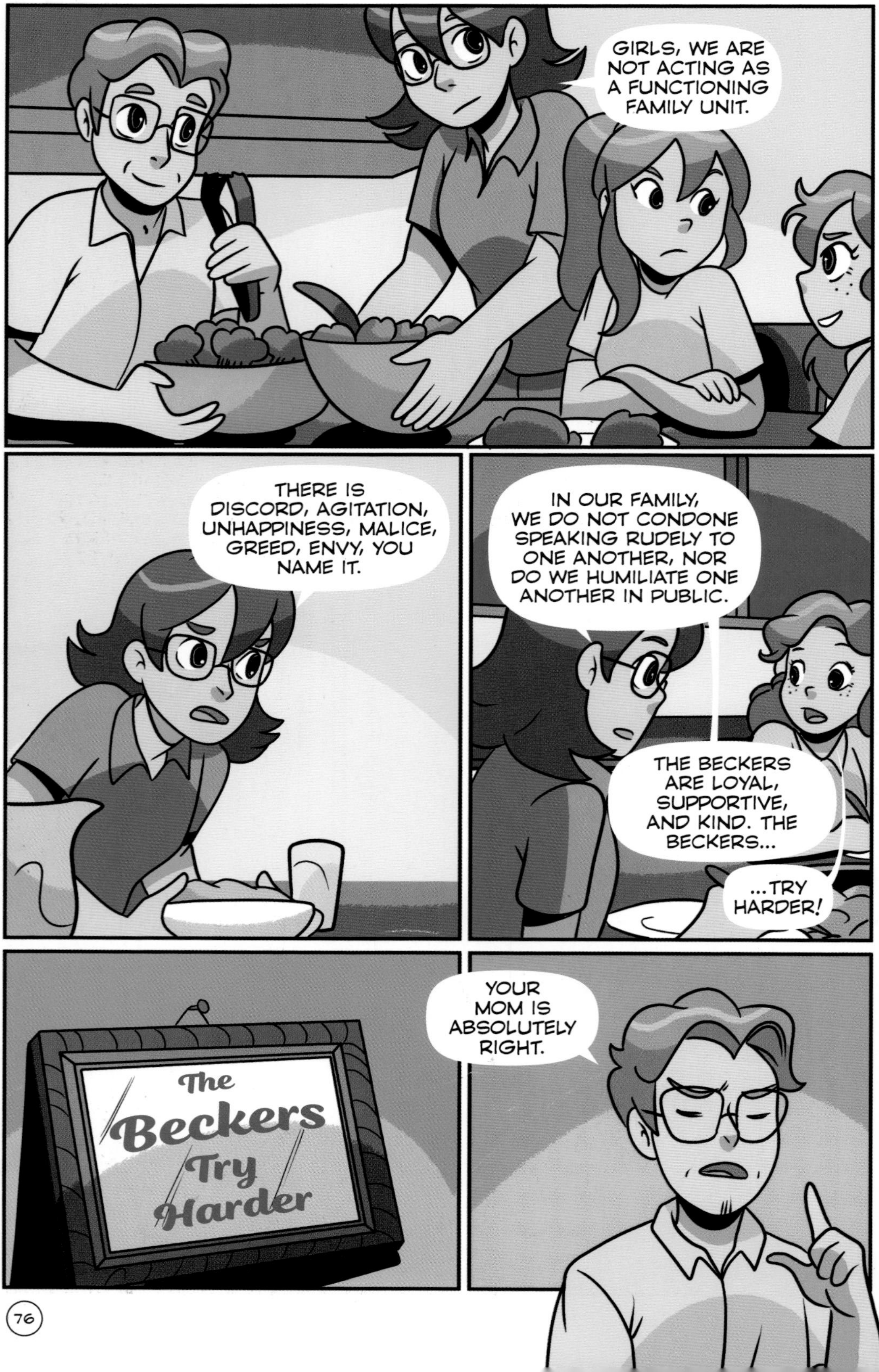
GIRLS, WE ARE NOT ACTING AS A FUNCTIONING FAMILY UNIT.
THERE IS DISCORD, AGITATION, UNHAPPINESS, MALICE, GREED, ENVY, YOU NAME IT.
IN OUR FAMILY, WE DO NOT CONDONE SPEAKING RUDELY TO ONE ANOTHER, NOR DO WE HUMILIATE ONE ANOTHER IN PUBLIC.
THE BECKERS ARE LOYAL, SUPPORTIVE, AND KIND. THE BECKERS...
...TRY HARDER!
The Beckers Try Harder
YOUR MOM IS ABSOLUTELY RIGHT.

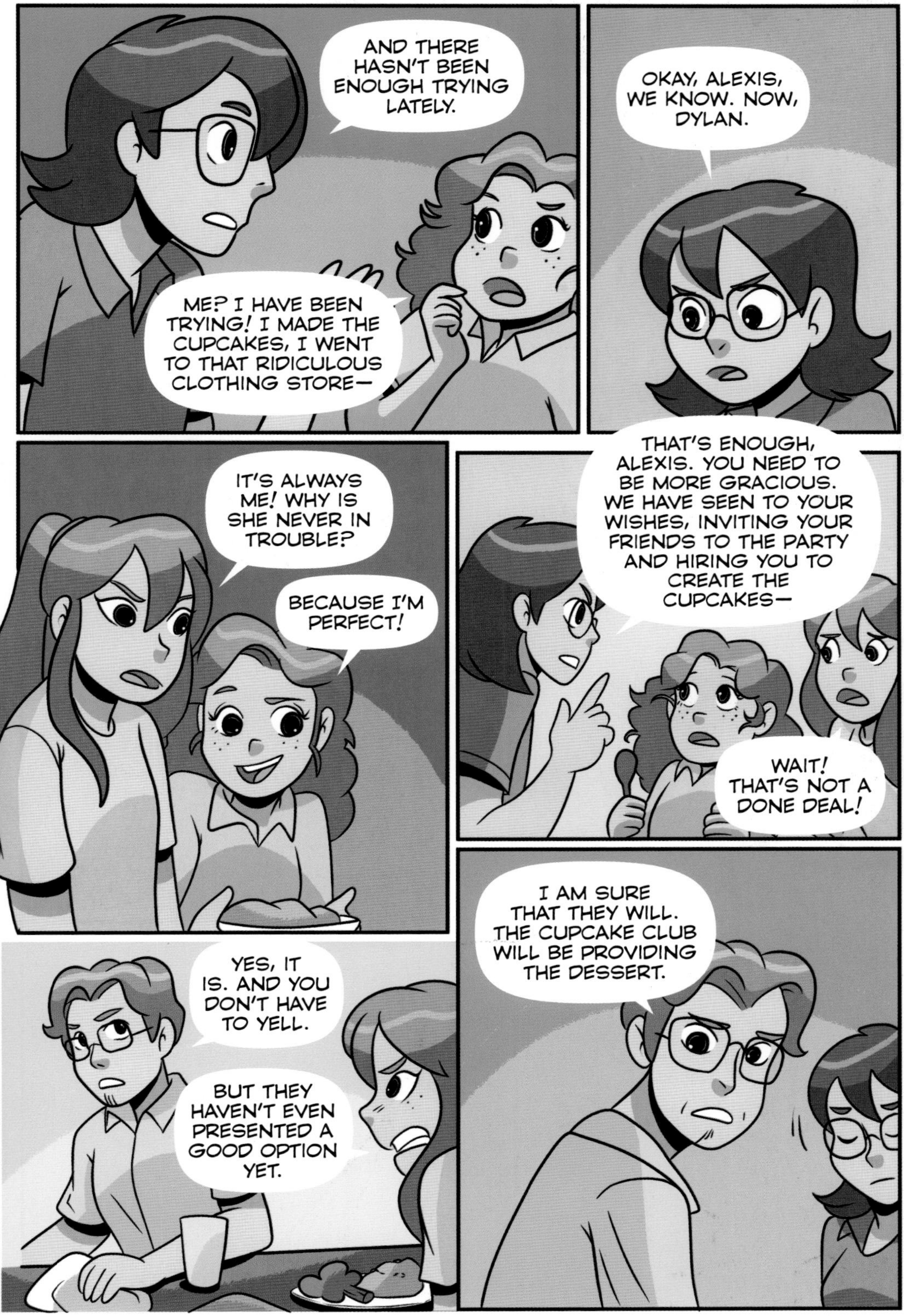
AND THERE HASN'T BEEN ENOUGH TRYING LATELY.
ME? I HAVE BEEN TRYING! I MADE THE CUPCAKES, I WENT TO THAT RIDICULOUS CLOTHING STORE—
OKAY, ALEXIS, WE KNOW. NOW, DYLAN.
IT'S ALWAYS ME! WHY IS SHE NEVER IN TROUBLE?
BECAUSE I'M PERFECT!
THAT'S ENOUGH, ALEXIS. YOU NEED TO BE MORE GRACIOUS. WE HAVE SEEN TO YOUR WISHES, INVITING YOUR FRIENDS TO THE PARTY AND HIRING YOU TO CREATE THE CUPCAKES—
WAIT! THAT'S NOT A DONE DEAL!
YES, IT IS. AND YOU DON'T HAVE TO YELL.
BUT THEY HAVEN'T EVEN PRESENTED A GOOD OPTION YET.
I AM SURE THAT THEY WILL. THE CUPCAKE CLUB WILL BE PROVIDING THE DESSERT.

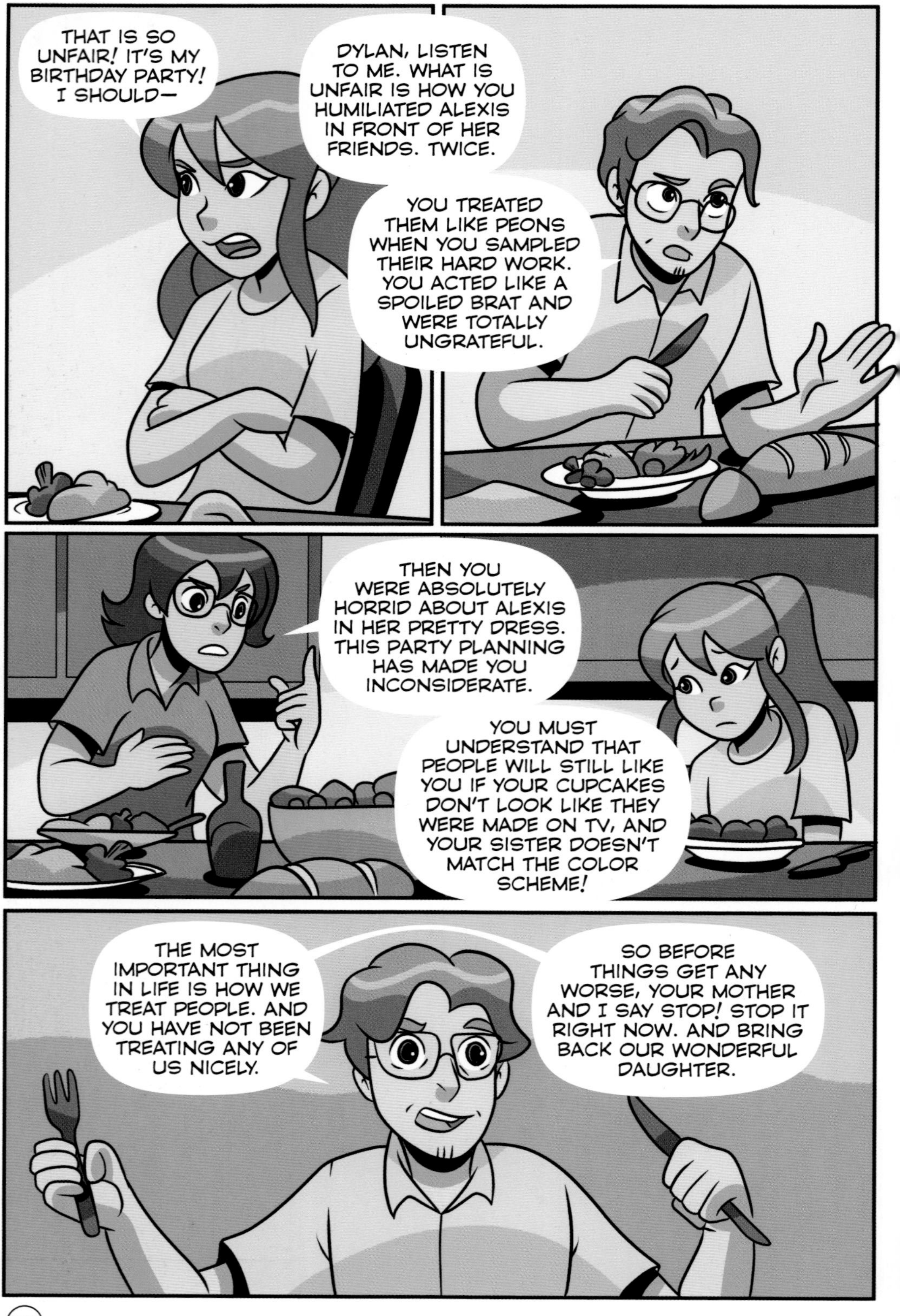
THAT IS SO UNFAIR! IT'S MY BIRTHDAY PARTY! I SHOULD—
DYLAN, LISTEN TO ME. WHAT IS UNFAIR IS HOW YOU HUMILIATED ALEXIS IN FRONT OF HER FRIENDS. TWICE.
YOU TREATED THEM LIKE PEONS WHEN YOU SAMPLED THEIR HARD WORK. YOU ACTED LIKE A SPOILED BRAT AND WERE TOTALLY UNGRATEFUL.
THEN YOU WERE ABSOLUTELY HORRID ABOUT ALEXIS IN HER PRETTY DRESS. THIS PARTY PLANNING HAS MADE YOU INCONSIDERATE.
YOU MUST UNDERSTAND THAT PEOPLE WILL STILL LIKE YOU IF YOUR CUPCAKES DON'T LOOK LIKE THEY WERE MADE ON TV, AND YOUR SISTER DOESN'T MATCH THE COLOR SCHEME!
THE MOST IMPORTANT THING IN LIFE IS HOW WE TREAT PEOPLE. AND YOU HAVE NOT BEEN TREATING ANY OF US NICELY.
SO BEFORE THINGS GET ANY WORSE, YOUR MOTHER AND I SAY STOP! STOP IT RIGHT NOW. AND BRING BACK OUR WONDERFUL DAUGHTER.

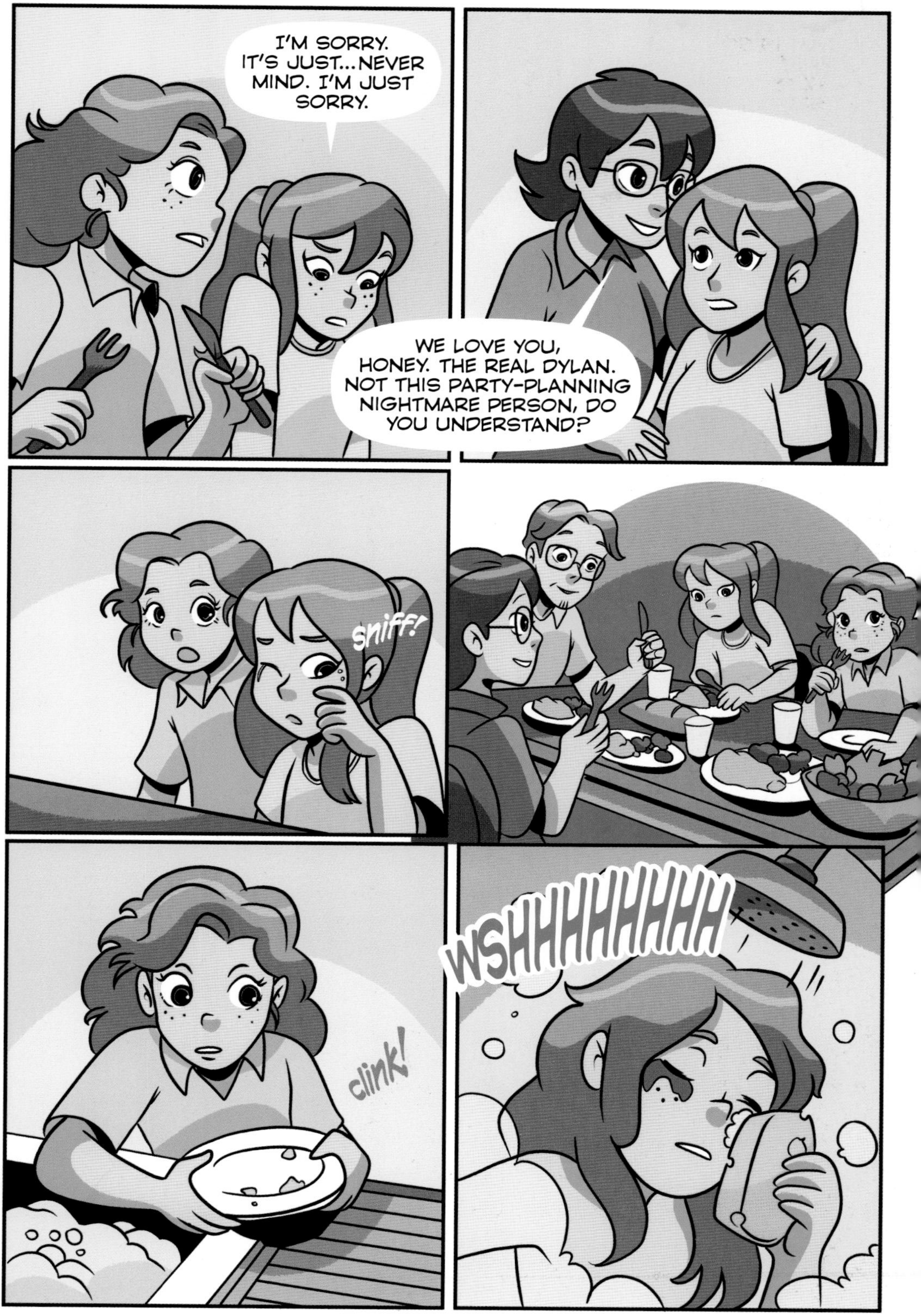
I'M SORRY. IT'S JUST...NEVER MIND. I'M JUST SORRY.
WE LOVE YOU, HONEY. THE REAL DYLAN. NOT THIS PARTY-PLANNING NIGHTMARE PERSON, DO YOU UNDERSTAND?
sniff!
clink!
WSHHHHHHHHH

Chapter 10

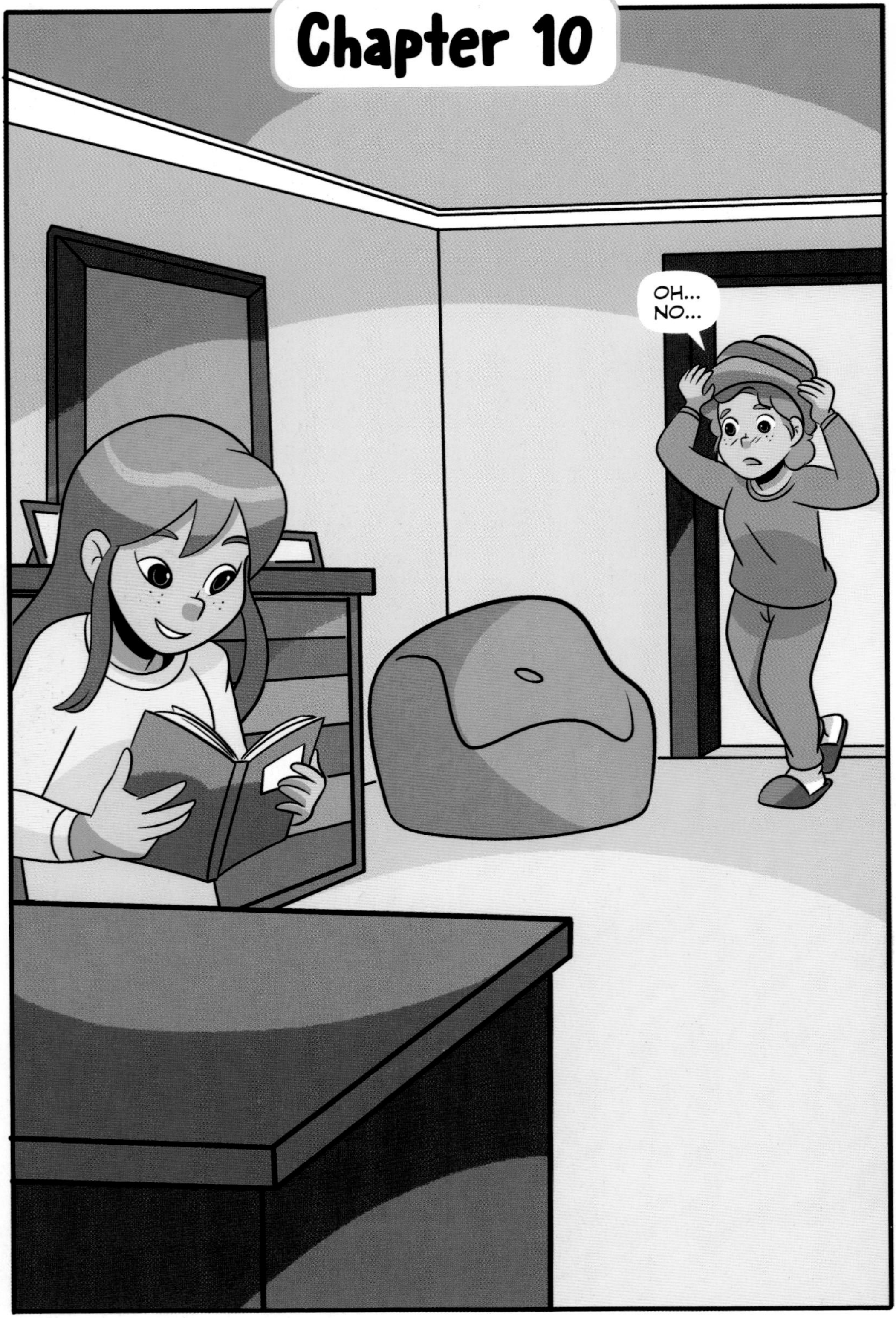
OH...
NO...

WHAT IS THIS? DO YOU LIKE SOMEONE?

DON'T THROW UP. DON'T THROW UP.

WHAT IF I DO?

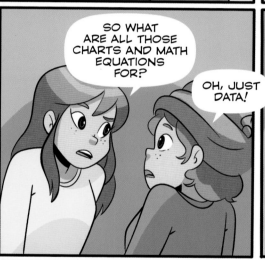

SO WHAT ARE ALL THOSE CHARTS AND MATH EQUATIONS FOR?

OH, JUST DATA!

SO WHO IS IT?

IS SHE BEING NICE, OR IS THIS A TRICK?

UM...

YOU CAN TELL ME. I WON'T SAY ANYTHING.

IT'S MATT.

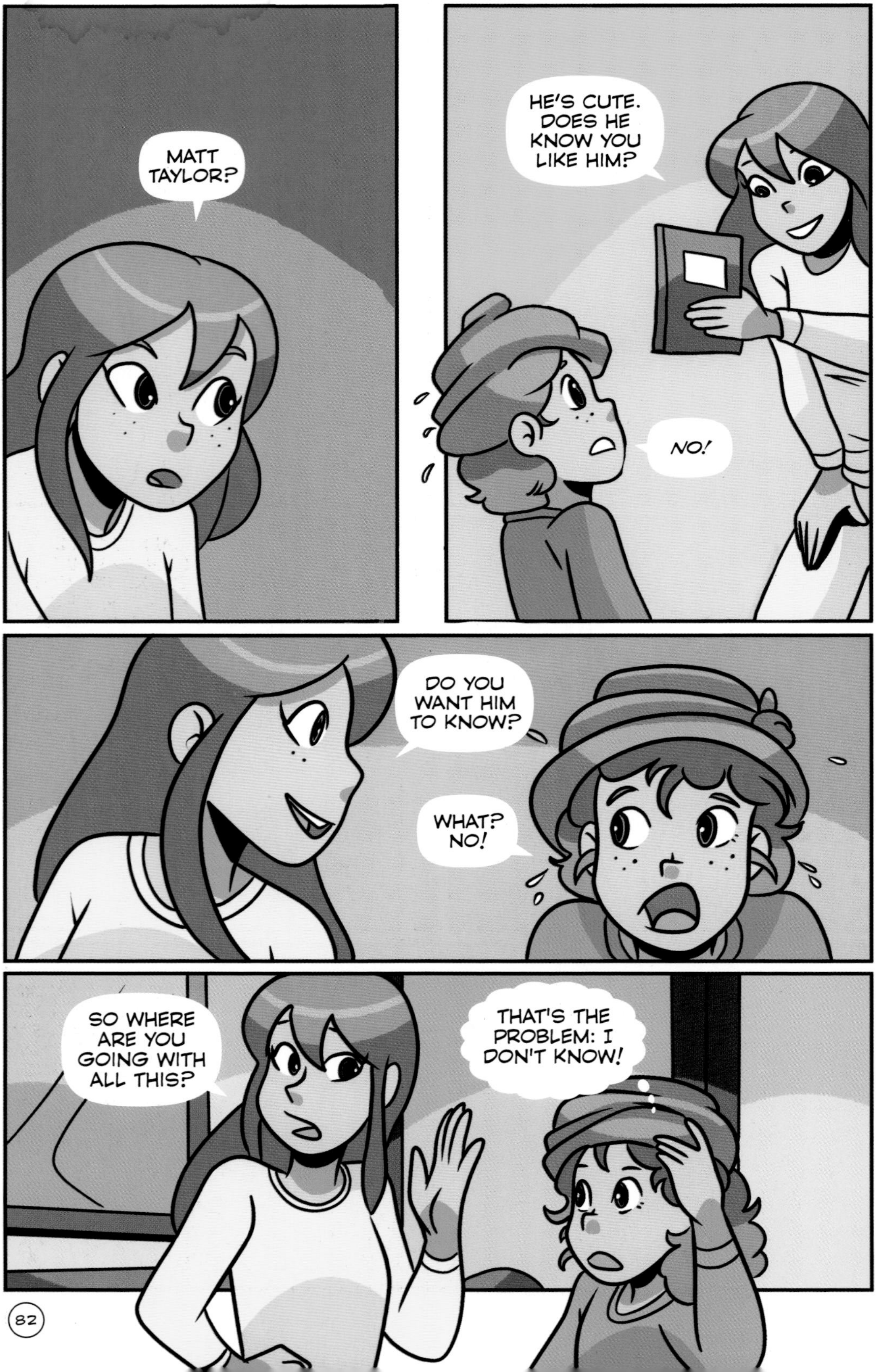
MATT TAYLOR?
HE'S CUTE. DOES HE KNOW YOU LIKE HIM?
NO!
DO YOU WANT HIM TO KNOW?
WHAT? NO!
SO WHERE ARE YOU GOING WITH ALL THIS?
THAT'S THE PROBLEM: I DON'T KNOW!

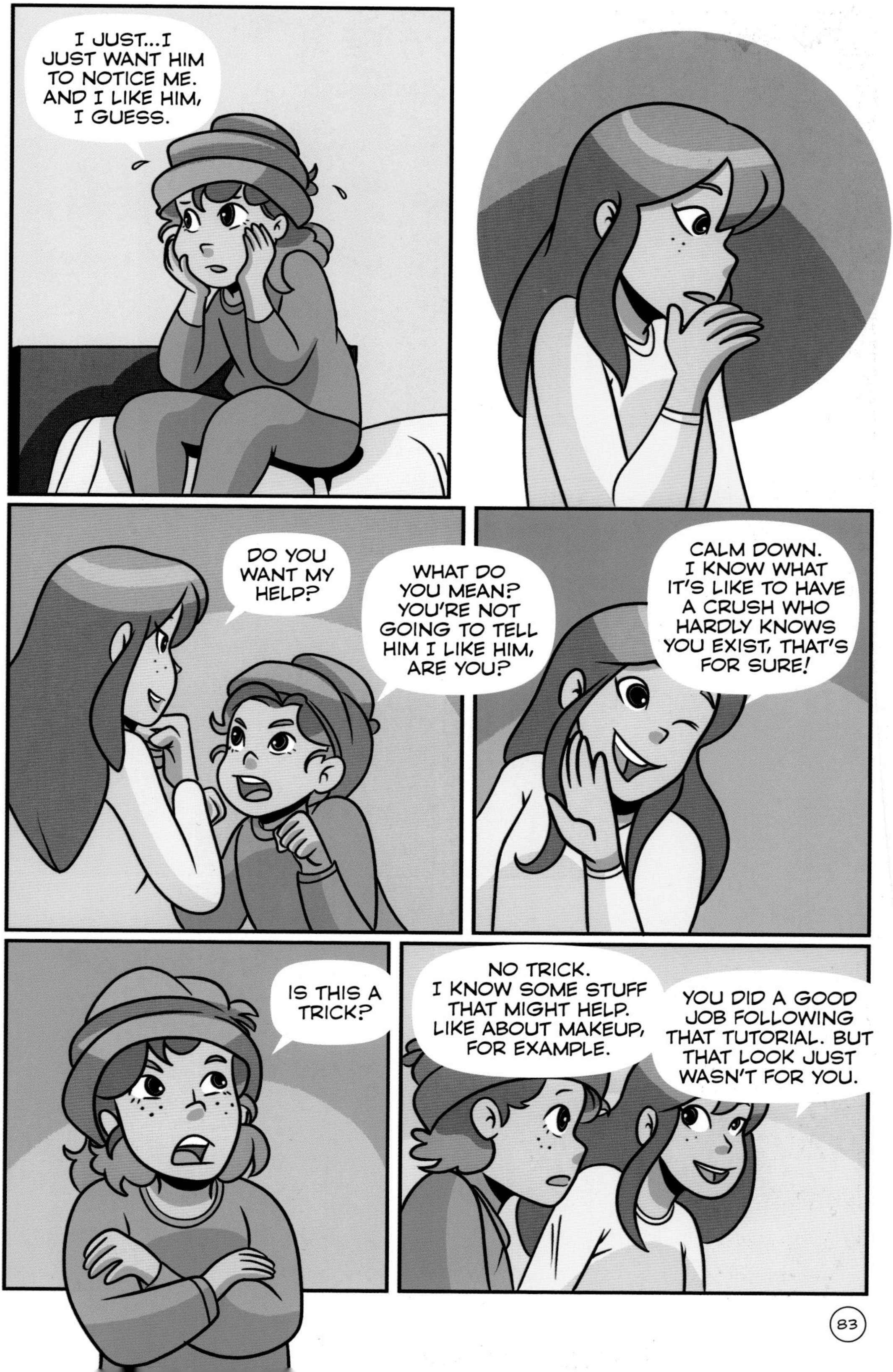
I JUST...I JUST WANT HIM TO NOTICE ME. AND I LIKE HIM, I GUESS.
DO YOU WANT MY HELP?
WHAT DO YOU MEAN? YOU'RE NOT GOING TO TELL HIM I LIKE HIM, ARE YOU?
CALM DOWN. I KNOW WHAT IT'S LIKE TO HAVE A CRUSH WHO HARDLY KNOWS YOU EXIST, THAT'S FOR SURE!
IS THIS A TRICK?
NO TRICK. I KNOW SOME STUFF THAT MIGHT HELP. LIKE ABOUT MAKEUP, FOR EXAMPLE.
YOU DID A GOOD JOB FOLLOWING THAT TUTORIAL. BUT THAT LOOK JUST WASN'T FOR YOU.

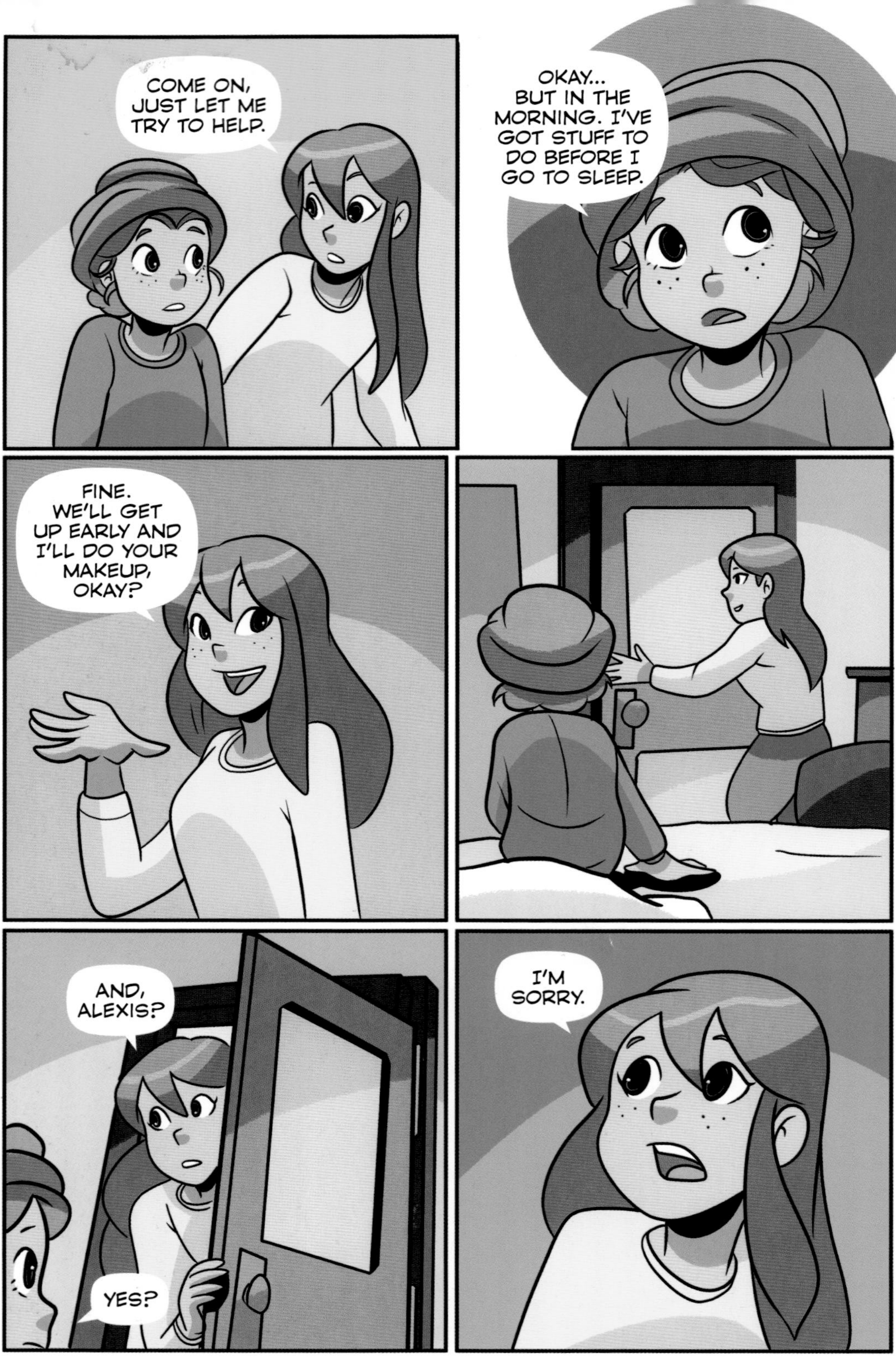
COME ON, JUST LET ME TRY TO HELP.
OKAY... BUT IN THE MORNING. I'VE GOT STUFF TO DO BEFORE I GO TO SLEEP.
FINE. WE'LL GET UP EARLY AND I'LL DO YOUR MAKEUP, OKAY?
AND, ALEXIS?
YES?
I'M SORRY.

FOR WHAT?

EVERYTHING.

CLICK

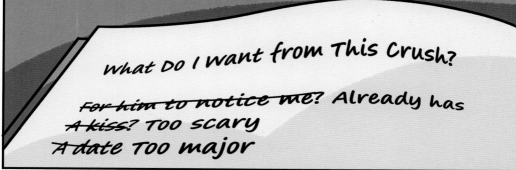

What Do I Want from This Crush?

~~For him to notice me?~~ Already has
~~A kiss?~~ TOO scary
~~A date~~ TOO major

PING!

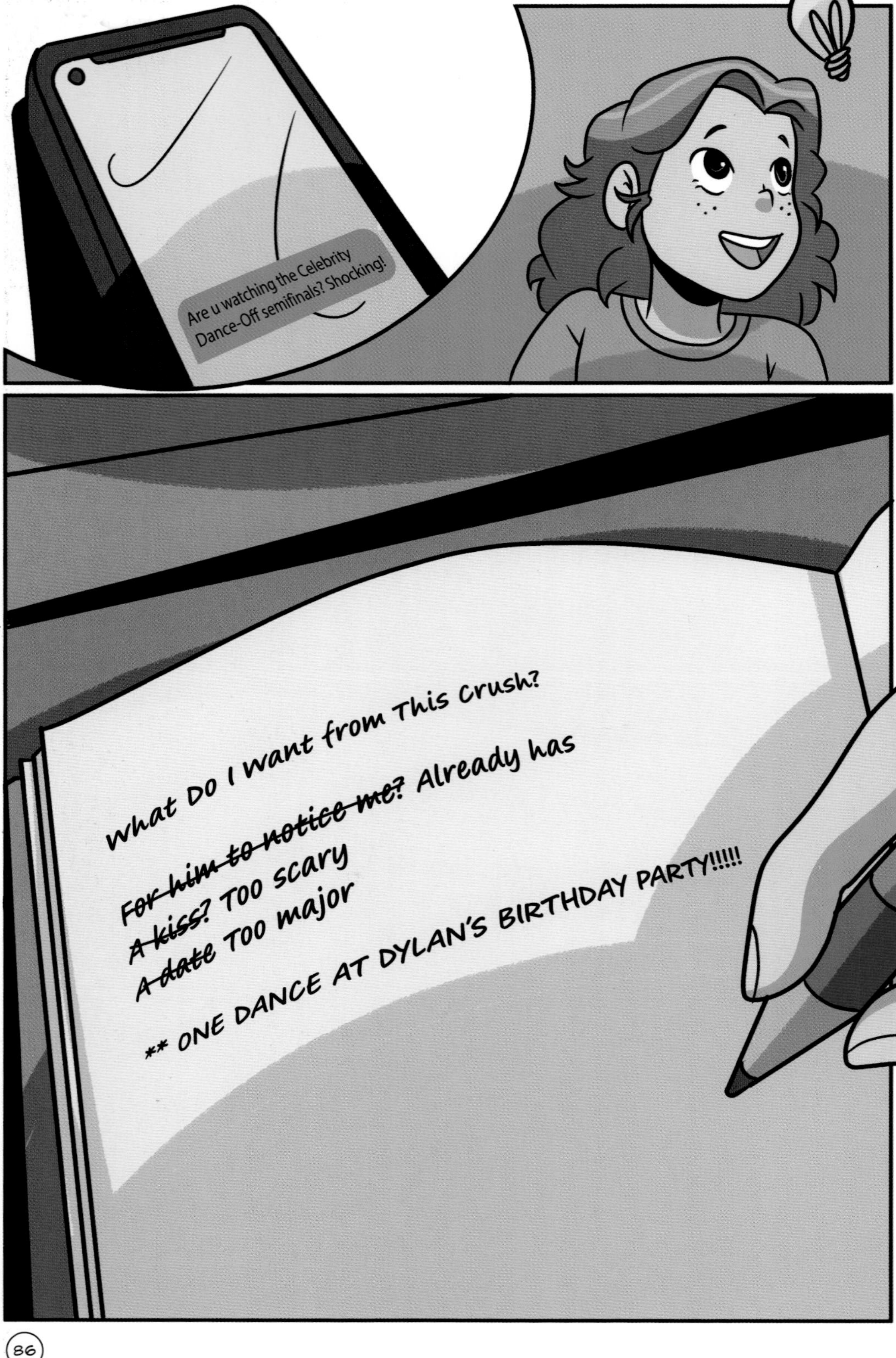
Are u watching the Celebrity Dance-Off semifinals? Shocking!
What Do I Want from This Crush?
~~For him to notice me?~~ Already has
~~A kiss?~~ TOO scary
~~A date~~ TOO major
** ONE DANCE AT DYLAN'S BIRTHDAY PARTY!!!!!

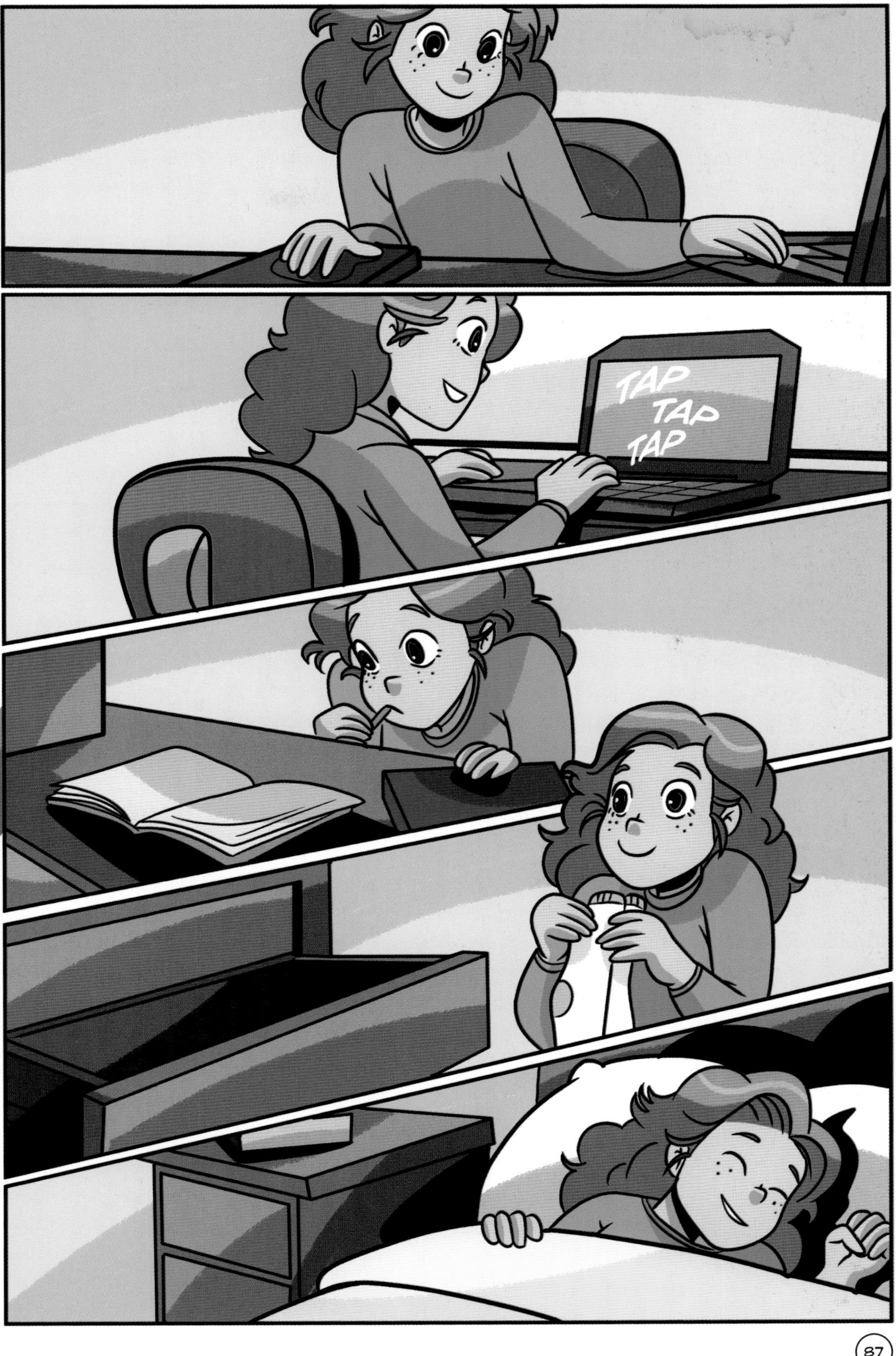
TAP
TAP
TAP

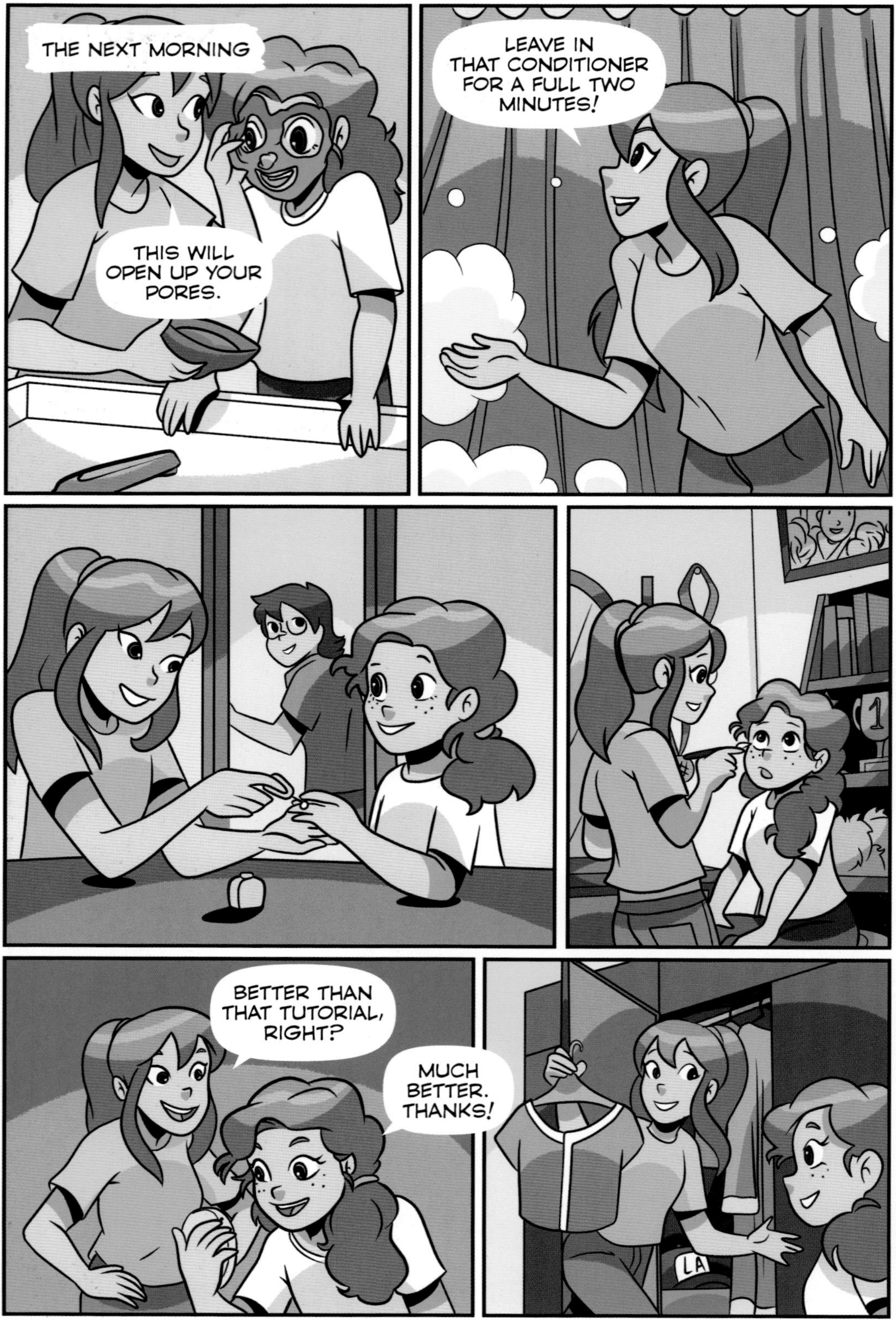
THE NEXT MORNING
THIS WILL OPEN UP YOUR PORES.
LEAVE IN THAT CONDITIONER FOR A FULL TWO MINUTES!
BETTER THAN THAT TUTORIAL, RIGHT?
MUCH BETTER. THANKS!
LA

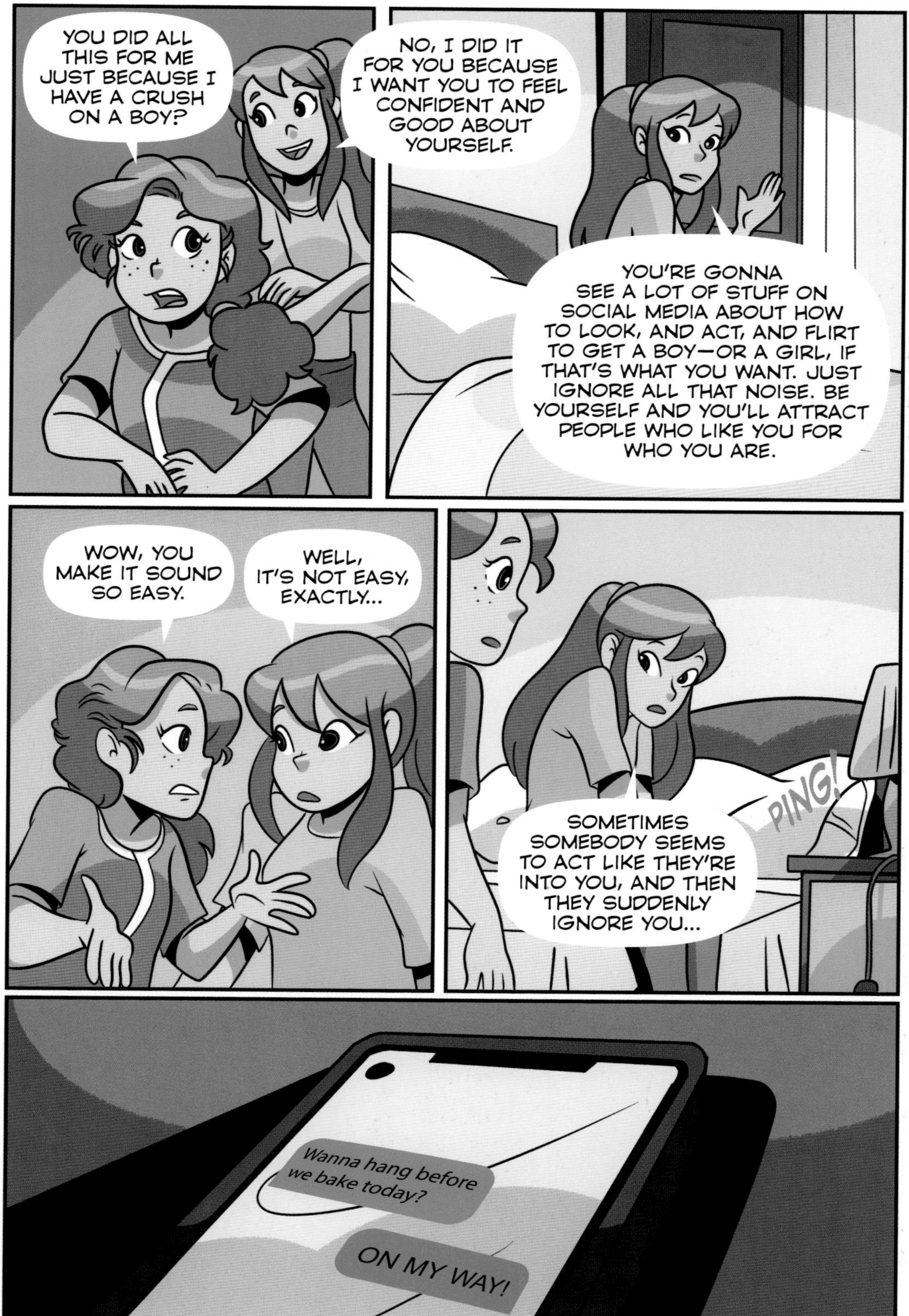
YOU DID ALL THIS FOR ME JUST BECAUSE I HAVE A CRUSH ON A BOY?
NO, I DID IT FOR YOU BECAUSE I WANT YOU TO FEEL CONFIDENT AND GOOD ABOUT YOURSELF.
YOU'RE GONNA SEE A LOT OF STUFF ON SOCIAL MEDIA ABOUT HOW TO LOOK, AND ACT, AND FLIRT TO GET A BOY—OR A GIRL, IF THAT'S WHAT YOU WANT. JUST IGNORE ALL THAT NOISE. BE YOURSELF AND YOU'LL ATTRACT PEOPLE WHO LIKE YOU FOR WHO YOU ARE.
WOW, YOU MAKE IT SOUND SO EASY.
WELL, IT'S NOT EASY, EXACTLY...
SOMETIMES SOMEBODY SEEMS TO ACT LIKE THEY'RE INTO YOU, AND THEN THEY SUDDENLY IGNORE YOU...
PING!
Wanna hang before we bake today?
ON MY WAY!

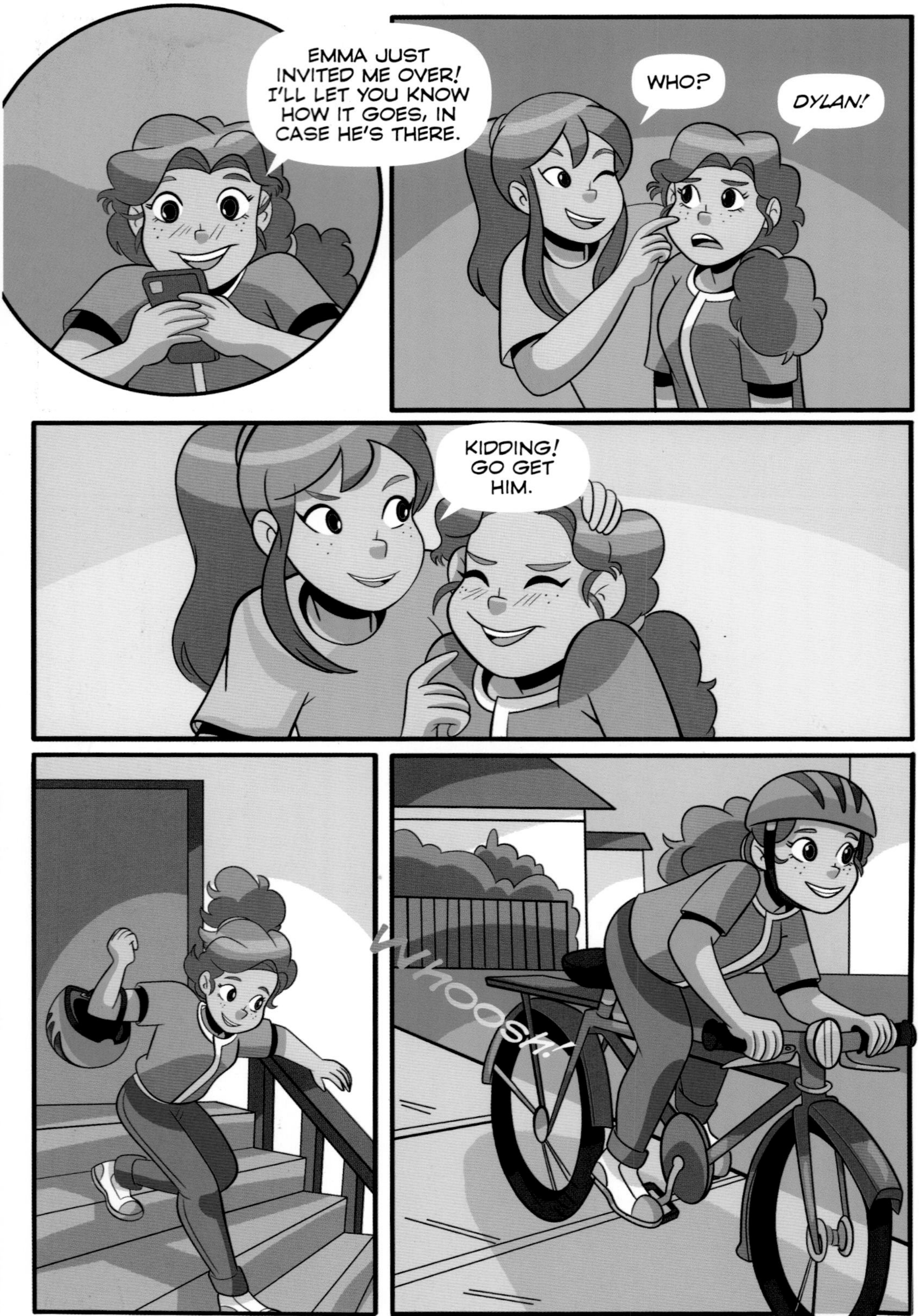
EMMA JUST INVITED ME OVER! I'LL LET YOU KNOW HOW IT GOES, IN CASE HE'S THERE.
WHO?
DYLAN!
KIDDING! GO GET HIM.
WHOOSH!

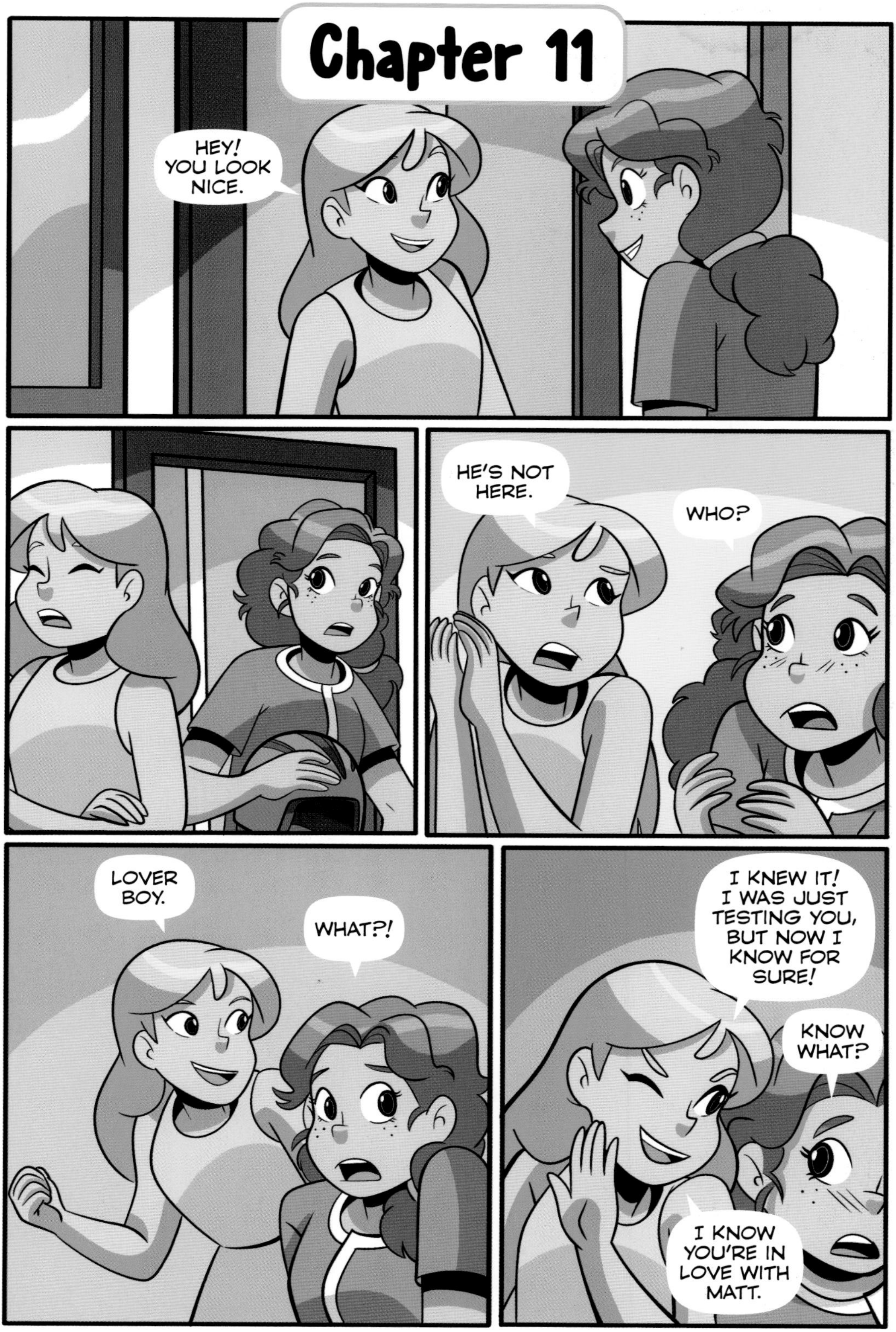
Chapter 11
HEY! YOU LOOK NICE.
HE'S NOT HERE.
WHO?
LOVER BOY.
WHAT?!
I KNEW IT! I WAS JUST TESTING YOU, BUT NOW I KNOW FOR SURE!
KNOW WHAT?
I KNOW YOU'RE IN LOVE WITH MATT.

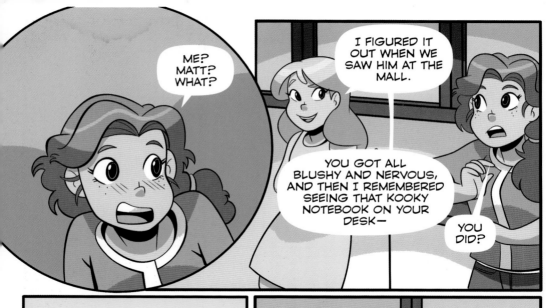

ME? MATT? WHAT?

I FIGURED IT OUT WHEN WE SAW HIM AT THE MALL.

YOU GOT ALL BLUSHY AND NERVOUS, AND THEN I REMEMBERED SEEING THAT KOOKY NOTEBOOK ON YOUR DESK—

YOU DID?

HA! SO YOU ARE.

YES, I AM. I'M SORRY. I JUST CAN'T HELP IT.

IT'S A LITTLE AWKWARD. AND WHY MATT? I MEAN, SAM, MAYBE. HE'S CUTE, AND GIRLS SEEM TO REALLY LIKE HIM. BUT MATT? SMELLY SOCK MATT? COMPUTER GEEK MATT?

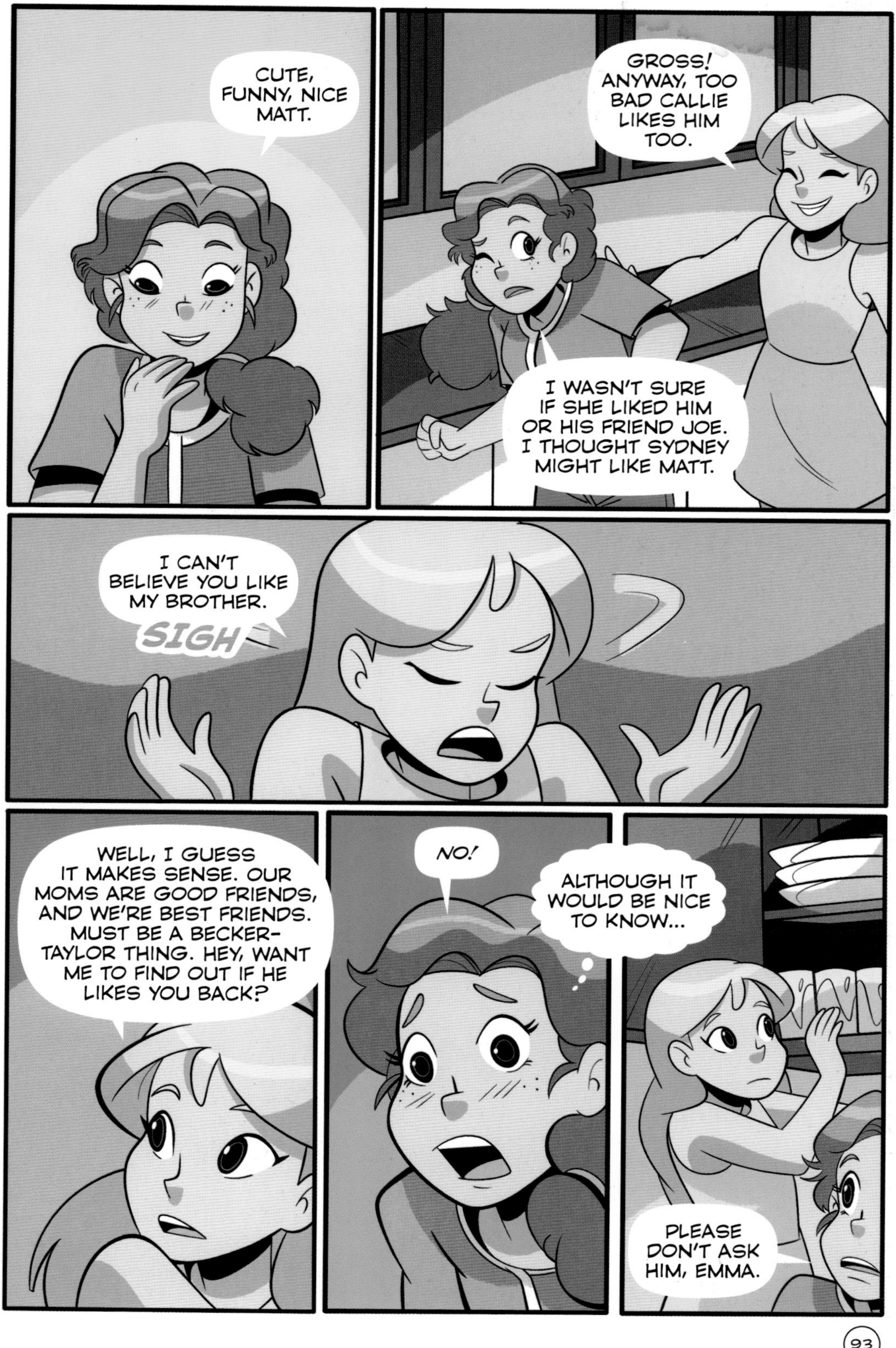
CUTE, FUNNY, NICE MATT.
GROSS! ANYWAY, TOO BAD CALLIE LIKES HIM TOO.
I WASN'T SURE IF SHE LIKED HIM OR HIS FRIEND JOE. I THOUGHT SYDNEY MIGHT LIKE MATT.
I CAN'T BELIEVE YOU LIKE MY BROTHER.
SIGH
WELL, I GUESS IT MAKES SENSE. OUR MOMS ARE GOOD FRIENDS, AND WE'RE BEST FRIENDS. MUST BE A BECKER-TAYLOR THING. HEY, WANT ME TO FIND OUT IF HE LIKES YOU BACK?
NO!
ALTHOUGH IT WOULD BE NICE TO KNOW...
PLEASE DON'T ASK HIM, EMMA.

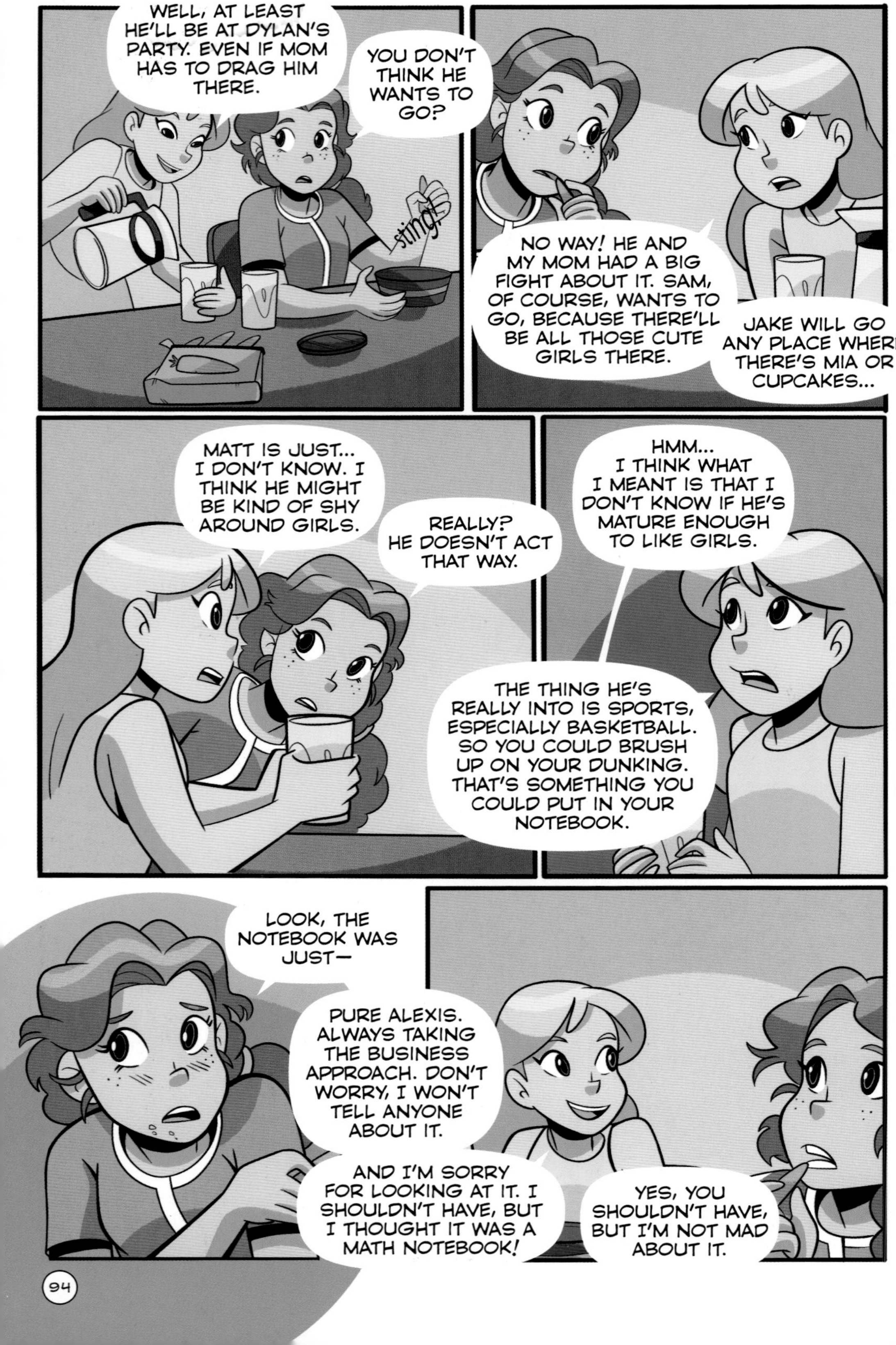
WELL, AT LEAST HE'LL BE AT DYLAN'S PARTY. EVEN IF MOM HAS TO DRAG HIM THERE.
YOU DON'T THINK HE WANTS TO GO?
sting!
NO WAY! HE AND MY MOM HAD A BIG FIGHT ABOUT IT. SAM, OF COURSE, WANTS TO GO, BECAUSE THERE'LL BE ALL THOSE CUTE GIRLS THERE.
JAKE WILL GO ANY PLACE WHERE THERE'S MIA OR CUPCAKES...
MATT IS JUST... I DON'T KNOW. I THINK HE MIGHT BE KIND OF SHY AROUND GIRLS.
REALLY? HE DOESN'T ACT THAT WAY.
HMM... I THINK WHAT I MEANT IS THAT I DON'T KNOW IF HE'S MATURE ENOUGH TO LIKE GIRLS.
THE THING HE'S REALLY INTO IS SPORTS, ESPECIALLY BASKETBALL. SO YOU COULD BRUSH UP ON YOUR DUNKING. THAT'S SOMETHING YOU COULD PUT IN YOUR NOTEBOOK.
LOOK, THE NOTEBOOK WAS JUST—
PURE ALEXIS. ALWAYS TAKING THE BUSINESS APPROACH. DON'T WORRY, I WON'T TELL ANYONE ABOUT IT.
AND I'M SORRY FOR LOOKING AT IT. I SHOULDN'T HAVE, BUT I THOUGHT IT WAS A MATH NOTEBOOK!
YES, YOU SHOULDN'T HAVE, BUT I'M NOT MAD ABOUT IT.

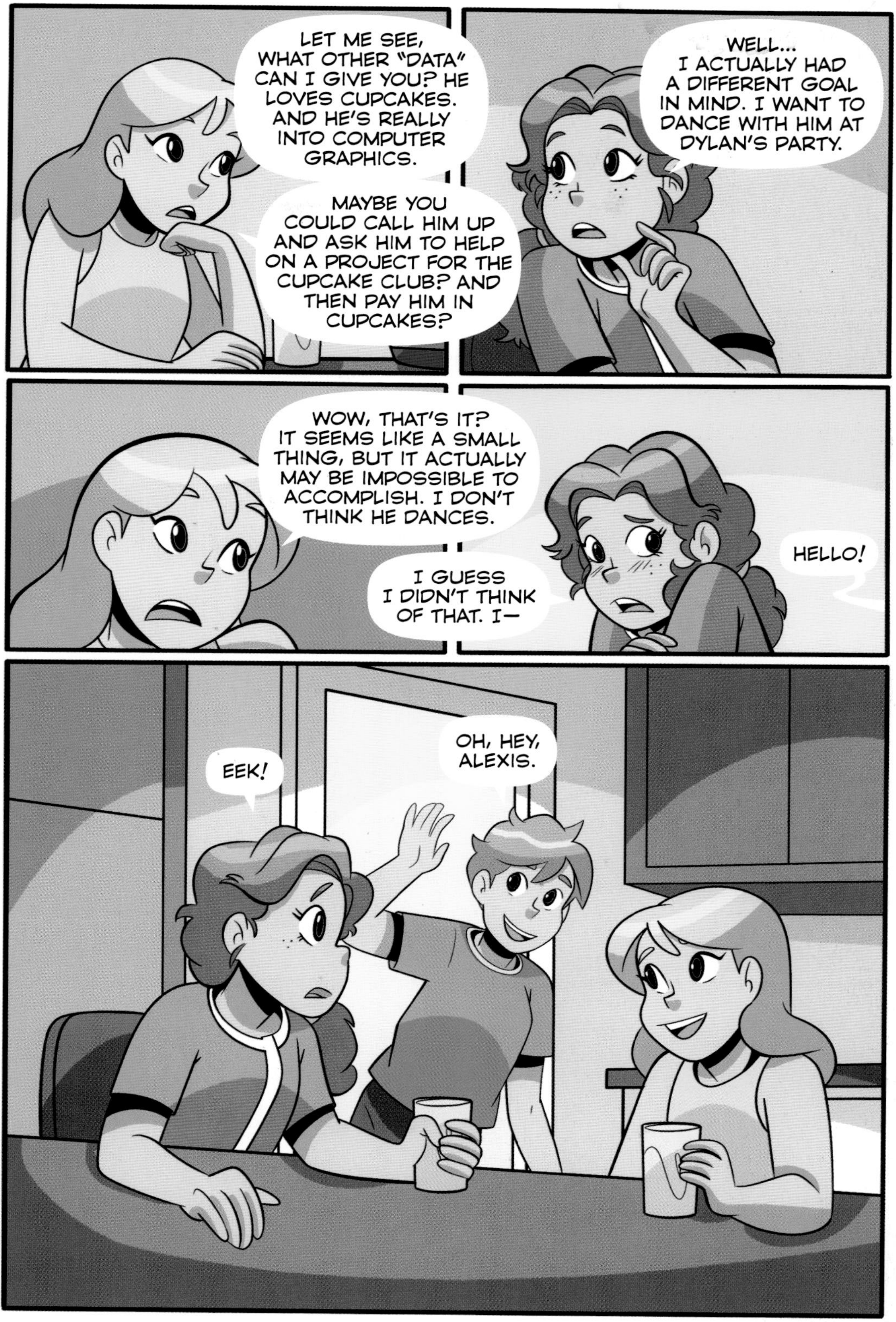
LET ME SEE, WHAT OTHER "DATA" CAN I GIVE YOU? HE LOVES CUPCAKES. AND HE'S REALLY INTO COMPUTER GRAPHICS.
MAYBE YOU COULD CALL HIM UP AND ASK HIM TO HELP ON A PROJECT FOR THE CUPCAKE CLUB? AND THEN PAY HIM IN CUPCAKES?
WELL... I ACTUALLY HAD A DIFFERENT GOAL IN MIND. I WANT TO DANCE WITH HIM AT DYLAN'S PARTY.
WOW, THAT'S IT? IT SEEMS LIKE A SMALL THING, BUT IT ACTUALLY MAY BE IMPOSSIBLE TO ACCOMPLISH. I DON'T THINK HE DANCES.
I GUESS I DIDN'T THINK OF THAT. I—
HELLO!
EEK!
OH, HEY, ALEXIS.

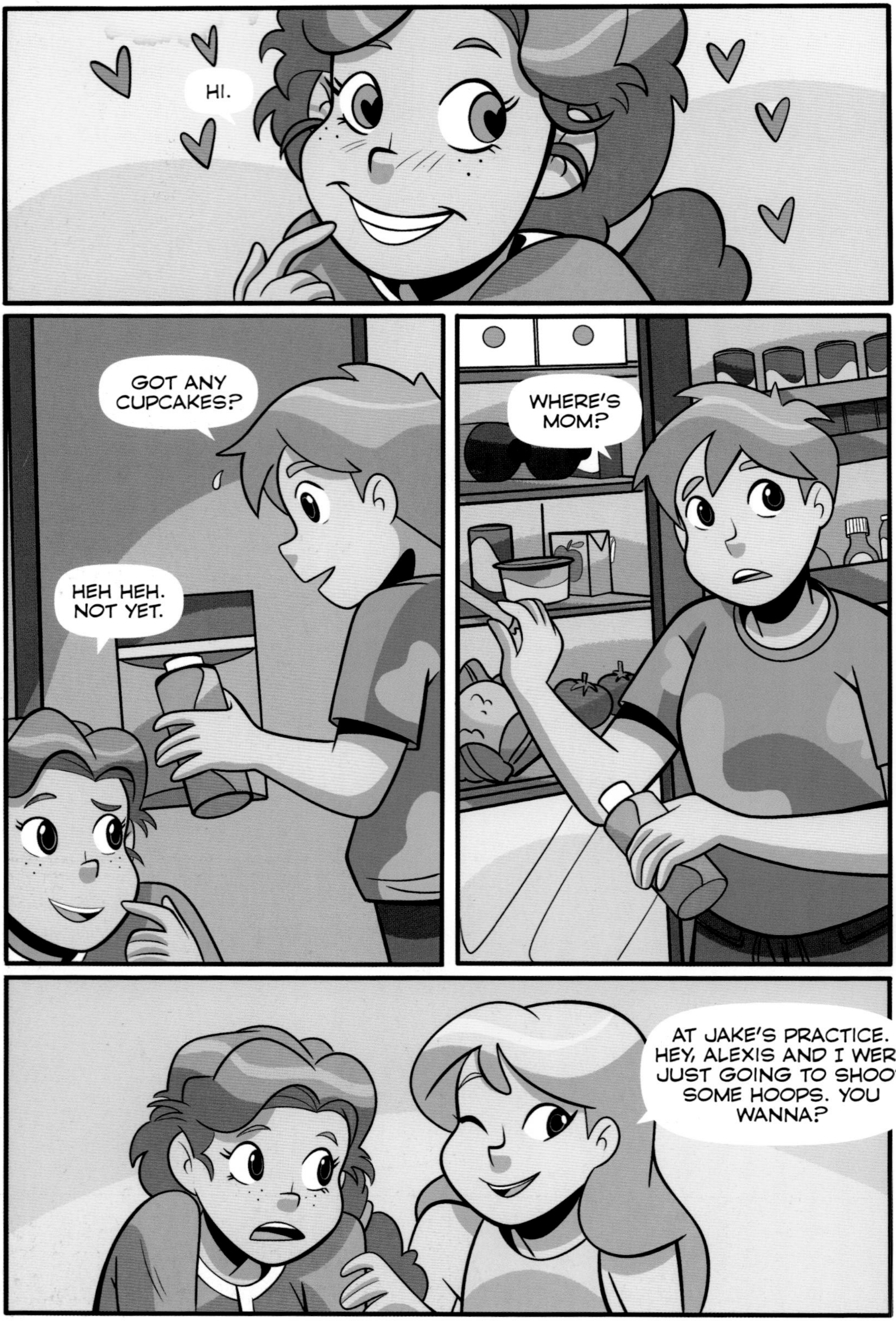
HI.
GOT ANY CUPCAKES?
HEH HEH. NOT YET.
WHERE'S MOM?
AT JAKE'S PRACTICE. HEY, ALEXIS AND I WERE JUST GOING TO SHOOT SOME HOOPS. YOU WANNA?

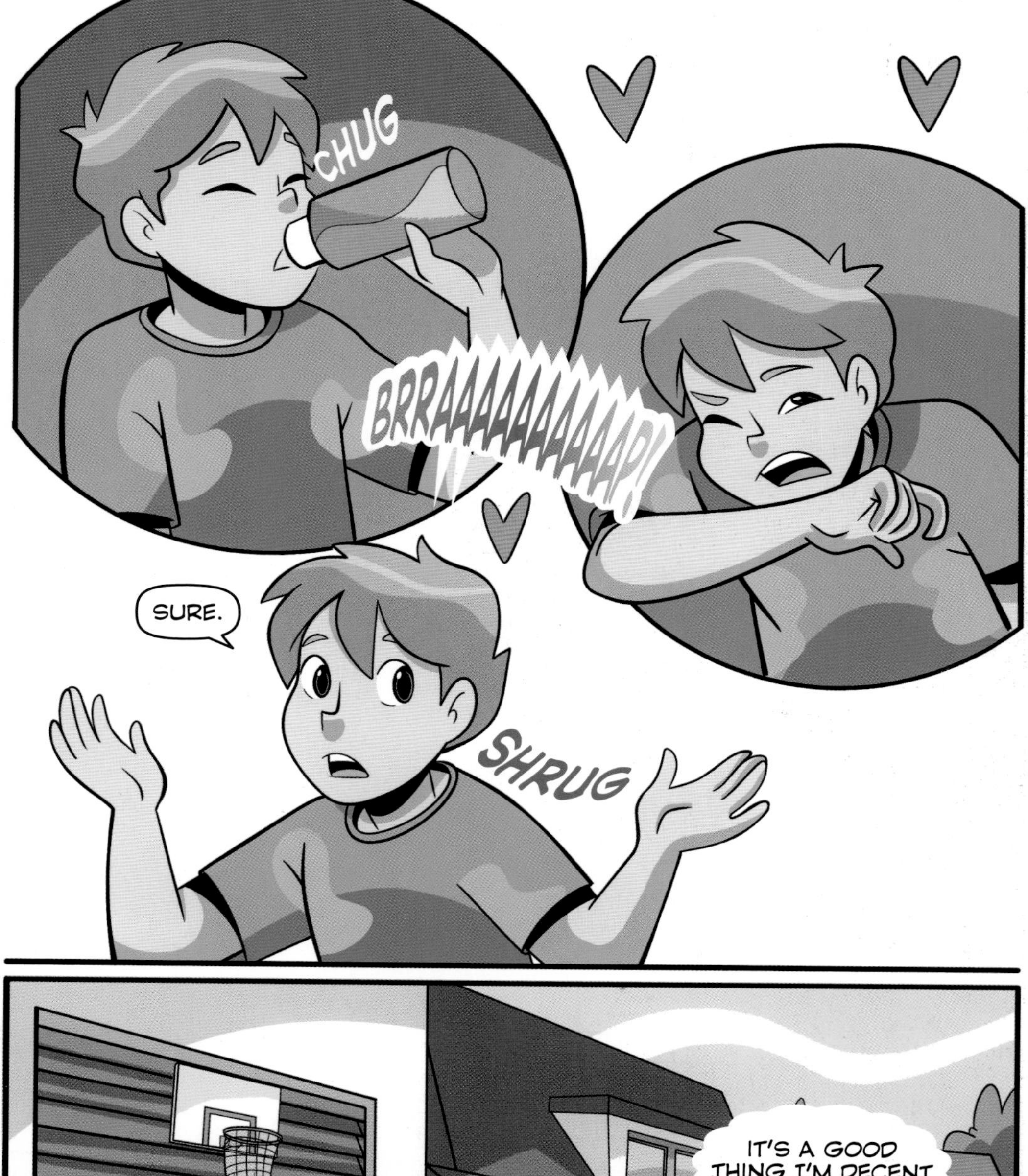
CHUG
BRRAAAAAAAAAAP!
SURE.
SHRUG

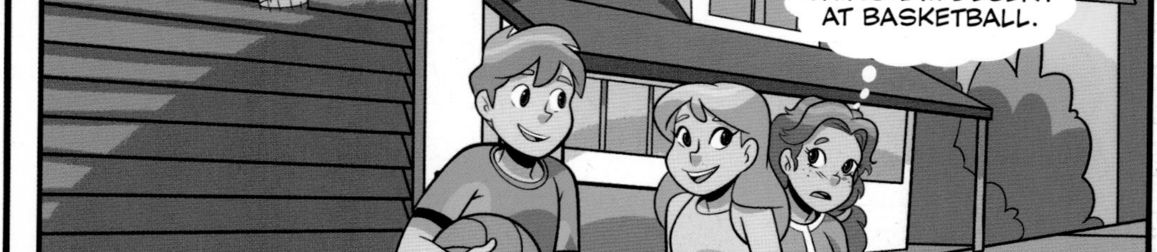
IT'S A GOOD THING I'M DECENT AT BASKETBALL.

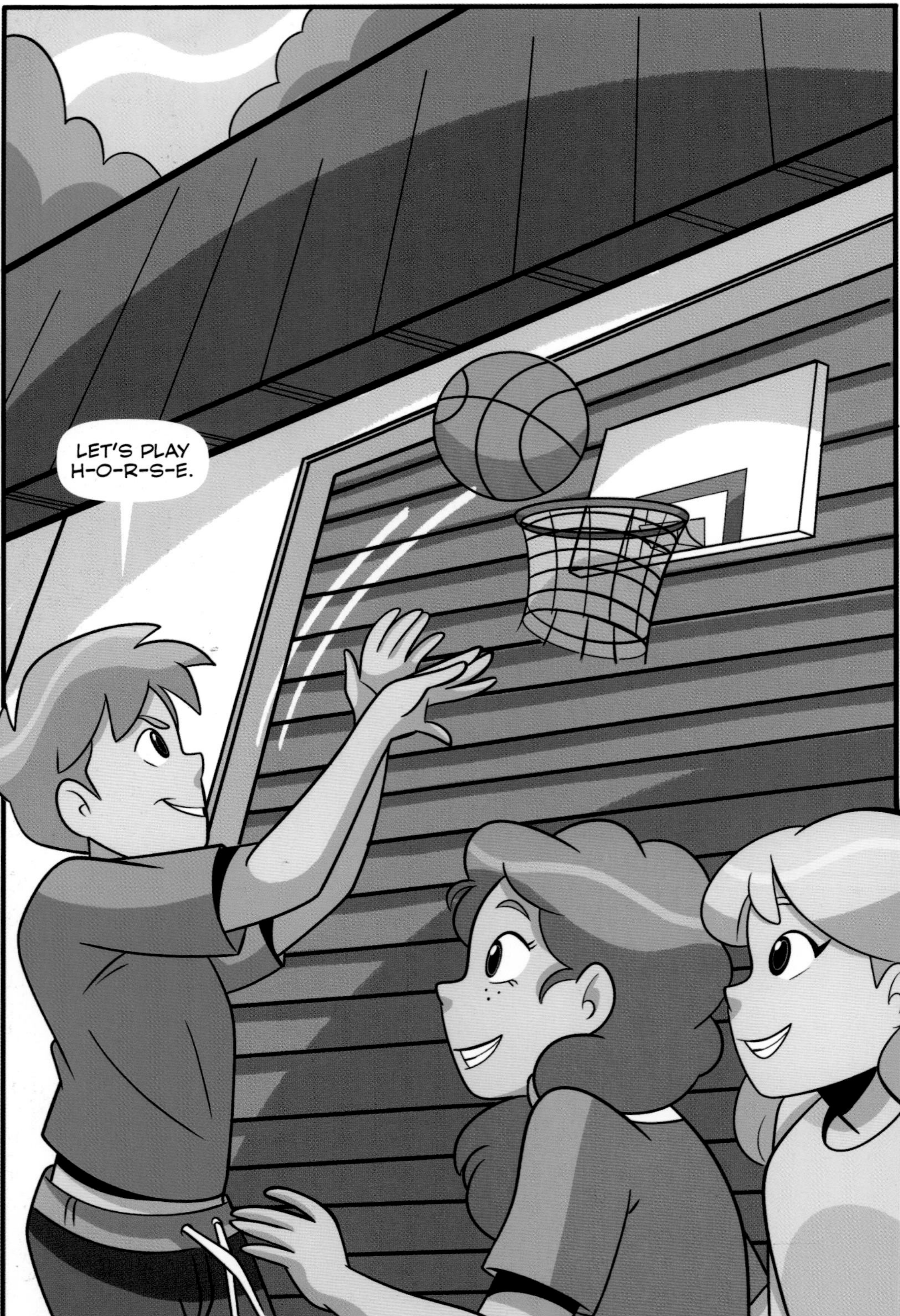
LET'S PLAY H-O-R-S-E.

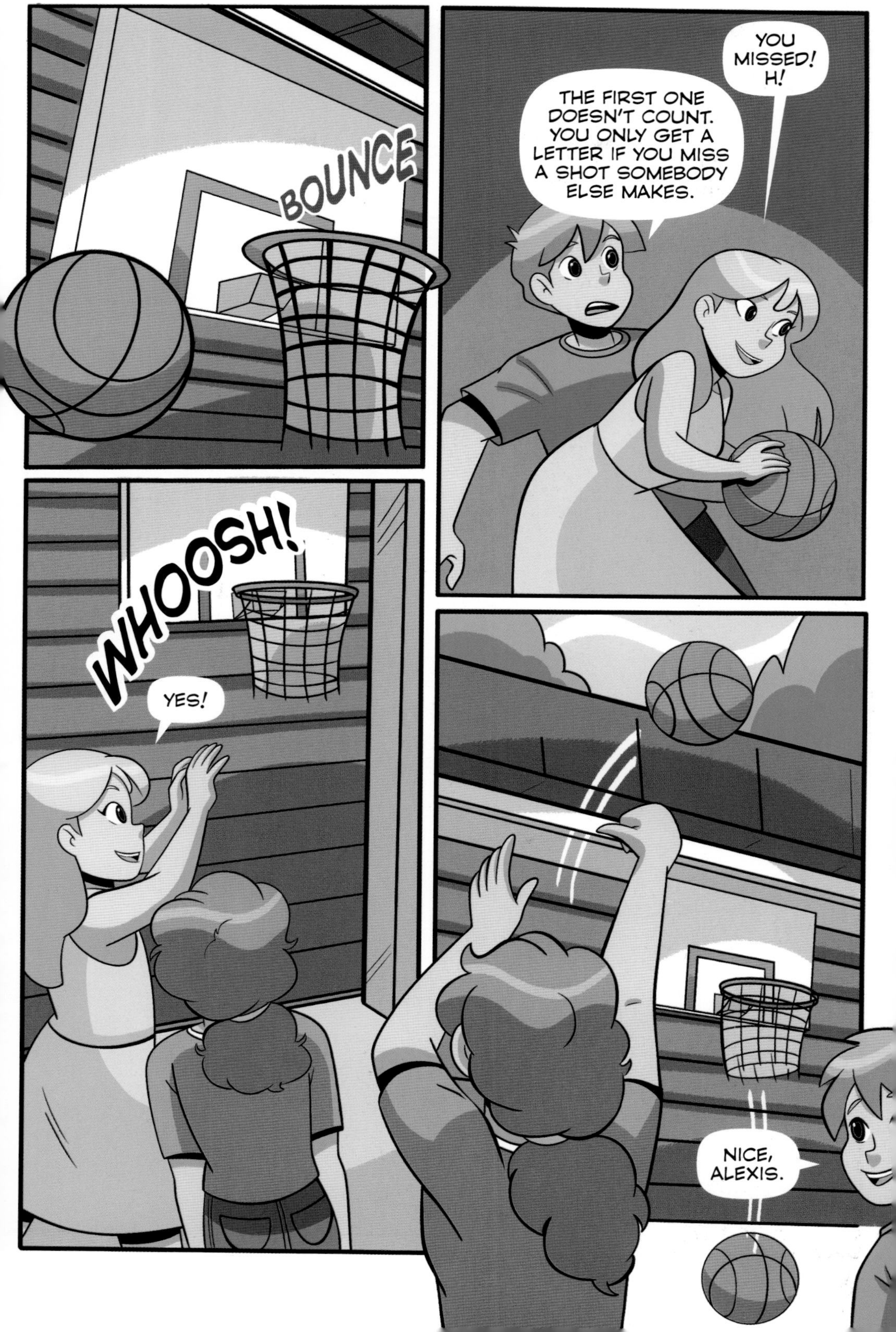
BOUNCE
THE FIRST ONE DOESN'T COUNT. YOU ONLY GET A LETTER IF YOU MISS A SHOT SOMEBODY ELSE MAKES.
YOU MISSED! H!
WHOOSH!
YES!
NICE, ALEXIS.

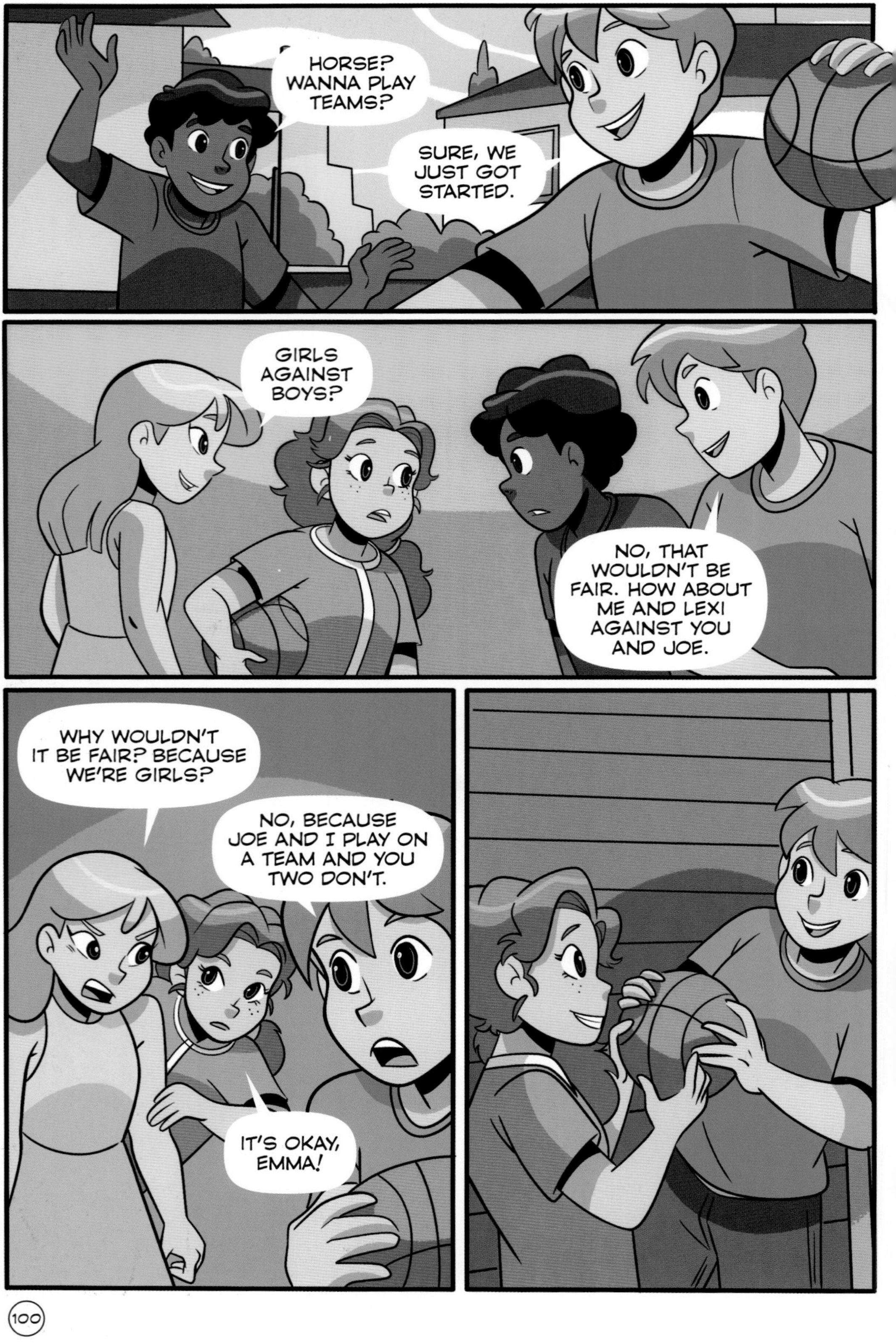
HORSE? WANNA PLAY TEAMS?
SURE, WE JUST GOT STARTED.
GIRLS AGAINST BOYS?
NO, THAT WOULDN'T BE FAIR. HOW ABOUT ME AND LEXI AGAINST YOU AND JOE.
WHY WOULDN'T IT BE FAIR? BECAUSE WE'RE GIRLS?
NO, BECAUSE JOE AND I PLAY ON A TEAM AND YOU TWO DON'T.
IT'S OKAY, EMMA!

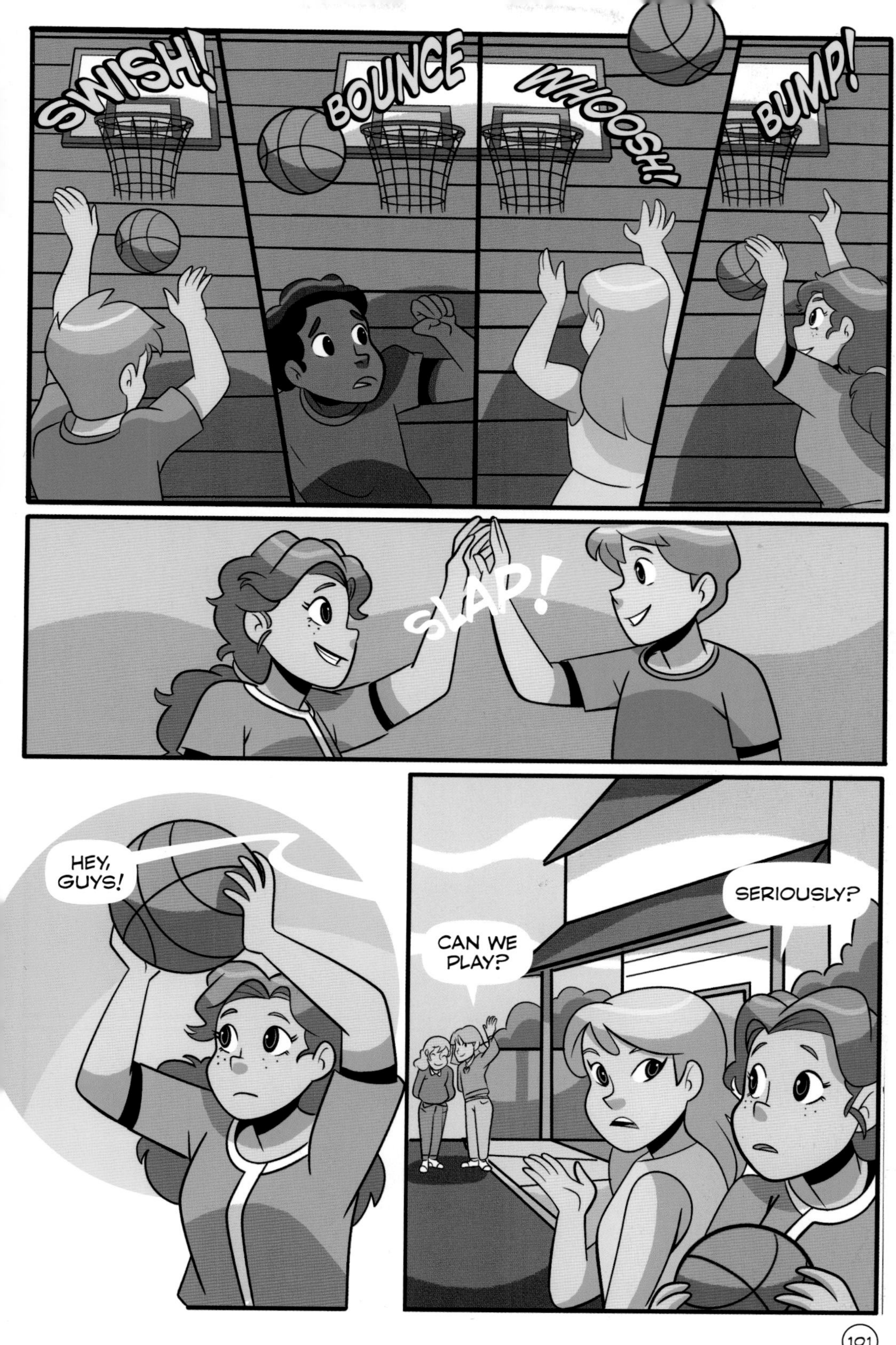
SWISH!
BOUNCE
WHOOSH!
BUMP!
SLAP!
HEY, GUYS!
CAN WE PLAY?
SERIOUSLY?

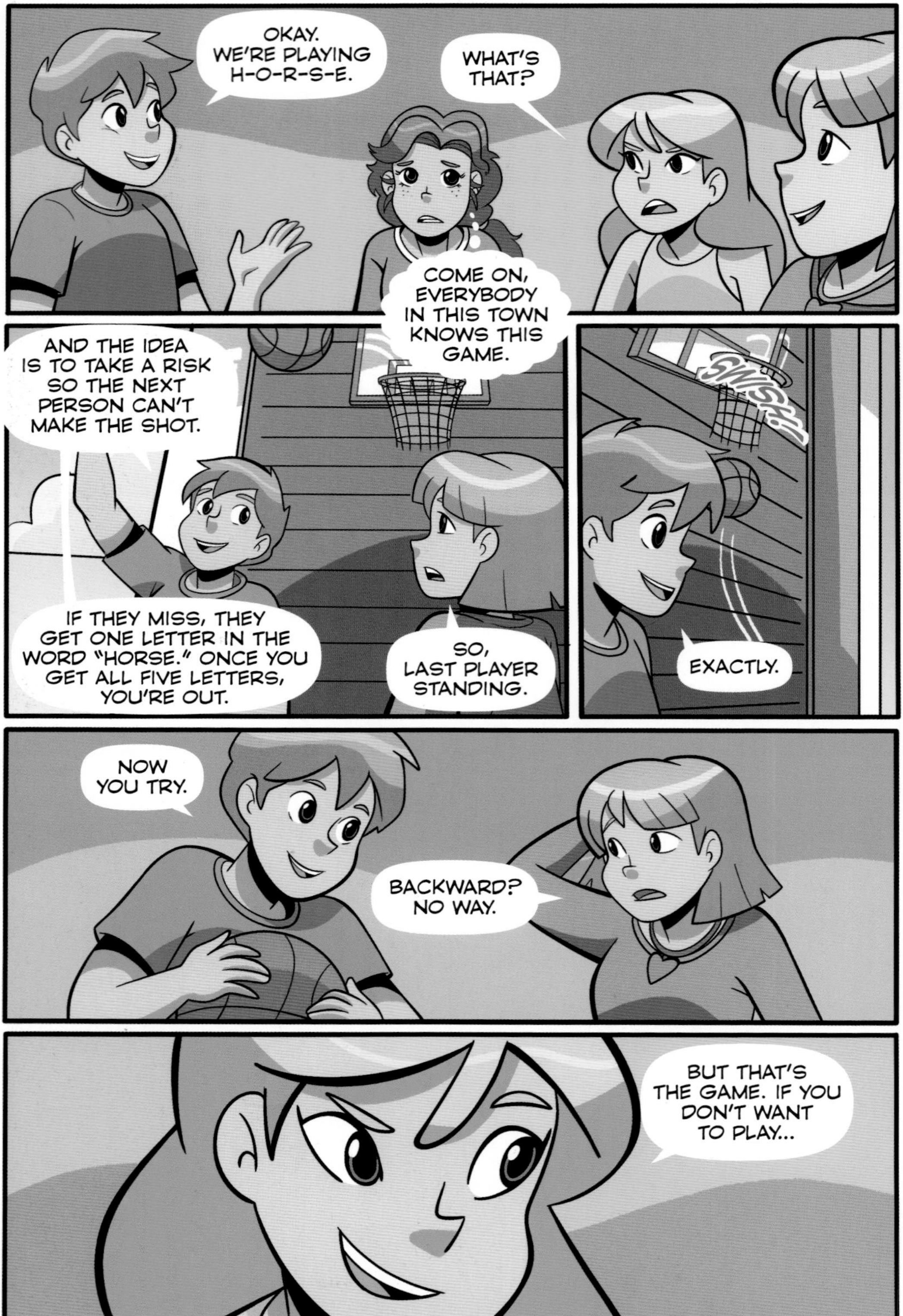
OKAY. WE'RE PLAYING H-O-R-S-E.
WHAT'S THAT?
COME ON, EVERYBODY IN THIS TOWN KNOWS THIS GAME.
AND THE IDEA IS TO TAKE A RISK SO THE NEXT PERSON CAN'T MAKE THE SHOT.
IF THEY MISS, THEY GET ONE LETTER IN THE WORD "HORSE." ONCE YOU GET ALL FIVE LETTERS, YOU'RE OUT.
SO, LAST PLAYER STANDING.
SWISH!
EXACTLY.
NOW YOU TRY.
BACKWARD? NO WAY.
BUT THAT'S THE GAME. IF YOU DON'T WANT TO PLAY...

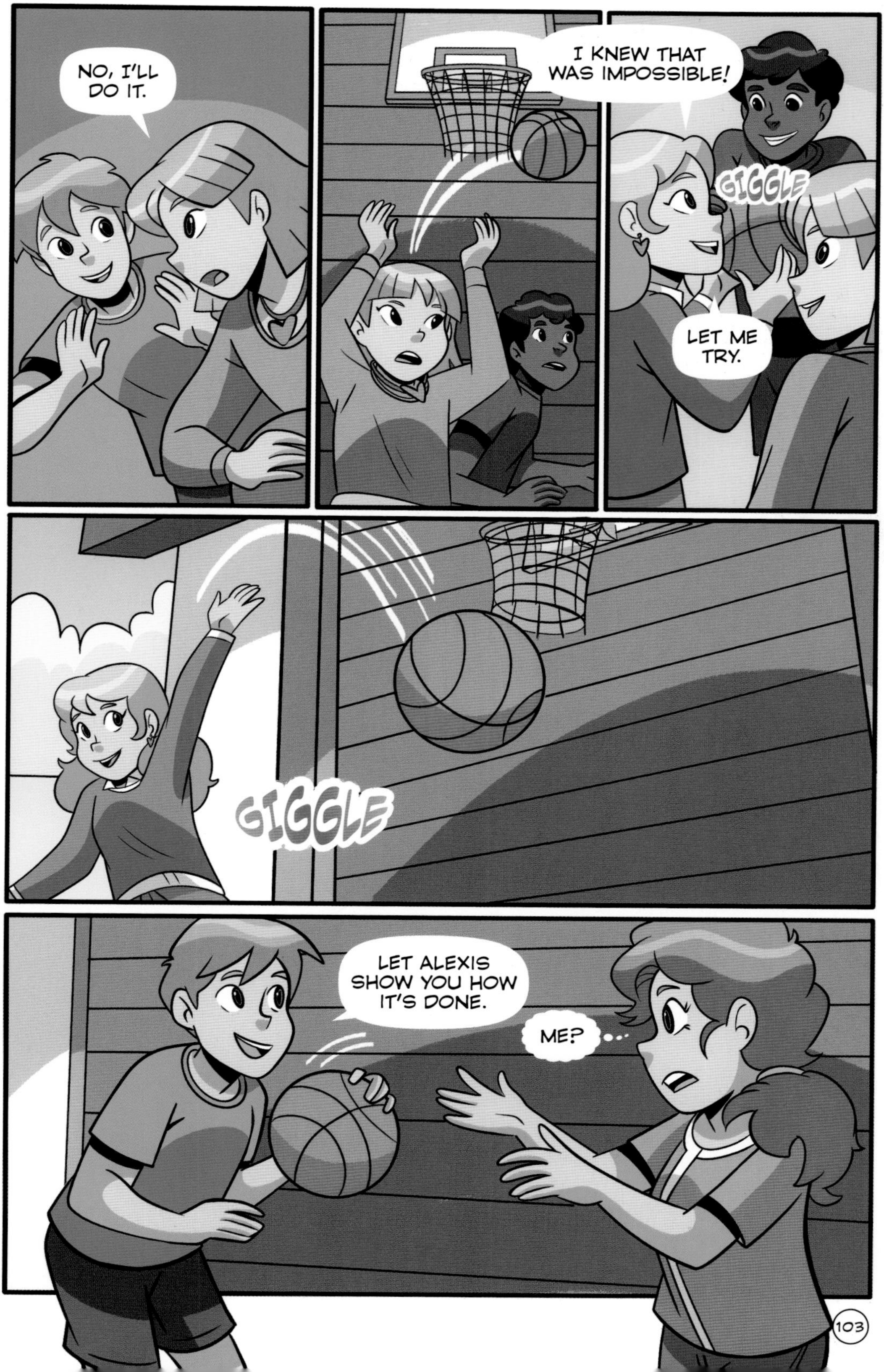
NO, I'LL DO IT.
I KNEW THAT WAS IMPOSSIBLE!
GIGGLE
LET ME TRY.
GIGGLE
LET ALEXIS SHOW YOU HOW IT'S DONE.
ME?

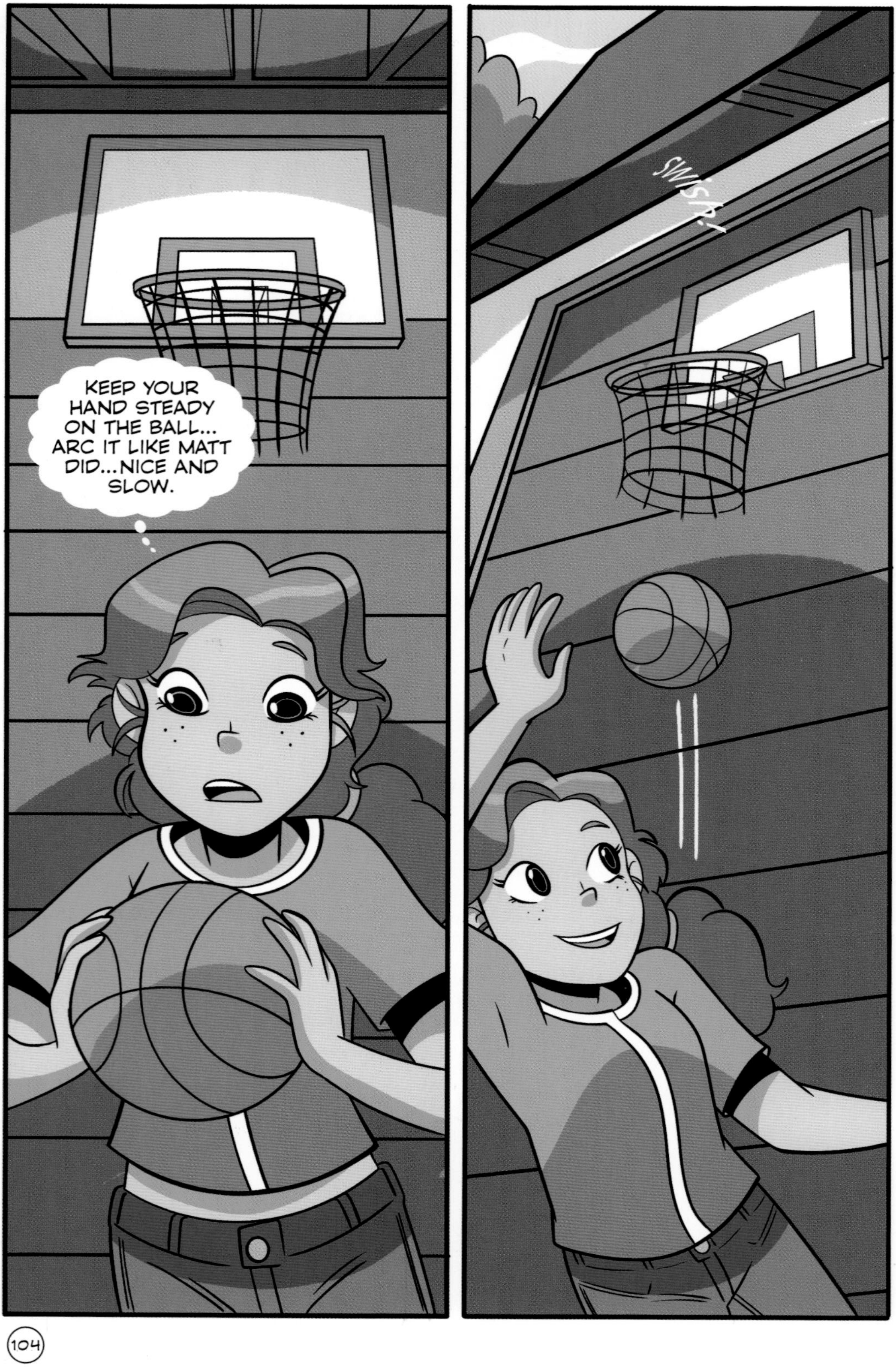
KEEP YOUR HAND STEADY ON THE BALL... ARC IT LIKE MATT DID...NICE AND SLOW.
SWISH!

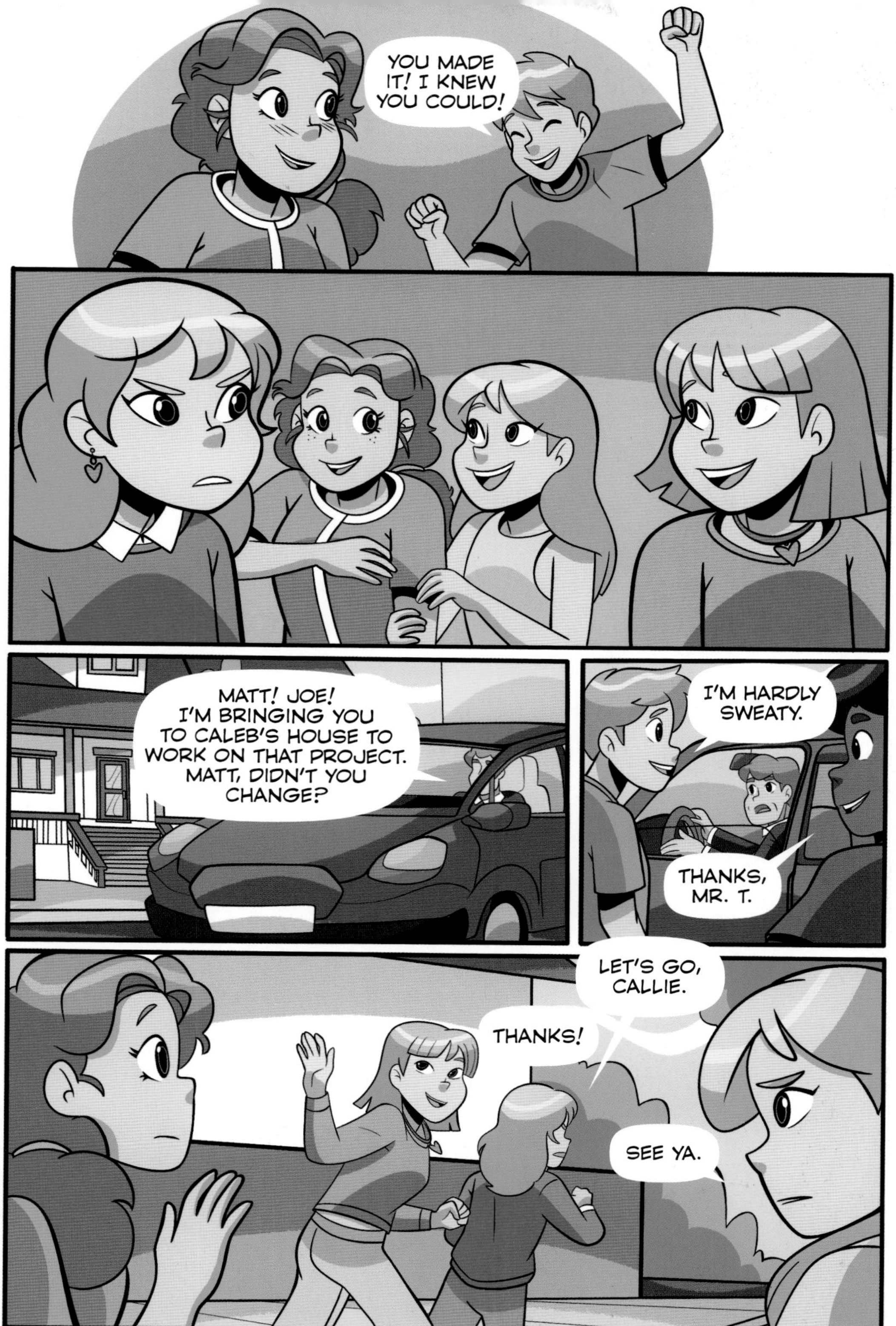

YOU MADE IT! I KNEW YOU COULD!
MATT! JOE! I'M BRINGING YOU TO CALEB'S HOUSE TO WORK ON THAT PROJECT. MATT, DIDN'T YOU CHANGE?
I'M HARDLY SWEATY.
THANKS, MR. T.
LET'S GO, CALLIE.
THANKS!
SEE YA.

I CAN'T BELIEVE YOU MADE THAT BASKET. THAT WAS EPIC!

I CAN'T BELIEVE IT EITHER. TALK ABOUT LUCK.

IT WAS SKILL. AND MATT WAS IMPRESSED.

YOU THINK?

WE STILL HAVE TO FIGURE OUT DYLAN'S CUPCAKES. LET'S GET KATIE AND MIA OVER HERE AND BAKE.

YES!

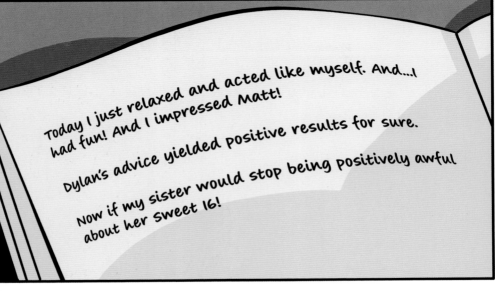

Today I just relaxed and acted like myself. And...I had fun! And I impressed Matt!

Dylan's advice yielded positive results for sure.

Now if my sister would stop being positively awful about her sweet 16!

Chapter 12

ALEXIS, YOUR MAKEUP SKILLS ARE ON POINT LATELY.

MY FRIENDS NOTICED SOME OF THE CHANGES I'D MADE. BUT I WAS HAPPY THAT EMMA HADN'T TOLD THEM ABOUT MY CRUSH ON MATT.

THANKS, I'M USING THAT KIT YOU GAVE ME.

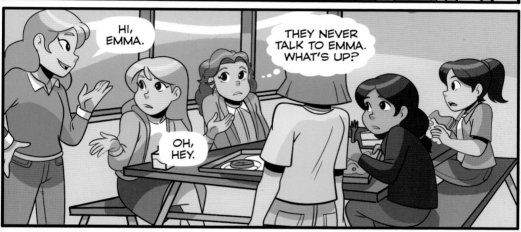

HI, EMMA.

THEY NEVER TALK TO EMMA. WHAT'S UP?

OH, HEY.

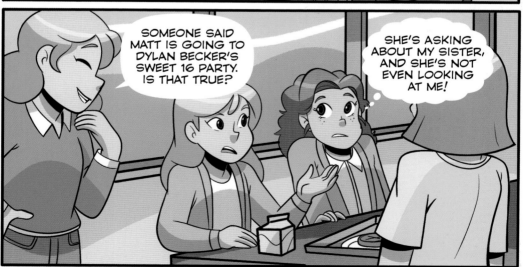

SOMEONE SAID MATT IS GOING TO DYLAN BECKER'S SWEET 16 PARTY. IS THAT TRUE?

SHE'S ASKING ABOUT MY SISTER, AND SHE'S NOT EVEN LOOKING AT ME!

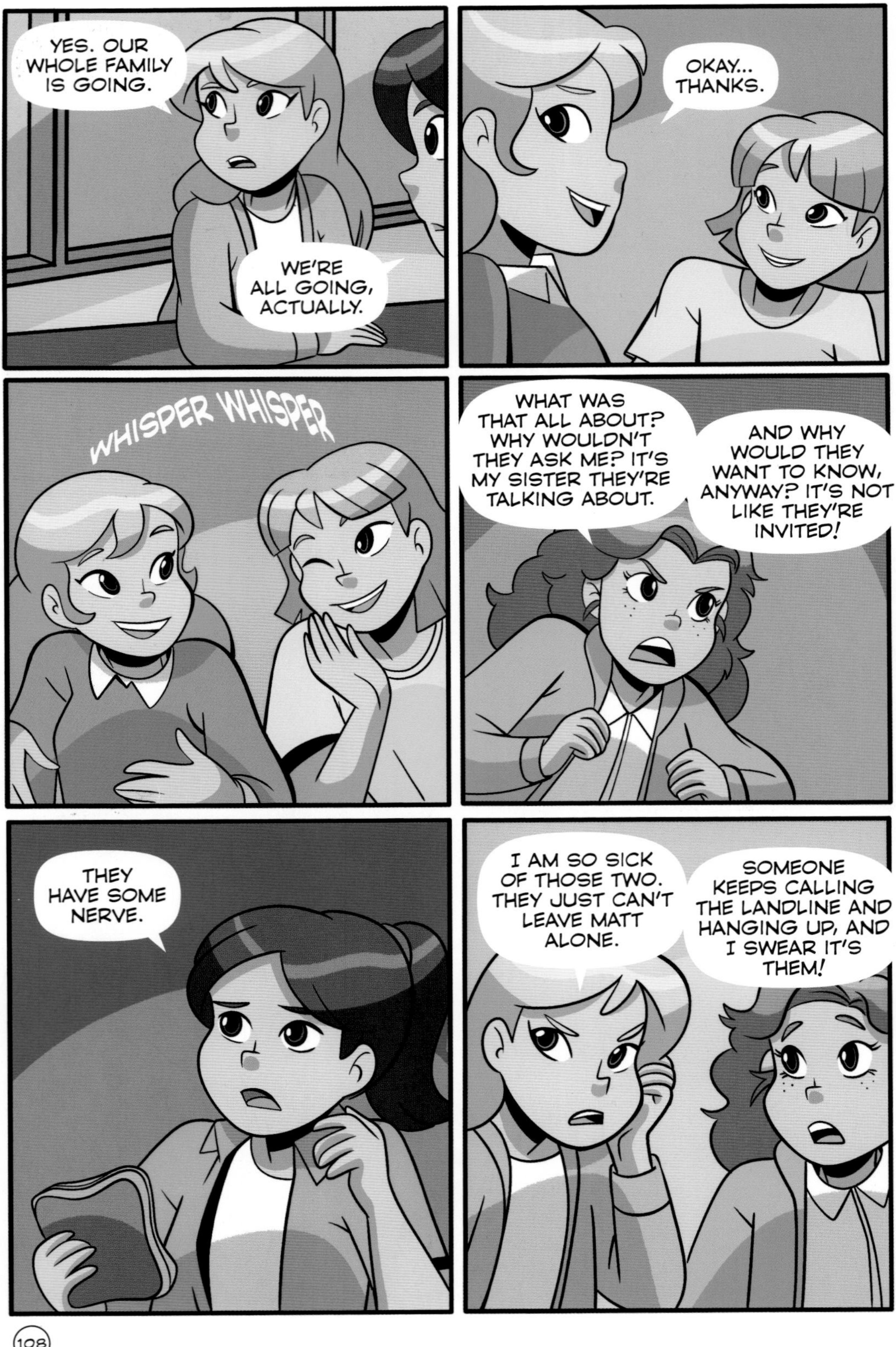
YES. OUR WHOLE FAMILY IS GOING.
WE'RE ALL GOING, ACTUALLY.
OKAY... THANKS.
WHISPER WHISPER
WHAT WAS THAT ALL ABOUT? WHY WOULDN'T THEY ASK ME? IT'S MY SISTER THEY'RE TALKING ABOUT.
AND WHY WOULD THEY WANT TO KNOW, ANYWAY? IT'S NOT LIKE THEY'RE INVITED!
THEY HAVE SOME NERVE.
I AM SO SICK OF THOSE TWO. THEY JUST CAN'T LEAVE MATT ALONE.
SOMEONE KEEPS CALLING THE LANDLINE AND HANGING UP, AND I SWEAR IT'S THEM!

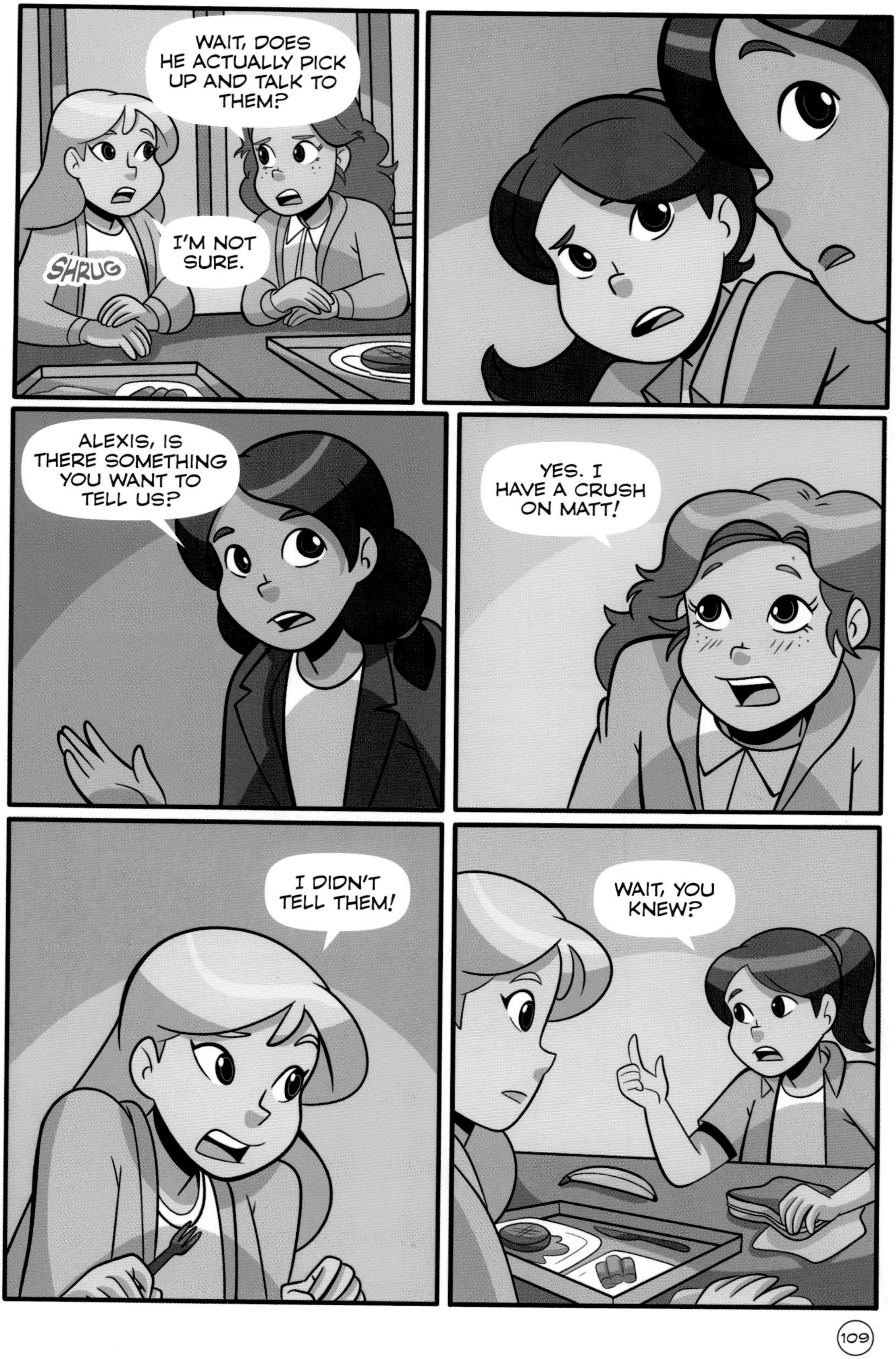
WAIT, DOES HE ACTUALLY PICK UP AND TALK TO THEM?
SHRUG
I'M NOT SURE.
ALEXIS, IS THERE SOMETHING YOU WANT TO TELL US?
YES. I HAVE A CRUSH ON MATT!
I DIDN'T TELL THEM!
WAIT, YOU KNEW?

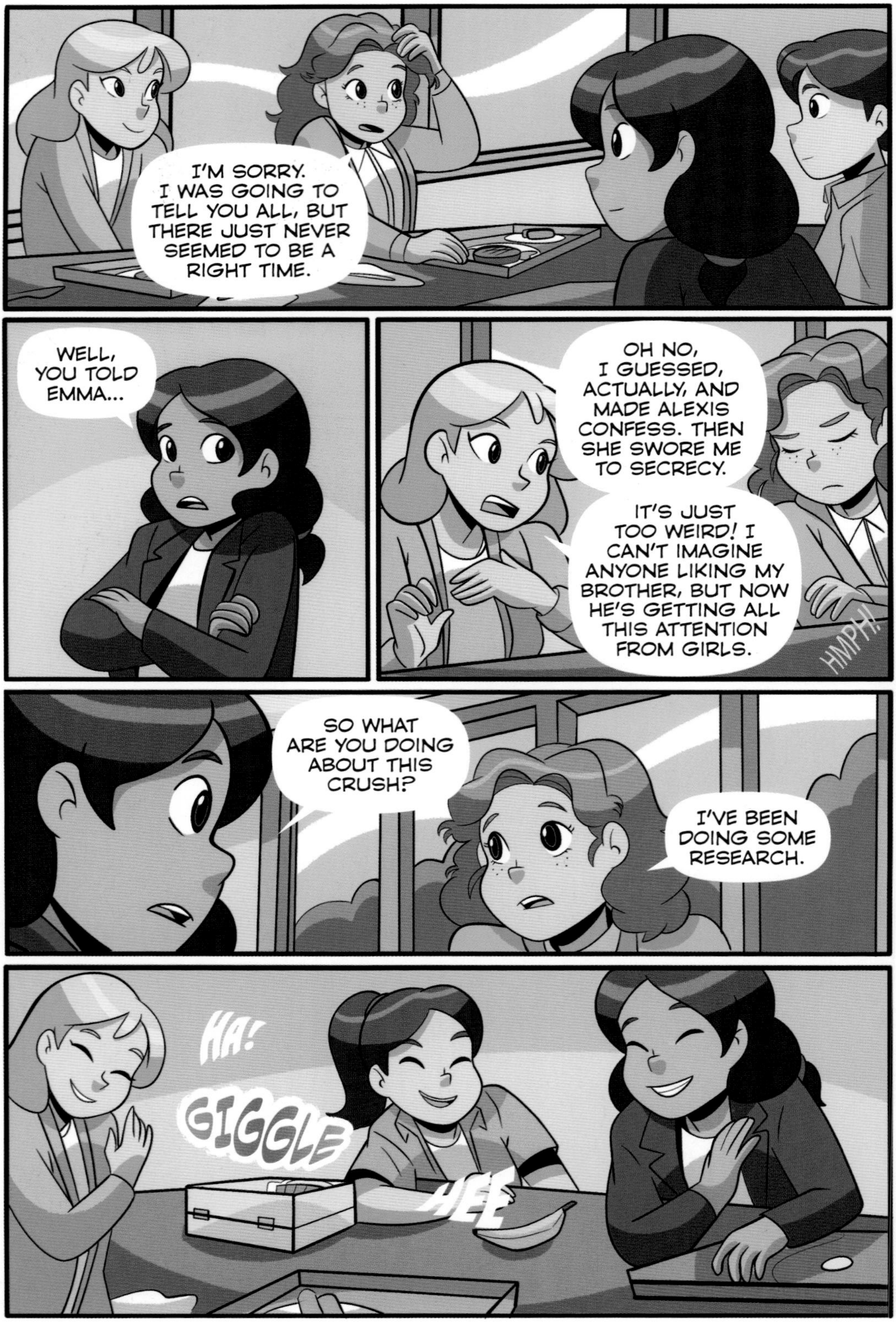
I'M SORRY. I WAS GOING TO TELL YOU ALL, BUT THERE JUST NEVER SEEMED TO BE A RIGHT TIME.
WELL, YOU TOLD EMMA...
OH NO, I GUESSED, ACTUALLY, AND MADE ALEXIS CONFESS. THEN SHE SWORE ME TO SECRECY.
IT'S JUST TOO WEIRD! I CAN'T IMAGINE ANYONE LIKING MY BROTHER, BUT NOW HE'S GETTING ALL THIS ATTENTION FROM GIRLS.
HMPH!
SO WHAT ARE YOU DOING ABOUT THIS CRUSH?
I'VE BEEN DOING SOME RESEARCH.
HA!
GIGGLE
HEE

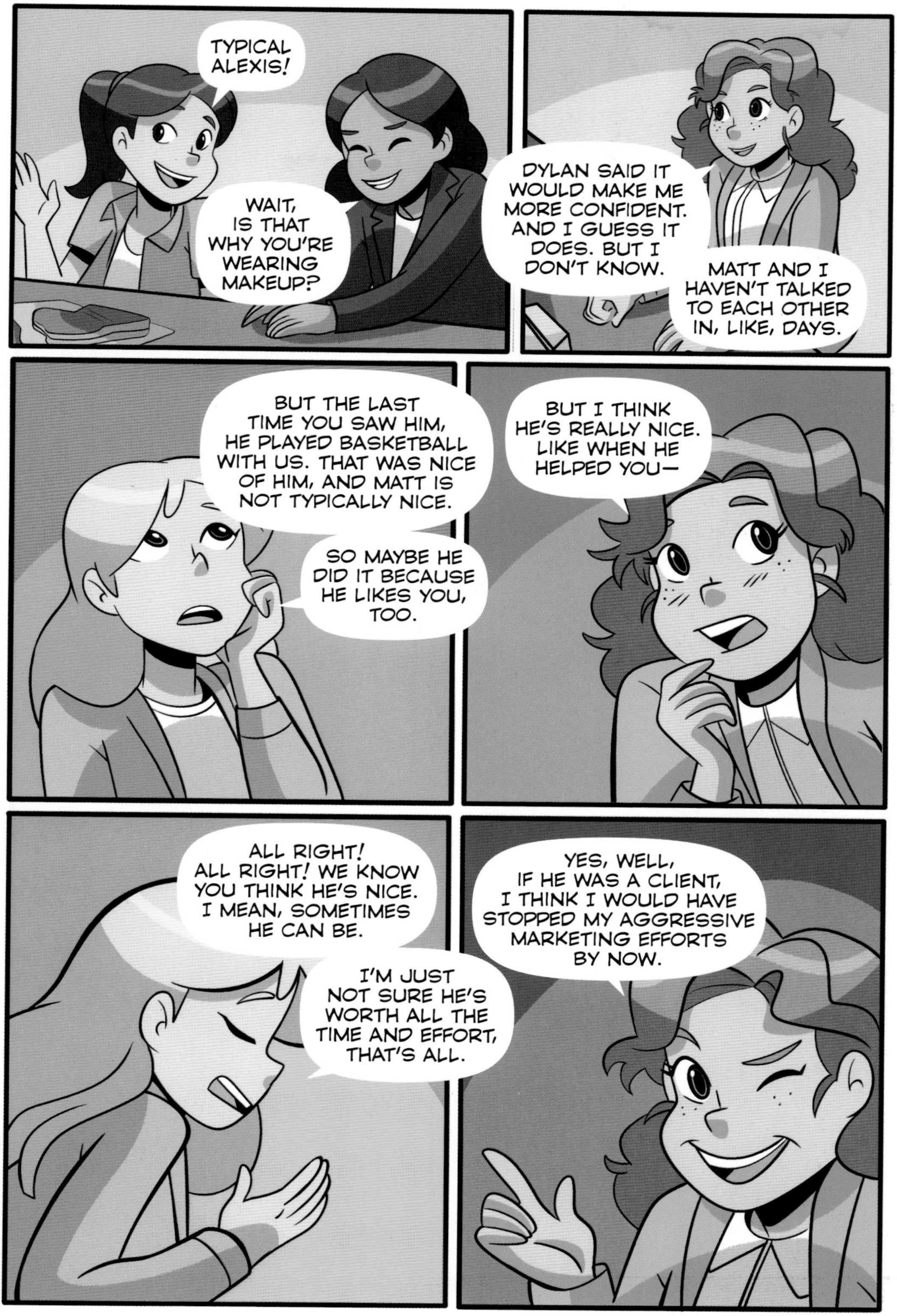
TYPICAL ALEXIS!
WAIT, IS THAT WHY YOU'RE WEARING MAKEUP?
DYLAN SAID IT WOULD MAKE ME MORE CONFIDENT. AND I GUESS IT DOES. BUT I DON'T KNOW.
MATT AND I HAVEN'T TALKED TO EACH OTHER IN, LIKE, DAYS.
BUT THE LAST TIME YOU SAW HIM, HE PLAYED BASKETBALL WITH US. THAT WAS NICE OF HIM, AND MATT IS NOT TYPICALLY NICE.
SO MAYBE HE DID IT BECAUSE HE LIKES YOU, TOO.
BUT I THINK HE'S REALLY NICE. LIKE WHEN HE HELPED YOU—
ALL RIGHT! ALL RIGHT! WE KNOW YOU THINK HE'S NICE. I MEAN, SOMETIMES HE CAN BE.
I'M JUST NOT SURE HE'S WORTH ALL THE TIME AND EFFORT, THAT'S ALL.
YES, WELL, IF HE WAS A CLIENT, I THINK I WOULD HAVE STOPPED MY AGGRESSIVE MARKETING EFFORTS BY NOW.

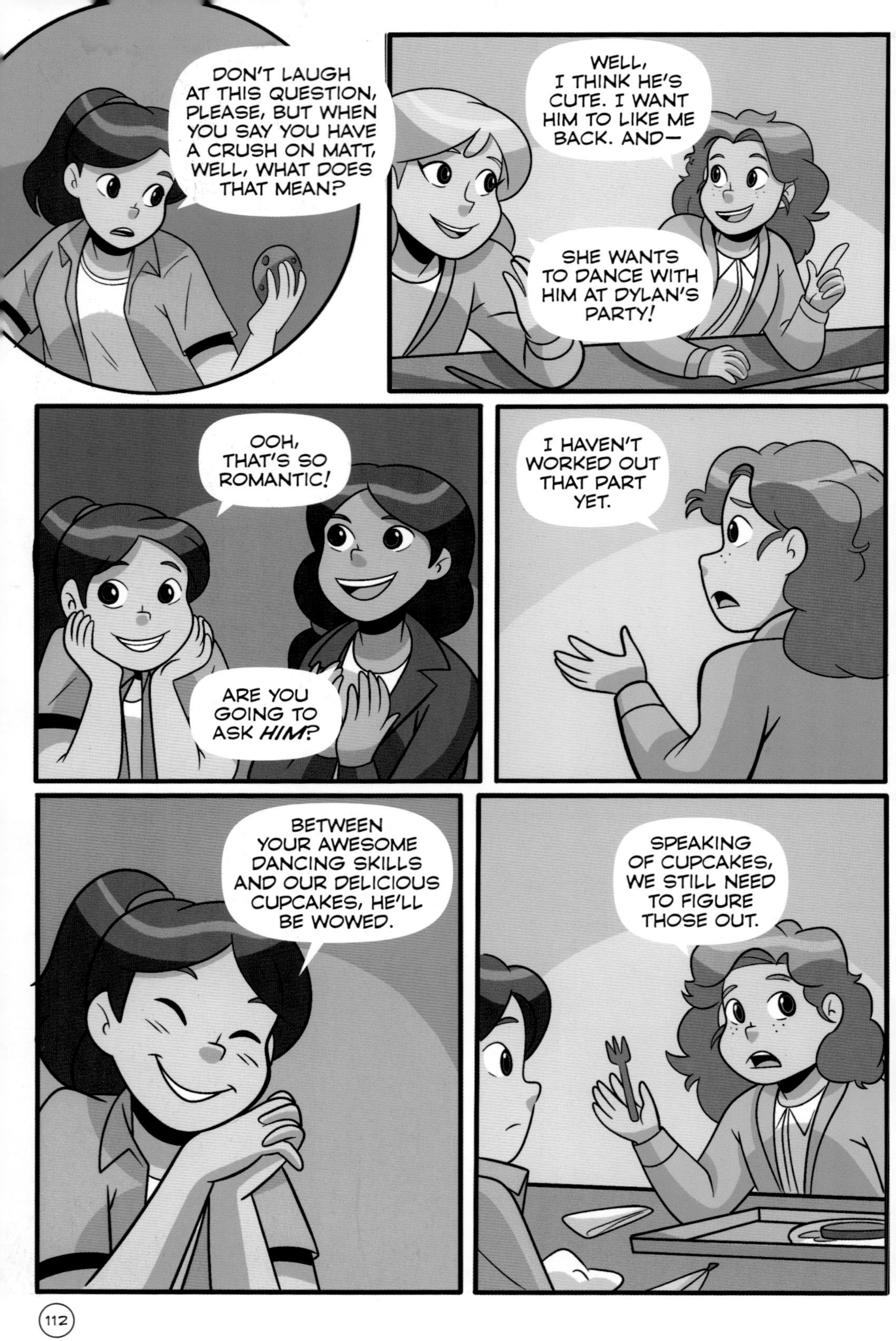
DON'T LAUGH AT THIS QUESTION, PLEASE, BUT WHEN YOU SAY YOU HAVE A CRUSH ON MATT, WELL, WHAT DOES THAT MEAN?
WELL, I THINK HE'S CUTE. I WANT HIM TO LIKE ME BACK. AND—
SHE WANTS TO DANCE WITH HIM AT DYLAN'S PARTY!
OOH, THAT'S SO ROMANTIC!
ARE YOU GOING TO ASK *HIM*?
I HAVEN'T WORKED OUT THAT PART YET.
BETWEEN YOUR AWESOME DANCING SKILLS AND OUR DELICIOUS CUPCAKES, HE'LL BE WOWED.
SPEAKING OF CUPCAKES, WE STILL NEED TO FIGURE THOSE OUT.

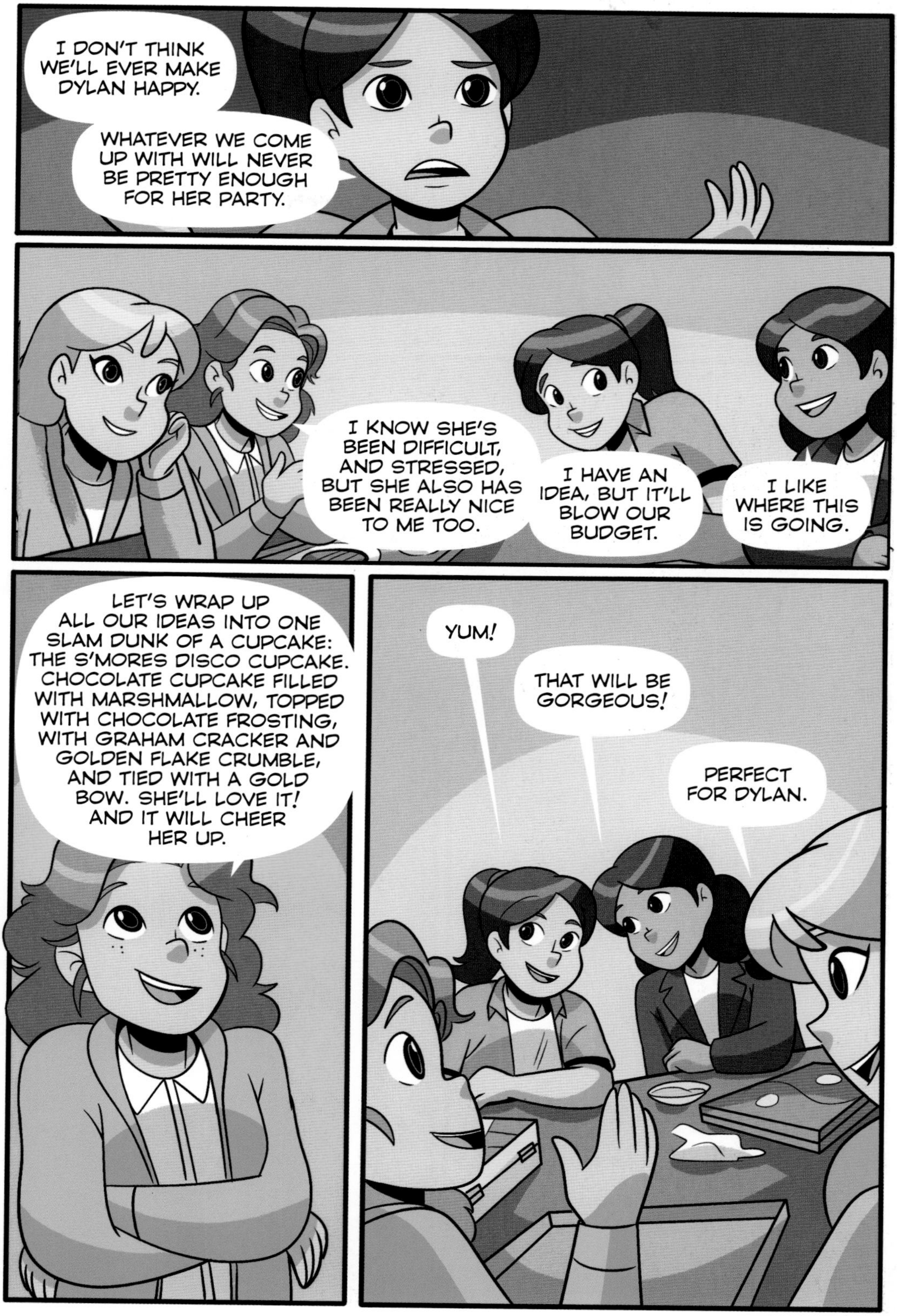
I DON'T THINK WE'LL EVER MAKE DYLAN HAPPY.
WHATEVER WE COME UP WITH WILL NEVER BE PRETTY ENOUGH FOR HER PARTY.
I KNOW SHE'S BEEN DIFFICULT, AND STRESSED, BUT SHE ALSO HAS BEEN REALLY NICE TO ME TOO.
I HAVE AN IDEA, BUT IT'LL BLOW OUR BUDGET.
I LIKE WHERE THIS IS GOING.
LET'S WRAP UP ALL OUR IDEAS INTO ONE SLAM DUNK OF A CUPCAKE: THE S'MORES DISCO CUPCAKE. CHOCOLATE CUPCAKE FILLED WITH MARSHMALLOW, TOPPED WITH CHOCOLATE FROSTING, WITH GRAHAM CRACKER AND GOLDEN FLAKE CRUMBLE, AND TIED WITH A GOLD BOW. SHE'LL LOVE IT! AND IT WILL CHEER HER UP.
YUM!
THAT WILL BE GORGEOUS!
PERFECT FOR DYLAN.

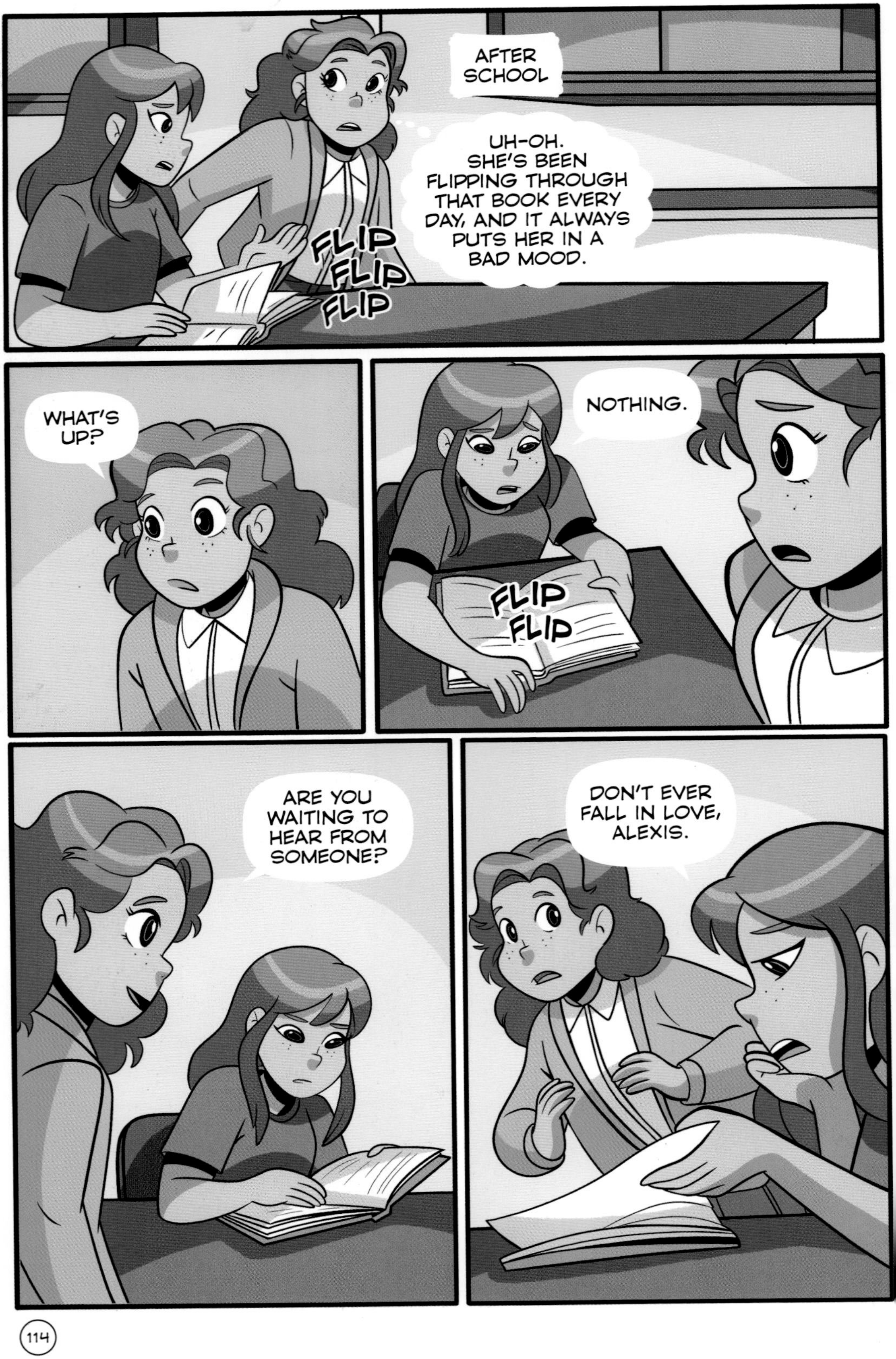
AFTER SCHOOL
UH-OH. SHE'S BEEN FLIPPING THROUGH THAT BOOK EVERY DAY, AND IT ALWAYS PUTS HER IN A BAD MOOD.
FLIP FLIP FLIP
WHAT'S UP?
NOTHING.
FLIP FLIP
ARE YOU WAITING TO HEAR FROM SOMEONE?
DON'T EVER FALL IN LOVE, ALEXIS.

TOO LATE, DYL. WHO ARE YOU IN LOVE WITH?

NEVER MIND. IT'S HOPELESS. HE HASN'T EVEN RSVP'D.

SOUNDS LIKE A JERK.

NO, NO, NO, HE'S NOT A JERK. HE'S JUST REALLY BUSY! I'M SURE HE'LL...HE'LL LET ME KNOW SOON.

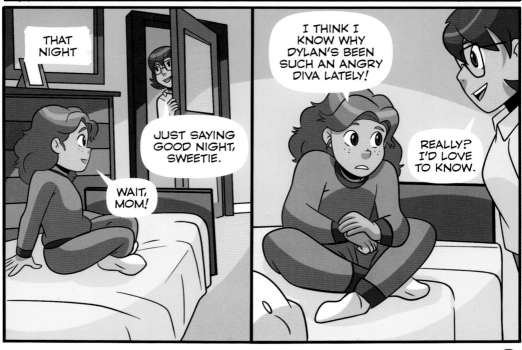
THAT NIGHT

JUST SAYING GOOD NIGHT, SWEETIE.

WAIT, MOM!

I THINK I KNOW WHY DYLAN'S BEEN SUCH AN ANGRY DIVA LATELY!

REALLY? I'D LOVE TO KNOW.

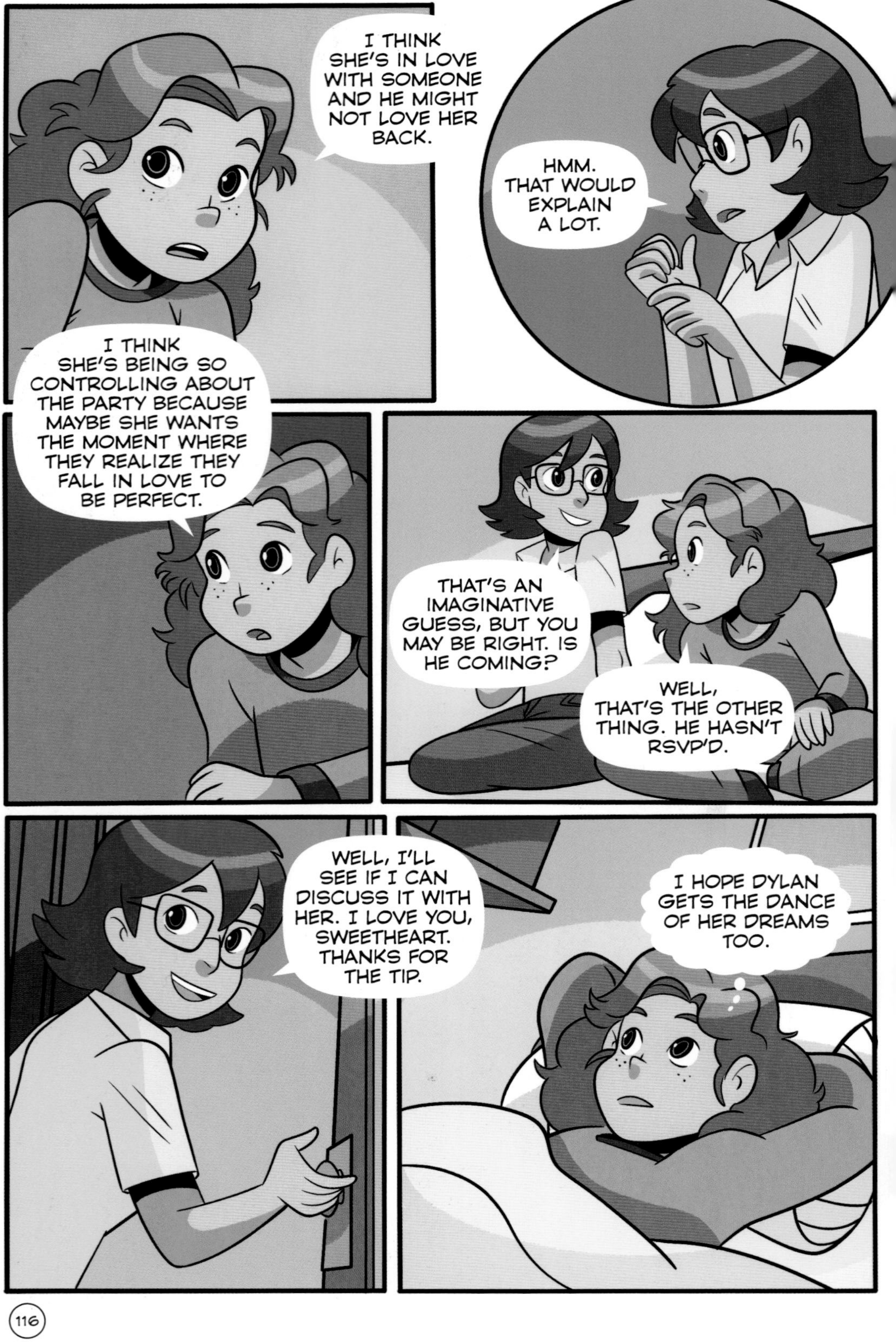
I THINK SHE'S IN LOVE WITH SOMEONE AND HE MIGHT NOT LOVE HER BACK.
HMM. THAT WOULD EXPLAIN A LOT.
I THINK SHE'S BEING SO CONTROLLING ABOUT THE PARTY BECAUSE MAYBE SHE WANTS THE MOMENT WHERE THEY REALIZE THEY FALL IN LOVE TO BE PERFECT.
THAT'S AN IMAGINATIVE GUESS, BUT YOU MAY BE RIGHT. IS HE COMING?
WELL, THAT'S THE OTHER THING. HE HASN'T RSVP'D.
WELL, I'LL SEE IF I CAN DISCUSS IT WITH HER. I LOVE YOU, SWEETHEART. THANKS FOR THE TIP.
I HOPE DYLAN GETS THE DANCE OF HER DREAMS TOO.

Chapter 13

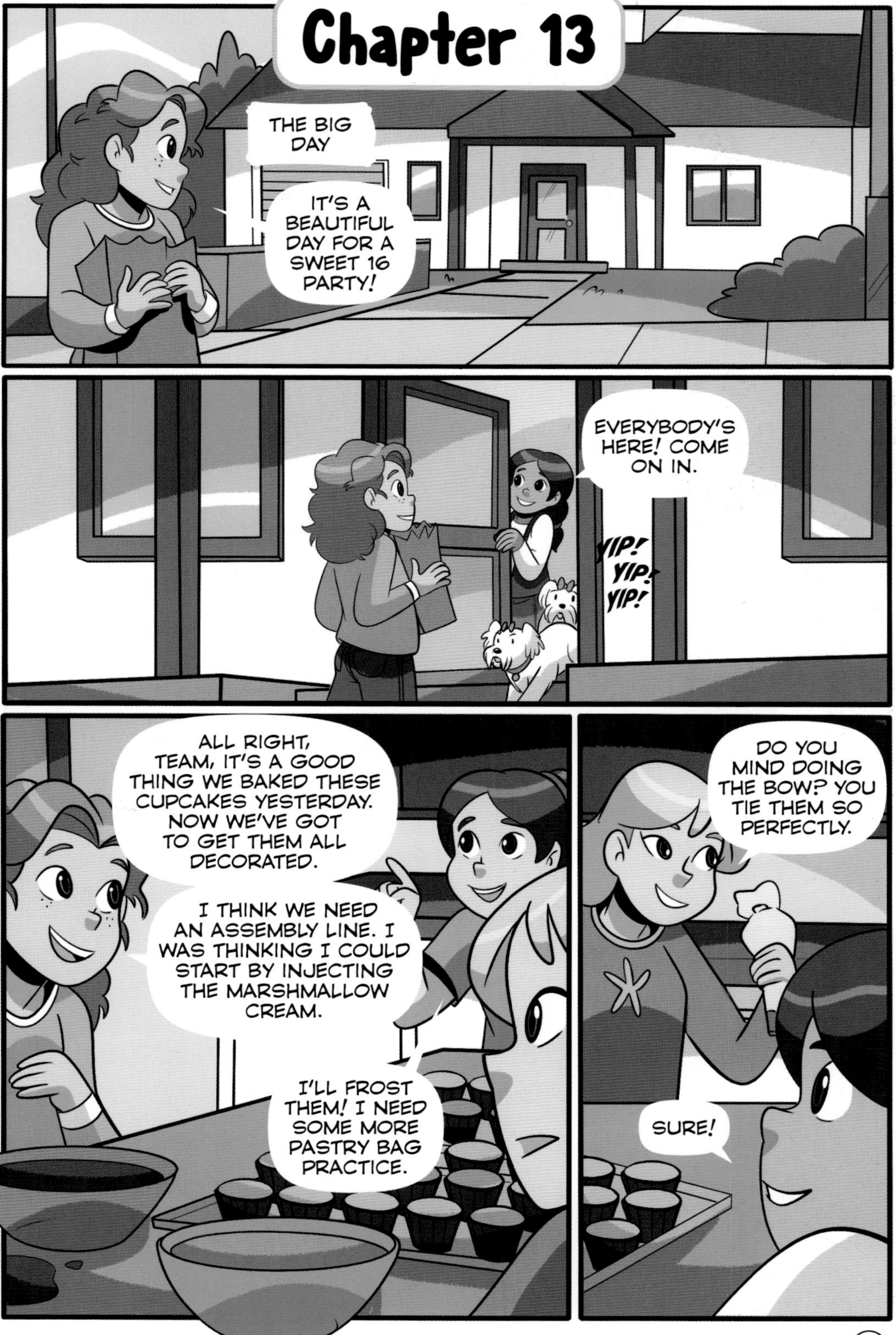

THE BIG DAY
IT'S A BEAUTIFUL DAY FOR A SWEET 16 PARTY!
EVERYBODY'S HERE! COME ON IN.
YIP! YIP! YIP!
ALL RIGHT, TEAM, IT'S A GOOD THING WE BAKED THESE CUPCAKES YESTERDAY. NOW WE'VE GOT TO GET THEM ALL DECORATED.
I THINK WE NEED AN ASSEMBLY LINE. I WAS THINKING I COULD START BY INJECTING THE MARSHMALLOW CREAM.
I'LL FROST THEM! I NEED SOME MORE PASTRY BAG PRACTICE.
DO YOU MIND DOING THE BOW? YOU TIE THEM SO PERFECTLY.
SURE!

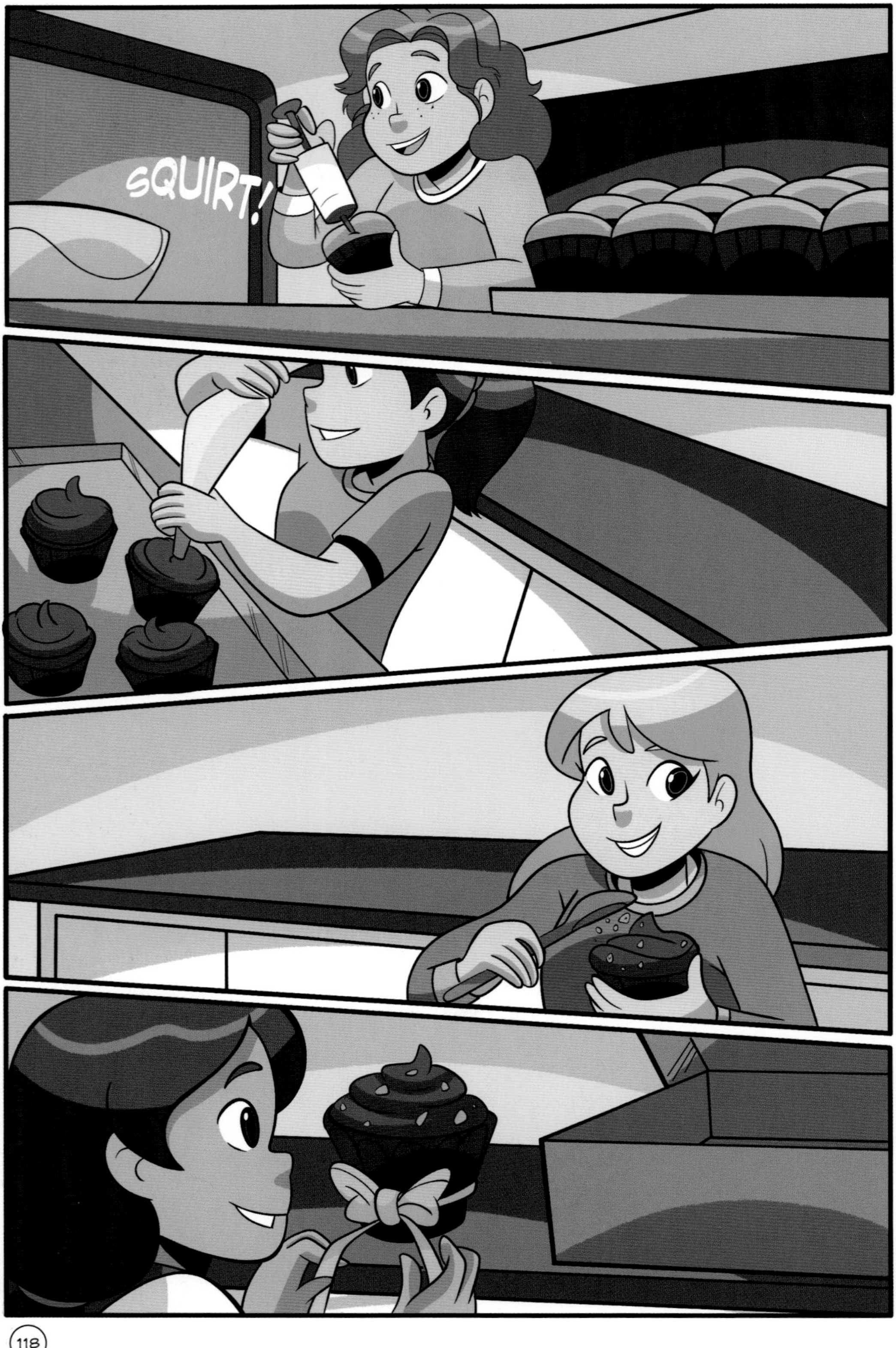
SQUIRT!

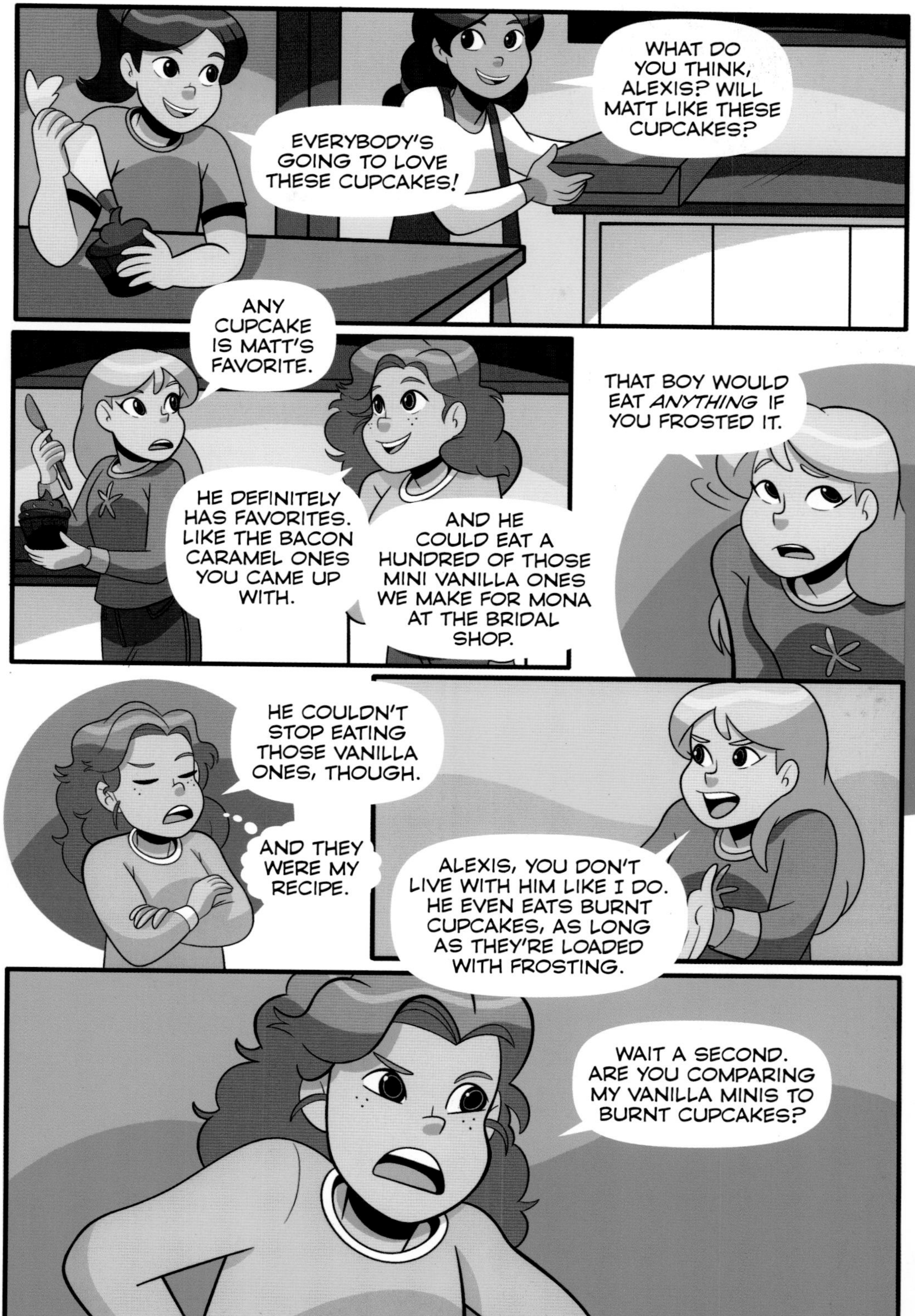
EVERYBODY'S GOING TO LOVE THESE CUPCAKES!
WHAT DO YOU THINK, ALEXIS? WILL MATT LIKE THESE CUPCAKES?
ANY CUPCAKE IS MATT'S FAVORITE.
HE DEFINITELY HAS FAVORITES. LIKE THE BACON CARAMEL ONES YOU CAME UP WITH.
AND HE COULD EAT A HUNDRED OF THOSE MINI VANILLA ONES WE MAKE FOR MONA AT THE BRIDAL SHOP.
THAT BOY WOULD EAT *ANYTHING* IF YOU FROSTED IT.
HE COULDN'T STOP EATING THOSE VANILLA ONES, THOUGH.
AND THEY WERE MY RECIPE.
ALEXIS, YOU DON'T LIVE WITH HIM LIKE I DO. HE EVEN EATS BURNT CUPCAKES, AS LONG AS THEY'RE LOADED WITH FROSTING.
WAIT A SECOND. ARE YOU COMPARING MY VANILLA MINIS TO BURNT CUPCAKES?

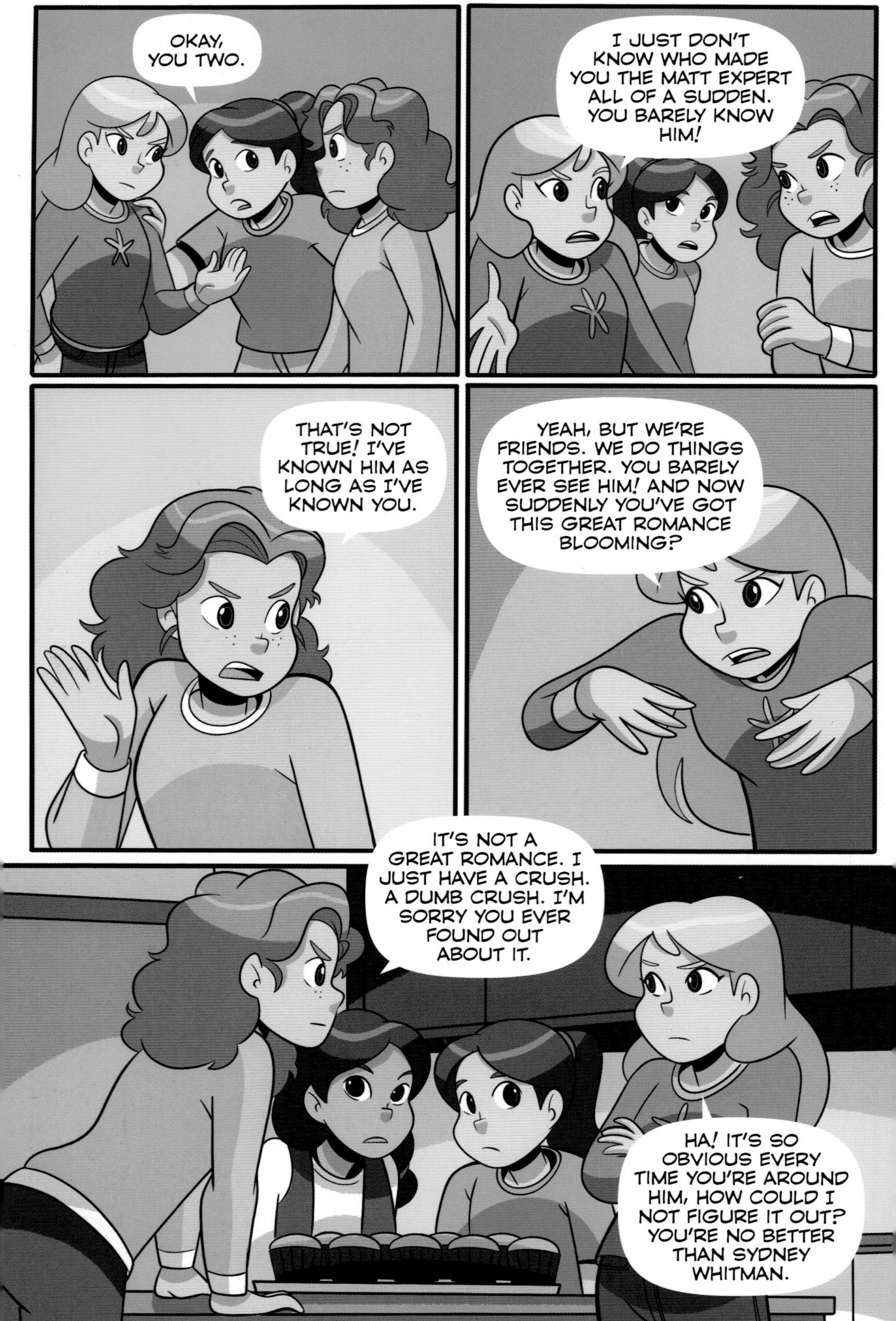

OKAY, YOU TWO.
I JUST DON'T KNOW WHO MADE YOU THE MATT EXPERT ALL OF A SUDDEN. YOU BARELY KNOW HIM!
THAT'S NOT TRUE! I'VE KNOWN HIM AS LONG AS I'VE KNOWN YOU.
YEAH, BUT WE'RE FRIENDS. WE DO THINGS TOGETHER. YOU BARELY EVER SEE HIM! AND NOW SUDDENLY YOU'VE GOT THIS GREAT ROMANCE BLOOMING?
IT'S NOT A GREAT ROMANCE. I JUST HAVE A CRUSH. A DUMB CRUSH. I'M SORRY YOU EVER FOUND OUT ABOUT IT.
HA! IT'S SO OBVIOUS EVERY TIME YOU'RE AROUND HIM, HOW COULD I NOT FIGURE IT OUT? YOU'RE NO BETTER THAN SYDNEY WHITMAN.

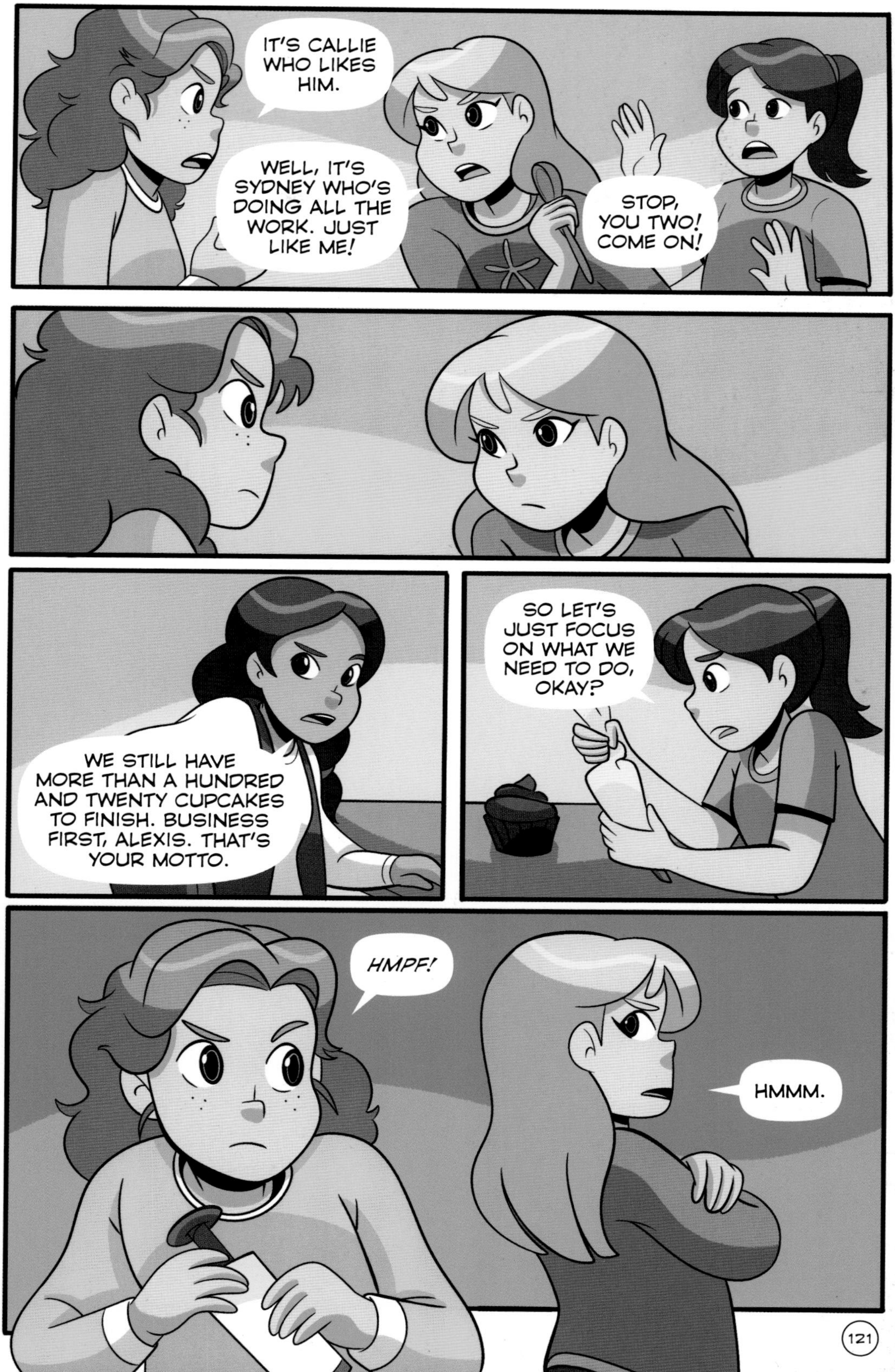
IT'S CALLIE WHO LIKES HIM.
WELL, IT'S SYDNEY WHO'S DOING ALL THE WORK. JUST LIKE ME!
STOP, YOU TWO! COME ON!
WE STILL HAVE MORE THAN A HUNDRED AND TWENTY CUPCAKES TO FINISH. BUSINESS FIRST, ALEXIS. THAT'S YOUR MOTTO.
SO LET'S JUST FOCUS ON WHAT WE NEED TO DO, OKAY?
HMPF!
HMMM.

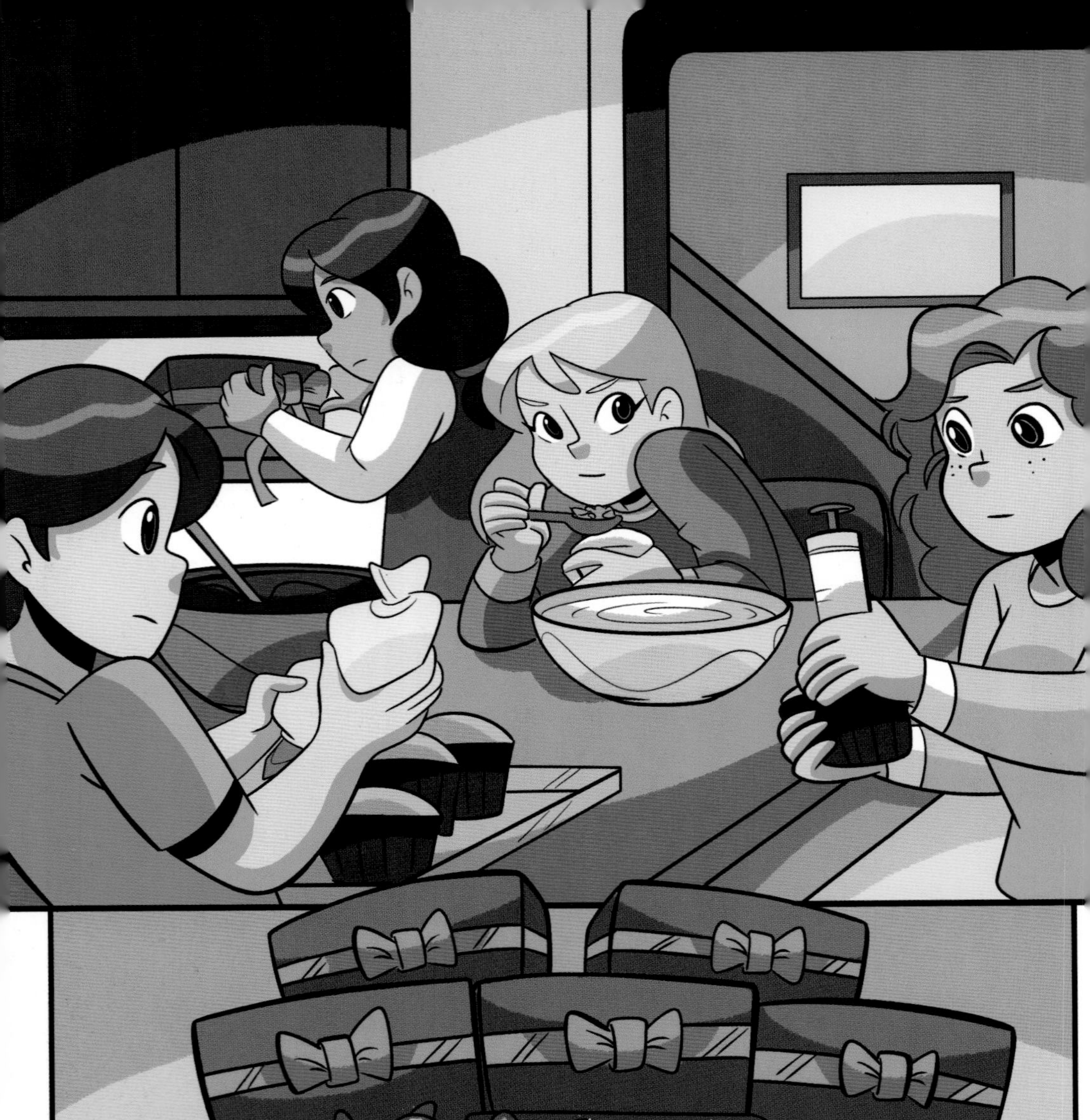

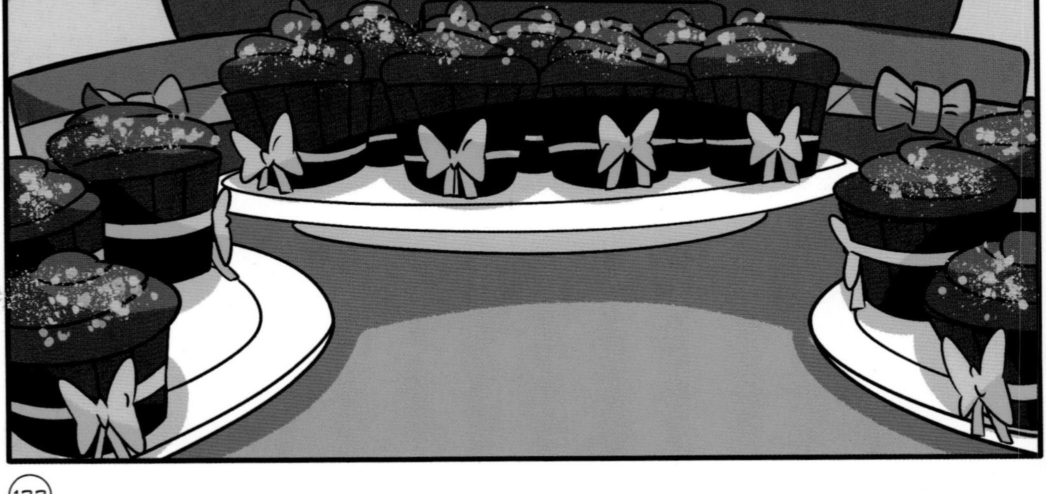

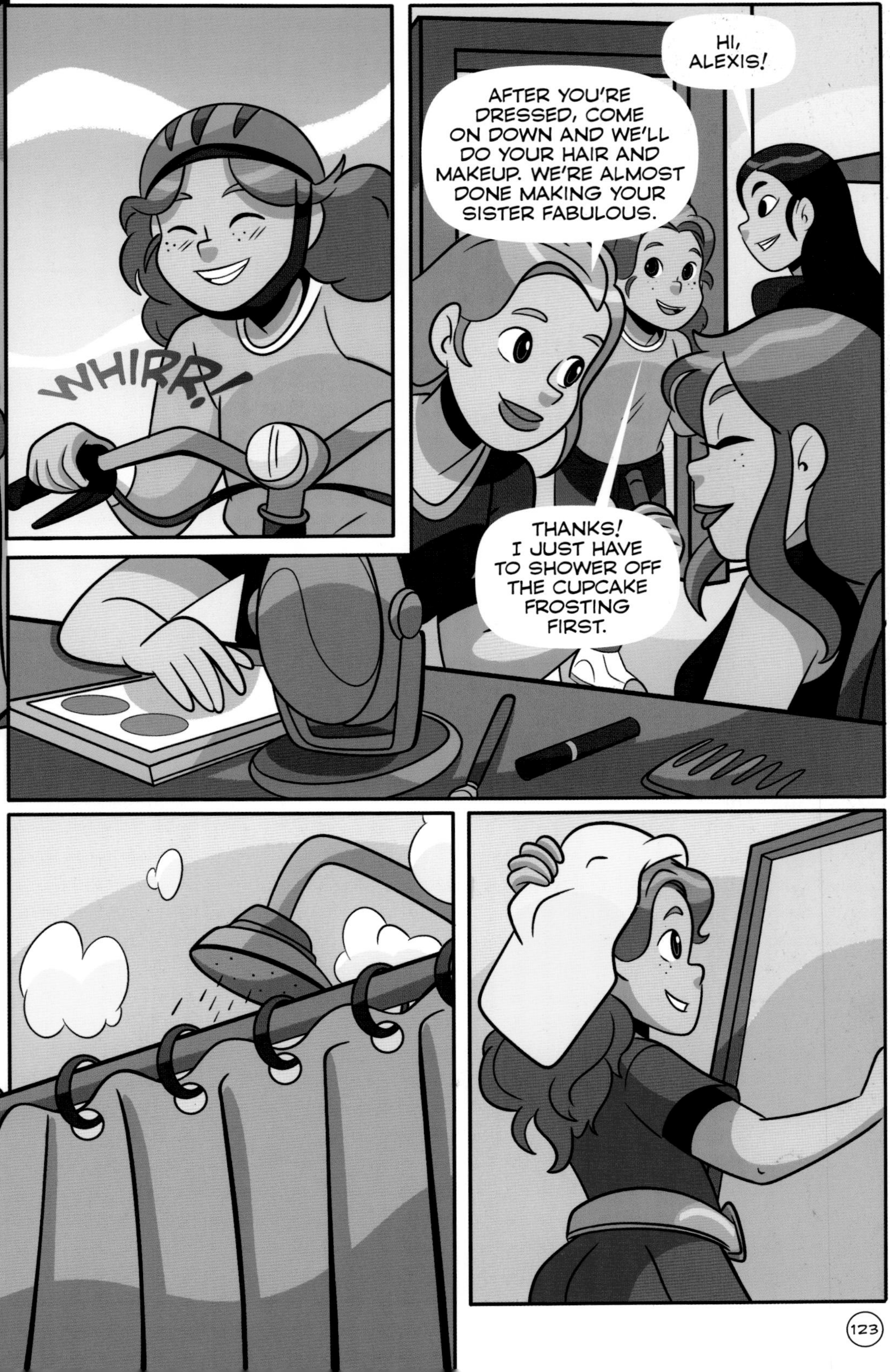

WHIRR!
HI, ALEXIS!
AFTER YOU'RE DRESSED, COME ON DOWN AND WE'LL DO YOUR HAIR AND MAKEUP. WE'RE ALMOST DONE MAKING YOUR SISTER FABULOUS.
THANKS! I JUST HAVE TO SHOWER OFF THE CUPCAKE FROSTING FIRST.

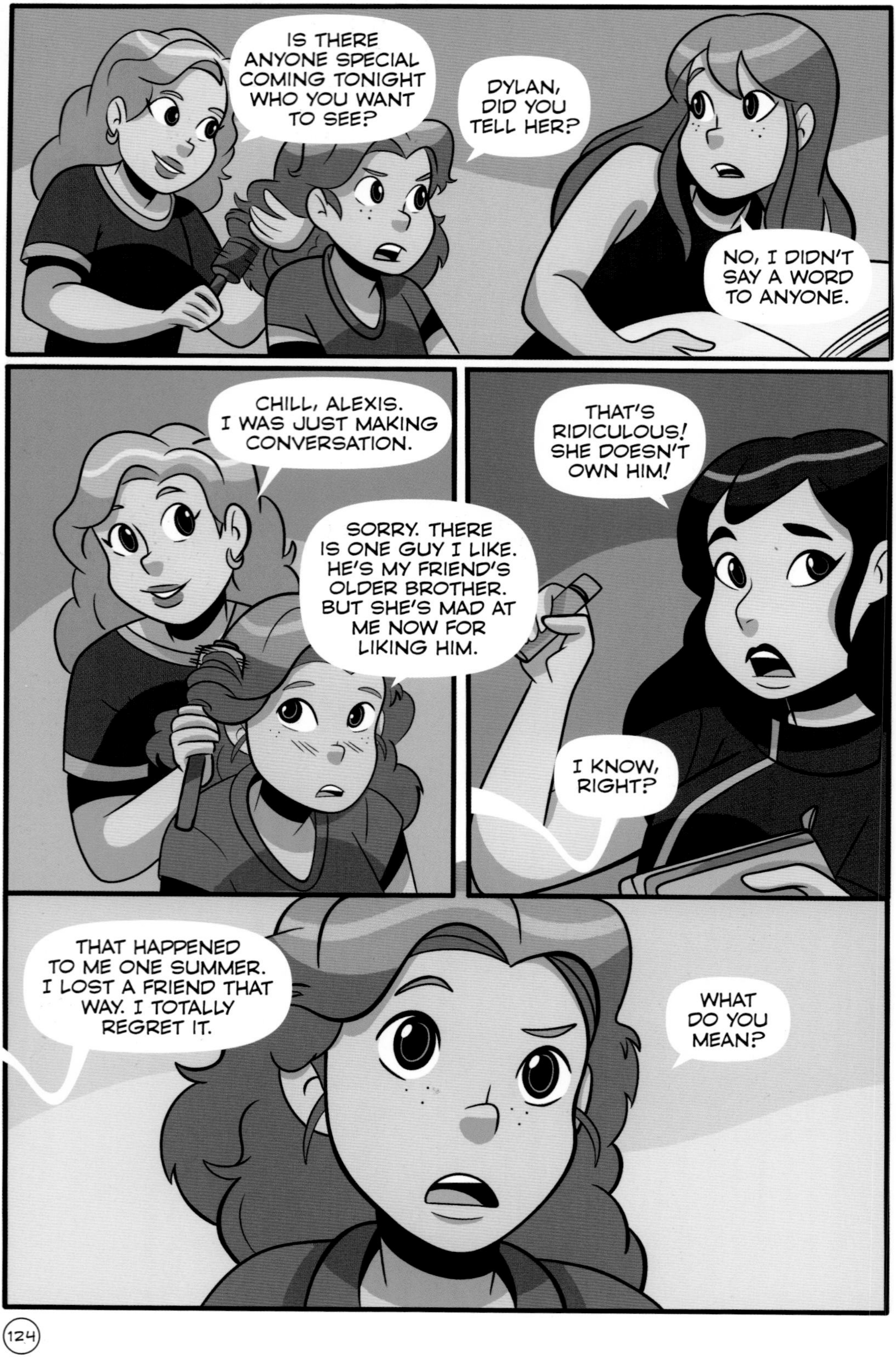
IS THERE ANYONE SPECIAL COMING TONIGHT WHO YOU WANT TO SEE?
DYLAN, DID YOU TELL HER?
NO, I DIDN'T SAY A WORD TO ANYONE.
CHILL, ALEXIS. I WAS JUST MAKING CONVERSATION.
SORRY. THERE IS ONE GUY I LIKE. HE'S MY FRIEND'S OLDER BROTHER. BUT SHE'S MAD AT ME NOW FOR LIKING HIM.
THAT'S RIDICULOUS! SHE DOESN'T OWN HIM!
I KNOW, RIGHT?
THAT HAPPENED TO ME ONE SUMMER. I LOST A FRIEND THAT WAY. I TOTALLY REGRET IT.
WHAT DO YOU MEAN?

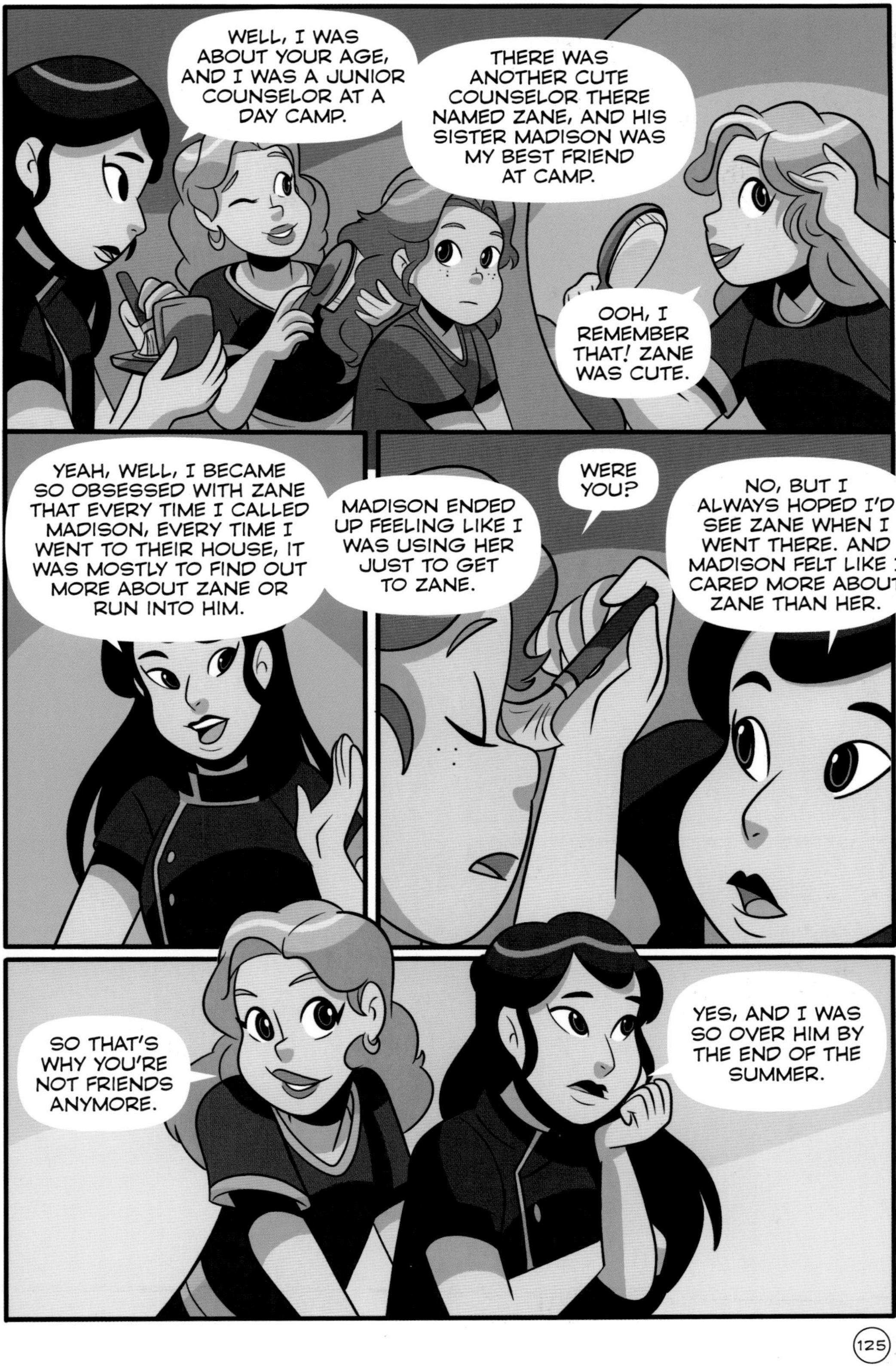
WELL, I WAS ABOUT YOUR AGE, AND I WAS A JUNIOR COUNSELOR AT A DAY CAMP.
THERE WAS ANOTHER CUTE COUNSELOR THERE NAMED ZANE, AND HIS SISTER MADISON WAS MY BEST FRIEND AT CAMP.
OOH, I REMEMBER THAT! ZANE WAS CUTE.
YEAH, WELL, I BECAME SO OBSESSED WITH ZANE THAT EVERY TIME I CALLED MADISON, EVERY TIME I WENT TO THEIR HOUSE, IT WAS MOSTLY TO FIND OUT MORE ABOUT ZANE OR RUN INTO HIM.
MADISON ENDED UP FEELING LIKE I WAS USING HER JUST TO GET TO ZANE.
WERE YOU?
NO, BUT I ALWAYS HOPED I'D SEE ZANE WHEN I WENT THERE. AND MADISON FELT LIKE I CARED MORE ABOUT ZANE THAN HER.
SO THAT'S WHY YOU'RE NOT FRIENDS ANYMORE.
YES, AND I WAS SO OVER HIM BY THE END OF THE SUMMER.

HOW DID YOU GET OVER HIM?

WE FINALLY WENT OUT ON A DATE, AND I REALIZED WE HAD NOTHING TO TALK ABOUT WHEN MADISON WASN'T THERE.

BRRRRRRRRRRRRING!

IT'S HIM!

ANSWER IT!

BRRRRRRRRRRRRRRING!

I...I CAN'T!

BRRRRRRRRRRRRRRING!

BECKER RESIDENCE.

UH... HI, UH, IS DYLAN THERE, PLEASE?

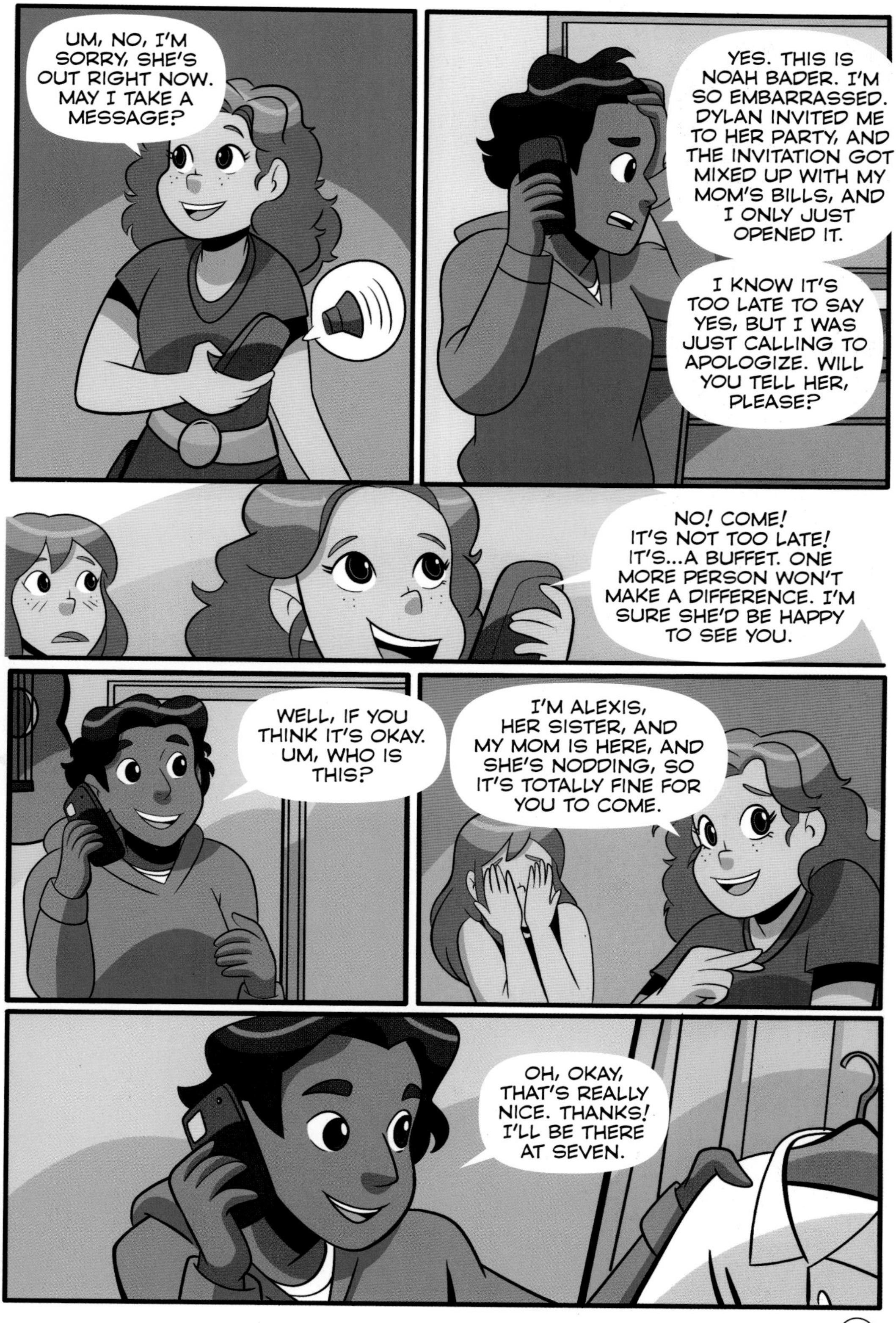
UM, NO, I'M SORRY, SHE'S OUT RIGHT NOW. MAY I TAKE A MESSAGE?
YES. THIS IS NOAH BADER. I'M SO EMBARRASSED. DYLAN INVITED ME TO HER PARTY, AND THE INVITATION GOT MIXED UP WITH MY MOM'S BILLS, AND I ONLY JUST OPENED IT.
I KNOW IT'S TOO LATE TO SAY YES, BUT I WAS JUST CALLING TO APOLOGIZE. WILL YOU TELL HER, PLEASE?
NO! COME! IT'S NOT TOO LATE! IT'S...A BUFFET. ONE MORE PERSON WON'T MAKE A DIFFERENCE. I'M SURE SHE'D BE HAPPY TO SEE YOU.
WELL, IF YOU THINK IT'S OKAY. UM, WHO IS THIS?
I'M ALEXIS, HER SISTER, AND MY MOM IS HERE, AND SHE'S NODDING, SO IT'S TOTALLY FINE FOR YOU TO COME.
OH, OKAY, THAT'S REALLY NICE. THANKS! I'LL BE THERE AT SEVEN.

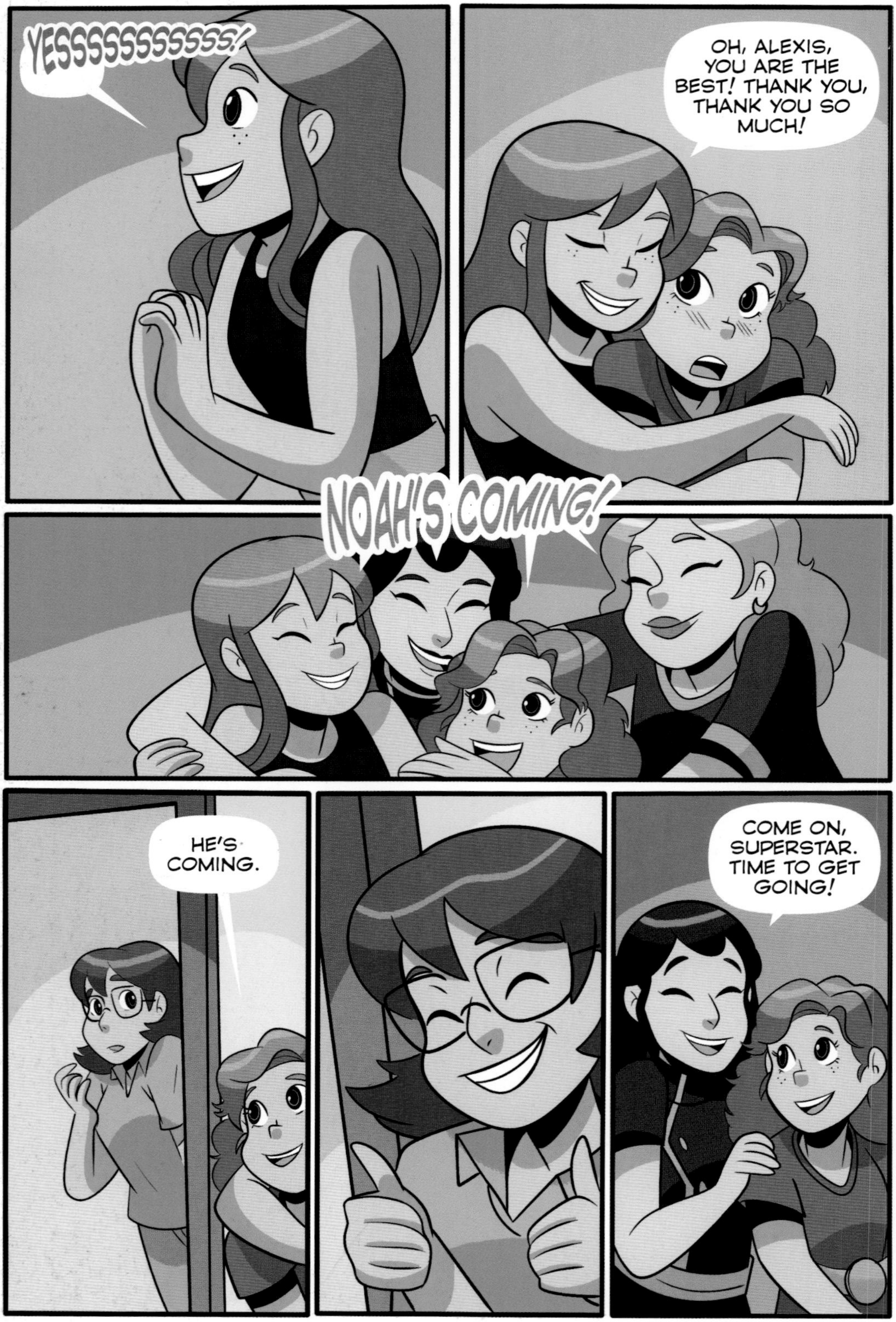
YESSSSSSSSSSSS!
OH, ALEXIS, YOU ARE THE BEST! THANK YOU, THANK YOU SO MUCH!
NOAH'S COMING!
HE'S COMING.
COME ON, SUPERSTAR. TIME TO GET GOING!

Chapter 14

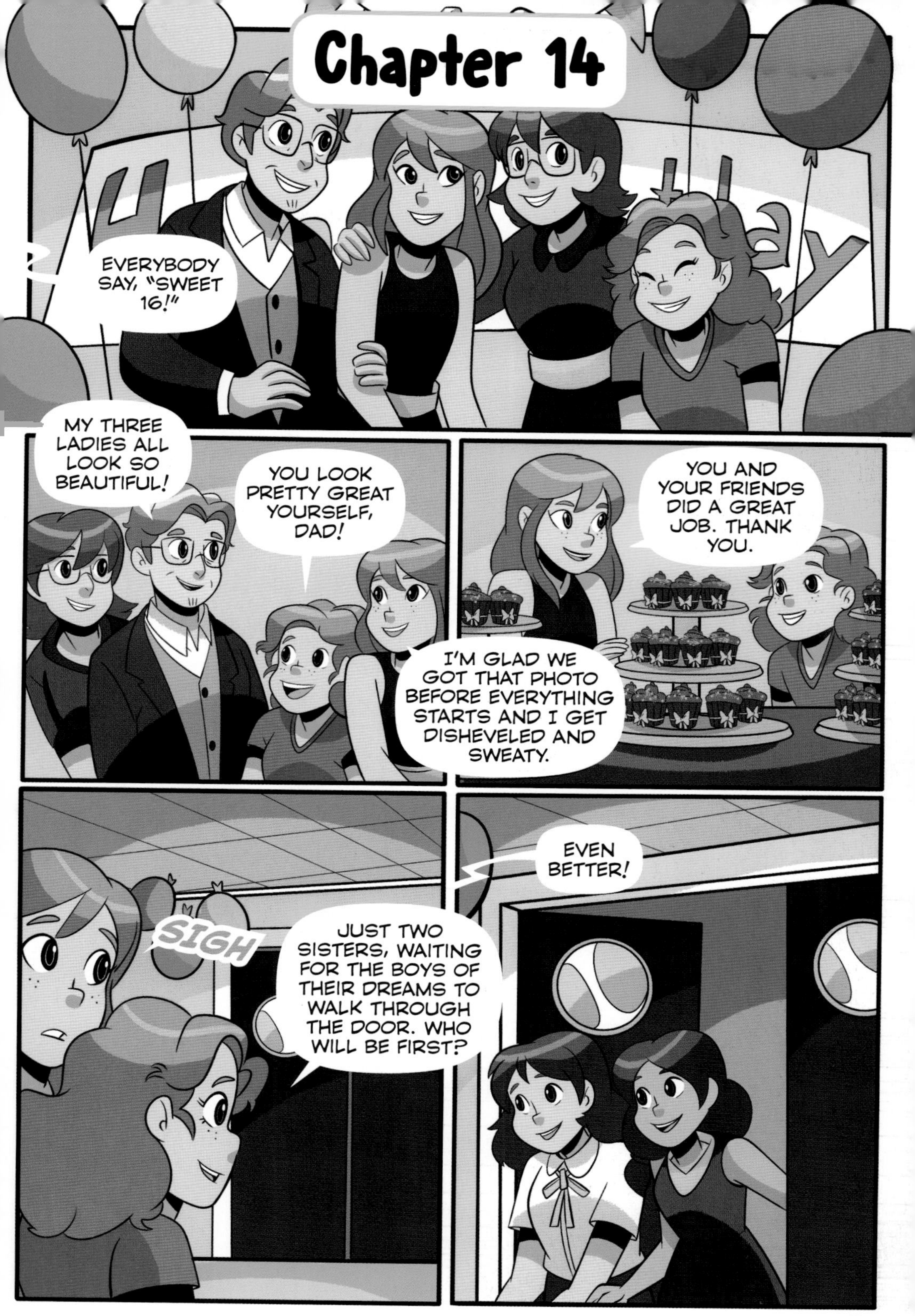

EVERYBODY SAY, "SWEET 16!"
MY THREE LADIES ALL LOOK SO BEAUTIFUL!
YOU LOOK PRETTY GREAT YOURSELF, DAD!
YOU AND YOUR FRIENDS DID A GREAT JOB. THANK YOU.
I'M GLAD WE GOT THAT PHOTO BEFORE EVERYTHING STARTS AND I GET DISHEVELED AND SWEATY.
SIGH
JUST TWO SISTERS, WAITING FOR THE BOYS OF THEIR DREAMS TO WALK THROUGH THE DOOR. WHO WILL BE FIRST?
EVEN BETTER!

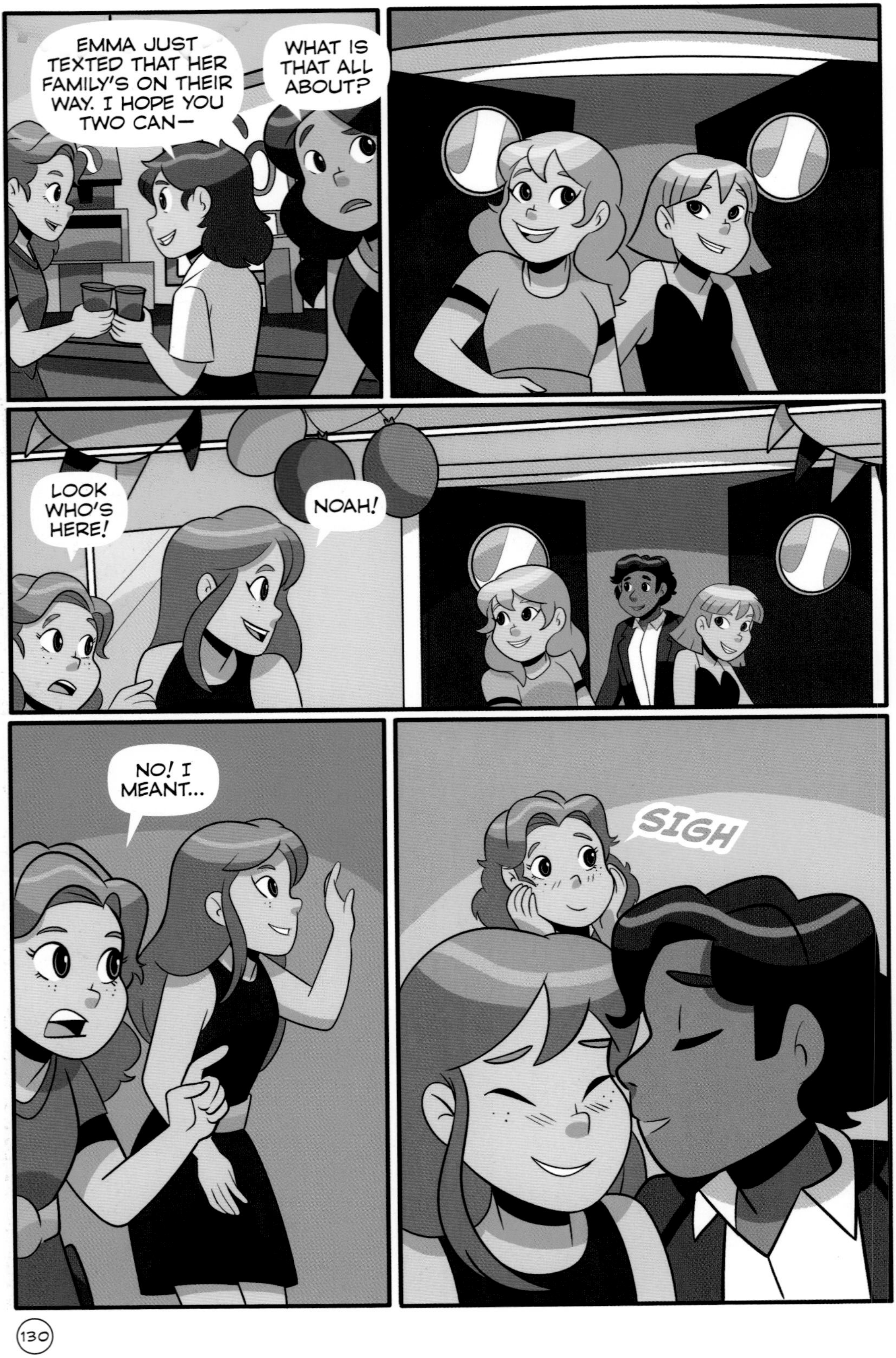
EMMA JUST TEXTED THAT HER FAMILY'S ON THEIR WAY. I HOPE YOU TWO CAN—
WHAT IS THAT ALL ABOUT?
LOOK WHO'S HERE!
NOAH!
NO! I MEANT...
SIGH

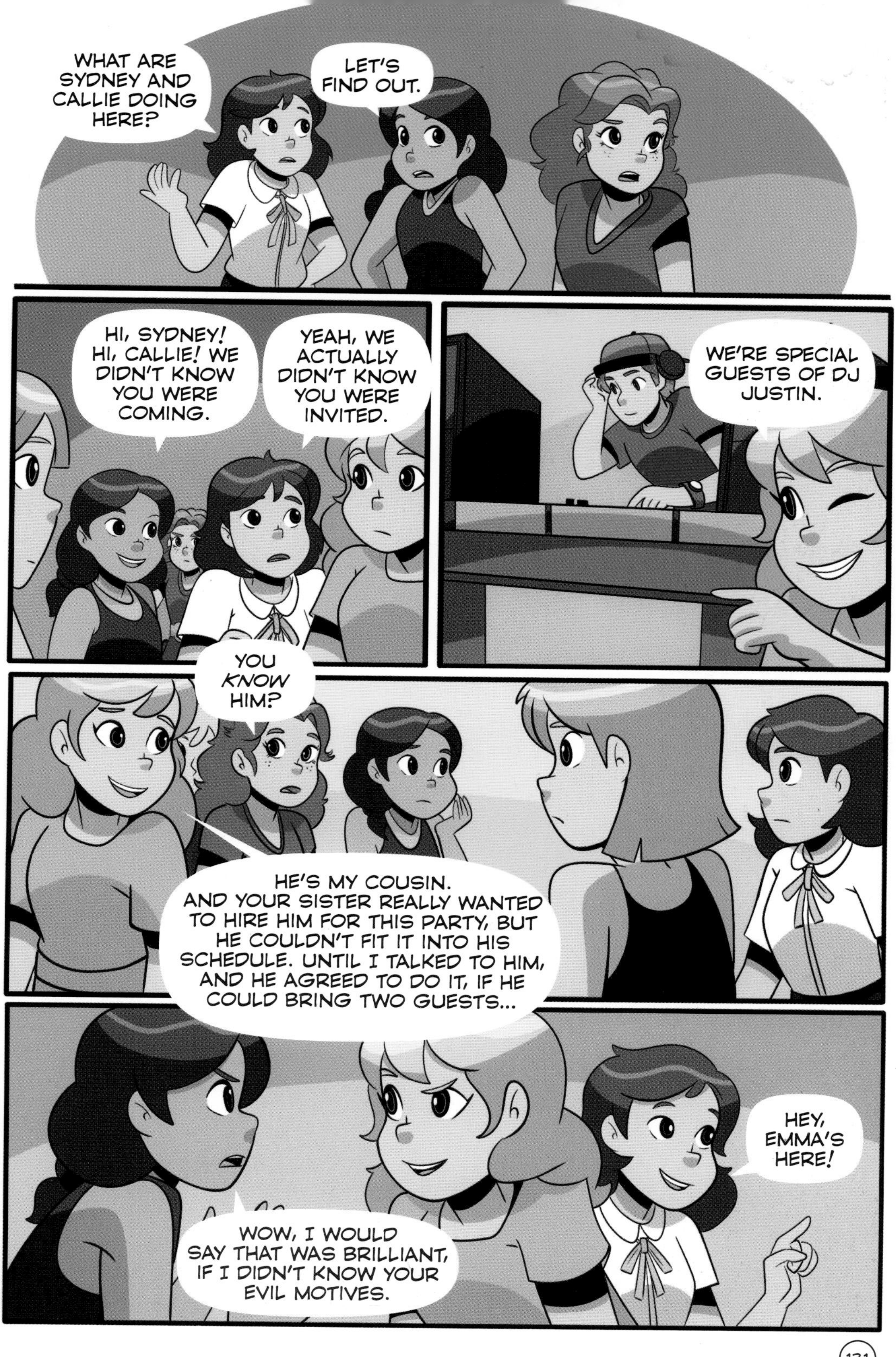
WHAT ARE SYDNEY AND CALLIE DOING HERE?
LET'S FIND OUT.
HI, SYDNEY! HI, CALLIE! WE DIDN'T KNOW YOU WERE COMING.
YEAH, WE ACTUALLY DIDN'T KNOW YOU WERE INVITED.
WE'RE SPECIAL GUESTS OF DJ JUSTIN.
YOU *KNOW* HIM?
HE'S MY COUSIN. AND YOUR SISTER REALLY WANTED TO HIRE HIM FOR THIS PARTY, BUT HE COULDN'T FIT IT INTO HIS SCHEDULE. UNTIL I TALKED TO HIM, AND HE AGREED TO DO IT, IF HE COULD BRING TWO GUESTS...
WOW, I WOULD SAY THAT WAS BRILLIANT, IF I DIDN'T KNOW YOUR EVIL MOTIVES.
HEY, EMMA'S HERE!

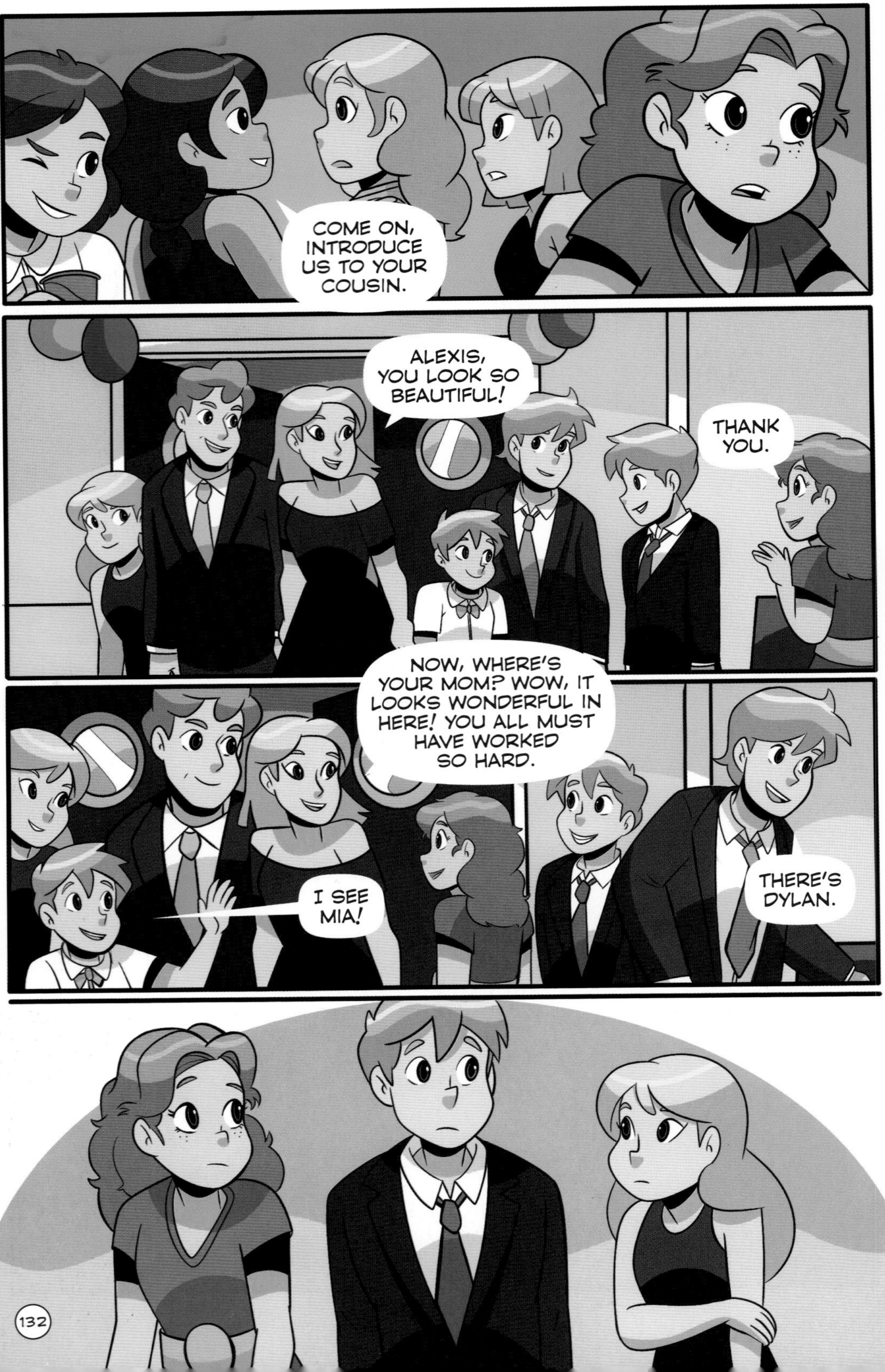
COME ON, INTRODUCE US TO YOUR COUSIN.
ALEXIS, YOU LOOK SO BEAUTIFUL!
THANK YOU.
NOW, WHERE'S YOUR MOM? WOW, IT LOOKS WONDERFUL IN HERE! YOU ALL MUST HAVE WORKED SO HARD.
I SEE MIA!
THERE'S DYLAN.

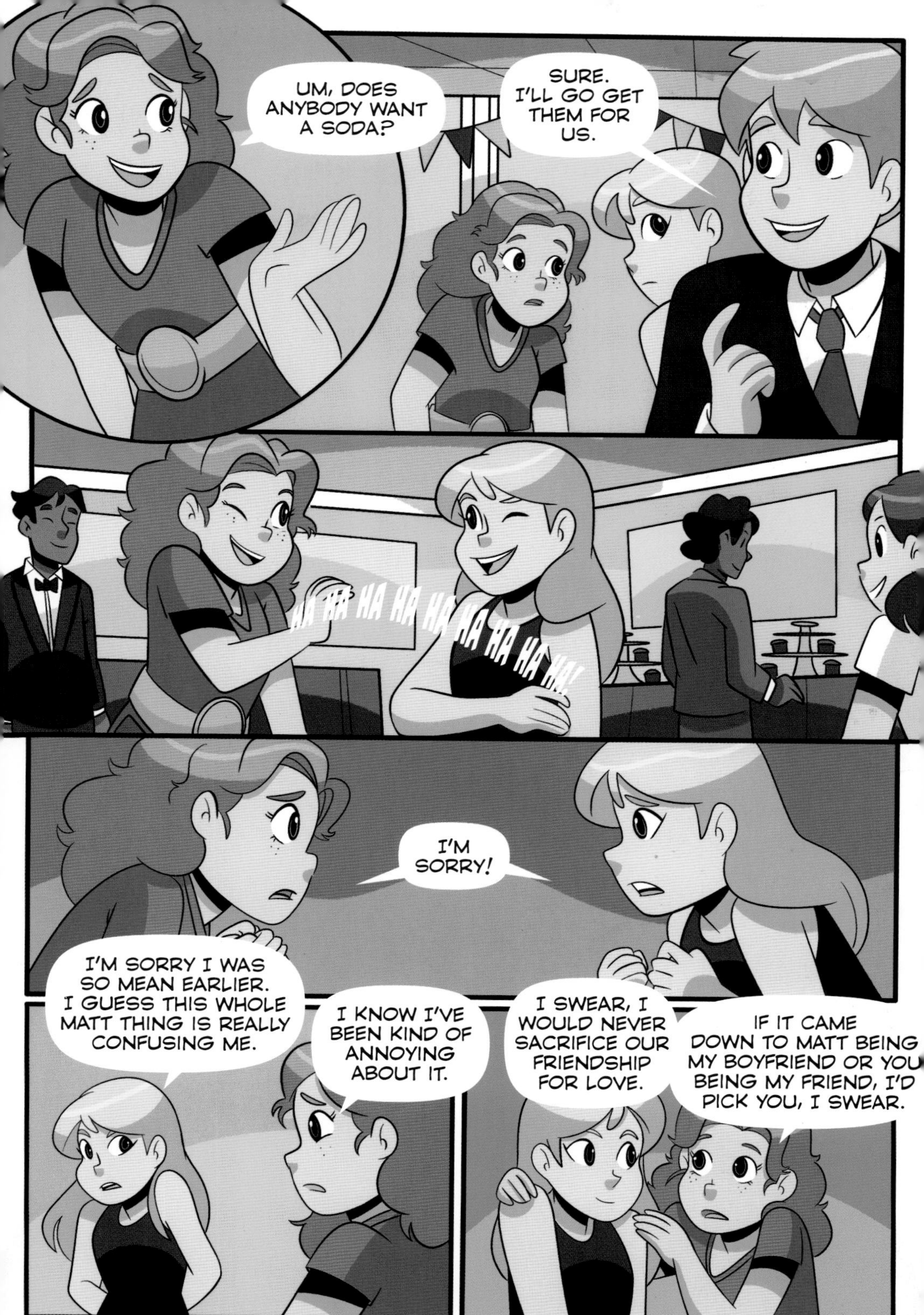
UM, DOES ANYBODY WANT A SODA?
SURE. I'LL GO GET THEM FOR US.
HA HA HA HA HA HA HA HA HA!
I'M SORRY!
I'M SORRY I WAS SO MEAN EARLIER. I GUESS THIS WHOLE MATT THING IS REALLY CONFUSING ME.
I KNOW I'VE BEEN KIND OF ANNOYING ABOUT IT.
I SWEAR, I WOULD NEVER SACRIFICE OUR FRIENDSHIP FOR LOVE.
IF IT CAME DOWN TO MATT BEING MY BOYFRIEND OR YOU BEING MY FRIEND, I'D PICK YOU, I SWEAR.

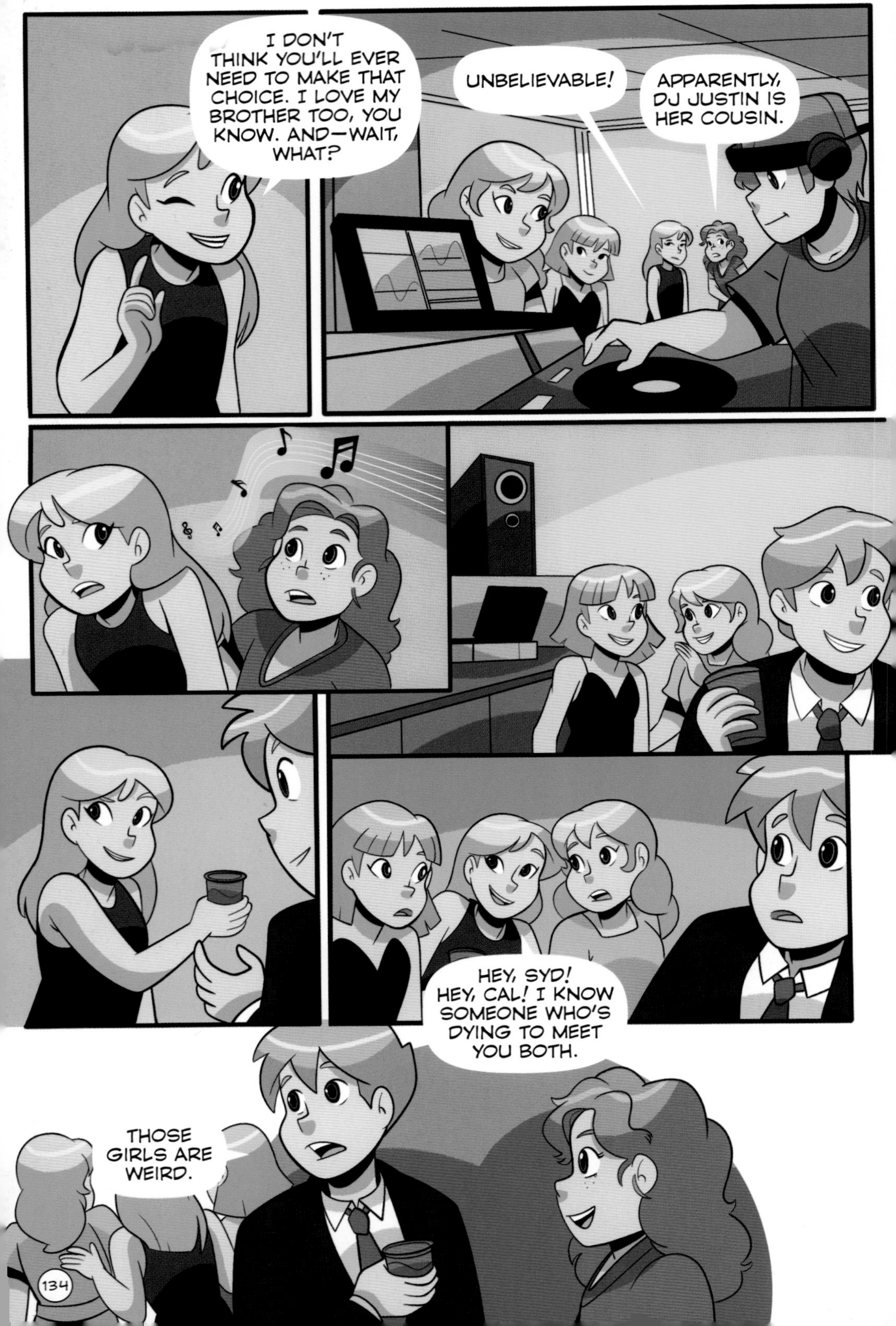
I DON'T THINK YOU'LL EVER NEED TO MAKE THAT CHOICE. I LOVE MY BROTHER TOO, YOU KNOW. AND—WAIT, WHAT?
UNBELIEVABLE!
APPARENTLY, DJ JUSTIN IS HER COUSIN.
HEY, SYD! HEY, CAL! I KNOW SOMEONE WHO'S DYING TO MEET YOU BOTH.
THOSE GIRLS ARE WEIRD.

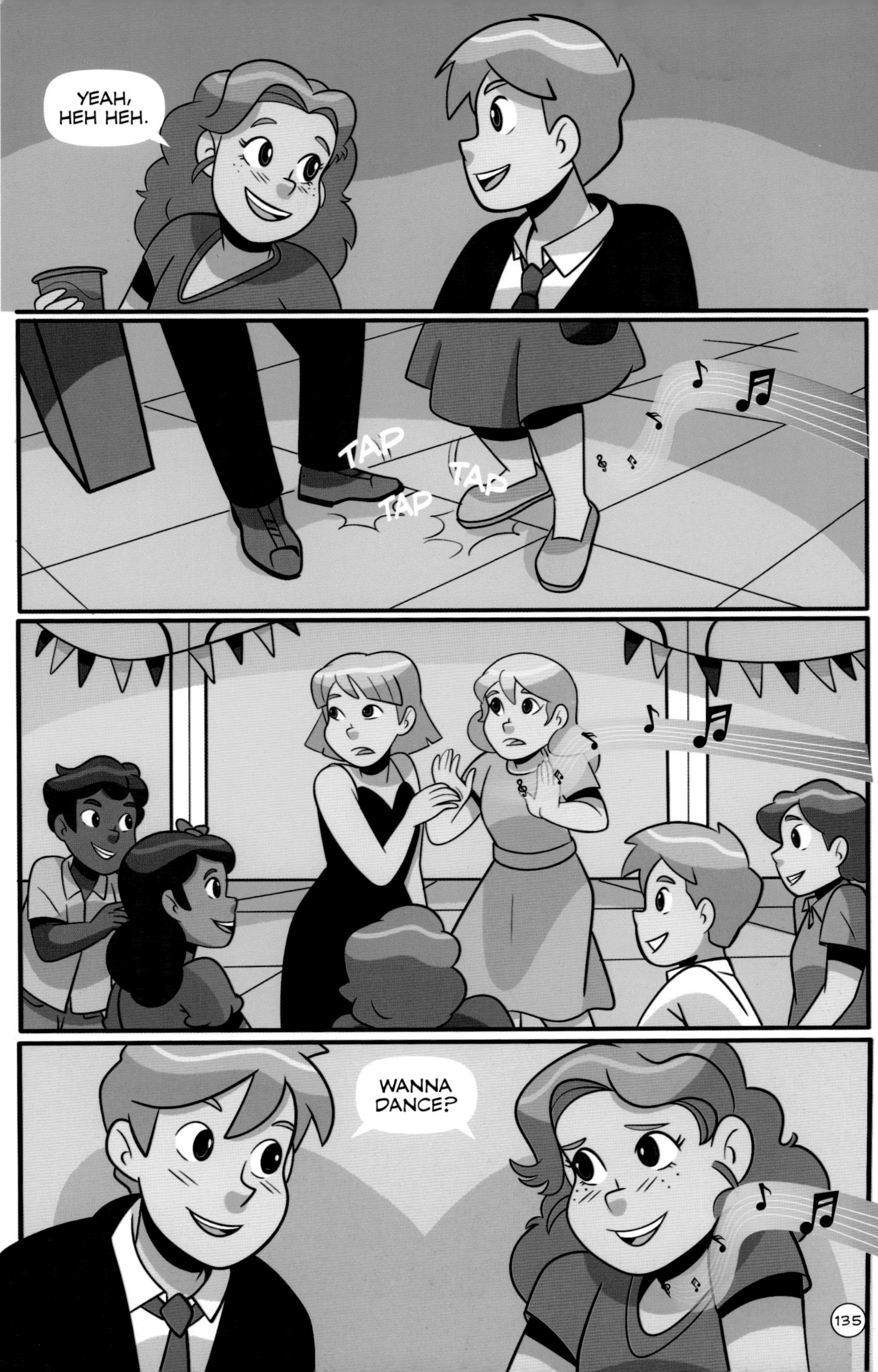
YEAH, HEH HEH.
TAP
TAP
TAP
WANNA DANCE?

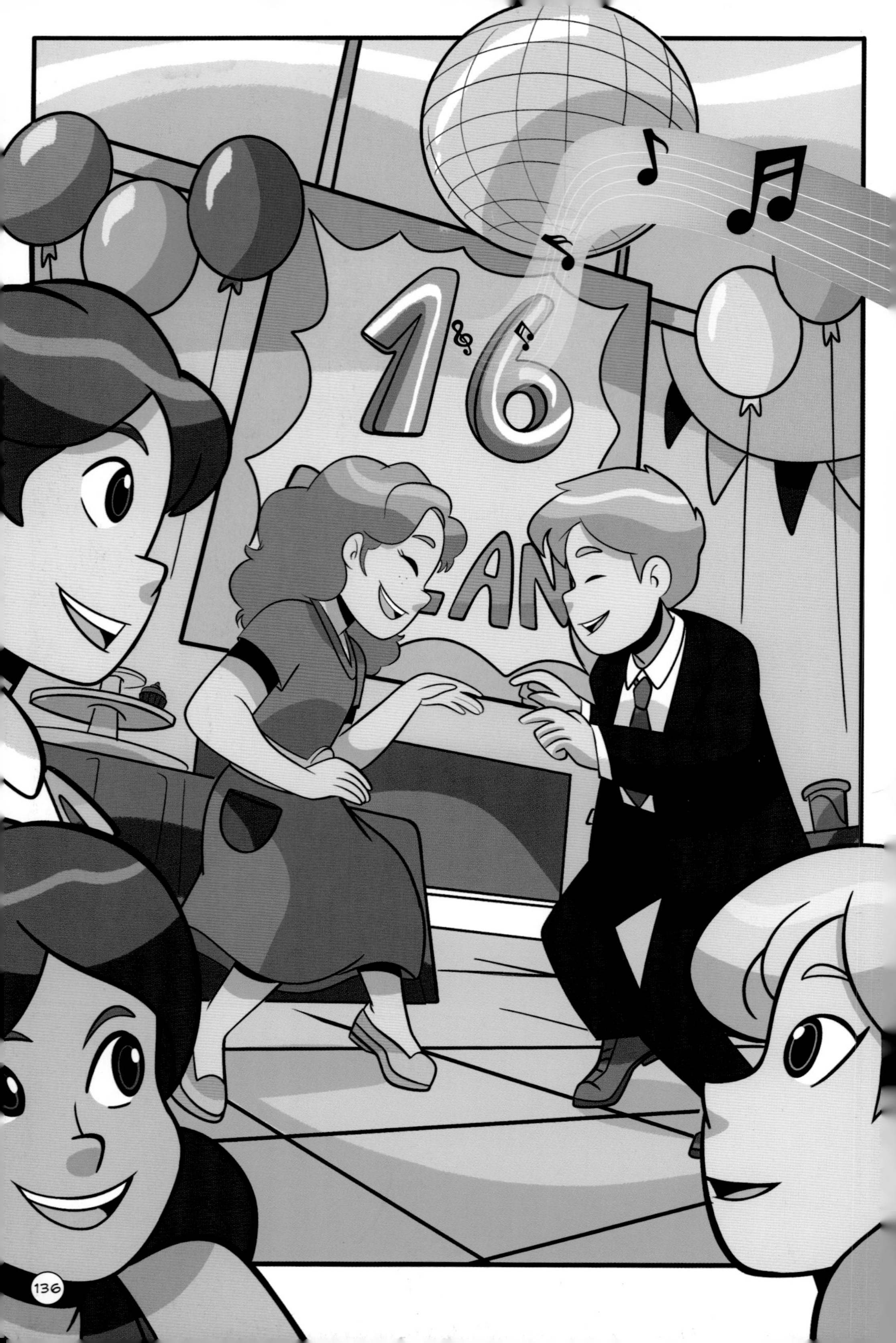
16

Chapter 15

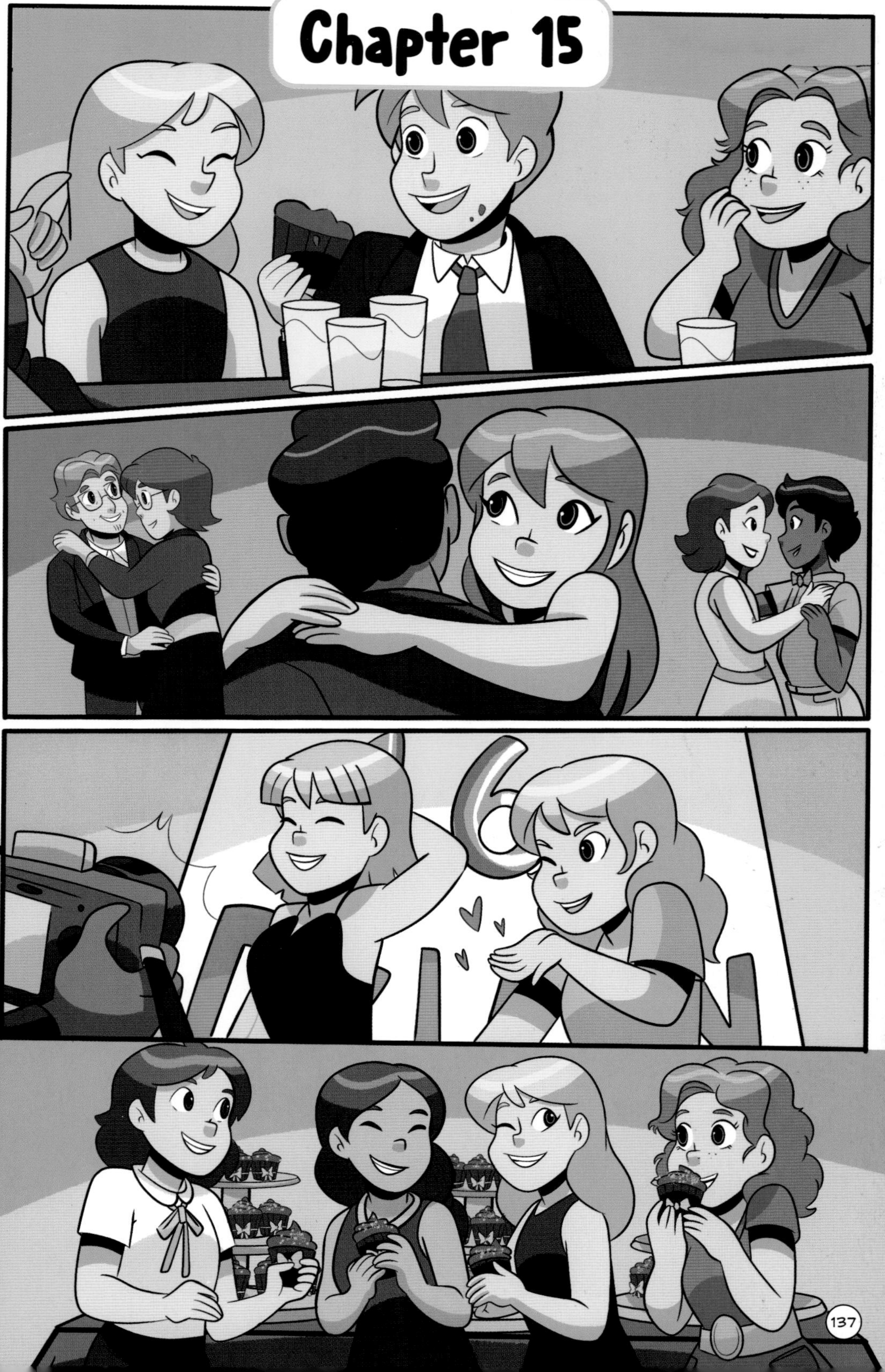

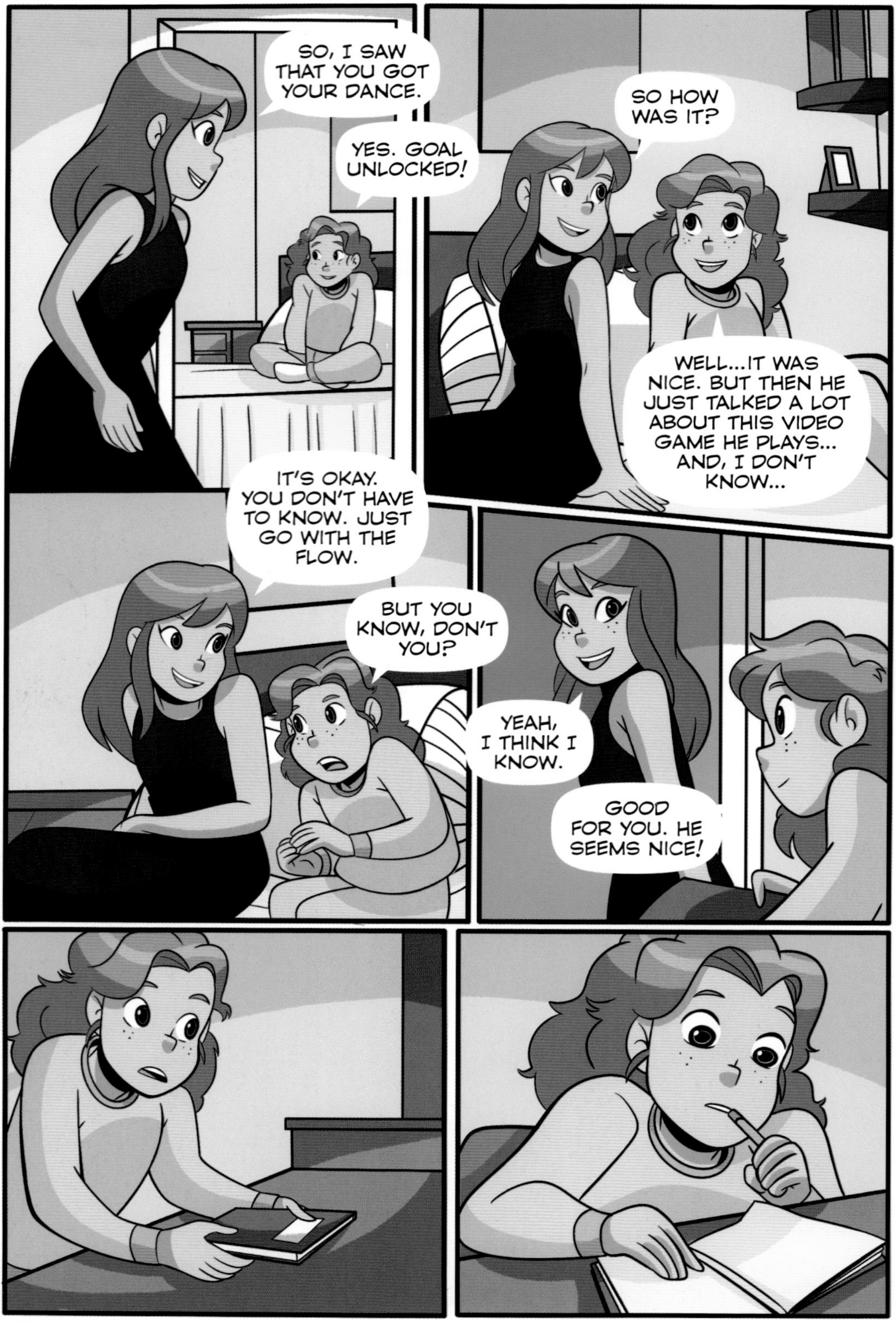
SO, I SAW THAT YOU GOT YOUR DANCE.
YES. GOAL UNLOCKED!
SO HOW WAS IT?
WELL...IT WAS NICE. BUT THEN HE JUST TALKED A LOT ABOUT THIS VIDEO GAME HE PLAYS... AND, I DON'T KNOW...
IT'S OKAY. YOU DON'T HAVE TO KNOW. JUST GO WITH THE FLOW.
BUT YOU KNOW, DON'T YOU?
YEAH, I THINK I KNOW.
GOOD FOR YOU. HE SEEMS NICE!

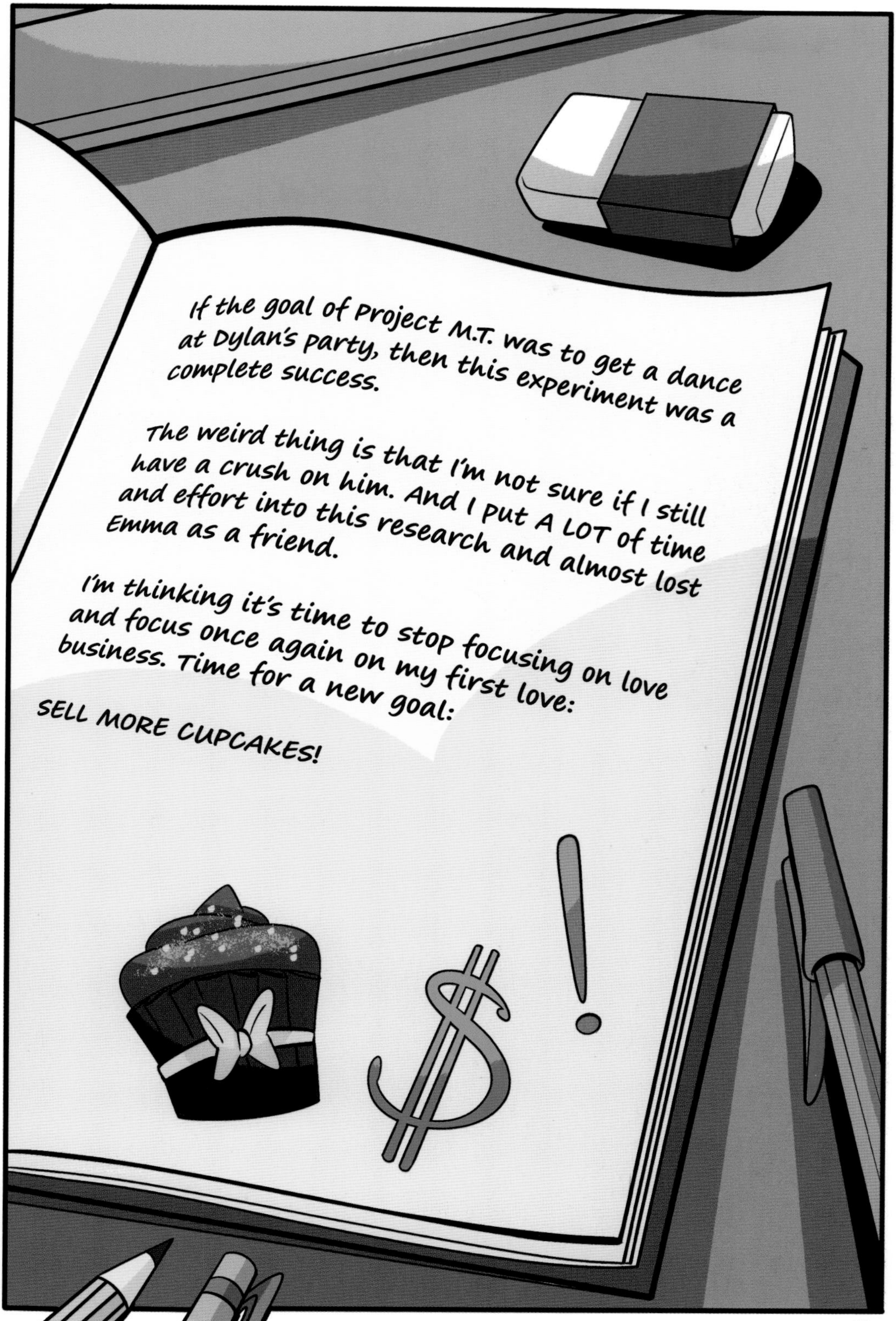
If the goal of Project M.T. was to get a dance at Dylan's party, then this experiment was a complete success.
The weird thing is that I'm not sure if I still have a crush on him. And I put A LOT of time and effort into this research and almost lost Emma as a friend.
I'm thinking it's time to stop focusing on love and focus once again on my first love: business. Time for a new goal:
SELL MORE CUPCAKES!

Make sure you read them all!

Cupcake Diaries

Emma on Thin Icing

From the bestselling author of Cupcake Diaries Coco Simon
Cupcake Diaries
#3
The Graphic Novel
Emma on Thin Icing

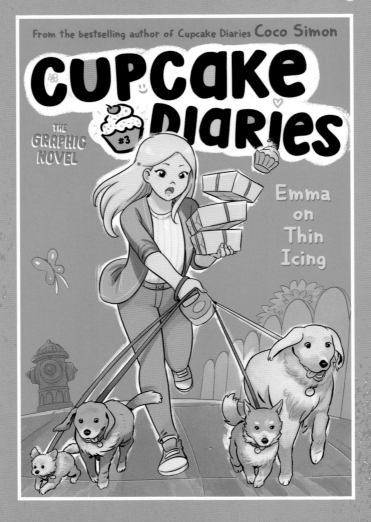

Chapter 1

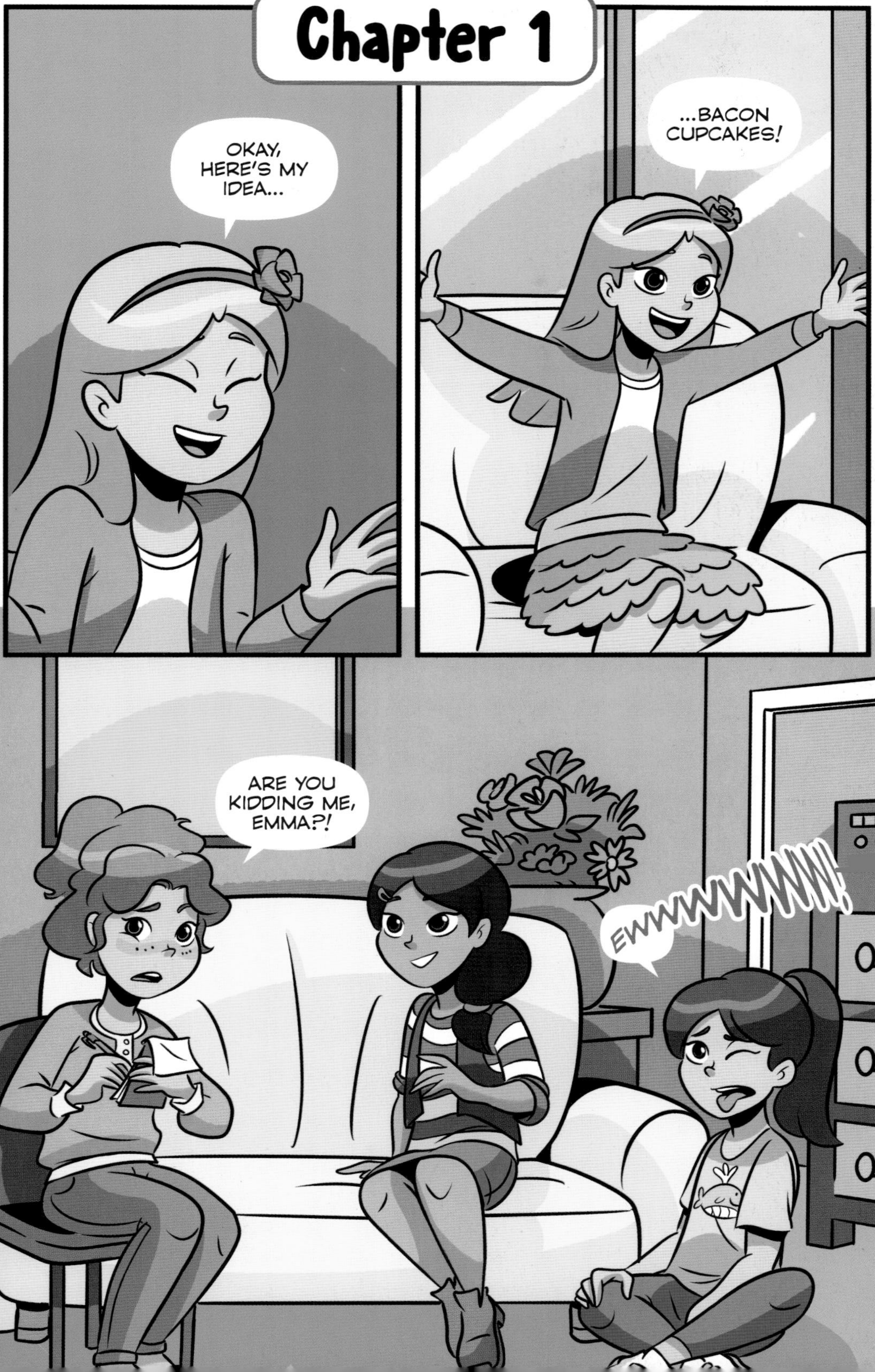
OKAY, HERE'S MY IDEA...
...BACON CUPCAKES!
ARE YOU KIDDING ME, EMMA?!
EWWWWWWWW!

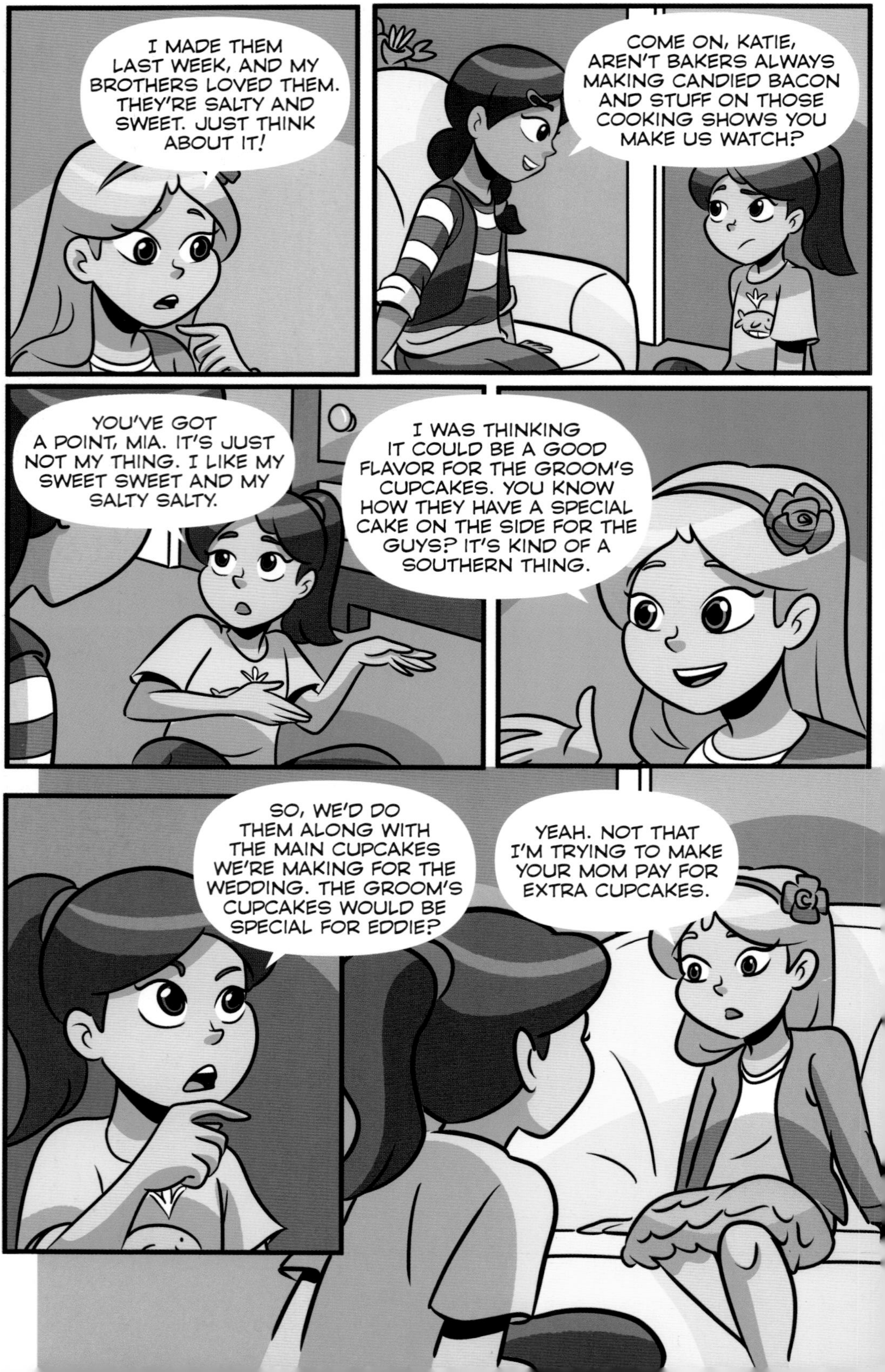
I MADE THEM LAST WEEK, AND MY BROTHERS LOVED THEM. THEY'RE SALTY AND SWEET. JUST THINK ABOUT IT!
COME ON, KATIE, AREN'T BAKERS ALWAYS MAKING CANDIED BACON AND STUFF ON THOSE COOKING SHOWS YOU MAKE US WATCH?
YOU'VE GOT A POINT, MIA. IT'S JUST NOT MY THING. I LIKE MY SWEET SWEET AND MY SALTY SALTY.
I WAS THINKING IT COULD BE A GOOD FLAVOR FOR THE GROOM'S CUPCAKES. YOU KNOW HOW THEY HAVE A SPECIAL CAKE ON THE SIDE FOR THE GUYS? IT'S KIND OF A SOUTHERN THING.
SO, WE'D DO THEM ALONG WITH THE MAIN CUPCAKES WE'RE MAKING FOR THE WEDDING. THE GROOM'S CUPCAKES WOULD BE SPECIAL FOR EDDIE?
YEAH. NOT THAT I'M TRYING TO MAKE YOUR MOM PAY FOR EXTRA CUPCAKES.

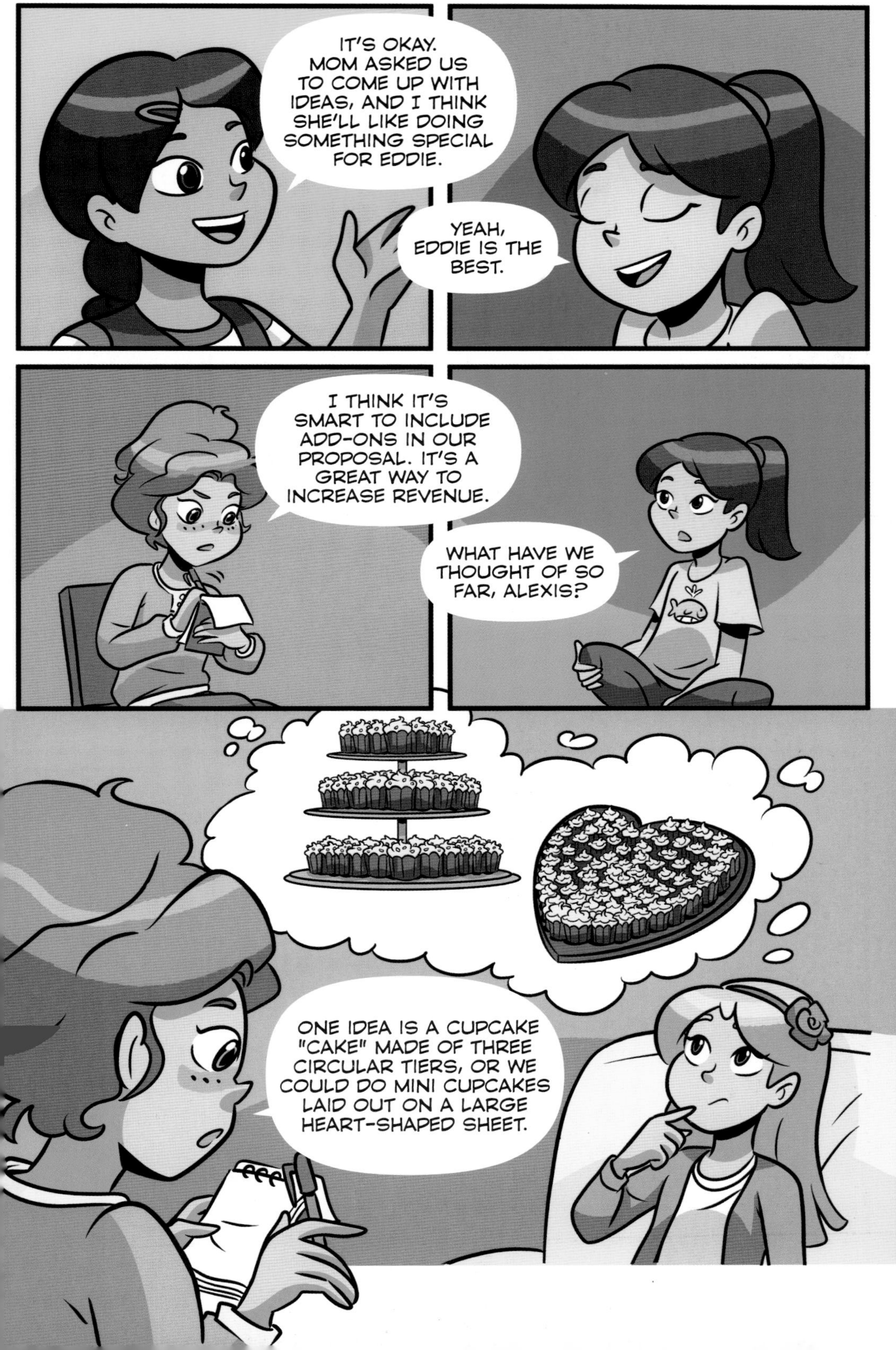
IT'S OKAY. MOM ASKED US TO COME UP WITH IDEAS, AND I THINK SHE'LL LIKE DOING SOMETHING SPECIAL FOR EDDIE.
YEAH, EDDIE IS THE BEST.
I THINK IT'S SMART TO INCLUDE ADD-ONS IN OUR PROPOSAL. IT'S A GREAT WAY TO INCREASE REVENUE.
WHAT HAVE WE THOUGHT OF SO FAR, ALEXIS?
ONE IDEA IS A CUPCAKE "CAKE" MADE OF THREE CIRCULAR TIERS, OR WE COULD DO MINI CUPCAKES LAID OUT ON A LARGE HEART-SHAPED SHEET.

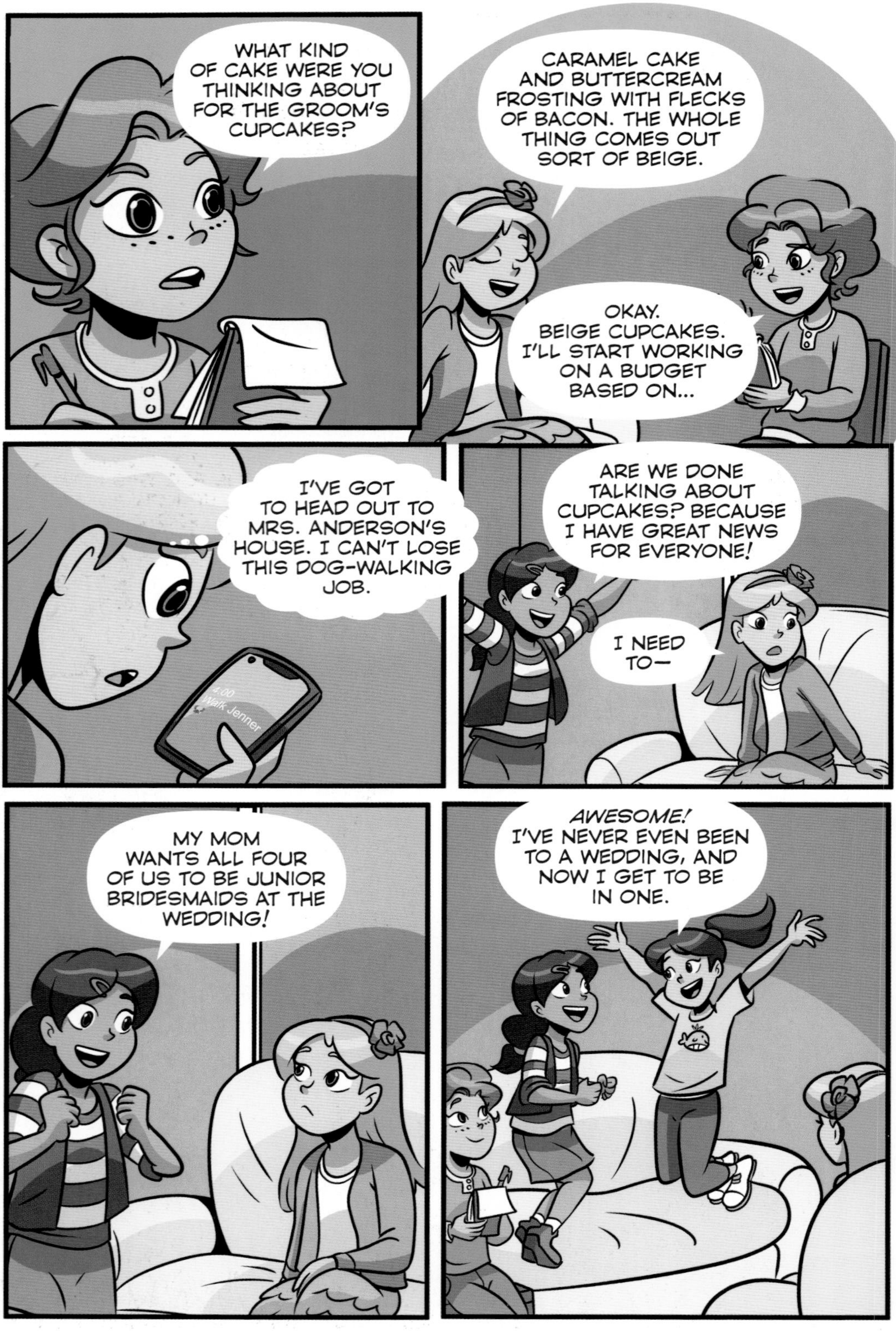
WHAT KIND OF CAKE WERE YOU THINKING ABOUT FOR THE GROOM'S CUPCAKES?
CARAMEL CAKE AND BUTTERCREAM FROSTING WITH FLECKS OF BACON. THE WHOLE THING COMES OUT SORT OF BEIGE.
OKAY. BEIGE CUPCAKES. I'LL START WORKING ON A BUDGET BASED ON...
I'VE GOT TO HEAD OUT TO MRS. ANDERSON'S HOUSE. I CAN'T LOSE THIS DOG-WALKING JOB.
4:00
Walk Jenner
ARE WE DONE TALKING ABOUT CUPCAKES? BECAUSE I HAVE GREAT NEWS FOR EVERYONE!
I NEED TO—
MY MOM WANTS ALL FOUR OF US TO BE JUNIOR BRIDESMAIDS AT THE WEDDING!
AWESOME! I'VE NEVER EVEN BEEN TO A WEDDING, AND NOW I GET TO BE IN ONE.

THAT'S EXCELLENT!

YEAH, THAT'S VERY COOL OF YOUR MOM. NOW I—

THE SALON WHERE MOM GOT HER DRESS HAS SUCH CUTE BRIDESMAID DRESSES!

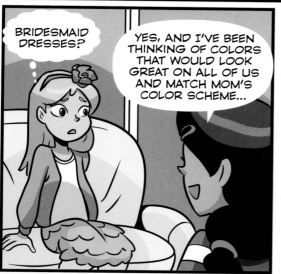

BRIDESMAID DRESSES?

YES, AND I'VE BEEN THINKING OF COLORS THAT WOULD LOOK GREAT ON ALL OF US AND MATCH MOM'S COLOR SCHEME...

I DON'T HAVE TIME FOR THIS NOW. AND HOW AM I SUPPOSED TO AFFORD A DRESS, ANYWAY?

THINGS HAD BEEN TIGHT SINCE MOM LOST HER JOB. SHE HAD TO TAKE A PART-TIME JOB AT NIGHT, AND MATT, SAM, AND I HAD TO PITCH IN AND WATCH JAKE AND TAKE CARE OF THE HOUSE.

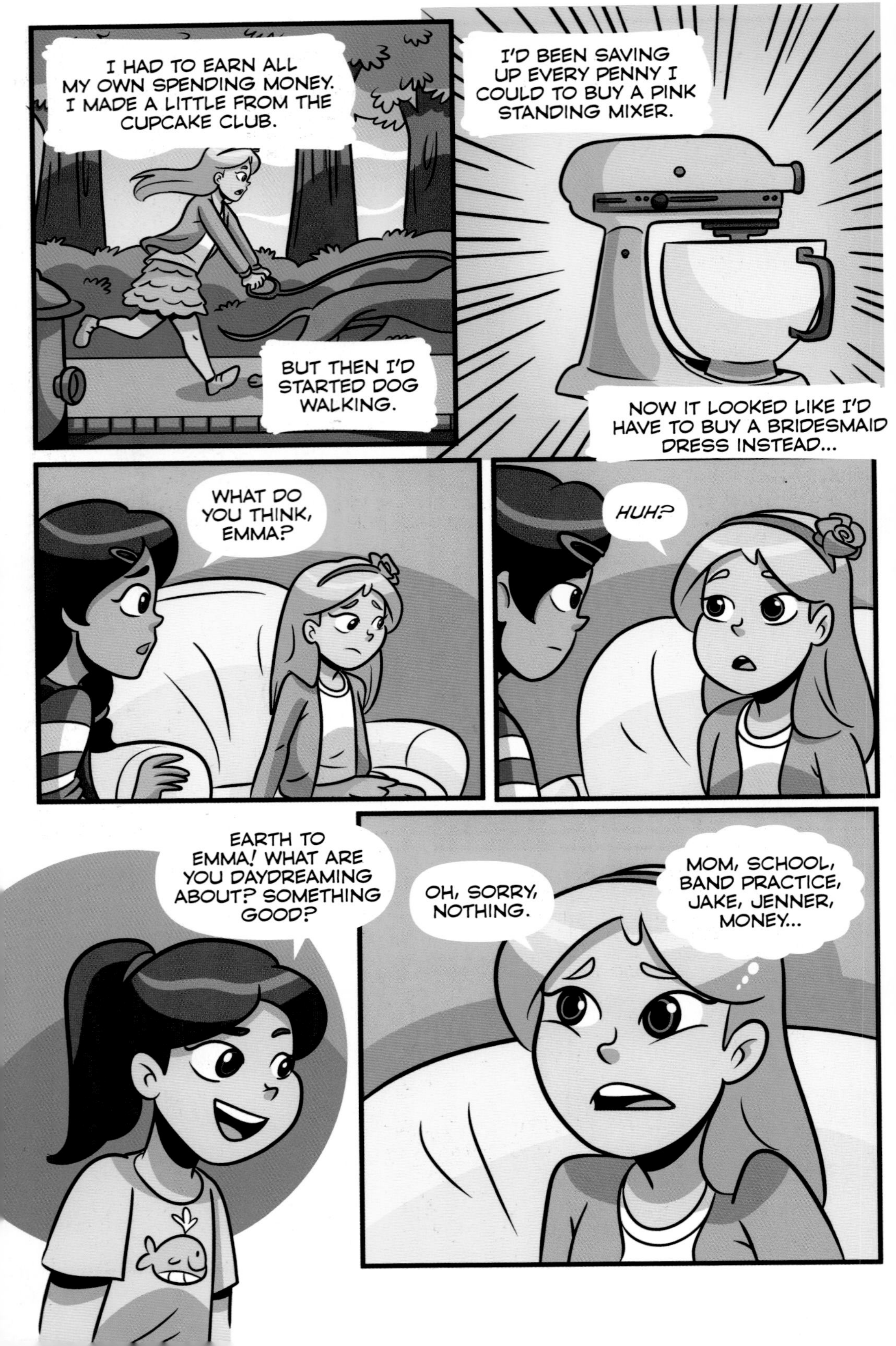
I HAD TO EARN ALL MY OWN SPENDING MONEY. I MADE A LITTLE FROM THE CUPCAKE CLUB.
BUT THEN I'D STARTED DOG WALKING.
I'D BEEN SAVING UP EVERY PENNY I COULD TO BUY A PINK STANDING MIXER.
NOW IT LOOKED LIKE I'D HAVE TO BUY A BRIDESMAID DRESS INSTEAD...
WHAT DO YOU THINK, EMMA?
HUH?
EARTH TO EMMA! WHAT ARE YOU DAYDREAMING ABOUT? SOMETHING GOOD?
OH, SORRY, NOTHING.
MOM, SCHOOL, BAND PRACTICE, JAKE, JENNER, MONEY...

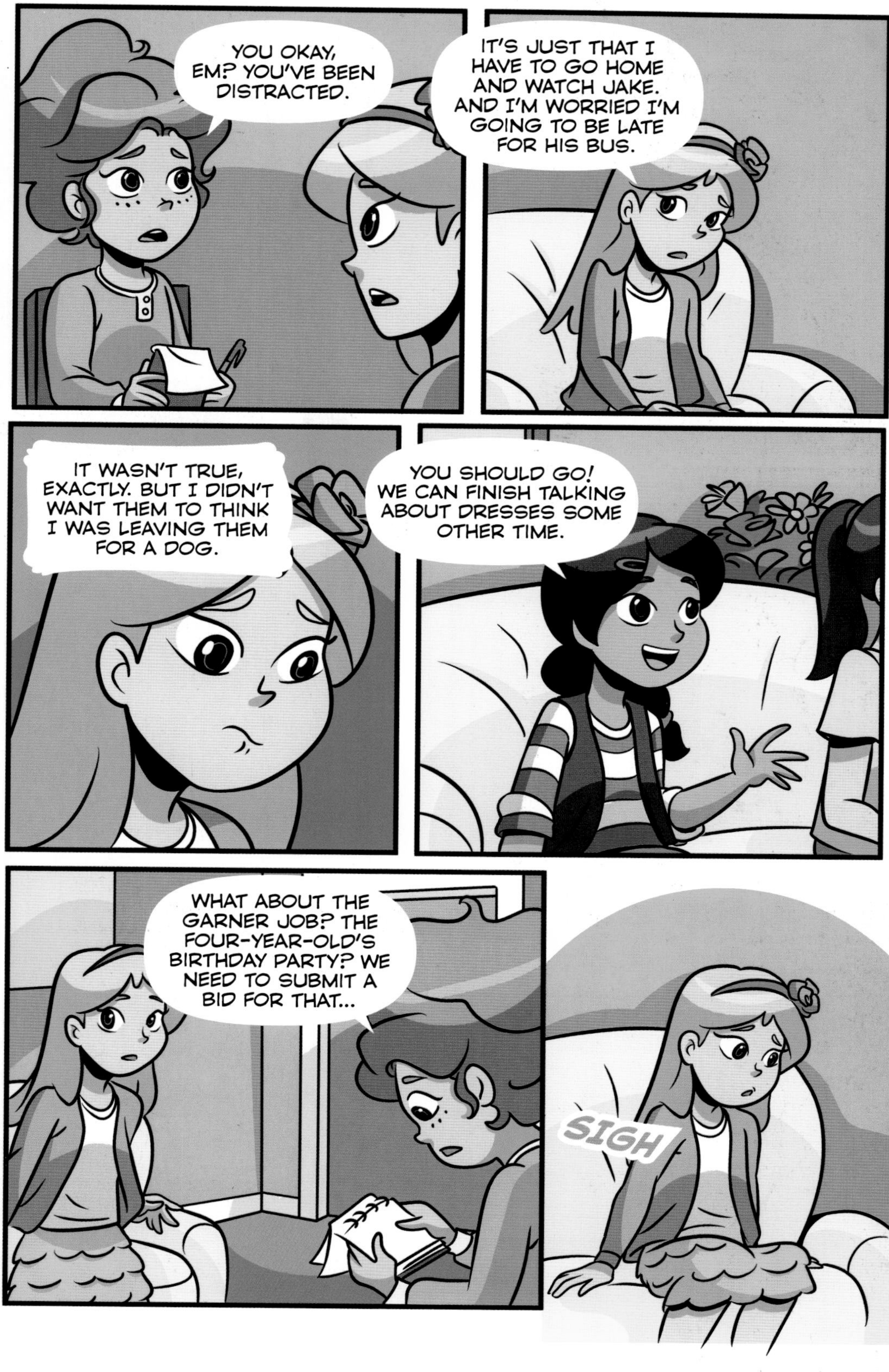
YOU OKAY, EM? YOU'VE BEEN DISTRACTED.
IT'S JUST THAT I HAVE TO GO HOME AND WATCH JAKE. AND I'M WORRIED I'M GOING TO BE LATE FOR HIS BUS.
IT WASN'T TRUE, EXACTLY. BUT I DIDN'T WANT THEM TO THINK I WAS LEAVING THEM FOR A DOG.
YOU SHOULD GO! WE CAN FINISH TALKING ABOUT DRESSES SOME OTHER TIME.
WHAT ABOUT THE GARNER JOB? THE FOUR-YEAR-OLD'S BIRTHDAY PARTY? WE NEED TO SUBMIT A BID FOR THAT...
SIGH

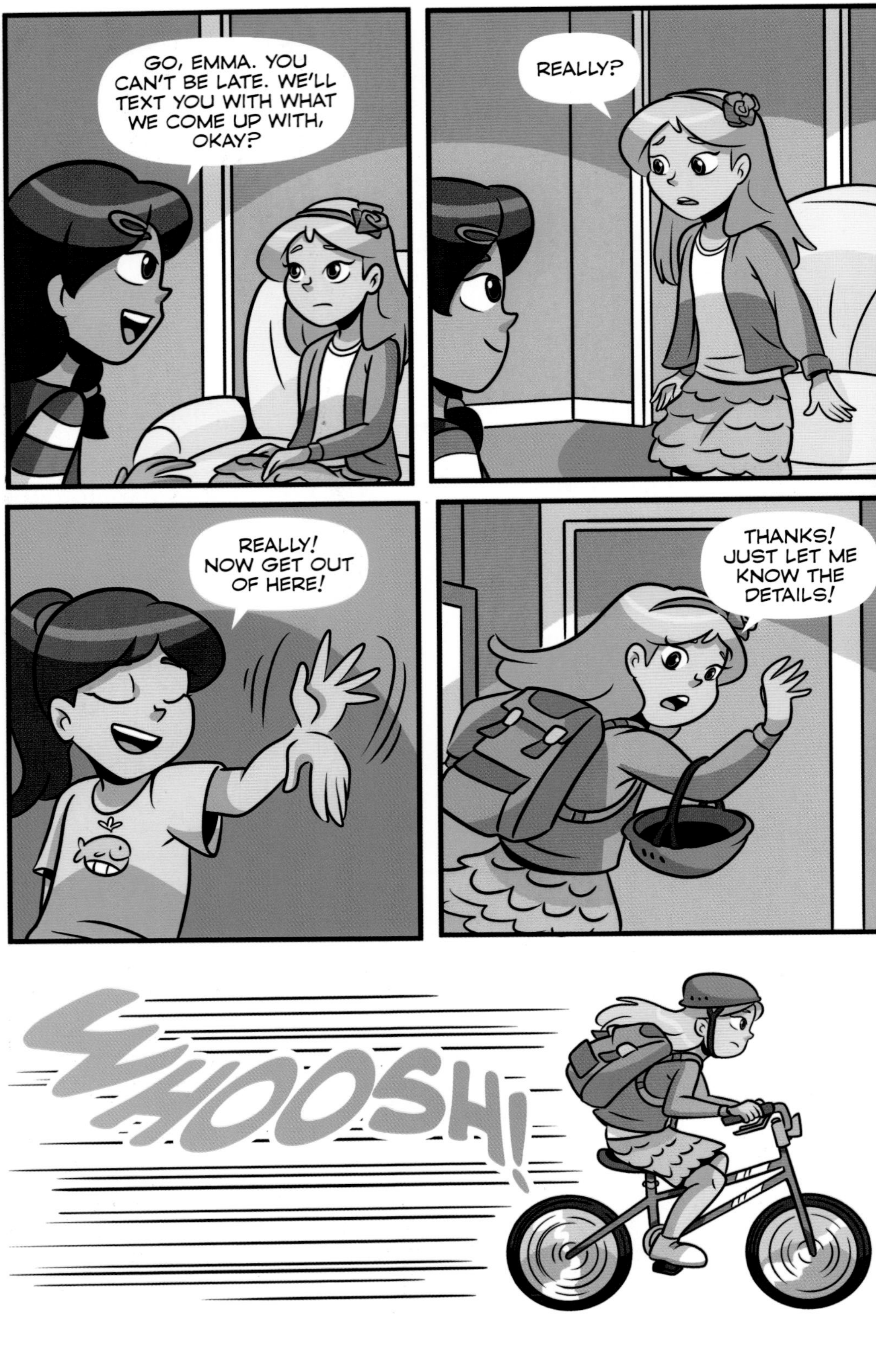
GO, EMMA. YOU CAN'T BE LATE. WE'LL TEXT YOU WITH WHAT WE COME UP WITH, OKAY?
REALLY?
REALLY! NOW GET OUT OF HERE!
THANKS! JUST LET ME KNOW THE DETAILS!
WHOOSH!

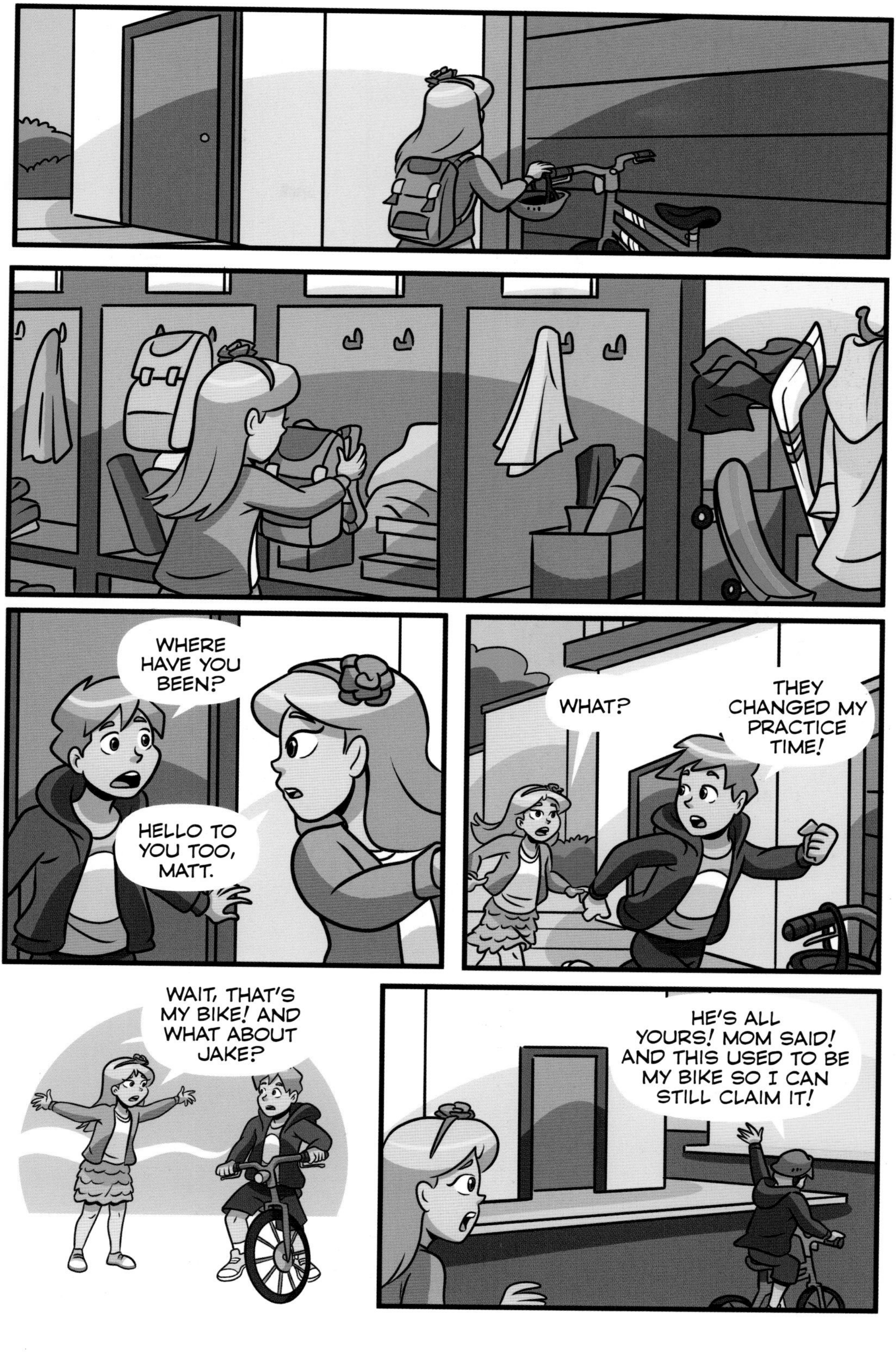
WHERE HAVE YOU BEEN?
HELLO TO YOU TOO, MATT.
WHAT?
THEY CHANGED MY PRACTICE TIME!
WAIT, THAT'S MY BIKE! AND WHAT ABOUT JAKE?
HE'S ALL YOURS! MOM SAID! AND THIS USED TO BE MY BIKE SO I CAN STILL CLAIM IT!

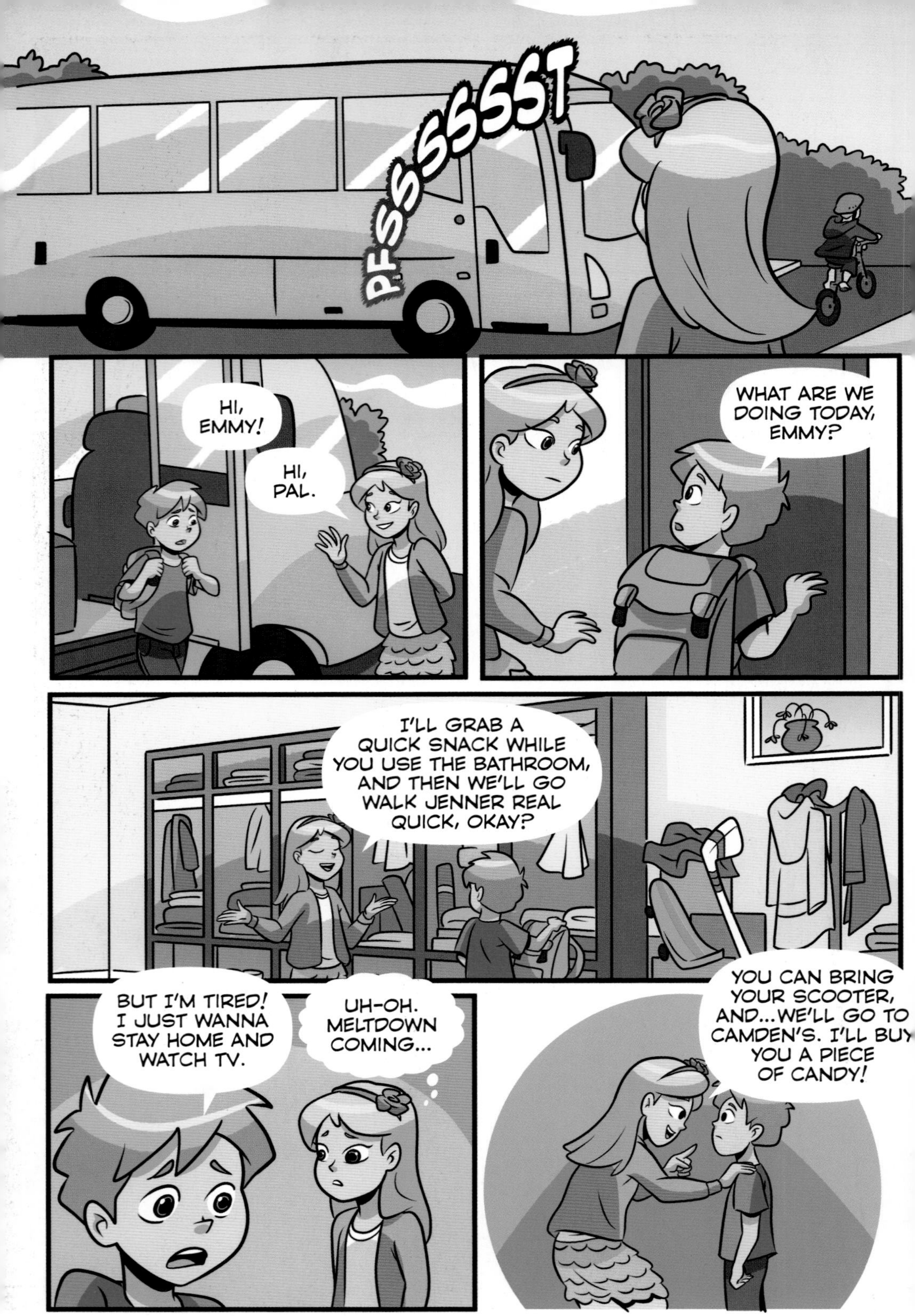
PFSSSSSST
HI, EMMY!
HI, PAL.
WHAT ARE WE DOING TODAY, EMMY?
I'LL GRAB A QUICK SNACK WHILE YOU USE THE BATHROOM, AND THEN WE'LL GO WALK JENNER REAL QUICK, OKAY?
BUT I'M TIRED! I JUST WANNA STAY HOME AND WATCH TV.
UH-OH. MELTDOWN COMING...
YOU CAN BRING YOUR SCOOTER, AND...WE'LL GO TO CAMDEN'S. I'LL BUY YOU A PIECE OF CANDY!

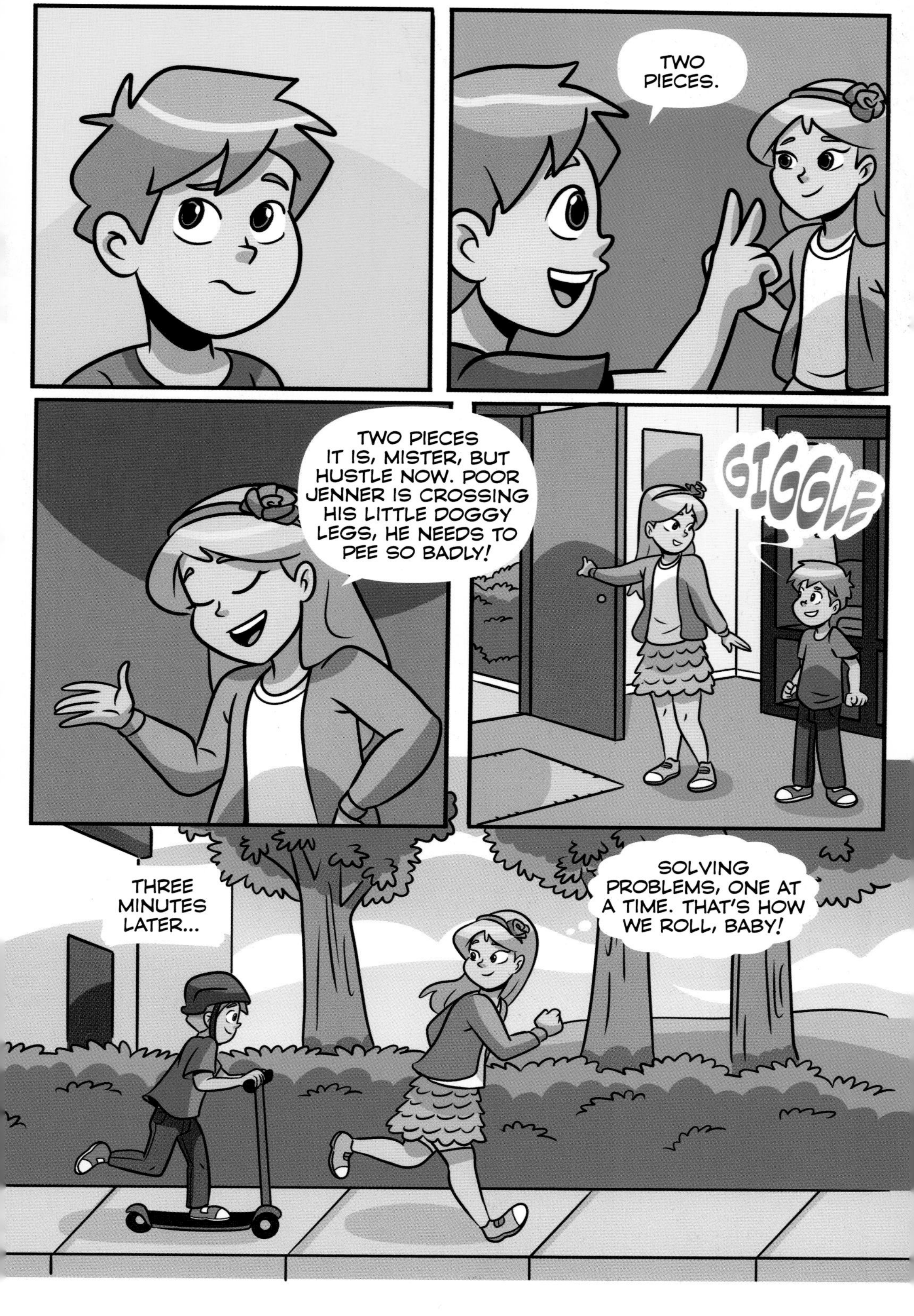
TWO PIECES.
TWO PIECES IT IS, MISTER, BUT HUSTLE NOW. POOR JENNER IS CROSSING HIS LITTLE DOGGY LEGS, HE NEEDS TO PEE SO BADLY!
GIGGLE
THREE MINUTES LATER...
SOLVING PROBLEMS, ONE AT A TIME. THAT'S HOW WE ROLL, BABY!

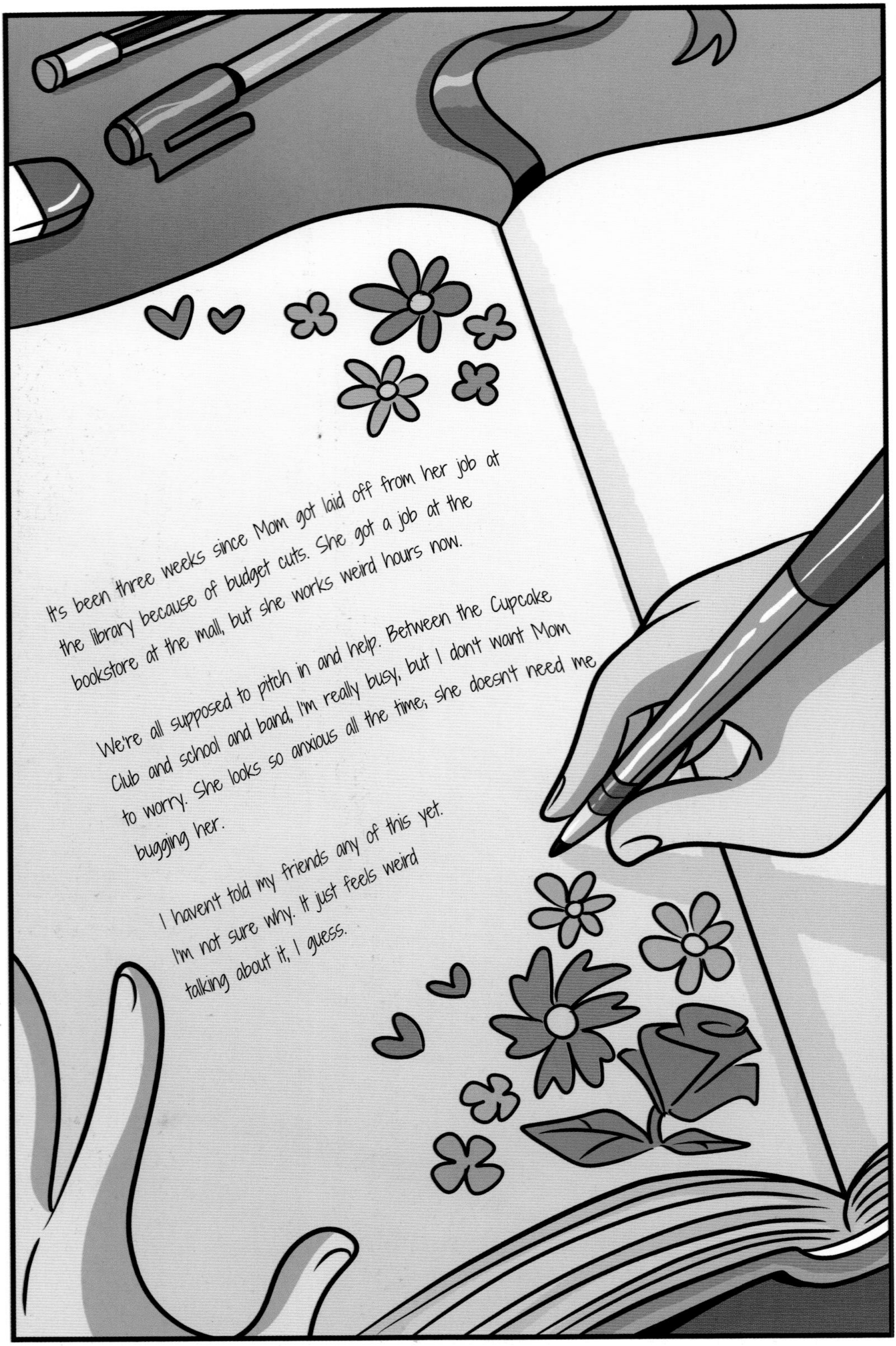
It's been three weeks since Mom got laid off from her job at the library because of budget cuts. She got a job at the bookstore at the mall, but she works weird hours now.
We're all supposed to pitch in and help. Between the Cupcake Club and school and band, I'm really busy, but I don't want Mom to worry. She looks so anxious all the time; she doesn't need me bugging her.
I haven't told my friends any of this yet. I'm not sure why. It just feels weird talking about it, I guess.

Chapter 2

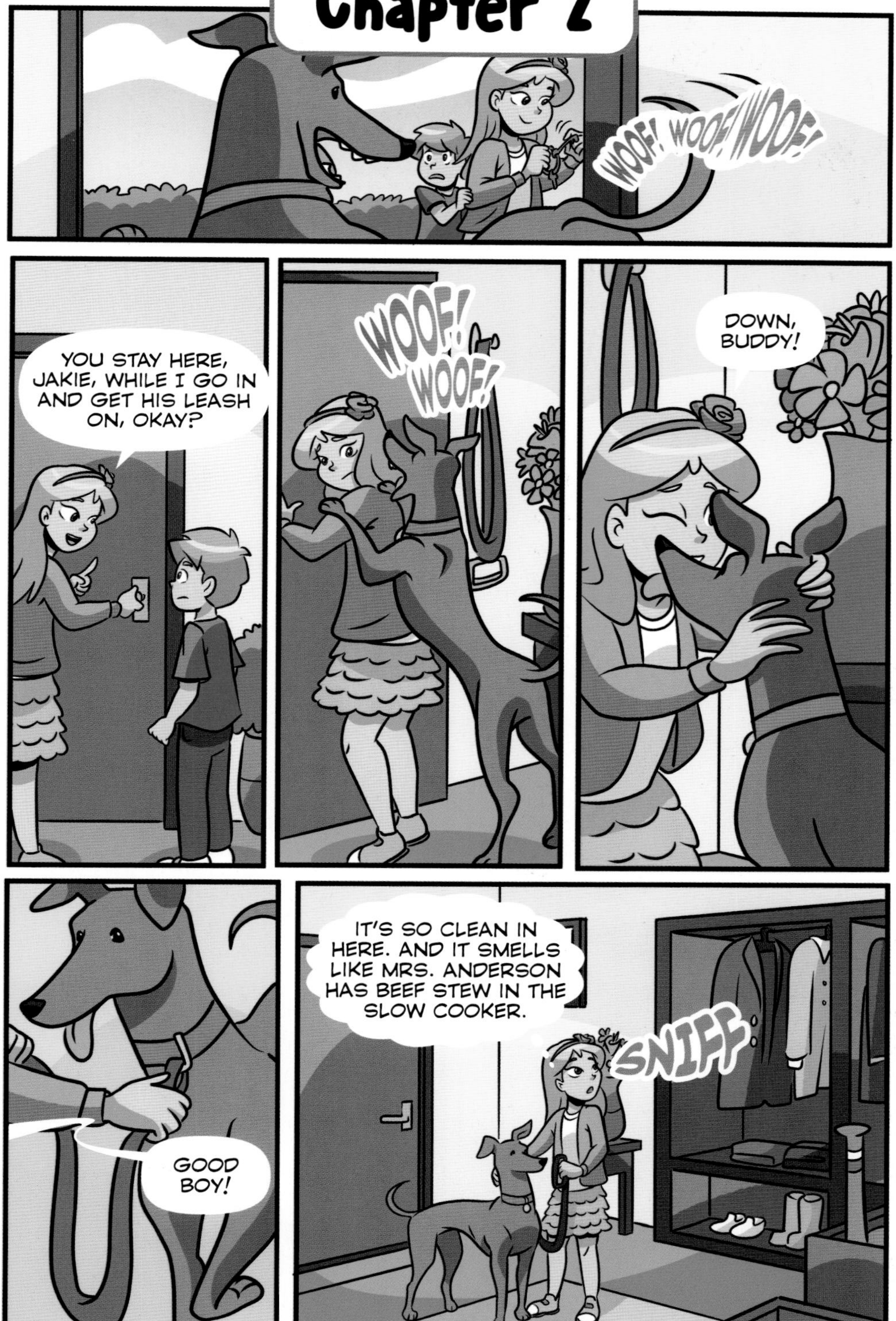
WOOF! WOOF! WOOF!
YOU STAY HERE, JAKIE, WHILE I GO IN AND GET HIS LEASH ON, OKAY?
WOOF! WOOF!
DOWN, BUDDY!
GOOD BOY!
IT'S SO CLEAN IN HERE. AND IT SMELLS LIKE MRS. ANDERSON HAS BEEF STEW IN THE SLOW COOKER.
SNIFF

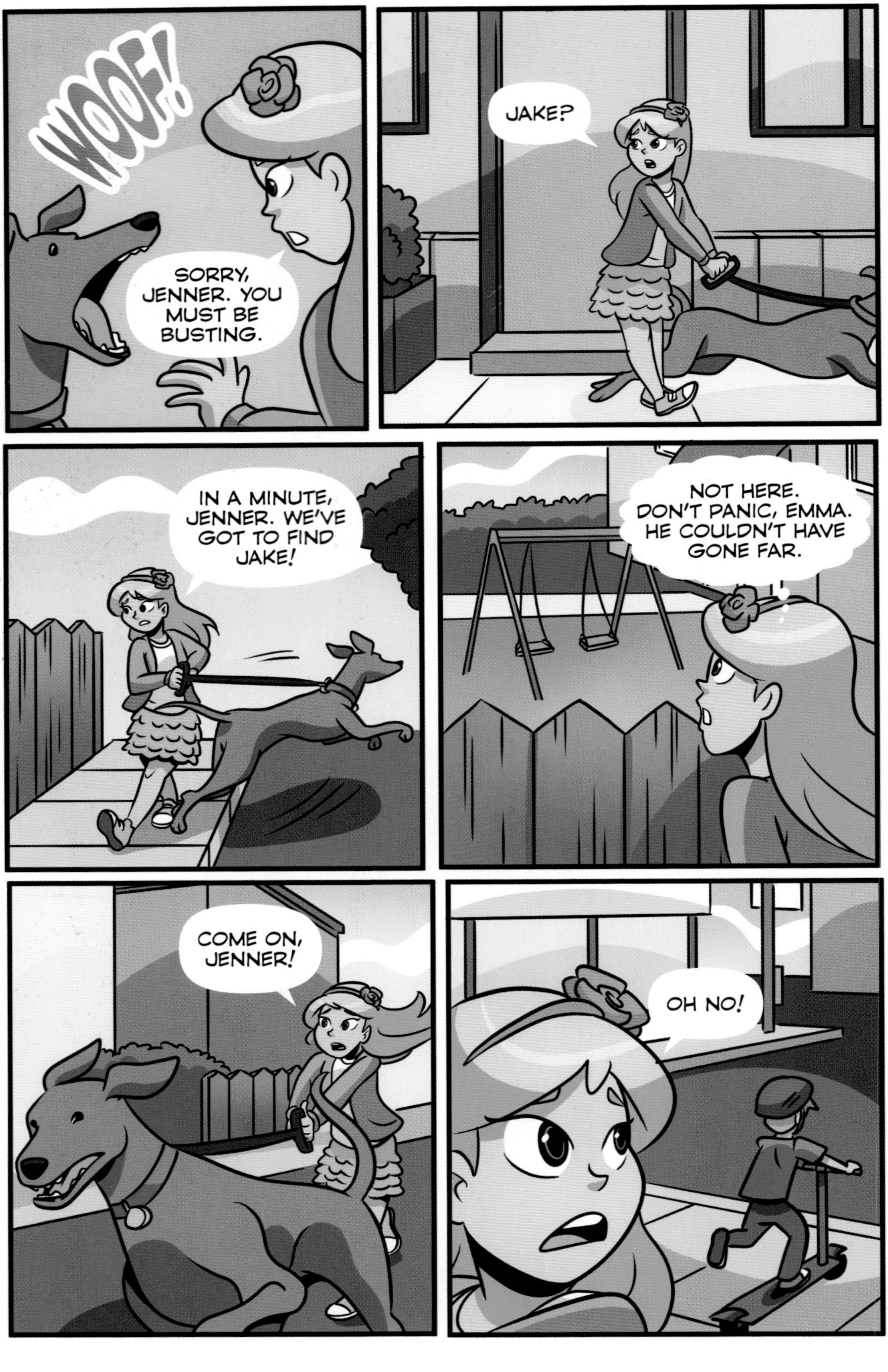
WOOF!
SORRY, JENNER. YOU MUST BE BUSTING.
JAKE?
IN A MINUTE, JENNER. WE'VE GOT TO FIND JAKE!
NOT HERE. DON'T PANIC, EMMA. HE COULDN'T HAVE GONE FAR.
COME ON, JENNER!
OH NO!

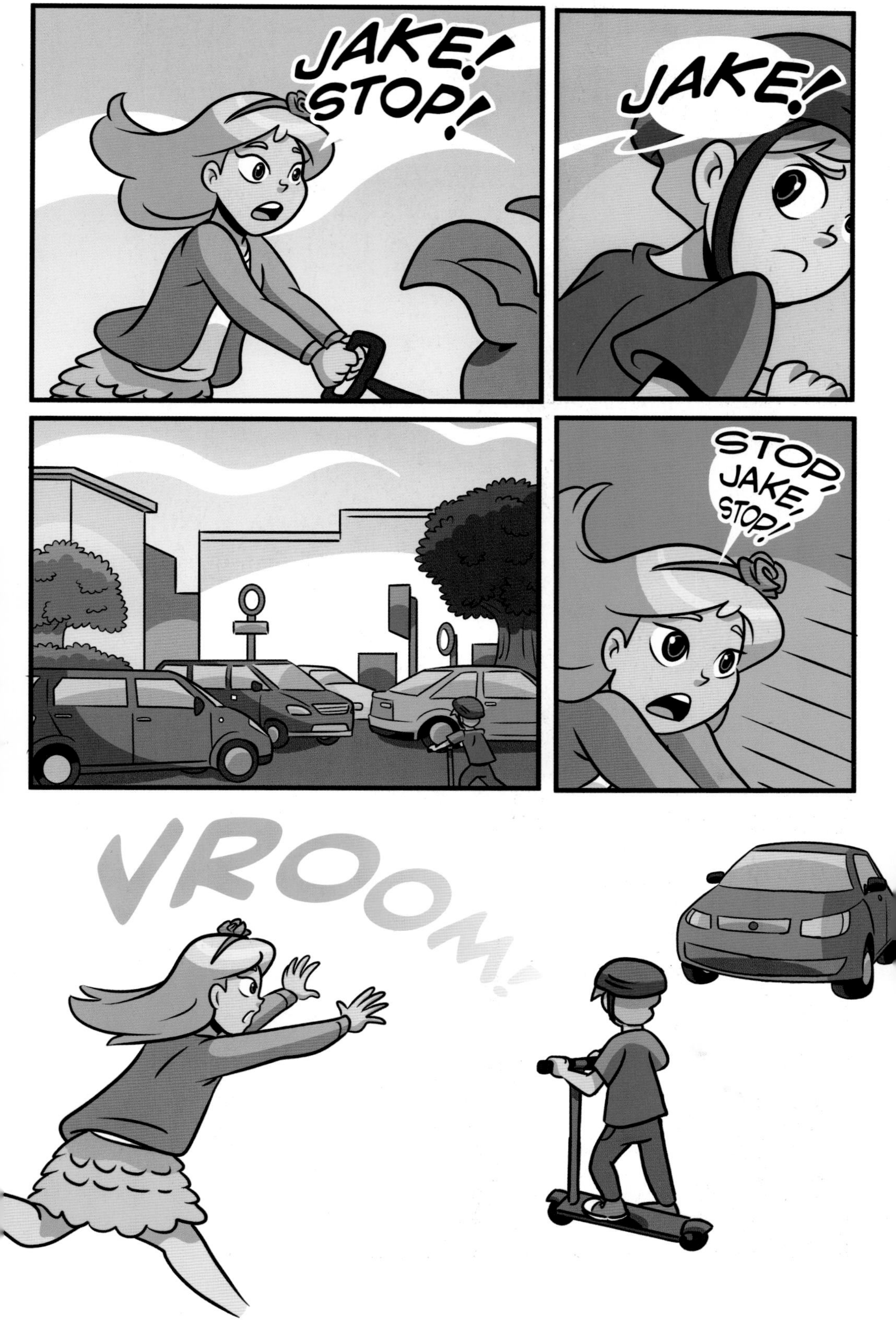
JAKE! STOP!
JAKE!
STOP, JAKE, STOP!
VROOM!

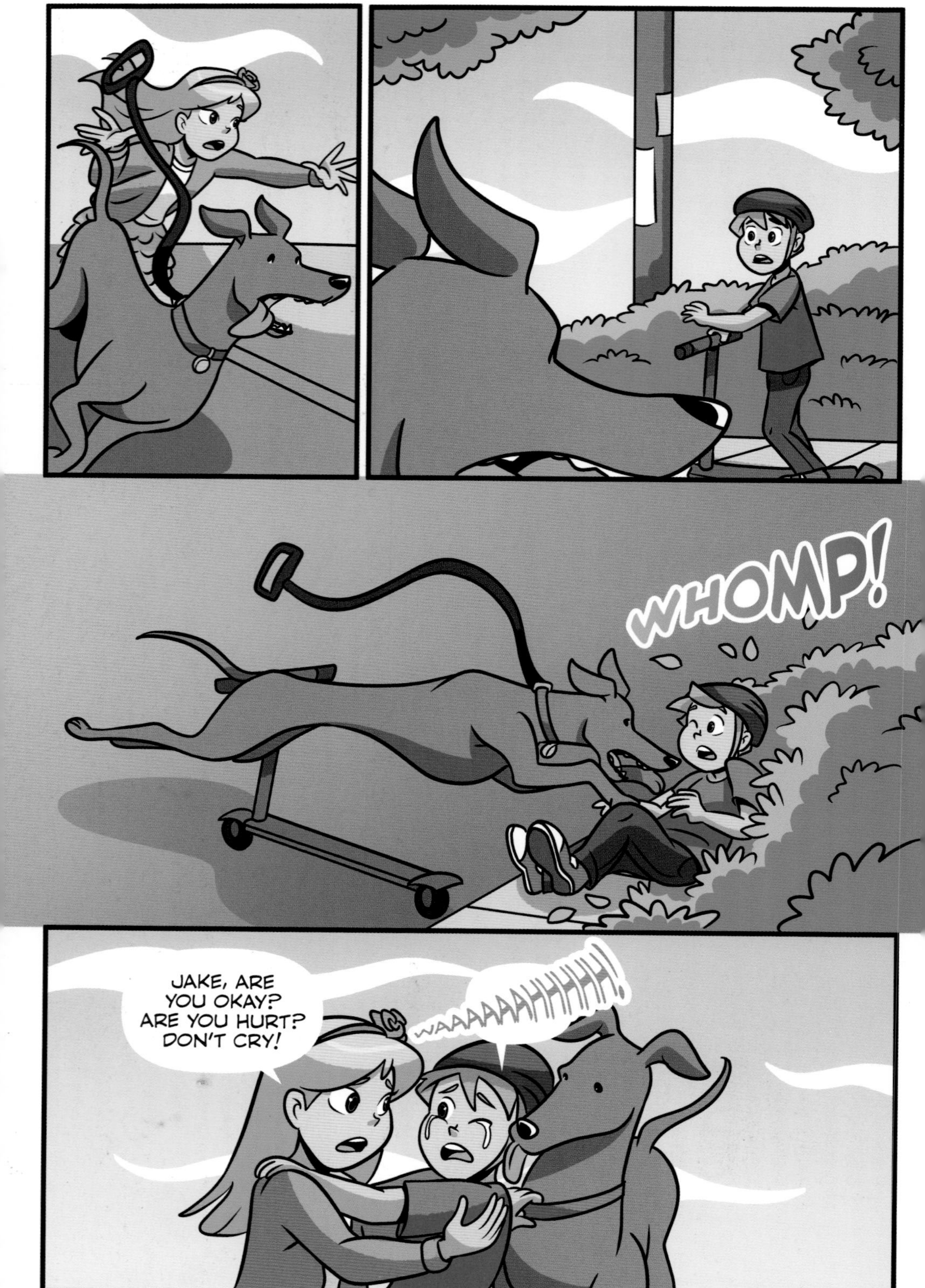
WHOMP!
JAKE, ARE YOU OKAY? ARE YOU HURT? DON'T CRY!
WAAAAAAHHHHHH!

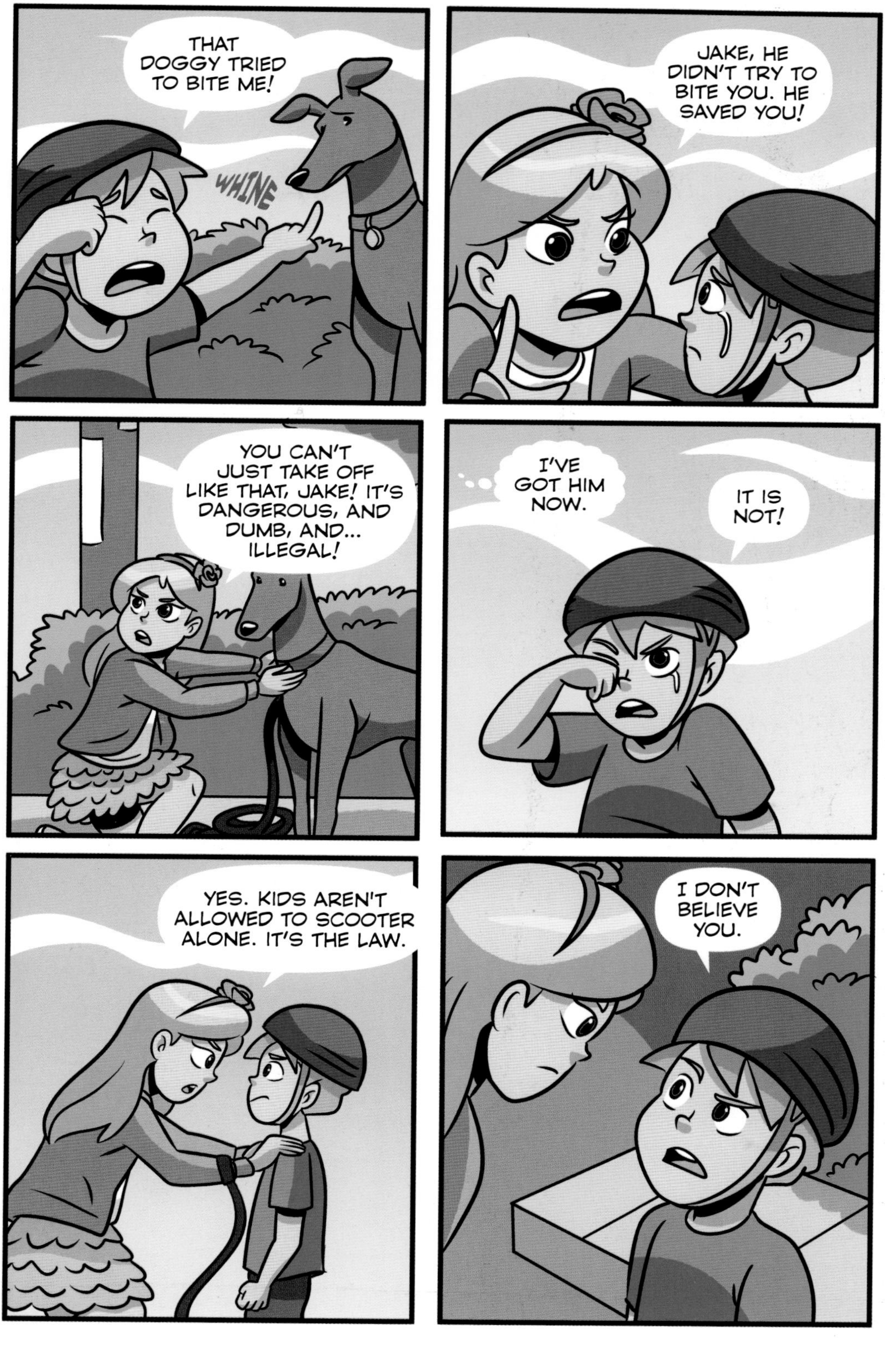
THAT DOGGY TRIED TO BITE ME!
WHINE
JAKE, HE DIDN'T TRY TO BITE YOU. HE SAVED YOU!
YOU CAN'T JUST TAKE OFF LIKE THAT, JAKE! IT'S DANGEROUS, AND DUMB, AND... ILLEGAL!
I'VE GOT HIM NOW.
IT IS NOT!
YES. KIDS AREN'T ALLOWED TO SCOOTER ALONE. IT'S THE LAW.
I DON'T BELIEVE YOU.

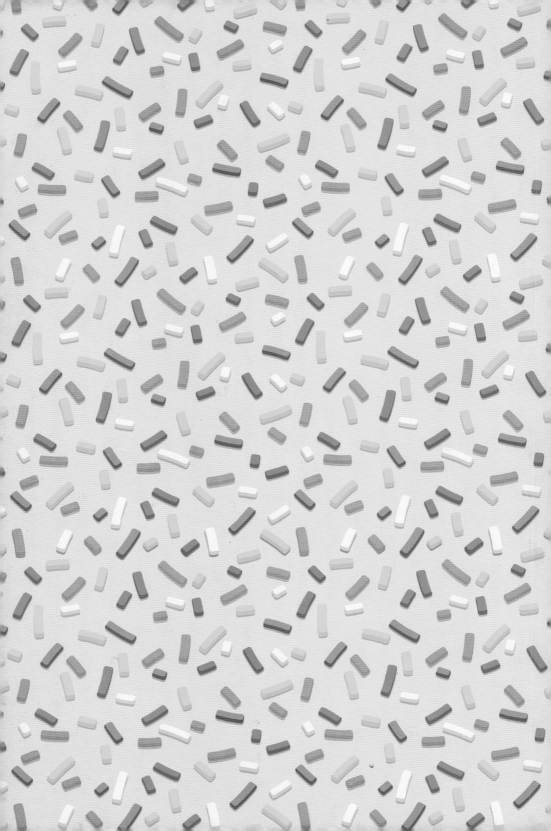

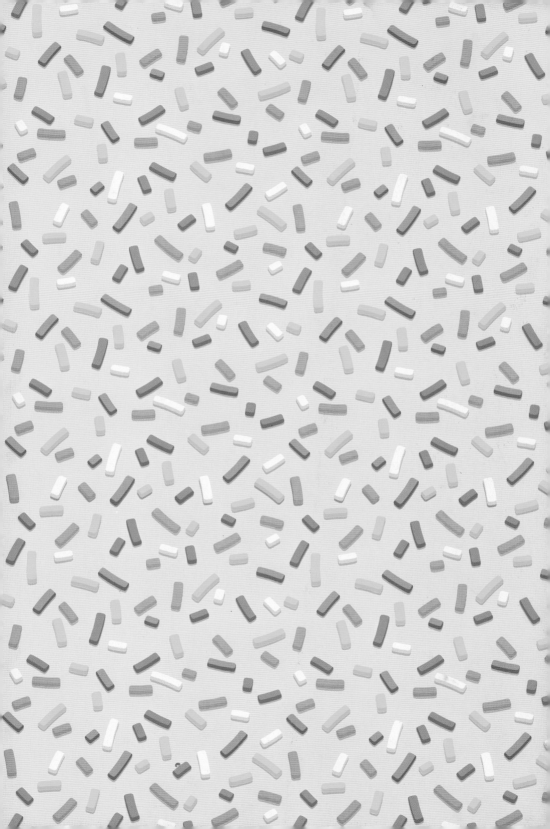

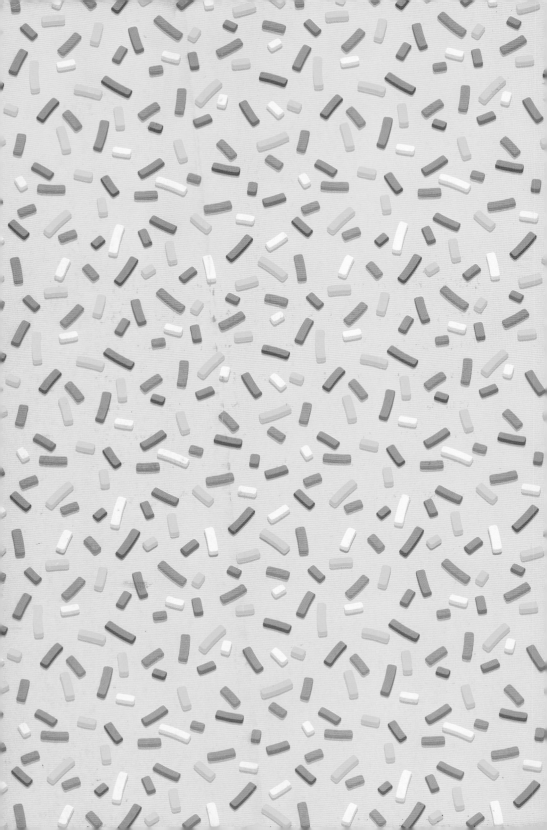